The Seary Line

NICOLE LUNDRIGAN

The Seary Line

a novel

Library and Archives Canada Cataloguing in Publication

Lundrigan, Nicole
The Seary line : a novel / Nicole Lundrigan.

ISBN 978-1-55081-248-0

I. Title.

PS8573.U5436S39 2008 C813'.6 C2008-903101-6

Cover Design & Layout: Monique Maynard

We acknowledge the financial support of The Canada Council for the Arts for our publishing activities.

We acknowledge the support of the Department of Tourism, Culture and Recreation for our publishing activities.

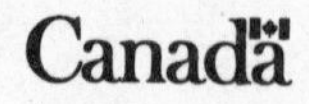

We acknowledge the financial support of the Government of Canada through the Book Publishing Industry Development Program (BPIDP) for our publishing activities.

Printed in Canada.

Printed on Rolland Enviro 100, contains 100% post consuming waste (PCW), EcoLogo certified, processed chlorine free, FSC recycled and made from biogas energy.

for

my father,
John Lundrigan,
a true character.

chapter one

Midday on a Tuesday afternoon, in the hallway of a weathered clapboard farmhouse, a man called Uncle waited outside a heavy wooden bedroom door. He did not lean against the doorframe or slouch. Instead, his shoulders were square, jaw clenched, shoed feet amply spaced on a braided rug lying askew on the floor. Uncle had been standing there for nearly two hours, had missed his morning tea and soon would miss his lunch. As the heat in the house climbed, he noticed the odour of leftover salt fish and potatoes, the dish of diced onions that had been abandoned on the kitchen counter. His belly rumbled, though he could not consider eating. He was much too preoccupied with the tension that had settled in the muscles around his skull.

Uncle turned his head to look out of the window at the end of the hall. Beyond the smudged glass, he could see Eldred Wood, holding the smooth handle of a hoe, trenching up a row of young potato plants. He was wearing a pale cotton shirt, and Uncle knew it would be buttoned up to the neck, cuffs snug around his wrists. The sun was strong today, likely burning the back of his bent head, his thin neck. Uncle had told him not to work during noon hour, but this was the only time Eldred would venture outside when the weather was fine. He was panicky over his shadow, claimed it followed him relentlessly. "Well, yes," Uncle's wife had once joked as she folded her arms across the cushion of her chest. "They do tend to do that." Eldred Wood never smiled.

If they had spoken of it, both Uncle and his wife might admit it had been a mistake bringing Eldred to live with them so many years ago. They might admit that fact even more readily today, at this hour. Though no good came from dwelling on it. Eldred was a man, after all. "And he did what men do best," Uncle's wife repeated frequently. Whenever Uncle reflected on this, he always felt a slight disgust, a slight shame.

The doorknob turned, and Uncle's head snapped around. Through a crack, he saw the faded eye of his wife, peering towards him, skeptically. She squeezed her round body out of the room, opening the door no more than necessary, and clicking it shut just as quickly. In that moment when the door was ajar, Uncle saw a naked leg, stubby and smooth, dangling over the edge of the bed. Damp earthy warmth taunted his face.

"What! You're still here?" Her words were clipped, like sharp slaps to Uncle's ears.

When she stood before him, he smelled the layer of tainted air that had wrapped itself around her, caught in her hair, her clothes. Slaughter came to mind, the scent that rose up when he was rinsing away the blood, stubborn bits stuck to the hard floor of his barn. For the second time today, he resented his sensitive nose, wishing its capabilities had diminished in turn with his soggy sight, his chalky mouth.

He tried to shrug, but he had stiffened. A shrug would have been insignificant anyway. How could he tell her what raced around inside his head? Worried that the worst might still happen. Angry that, likely, it already had. How could he tell her that he had grown old and complacent? That this was his fault, his fault. And more horrible than anything else, in a dark fold of his mind, he firmly believed he had planned it all. He had brought that woman here, introduced the two of them, in hopes that this very thing might happen.

"Go," she commanded. "Do something." Her hands were behind her, still gripping the doorknob.

Uncle stared at his wife. Her dull hair was disheveled, skin on her plump face shiny. An extra button on the front of her dress was undone. He noticed a trace of red currant jam at the corner of her mouth, still lingering from a rushed breakfast. As if she had read his mind, her tongue darted out, swabbed the sticky spot, and then retreated. She looked indignant. They had been married fifty-three years.

"You've nothing to do? Imagine that. A farm to run, and nothing to do."

Her cheeks flushed, and he hoped she would regret chiding him. Though that was unlikely. Regret involved sentiment, and any notion of that had dried up, withered ages ago. For the most part, she hardly seemed to notice him anymore. He had become a nudge in the morning, a white plate opposite her own, a steaming cup of milky tea perched on the wide arm of a chair. She had been living around him for so long now. So, so long.

He remembered her whistling when she was a young girl. High and shrill, it was like the raucous screech of a sailor who was happy to be on solid ground. The first time he heard it, he was walking down the lane beside the Gill sisters' house, and spied a young girl, a cousin he'd guessed, working in the garden. She glanced over at him, smiled, then pursed her lips and resumed her work – and her whistling. She was pretty, in a homely way, but it was the whistling that caught him. He adored it. Went so far as to suppose he was charmed by it. Maybe cursed by it, for all he knew. It caused him to break solid promises he had already made.

How funny, his remembering this now, though the recollection sparked nothing within him, no desire to reclaim her, even touch her. Living together, mixing air and breath, that seemed personal enough.

"Go, then. Watch for Miss Cooke. She should've been here an hour ago."

Ah yes, Miss Cooke. Was he trying to trick himself into thinking he had forgotten?

When his wife reentered the room, he could hear moaning followed by a never-ending string of "Lord Jeesus, Lord Jeesus, Lord Jeesus." The occasional "Mother Mary" thrown in for good measure.

Uncle's ears burned, and he felt an unpleasant twinge move through his body. As he exhaled, his empty stomach rolled over again, and he pushed his fist up underneath his ribs to calm it. Then, shuffling his feet, he managed to move away from the bedroom door and make his way to the back of the house.

On the painted stoop, he reached for the rails, gripped them. No sign of her. Miss Cooke. She would come through the wooden gate at the top of his property, wind her way down through the shivering field of tall grass. Her gait would be purposeful, a no nonsense sort of stride, and he imagined the grass shying away from her slender body. Uncle knew she would be wearing her weekday dress – the yellow one, a smattering of something blue, maybe flowers, gathered at the waist.

A breeze came around the corner of the house, and his

throat asked for a cold drink of water from his well. He considered offering one to Eldred. Did the man know what was happening? Or did his thoughts end at the bottom of his hoe, where metal touched soil? Uncle felt a pang of jealousy for that simplicity. His mind was slipping too, no doubt, though not in the ways he had anticipated. He had always been something of a dour man, but had recently grown prone to folly. Prone to dreaded introspection. He should stop, but could not. Apprehension had overtaken him, and he spent valuable hours every day standing stone still, trying to undo the considerable mistake he had made decades ago.

While he waited, he watched a trap-skiff out in the harbour, laden with barrels of flour for the general store. Moving swiftly across the water, it was decisive, doing the job it was meant to do. Then Miss Cooke appeared on the hill, his hill – he knew she was there before he saw her. In her arms, she held a clutch of fabric tied up in a knot. His hand surprised him, when it lifted, waved slightly to her like a friend might. He was not offended when she did not return the gesture.

Before he could commit her to memory, she was beside him. Time had been kind to her, even though her nose and earlobes were significantly larger, the fine skin on her chin now loose. Her hair was shiny white, and if she had faced him directly (which she didn't), he might have said she had a welcoming lean. No doubt, she had grown into a beautiful old woman. An honest spinster. Uncle could not deny that any other state of union for Miss Cooke might have killed him.

Though her body had aged, her voice was just the same. He heard it only for an instant when she said his Christian name. As quickly as she spoke, he locked those two syllables away. Knew he would replay them time after time when he was still, when he was silent. He thought she wavered when their old eyes met, and he considered that she was building up to their meeting as well. How long had it been? An easy number to recollect. Fifty-three years.

Once she was well inside his home, Uncle's knees buckled, and he collapsed against the sun-warmed door. He was light-headed, overwhelmed by the weight of emotion within him. Joy and sorrow. Looping, weaving. Mending. Tearing apart. Many, many strands of both. And these strands had nothing to do with the fact that right now, in the home where he had lived his entire life, a child was being born.

"How bad is it?" Percy Abbott asked as he sat knee to knee with his wife Delia at their kitchen table.

"Not too bad," she replied. "I don't think."

Percy took her hand in his and sighed. Another mishap, just enough to make him teeter. He wiped his sweating face on the shoulder of his plaid shirt, then noticed the skinned rabbit lying on a wooden cutting board beside him. Its furry paws were removed and pushed off to the side. One desiccated black eye stared up at Percy. *She didn't listen to me either,* it seemed to say. *Didn't heed a peep.* With his elbow, Percy nudged the board, re-orienting the dead rabbit's gaze.

Now holding her hand up to the light, he saw the tip of her index finger, firm and ready to burst, offering up a blistering heat. A spider web of redness threatened to take over her palm.

"Can you move it?"

"Not since this morning."

"Jesus, Del. Why did you hide this?"

"Don't yop my head off," she snapped.

A rush of air from his nostrils.

"I didn't hide it exactly," she continued, eyes focused on the calico fabric of her dress. "You just didn't notice."

There you go, he thought, *turning it around.*

"Did not," she said flatly.

He chose not to respond.

Percy knew something was wrong when she met him at the door. He arrived for his afternoon lunch, but there was no steaming tea, no plate of squares or bread on the table. Not even a dry cracker to calm his cranky belly. Instead, she was standing in the doorway, holding her hand against her chest, chirping through a nervous smile. "You're going to be mad."

"Not again, Del. Poking around in my shed."

"I wasn't, then. I was...I was cleaning."

"Poking around."

"Okay. Poking around."

"Again."

Only last winter, he had found her trapped there, unable to move. He'd been cutting wood most of the day, but when fat snowflakes began to sift down through a darkened sky and the air grew dense, he decided to haul his sleigh out before the path was erased. When he arrived home, the house was strangely quiet, the fire low. He called to his wife, but she didn't answer. All of the rooms were empty. Lonely. For a fleeting moment, as he sat down in the kitchen, he had the notion that his wife may have left him, and he glanced about for a scribbled note.

Then, from the window over the kitchen sink, he saw his shed, the colour of blooming poppies, permeating the storm. Brazenly, it called to him, Come take a look.

Sure enough, she was there, hunched over his lathe, head and neck twisted like a chicken's just before the snap.

"Percy? Hand me the sickle, will you?" she said in a relaxed voice, as though the scene were somehow banal. Her arm stretched out behind her, pale fingers wiggling. "Can you pass that to me? I can't quite get it."

He reached around her, felt her hair, a gnarled mess coiling a length of wood, firmly secured in the lathe. Then, stepping back, he roared, "Sickle! A sickle! I got half a mind to hand you the scythe."

Her hand crawled up over her shoulder, and she tugged at her shawl, covered up her head. The whole works began to shake, and he could hear her muffled crying. He paced back and forth in the tiny shed, hoping his anger would scatter with each livid scuff of his boots.

That morning, he had fixed a piece of knotty pine in the lathe, taken it down using the barrel of an old gun as a roughing gouge. When he left it, the newly formed spindle was still jagged, hitching onto his sweater when he brushed his arm against it.

He could just imagine what had happened. Tentative at first, she would have pressed the treadle slowly with her buttoned boot, and pressing it again, she might have leaned her face closer to feel the sweetly scented wind rising up from the dry wood. Then her hair would have fallen over her shoulder, and in a shocking instant, her head would crack downwards with a sudden awful force. Astounded foot like ice on the treadle.

He stared at his wife's backside and thought about her hair out loose like that in the middle of the day. Unpinned and unbraided, a nighttime style. Bedtime. The more he thought about her handfuls of hair, the harder he scuffed his feet along the worn wooden floor. Some part of him felt slightly sick, as though an unspoken confidence had been broken.

Then to find her in this most vulnerable position.

Certainly most men would think her stupid, might even strike her as though she were an errant animal. He shuddered at the thought of a bruise on her fair skin, and for the moment, his anger was outweighed by relief – that he was her husband, that he was the man coming upon her like this.

"What a mess," she mumbled, and her feet danced slightly. "I don't know what else to do. I've tried everything, but I's stuck. I've near scalped myself, I yanked so hard. Cut my hair, Percy, for God's sake. Cut it."

"That I won't."

She moaned. "Please, Percy. I's frozed, right down to the bone, been out here now God only knows how long. And...and. God, I don't care what you thinks of me no more, if you don't cut me free this instant, I's going to...I's going to lose my water all over myself."

Percy paused.

"For God's sake, have pity on me," she squealed.

He bent over her, released the tailstock, and pulled up on the piece of wood. Once freed, she bolted from the small room, darted up the slippery path through the woods towards the outhouse. Percy watched her, and even though his heart was still beating against his chest, he couldn't help but smirk. Bounding over the icy hill, the unfinished spindle offered its own form of punishment – a whack to the backside every time her springing feet touched the frozen ground.

Inside their home, he stoked the fire and waited for her to return. She never spoke when she entered the room, but sat in the chair beside him. Not a flinch as he began to untwist the wood, loosen her hair, snipping scattered stands. The tangle looked worse than it was, and in only minutes, wood and woman were separated.

She rubbed her neck, then stood, smoothed her apron. "How about I put that soup on the stove. Warm our bones?"

My bones is plenty warm.

Her cheeks glowed with his unspoken scolding, and she turned away from him, walked to the back stoop.

Percy was bewildered, wondered why she was so unsettled. After all these years of marriage, her landscape was familiar, but the earth beneath was always a surprise. Didn't women have their place? A place that had nothing to do with their husband's livelihood? A safe place: kitchen, church, vegetable garden, bedroom?

Then again, how was he to know? Percy had grown up with a silent father and four brooding brothers, and he understood nothing of the desires of a woman. Who was he to tell her what to do? Did he really have that right? He was uncertain, and hadn't said a word whenever she hovered in the doorway, lingered beside him as he worked. But soon, she began slipping in while he was away – his mallet might be in a different location, the dusty planer cleaned, a piece of furniture shifted. He was a precise man, and he noticed these things.

Delia returned with the frozen soup. Percy watched her hold the frosty pot to her abdomen with one hand, rub the other hand over it, a glitter of frost falling onto her skirt. And he was bewildered no more. Children. A child, even. Missing from her life. That would have changed everything. He had failed her.

"As the man–" he began, then coughed, reached for a handkerchief in his back pocket. His voice was like a wilted plant, and inside his head, he could hear his brothers mock his softness. *Oh, have mercy, little Percy.* He cleared his throat, then continued more forcefully than intended, "As your husband, I forbid you to ever go in there again. It's no place, no place for a decent woman."

He remembered her wincing when he'd said the word "decent." But the sting didn't last long. She had responded soberly, "If I hadn't gotten stuck, you'd never have known."

Percy shook his head, released the memory, tried to focus on Delia's finger. He laid her hand back in her lap, patted it, and stood. In the porch, he poured water in the basin, lathered his hands with a swipe of dark lye soap. A fly landed on his forearm, and he turned to see a tear near a nail in the screening on the door. An open invitation. He made a mental note to repair it next chance.

Delia extended her finger, but looked away when he approached holding a thin blade. With a quick flick, he sliced open the tip of her index finger, then squeezed and pressed until the pus-coated shard of pine oozed out. He could see the blush of her pain climbing up over her collarbones, then painting her thin neck, taking hold of her pretty face.

"Almost done," he whispered.

At the counter, he mixed a poultice of old bread, a few drops of water, and patted it onto the wound. Then he wrapped her finger with clean rags, bound the hand tightly, layer upon layer, tucked the tail of the fabric close to her palm.

"You was doing such a grand job, I's surprised you stopped at my wrist."

"Your wrist is fine, though I was wishing I had enough to wrap your mouth."

She smiled at him, then looked down at her hand.

"If it's not on the mend by tomorrow," he announced

after several moments of silence, "I'm going after Dr. Barnes. Get him to take a look at it."

"Oh no, Percy. I swear I's his best patient. Come fall, we'll have nar vegetable left, and his cellar'll be overflowing."

Percy's coarse eyebrows knitted together.

"I'll be fine, Percy. Honest."

You'll have to be.

"Now who's being dramatic?"

"I never said a word."

"Didn't have to."

He gazed about the room, focused on the rabbit, imagined the legs and body reunited, innards once again tucked neatly inside, thimble-sized organ pumping, head slipping through the neck of its furry sweater. Springing away. *Too late now,* he thought. *Once you're overtaken, once someone has got hold of all of you, there's no way to ask for nothing back.*

Uncle waited on the stoop while Miss Cooke was deep inside his home. Along with his wife, she was now witnessing a woman, splayed, stray child emerging from the bloodied flesh between her legs. Images of the crinkled female arrangement crept upwards, tap-tapped on his consciousness, but he pressed them down the back of his neck. He would be first to admit he struggled with that sort of thing. Whenever he heard a shrill cluck from a hen, he couldn't help but visualize a glistening egg emerging from a hidden mouth stretched beyond. And once, when he had to reach into a mare, grip the greasy legs of a breech foal, he came close to fainting when the wet animal was finally standing beside him on rubbery legs.

As he grew older, even relations with his wife became increasingly difficult. The morning afterwards, he always found his skin sensitive to any lick of wind, the brightness of the sun a terrible distraction. As he worked the field, a spicy scent would leach through the fabric of his clothes, be carried off on the breeze, and he was bothered by the notion that it might meet someone else's nose. This discomfort intensified to the point where he abandoned that nighttime struggle altogether, and was more settled because of it.

Behind him on the stoop, Eldred had taken a seat in a patch of certain shade, whittling a branch of a cherry tree with a small curved knife. Every now and again, a shaving would flick off, land on Uncle, and Eldred would leap up from his seat, dash out into the sunlight, pluck it from Uncle's sweater, saying, "Sorry, sir. Sorry." But Uncle was barely aware of the words, like bubbles within hardening resin, going nowhere.

Uncle lowered his head. How had this happened? How had his life, his entire life become composed of a series of unyielding lines? The edges of a grain of sand, the cliff that jutted out before him, the roof of his own home, the coastline on the map of where he lived. All lines. Complex, jagged sometimes, but still straight, steadfast. And no matter how hard he squinted his eyes, no matter how hard he clenched his jaw, he could identify no curve, no honest bend, where he might pause, reflect, and jaunt back to years gone by.

Uncle remembered their very last conversation. Between himself and Miss Cooke. Stilted, and unfinished. It was the day his mother died, a day very much like today – sticky, hot. The sort of weather when salt left trails on dry skin, and a foul mould would grow on any morsel left to linger on a plate.

Problems started when his mother complained of a tickle in her throat. The tickle turned to a rattle in her lungs, and the rattle to a hack. For three weeks, she languished in the bed, and the whole house smelled of her, faintly, like composted peelings. On the morning that she left him, she was consumed by fever, and Uncle had cursed the weather, called out for snow and ice, something to cool her body. But the heat in the house did not relent, and it sunk her eyes, hollowed out her cheeks, pulled back her withered lips. Early that evening, when damp day gave away to misty twilight, his mother turned from person to corpse. And in that moment, she was staring straight at Uncle, and he knew she wasn't ready to leave.

At the funeral, his father made him wear an oversized black wool suit, and his skin itched as sweat dripped down the sides of his trunk, down his spine and into the crevice of his backside. He hated his father that day, even though his father was a decent man, shaking hands with his neighbours, a grimace smile, displaying a stoic sort of grief.

Afterwards, Uncle had sat in the corner of the hot kitchen. His feet bounced underneath his chair, and he waited while funeral-goers milled about, chomped on cold sliced meat and raisin tarts. At one point, two neighbours stood directly in front of Uncle, and he listened as their conversation steered quickly away from the virtues of his dead mother, onto the subject of colicky horses. Uncle arose, feigned unsteadiness, jostling one man. He swiftly tore a loose button from the back of the man's good trousers, and a moment later, Uncle dropped it, crushed it to powder with the heel of his shoe.

When he heard the clack of dishes, the ladies scraping uneaten food into a pile for the dogs, Uncle left his home, went down to the beach, and sat on the stones. Gulls were squawking, the noise like a knife to his head. Almost unaware, he felt his fingers move over the smooth stones, until they found the perfectly sized one. He plucked it up, gripped it, let the trapped warmth of the sun seep into his palm. With a high arc, he flung it out over the water, closed his eyes when he heard the dull thud, the watery plop.

"What have you done?"

A shriek from the cliff behind him. Oh God. Annabelle.

"Willard! Willard May! What have you done?"

She was coming towards him now, making her way along the edge of the rock until she found the slender path that led down to the beach.

"Did you do that on purpose?"

"No."

"Yes, you did. I saw you take aim as clear as day."

"Then why'd you ask me for?"

She drove her hands into her hips. Lifted her feet, and turned to glance at her heels.

"God, you're heartless, Willard. Heartless and cold."

Another gull circled above, dove down towards the feathery white mass in the water. Then, as if stunned, it recoiled. Memory slipping moments later, it dove down to check again.

"Oh, look. What a sin. That must be his friend."

She was a slight woman, all neatly packaged, dress, shoes, pinned hair. She reminded him of his mother.

"For Christ's sake. It's only a dumb bird."

"A dumb bird, you says. And what gives you the right to take its life?"

Head to his knees, a cry from deep inside quivered at the edge of his dry throat. Making him gasp. He focused on the image between his legs, the tide sneaking in, moistening the gaps among the stones. When he glanced up, through the tangle of his wiry eyebrows, he could see the splayed gull, gliding from wave to wave towards him. Dead. Why had that happened? Why had the bird hovered just so, the wind lifting it, his own arm angled in just the right position.

Nearly impossible, the design of it all.

Annabelle crouched down beside him, pulled her ash-coloured dress over her knees. Rubbing his back, she whispered, "Oh Willard, today of all days, and listen to me."

He hadn't meant to knock her over when he jumped to his feet. But he had to get away from her. She understood his ways, balanced him evenly. And this agitated Uncle, as right now, he craved that unbearable lightness, wanted her side of the scale to crash down to the table below.

He turned only once to look at her as he stumbled away, and she was just standing there, plain face sad now, her questioning palms towards him. "I love you. Forever, Willard May. I promise I will." And his heart shriveled against his chest when he recognized an inkling of doubt had settled there. Could he do the same? Today, this moment, he wasn't sure.

Taking long strides up the lane, he had no idea where he was going. Away was the only direction he could grasp. He was rounding the bend that passed by Farmer Gill's when he heard that whistling. Stopped him in his tracks.

Plump, she was, with a mess of curls that the wind lifted and whipped about her face. Her legs were widely parted, and she was bent over at the waist in the garden. Grasping turnip tops with both hands, she tugged promptly, grunting now, and smirked as the earth renounced its treasure. When she stood, shook clumps of dirt from the root, the whistling resumed. He waited for her to notice him staring, and when she did, she smiled at him, and swiped a muddy hand across her forehead. "Afternoon," she sang, oblivious to the day he'd had. When her lips relaxed, they reminded him of the flaring mouth of a pitcher plant,sensual. A watery place where he might want to place his finger. "Yes," he'd replied. "It is." *She's seamless,* his mind announced, and he was almost crushed by a desire to take her up behind the rotting barn, lay her down on the knobby earth, and own her. She looked so damned happy.

When he heard Miss Cooke's shoes on the stoop, a neat clip of the heel, he was released from his stream of speculation. Her smell surrounded him, sun-warmed line-dried clothes, lilies, a hint of rancidity from old animal fat in lye soap.

"It's okay, Eldred," Uncle heard her say. "You can go on in now. She's fine. Everything's fine."

He had expected her to walk past him, but she didn't. She stood beside him on the step and scanned the water. A burst of sunlight skidded over the swells, and the radiance nearly blinded him. *Please, not now,* he thought, *not at this moment.* He bowed his head, closed his eyes, silently begged for another veil of clouds. An obliging south wind granted his wish.

In his peripheral vision he was able to admire her. His mind's eye peeling away the wrinkles, plucking out the errant whiskers, softening that silvery coarse hair back to bittersweet chocolate. With little effort, Annabelle was the same as she ever was.

"Who painted them?" Annabelle said abruptly, waving her hand towards the coloured beach stones that lined his walkway. Lemon yellow, green, sky blue. "Or, dare I ask?"

"What, those rocks?"

"Yes."

He cleared his throat. "She did. She. My wife. With left-over paint."

"Even so. Seems a bit of a waste to me. Perfectly good paint and all."

After a moment, he nodded, replied swiftly, "Yes. Yes. You might be right." He closed his eyes when he said this – an out-loud betrayal.

"Hm."

Uncle turned slightly, reached up and, with a tentative finger, touched the billow of skin at the back of her elbow. Felt a coolness there.

"Miss Cooke. Annabelle. Please."

"Please what, Willard?" Both elbows snapped inwards as though on elastic strings. Her next words were barely audible. "I'm an old woman now. But, I still remember."

How he had wished for pure anger or resentment, but there was no disguising the sadness in her voice, and that made it all the worse. Disgrace prickled his skin, and he felt pain rinse across his chest, then down towards his thighs. If cowards were supposed to be sickly yellow, then why was his old body currently glowing in hidden places?

"I am, I'm sorry," he somehow managed.

She leaned towards him ever so slightly, and her slender hand darted up, plucked a curl of bark from his straggly hair. Then her lips parted, and Uncle halted his wheezy breath so as not to miss a word. But instead of speaking, she took a deep step away from him, moved around the back of his home, floated up through the field, and disappeared. Immediately, his knowing hand moved to the spot where she had touched him.

"Don't tell me you're still standing around, Uncle. How can that be? How in God's name is that possible?"

His wife was watching him from behind the screen door and he could not turn to face her.

"Well, I'm beat," she continued. "Suppose you can pull

yourself together and take the child over to the Abbotts'? Or do I got to do that too?"

Uncle waited until his shoulders sensed her absence, and then he brought his earth-stained hands to his face. Right now, all he wanted was to be somewhere where he could see no part of himself. Where no reflection or reminder existed. Uncle pressed his fingers into the deep wrinkles around his eyes, rubbed until he saw dancing stars beneath his lids. And while he waited for the mist in his eyes to recede, he considered that perhaps he understood Eldred a little better – not quite the fear that lived within him, but something of the sentiment.

Percy was on the way up from the dank basement, an onion in either hand, when he heard a tapping at the back door. He knew who it was before he even answered. Every other member of Bended Knee Bay would have pulled open the door, strolled in, and gotten on with the visit. But not Uncle. There was nothing casual about that man, nothing informal or intimate.

"Good to see you, Uncle," Percy said, as he pushed open the screen door with his foot. "Come on in. Never mind the boots."

Uncle glanced at the onions, then at Delia seated in the rocker, and Percy noticed his face droop with a look of displeasure. His shoulders drooped too, large stomach jutting. Over a soiled beige shirt, his suspenders, decorated with jumping clovers, seemed almost whimsical. Percy stared at those suspenders, wondering what was out of place, when he realized Uncle was carrying a tiny bundle in the crook of his elbow, a cupful of pure white against the dull fabrics of his clothes.

Delia saw the child at the same time. "Oh, oh my. Oh my."

Percy dropped the onions onto a chair; they rolled down the incline, tan skins coming loose. Getting as close as he'd ever been to Uncle, Percy eased the warm knitted parcel into his own arms. Placing a hand underneath the pug nose, Percy sensed a warm breeze, smiled, and passed the baby to Delia.

"We'd have taken it on ourselves, if we wasn't so old. 'Twas our mess. No two ways about it."

"Oh, no mess, Uncle. 'Tis an honest joy for us. Idn't that right, Percy."

"We's right blessed. You've gone and blessed us this day." Percy went to clap Uncle on his back, but his hand stopped just short. "Take a load off, for God's sakes. What can I offer you? A drop of something. The best of whatever we has."

Uncle seemed to ignore the proposal, said firmly, "A bit earlier than expected, but if you're not ready, Berta can handle it for a day or two. Though she says it would be awful hard on the girl."

"We're ready."

"Yes, Uncle," Delia replied. "We've been ready since the day you told us the child was coming."

"Grand, then. Bert is wonderful tired, and I don't know nothing about tending to young'uns."

Delia leaned down to smell the child's head, and Uncle clenched his jaw, scowled.

"What is it? Boy or girl?"

"I don't rightly know now, missus."

Delia slid to the edge of her chair. "What do you mean, you don't know? Is there something wrong?"

"No. Just I didn't take the time to ask is all."

"Well, now."

"'Tis not my business what it is."

"I sees."

Percy piped up when he detected a slight sharpness in his wife's tone. "Of course you're going to stay for a drink. What can I get you?"

"No. Bert's got dinner on the table, and she's in no mood to wait. A long day we've had."

"As we can well imagine."

"So I'll be on my way."

"That's it, then?"

"Far as I sees."

"Well, thank you. Thank you kindly, Uncle. Hardly seems enough, though, don't it?"

Old Uncle moved his mouth as though he were a cow chewing its cud. Then, he tipped his hat and walked out into the porch. As he pushed the screen door open, he turned back, leaned in through the doorway.

"No guarantees, missus," he said, shaking his head. "No guarantees."

Delia met his tired eyes, then replied with conviction, "Is there ever?"

"Can you believe that man?" Delia said just after the door knocked against the frame.

"What do you mean?"

"Got neither soul at all. Handed this over as though 'twas a scrap of lost mail. Like driftwood, he is."

Percy swiped the damp hair on the back of his neck. "Who's to know what goes on inside another man's head?"

God. You can't say a poor word about no one.

Really, Del. Come now.

"You're right," she snorted. "That old man should be the last thing on my mind."

Delia's good hand hovered just over the baby, and she cried, "Oh Percy, I don't even know what to do with it."

He chuckled lightly. "Well, how about we figure out whether *it* is a he or a she."

Delia inspected the room from her chair. "Close the back door. Check the windows. Put another junk on the fire."

"It's plenty warm in here," he replied, but did as he was told.

"For us, it is. But I don't want no drafts. I idn't taking a single chance on this one."

She pulled away the soft flannel, ran a finger over the scrunched up face, the sparse strands of hair, and paused when she touched the indentation on the top of the skull, life beating beneath. She unwound the blanket, and the baby was dressed in a full-length cotton sleeper, secured at the shoulder and underneath the arms. Tucked inside, near the child's hip, was an impossibly small pair of shoes, soft leather, sewn around the edges.

"Oh look, Percy. Adorable. Pampooties."

"A tight squeeze on my toes," he replied as he danced a quick jig. "But I'll get as much use as I can out of them."

"Foolish old goat," she said as she fumbled with the strings, yanked gently. "God. Who tied this up?"

She could not disguise her frustration, though Percy understood she was really aggravated with herself.

"Could you," she said, "help me?"

He knelt beside her, and with his thick fingers, he untied the knots she had made. Then he waited beside her as she unclipped the single pin that held the diaper in place and peeked inside.

"A girl, Percy. It's a she. She's a she."

"Now then."

"But look. That black stuff. Right tarry. Like James. Don't you remember?"

Of course I remember. He could not actually speak these words as the sorrow in his voice would upset her. How could he not remember his first son? No fatter than that skinned rabbit, still piled on the cutting board. So often, when he was alone in his shed, he would close his eyes, cup his hands together, and recall that weight, that warmth pressing against his palms. Limp legs resting on his forearms. Toes like bird claws. He had watched the body for hours, until the pink mottle began to fade, settling underneath.

"God, I'm so angry at myself." Delia lifted her bad hand, let it knock down on the wooden arm of the rocker. "I can't even clean her. How stupid could I of been?"

Percy sighed, felt the muscles around his heart slacken ever so slightly. He was relieved that something inside his house might finally ground his wife, when all her life she'd lived without forethought. Letting the forces tug her any which way. A leaf in the wind.

He laid a blanket in front of the stove, poured some warm water from the kettle in a bowl, and cooled it. Bony ankles clipped between his fingers, he swiped and swiped, folding the cloth over upon itself each time.

"Right stubborn," he whispered. "But that's the best I can do."

"Is she okay? Shouldn't she have woken up?"

"She's just fine, maid. I just got a gentle touch is all." He swaddled her in the blanket, handed her back to Delia, and the baby squirmed slightly, lips yawning into a perfect O. "Should I make a little pap?"

"Ah. Just a bit of the milk'll be fine. Got a bottle this morning. Was going to make a custard. Surprise for you."

"Far better surprise we's getting now. Idn't we?"

As evening spread its dull wing over the trees outside the kitchen window, Delia rocked slowly, humming, child like the comfort of a warm stone on her lap. Her child. And no one would ever suggest any different. Even though the girl did not come straight from her body, such accommodations were made frequently. No gossiper would dare prod a woman's most tender bond, doubly so when that woman happened to be barren.

Percy smiled, chopped and browned the cut-up rabbit, added onions, salt, and covered it with an inch of water.

"Calm out," he said. *Calm in.*

"Yes. Beautiful."

On cue, the true night sky brightened, and stars began to wink.

"What do you think of Stella?" Percy asked.

"Stella? Who's Stella?"

"For a name, Del."

"Can you believe I'd forgotten about that?" There was a joyfulness tangled in around her words.

Deep within Percy, a mouth was beginning to form a toothy smile, creating a permanent inner fissure that was crammed with optimism. Risky, he knew, allowing that crack to develop, creating a sure nest for hope. But the air was so weighty with love, there was no other choice.

"Are you happy, Mother?"

"Yes," she replied, revelling in the name he had used. "So happy I feels sore all over."

chapter two

As a baby, Stella's birth mother also made people feel sore all over. When Miriam Seary was only six weeks old, she gurgled and cooed constantly, curled her raspberry lips into a variety of crowd-pleasing expressions for visitors. The skin on her plump face was a spring snow, set off by a crown of butterscotch curls. "Some sweet," second cousin Bea said, touching the baby's hair. "You almost want to dissolve a lock or two, drink it." Being the first child of an avid knitter, Miriam was always dressed smartly in caps and sweaters, booties to match. Neighbours called her stout pink digits irresistible, threatened to nibble them clean off.

But even though Miriam was adored, people sensed she was bound for a luckless existence. Amongst themselves, they prophesized, *God don't offer up that kind of face without robbing you of something else.* 'Tis only fair. Miriam's mother and father never heard a breath of the murmurs, and they continued their praise, stared at Miriam with jaws agape, chests clutched, toothy smiles plastered across their faces.

Scrunched-up Aunt Opal, settled in the rocker beside the cradle, felt a constant irritation over the chitchat. She believed it was un-Christian-like for her niece and husband to spend so much time admiring the product of their own loins. The heights of conceit. Evil vanity. And so, Aunt Opal decided to cut through the drivel with a dire prediction. After swirling the empty cup of tea she was holding, she peered in and saw the leaves clumped together in a dark dot at the very centre of the base. Though this meant nothing to her, she held it up, announced with thinly veiled satisfaction, "Just as I thought. No good'll come to that child. Not today. Not tomorrow. Not ever."

And old Aunt Opal was right. When Miriam was nine months old, Uncle Charlie had the drunken notion to play a rousing game of birdie with her. Just as his niece was reaching peak altitude during her inaugural flight, Uncle Charlie's belly began to sputter and spew, and he redirected his hands to his heaving abdomen. Down, down little Miriam flew. All four wings outstretched, but still, she landed squarely on her precious downy head. Two of her vertebrae were crushed and she lost consciousness for a nerve-wracking number of minutes. Grabbing her up, her mother placed a hand on her head, sweet brown curls overshadowed now by bulbous swelling, purple bruising on a compressible skull. She survived the tumble, but when her back healed, she was left with a noticeable hump, a persistent crook in her neck. And soon after, people began to notice the babbling had ceased, a smile could not be coaxed, and Miriam Seary grew prone to staring off into sideways space.

Miriam's parents were never the same. Her mother fell into a deep unyielding depression, and she faded away to nothingness, died when Miriam was six years old. Her father's despair was similar, though grittier, sloppier, and he was soon reunited with his wife when his liver grew scarred beyond repair. Now alone, the care of Miriam fell to a handful of gracious relatives. She started out with Nanny Joyce, then moved to Aunt Alfreda's, next on to Auntie Margaret's, and finally, she resided with second cousin twice removed, Fern. Kind people, all of them, but it always came down to the same thing. She wasn't a bother, really, but simply a distraction within the family. Attracting unwanted attention. A disagreeable disturbance. And after a reasonable amount of time had passed, a time when tongues were less likely to wag, Miriam was helped to find other accommodations.

During her teenage years, she was lucky enough to be taken in by a blissful, but deeply faithful elderly widow named Verna Hood. Miss Hood was one of the few in her community who owned two cows, and she traded both milk and butter for provisions. At once, she explained to Miriam that her cows were renowned for producing the sweetest milk and the smoothest butter. According to Miss Hood, a few gentle words to her animals and the Lord's grace were the reasons behind it.

On her second day there, Miriam learned to perch on the edge of a stool, reach beneath one of the old girls, and slide her pinched fingers down the tough teats. She enjoyed the sound as warm milk splattered off the bottom of the tin, sometimes splashing up onto her cheek. Her curved back made this a perfect task for her as she never had to hunch or lean. Miss Hood told her she was also well suited to floor-scrubbing, weeding, peeling potatoes, dusting, but milking the old girls remained a favourite chore.

On her third day there, Miss Hood showed Miriam how to churn butter. For several days, Miss Hood collected the cream that floated to the surface of slightly soured milk, and she emptied it into the churn. She directed Miriam towards a chair, and Miriam sat and nestled the wooden barrel between her solid thighs. Gripping the wooden plunger, she tugged it up, then shoved it down again and again until the plunger felt heavier and Miss Hood nodded, "You're getting close, maid."

Miriam's bands of muscle were tireless. She churned butter every three days without complaint. Her shoulders grew broader and her hands roughened. She churned the bright yellow butter of summer when the old girls ate grass, and the sallow cream of winter when the old girls survived on hay. Miss Hood showed her how to squeeze the juice from a grated carrot into the churn to brighten up dull winter butter. "My customers likes it better," she had confided. "Though it tastes just the same."

After Miss Hood had worked the butter with a paddle, removed the buttermilk and rinsed the contents with cold water, she produced several tin moulds. Miriam pressed the butter into the moulds. "Work out the air," said Miss Hood, "or they thinks we's cheating them." Removing the false bottoms, Miriam tapped pats of butter in the shape of miniature rosettes onto a plate. Miss Hood would place a pat on every cube of butter she produced, and saved the remainder for herself. So perfect, Miriam thought as she placed a whole pat on her tongue, let the grease melt and coat her insides. "Go ahead, dear," Miss Hood said as Miriam reached for a second pat. "I believes butter'll heal whatever ails you." Then, under her breath, she added, "Well, maybe not everything." Miriam had been curvy when she arrived at Miss Hood's, solid hips, hefty breasts, but when she discovered her cavernous fancy for butter, her weight began to balloon.

Miss Hood might have supposed that Miriam was a hard worker and that was why she churned butter so religiously. But while Miss Hood would have been partly right, she was mostly wrong. Miriam would never have been able to articulate it, but that gentle motion of churning had awakened something in her. The rhythmic vibration that rippled up through the flesh in her legs had settled somewhere down there, and she dreaded the moment when the plunger would stick, the cream already transformed. Sometimes Miss Hood would have to pry the handle from Miriam's hands, saying, "My goodness, child. You're all flushed. Quite the job, this is." And Miriam would pant, "Uh-huh."

Miriam liked to stay very close to home, but as she got older, Miss Hood encouraged her to run errands. Once, when Miss Hood sent her to the general store for molasses and flour, Miriam was stopped; a group of young men blocked the door. They were the three Billys: Billy Targate, Billy Gosse, and Billy Keilly. Neither Miriam nor Miss Hood knew much about the three Billys, though around the cove they were often referred to as "bloody rabble-rousers" or "the agitators."

"My, aren't you a pretty little girl," one snickered.

"Little girl?" howled another.

"She looks right like a proper lady to me."

"Lovely, grand," said the third after a low shrill whistle.

"Now, fellers," the storeowner cautioned. "Leave the Seary girl alone. And get on about your day. This is a business, not a hang-out."

A curious pride sprang up inside Miriam. She was scraping the five-foot mark, and as she passed through the cluster of men, one holding open the door, she tried her best to straighten out her hump. After that, she was eager to run errands, and Miss Hood began to joke, saying Miriam was doing fine after all with three handsome gentlemen suitors at her beck and call.

They were always there. At the general store. Sometimes, as she passed amongst them, they would poke her in the chest, run a hand or two down over her rump, but it was only in fun. They were always smirking and Miriam liked that. Liked that a lot.

One summery afternoon, they asked her if she would like to go for a walk. Even though Miriam had heard of this before, remembered when her cousin Sally went for Sunday walks with a brown-haired boy, she was still unprepared for the thrill that rushed in. They led her through a thicket of leafy dogwood trees and out into the middle of an overgrown field of wild grass. The Billys crouched down and patted a flattened area for Miriam.

"We idn't going grassing, is we?" Miriam asked. She understood from overhearing conversations between her cousin and aunt that strolling was fine, but grassing was naughty.

Bursts of laughter erupted from the three Billys, they smacked their legs.

"Christ, she's a card," they said amongst themselves. "Grassing. Is we going grassing, she asks. She idn't blunt, is she?"

Miriam watched the spectacle. It was the first time she recalled being so funny, and so she sang through her crooked smile, "A grassin' we will go, a grassin' we will go. Hi ho the dairy oh, a grassin' we will go."

More laughter, and Billy Targate rolled backwards onto the knobby ground, his watery eyes almost crossed.

Billy Gosse wiped his face and cleared his throat. More serious now, focused in on Miriam. "What do you like to do, missus? You knows, to have a bit of fun."

She paused, stuck her tongue out onto her bottom

lip. "I loves butter," she said, and then blushed. "Milking the old girls. Churning up the cream. Churning."

"Uh-huh." Nodding.

"Sometimes when I's helping Miss Hood, I gets it on my hands, and I licks my fingers."

"She likes licking, fellers," Billy Keilly said, but Billy Gosse swatted him on the back of his head, said to Miriam, "Churning, hey?"

"Uh-huh."

Billy Gosse chewed skin from the cuticle on his thumb, spat the fleck over his shoulder, and eyed the blood that flooded his nail bed. "Might you want to try a different way to churn now, missus?"

"Umm."

"A real special way?"

"Umm. All right?"

"The best butter in the world is when a feller churns with a missus. Did you know that?"

Miriam shook her head.

"Well, 'tis true. That makes the sweetest butter."

"Miss Hood's butter is right sweet. She makes butter flowers for me to eat. And I loves them."

"Is that right?"

"Uh-huh."

"Do you want to make some other butter?"

Miriam nodded. "I loves butter."

"You can count on us."

"We've all done this hundreds of times," Billy Keilly announced just before receiving a second, sharper swat.

Miriam nodded again.

"But to make this special butter, you got to lie down. Can't churn sitting up, maid." Guffaws.

As Miriam leaned back on her elbows, he flashed her a

wet grin, and she did the same without even realizing it.

"You got to go like this."

She did.

"And haul down those."

And she did that too.

One of the Billys climbed on top of her while the other two watched intently. He began to move his hips, using what he explained was his own personal plunger. She spread her arms out, let her fingers wander through the cool grass on either side of her body. It all began to make sense. Those feelings she had when churning for Miss Hood, now churning with a Billy.

"This is hard work," he said as he grunted. "Churning. Churning."

"I loves butter," Miriam cried out shortly after the second Billy began his work. "Oooo. Butt-errrrrr."

Over that summer, Miriam couldn't quite understand what had happened to her, what was happening to her. Her hair lost its soft curl, she developed strange bruises upon her bottom and thighs, and her lips were often chapped. Plus she had a powerful ache in her hump that was never there before.

Miss Hood never took the time to address the summer romps, simply announced one day that Miriam was going to leave. "That business. 'Twas bound to happen," she said, as Miriam placed her neatly folded belongings into her dead mother's trunk. "Bound."

Not long afterwards, Miriam Seary landed on the doorstep of Uncle and his wife Berta. They had long since given up taking in orphaned or unwanted children, but Berta had expressed the desire for additional companionship, another woman about the house, and Uncle had readily agreed. Though the girl had had some troubles, she said, Berta's cousin described Miriam as being a quiet, hard-working woman who was eternally pleasant.

Miriam was nearly twenty-three when she pressed her bulk into the closet-sized room on the main floor of Uncle's home. This presented an immediate problem as Miriam's body was composed of a significant amount of material. Mounds and mounds of it. After butter, her second love was sugar. She revered it, sucked her fingers and jammed them into the middle-sized canister as often as she could without getting caught. One of the things she missed most about living with Miss Hood was the sticks of candy the Billys used to offer her after they churned. Either mint or lemon flavoured, a green or yellow swirl would always give it away. Sometimes they were sticky from being sampled, but tasted just fine nevertheless.

Though she didn't notice, Uncle's face adopted a severe look when he first saw her. A woman of such mass and twisted proportions would be little help on the farm, he decided. She was even larger than his wife. Very likely she would consume as much food as all of them combined, and he knew he would smell her sweat in the summer heat just as he smelled his wife's – all things that turned his sensitive stomach – but he kept his inner eye on his most coveted wish and did his best to accept all that she was.

Uncle was in the porch washing his muddy hands when he heard Berta speaking to the new girl. Uncle envisioned his wife's words as rotting leaves of cabbage and, as he lathered brown soapy scum between his fingers, he imagined hoeing them into the ground. So many years of scolding he'd endured, every move berated. Over the course of their marriage, everything had become his fault – even the weather, which never seemed to satisfy her. He rinsed quietly, dried on an old rag, and peered through the door left ajar.

"So lovely to have a woman in the house," Berta clucked as Miriam lay dinner plates around the sturdy harvest table. "A wonderful comfort to me, it is. A wonderful comfort."

Miriam grinned, snorted lightly.

"Do you know I had nine sisters?" Berta continued as she dredged the last piece of damp fish in flour, slid it into the crackling pan. "No, of course you don't," she said. "Six passed on now, but you can imagine I was used to having women about the house. The chatter. Don't seem right living with just a couple of men."

Miriam nodded, said, "Uh-huh." Then she plucked up the forks and laid them to the right of each plate.

"It's to the left, dear," Berta whispered, shaking a floury hand towards the table. "To the left."

Miriam twisted slowly, grimaced, a spring forced to uncoil.

"Ah, never mind," Berta said. She wiped her hands in her apron and returned to her fish fillets. The edges were slightly burnt, and she moved the pan to a cooler section of the stove. "The table looks lovely. You did a grand job."

Moving swiftly around her kitchen, Berta placed a fluted dish of beet on the table, dumped the steaming boiled potatoes into a bowl. "Eldred is a nice man though. Real gentlemanly. Don't know how that happened, considering the way he was raised. Mother had a streak in her, beyond mean. Used to beat the daylights out of him, always outside, just in case he lost control of hisself, I reckons."

A sneeze erupted in the porch.

"Well, we's all set."

"Uh-huh."

"Just in time too. His Lordship is home."

At dinner, Uncle sat at the head of the table, lifted his hands for the prayer. Afterwards, he cleared his throat, said to Miriam, "Have you met Eldred yet?"

She leaned over in an odd way, giggled as she glanced quickly at Eldred without moving her head. Uncle felt a distressing jolt of excitement over the meeting, and considered changing the seating so that if Eldred should gaze upon Miriam, the dreadful bulge on her back might not be so noticeable.

"We all knows who Eldred is," Berta snapped. "I told her this morning."

"He's my best worker," Uncle continued as he unwittingly adjusted his posture.

Berta's eyes narrowed. "He's your only worker."

"That too, missus. And he plays the piano. Taught hisself."

"She would've figured that out."

"Folks come for miles around to listen to him. Sits right outside the window in the summers. Beautiful music. He's got a lot of talent, he do."

"Awfully chatty today, Father."

"And he don't always eat like that," Uncle added, as Eldred hunched over in his seat, only inches between plate and mouth.

"That's an absolute lie," Berta shrieked. "Don't heed a word that old man says. Eldred's been like that since he come into this house. We tried to break him of it now, teach him right. But, well. Eats like he thinks someone is going to steal his food. I allows he looks even worse perched next to a pick and nibble person like myself."

Uncle stared at his wife through watery eyes, kept his face calm while a sneer spread inside of him. That was one thing he always despised about his wife. She was not an honest eater. Every meal they shared, she poked at her food, scraped it across her plate. Each morsel would spend an eternity inside her mouth, chewed and chewed into paste, before being washed down with a dainty sip of water. But still, somehow when he was out of sight, she managed to cultivate and nourish a weight that frightened him. When they first married, he had craved those curves, cherished how each place on her body filled his empty hands, blurred his mind. Now those pounds threatened him, could smother him, make him vanish. Every night, while kneeling in prayer, he thanked the Lord above for the significant mattress bulge that separated them while they slept.

Berta looked up from her plate, stared back at him, and he felt her scrutiny like a mildewed cloth over his face.

"Just trying to make her welcome, missus," he said.

"A moment to take a bite might be helpful, Father."

The remainder of the meal was eaten in silence, other than Uncle's constant humming – a necessary diversion he'd adopted years ago so that he wouldn't hear his wife's chewing, bovine teeth moving through fodder.

"Tea?" Berta asked, lifting the teapot, moving it towards Miriam.

"Yes, Missus Uncle."

"Call me Berta, maid. Or Bertie. Anything'll do."

"Yes, Missus Uncle."

They sat at the table, steaming cups before them. Berta drew the hem of her skirt up over her bare knees to cool herself.

"Queer old day," Berta said. "Hot like this."

"Queer. Uh-huh."

"Be cold soon enough though. So we shouldn't complain."

"Shouldn't complain. Uh-huh."

"Well."

"Well."

First Berta, then Miriam, blew ripples across her tea.

Berta cleared her throat, slid to the edge of her chair, and spoke delicately, "Did you have a friend growing up, Miriam? A boyfriend, perhaps?"

Miriam stretched her arms out, yawned slightly. "Uh-huh, I did. Three of them."

"Well, now. Three. Well. That's something. I had a few when I was younger. No rush to settle now." She lowered her face towards her cup, relished a steamy twinge of pain on the loose skin of her neck. "What was they named?"

"Ah. The three Billys." Miriam pulled up her hem as Berta had done.

"Oh, imaginary friends. How sweet."

"They was."

"That's nice."

"I likes sweet."

"Do you like that story? About the goats? And the bridge? I thinks I got it here somewhere in one of our books. We used to have quite the number of children here back in the day – God never gave us any of our own. They used to have the run of the place, they did. Never say it now though."

"Noooooo," Miriam giggled. "The three Billys. They wasn't goats. But Miss Hood didn't like it."

"She didn't, did she?" Berta replied with a smile, full face of wrinkles. "Maybe they was too gruff?"

"Maybe." Miriam scrunched her eyes in similar fashion.

"How do you find Eldred?" Serious now.

"I finds him good," Miriam replied. "He got a nice, ah, a nice, um, a nice mouth." She began opening and closing her legs so that her thighs slapped.

Berta noticed. "Eldred is older, but I finds he's young in his head," she said, sliding back in her chair. "And I reckons I don't see every side to him, if you knows what I means."

Miriam nodded. "Uh-huh."

"I just wants to tell you, you've got to watch the men nowadays."

"All right. If you says so. I can watch."

"Some of them got their minds in the gutter."

"They do?" Eyes a little wider.

"Silver tongues."

"What?"

"They'll salt your brain."

"They will?" Mouth open.

"Best to steer clear."

"Steer clear."

"That's a good girl. For listening."

"Yes, Missus Uncle."

And Miriam did. She listened to Berta for the rest of that year and through the long winter. In spring, it was harder. Miriam was no longer drowsy, and the smell of new grass poking through the earth, swells on the ocean, and crackled mud did something to her. She didn't exactly look for Eldred, but when she came upon him in the loft of

Uncle's barn on a fresh summery day, she couldn't bring herself to leave him either.

She had been in the garden, plucking an armful of wild purple lupines, when she heard a small noise like a snuffling piglet. She followed it into the barn, and it came from above. Pinching the flowers in the crook of one elbow, she took each step slowly, hoisting her enormous frame up a thin ladder that led to the loft above. In the dimly lit corner, she saw Eldred, kneeling over a bundled scrap of fabric. Miriam edged closer, aware of the creaking boards beneath her flat feet. She placed her hand on his bony shoulder, and he leaned backwards to reveal a panting tabby cat, two wet kittens, another mottled mass emerging from underneath the mother's twitching tail. Eldred was sweating, face contorted. Panic lit up his eyes as though he himself were the expectant father.

They sat shoulder to shoulder on the hay-strewn platform, waiting. Eldred continued to snuffle, wiping his nose in his sleeve. Miriam, transfixed by the births, didn't budge, breathed through her stubby fingers clamped over her mouth. When all of the blind kittens were licked cleaned and latched on, Eldred slumped, sighed and opened his mouth. His bottom teeth were blackened. Miriam was reminded of candy, and wanted to do something to make him happy.

This was the first time they'd been alone together. She nestled in closer, crushing the lupines that had fallen between them. Wet words in his ear. "Have you ever churned the good butter?"

Once the child was born, Uncle had thought that would be the end of it. All his efforts, culminatng in one meeting, one subtle confrontation, the staggering possibility of exchanging a few words. But in the weeks that followed, he was paralyzed with misery, unwilling to move forward, unable to step back. Deep inside, he felt as though he was the butt of a cruel joke, and worst of all, he himself was the culprit. The perpetrator, in a sense, of a lifelong gag with neither punchline nor ripple of laughter. How could he have chosen so poorly? Now there was no son to carry on his name, no daughter to carry on his blood. Taking in those children had helped at the time, they were so needy and forgiving. But they had faded away, and in his old age, he had grown to resent each and every one of them. When he finally sensed their absence, it was so startlingly cold, it burned.

As summer began to wither, Uncle became preoccupied with his breathing, with the twitches in his muscles, the blue veins still full beneath his skin. He could no longer eat. Although he sat at the table during meals, he was unable to place a single morsel of his wife's cooking on his tongue. He lost weight rapidly, and his clothes dangled from his scarecrow frame. Eldred began to stare at him with the same frightened expression he reserved for his shadow. Though he wanted to, Uncle was unable to weep. Instead, while weeds multiplied, blight disfigured, and animals ran rampant, he sat for hours on the flaking chair on his back stoop, two fingers constantly assessing the faint pulse on his wrist.

"You got to snap out of it," Berta had told him. "No ifs, ands, or buts about it. This place is gone right to the dogs."

Uncle sighed.

"Did you hear me, Father? Right to the dogs, I said. The crop is near ruint, and I can't keep up with it all. Don't know what you expects."

Berta had had enough, and took it upon herself to meet Dr. Barnes directly at the boat when he arrived for his community visit.

"I don't know what's got into him," she told the doctor. "Like he come face to face with his own ghost."

Dr. Barnes took Uncle to the bedroom and asked him to sit on the bed.

"Can you tell me what's troubling you? Your wife is awful upset."

"My heart."

"Your heart?"

"Yes."

"Any discomfort? Sharp or dull pain?"

"No."

"Shortness of breath?"

"No."

"Light-headedness? Feel like retching?"

"No, sir."

Dr. Barnes listened with his stethoscope.

"Your heart sounds plenty strong to me. Given your age."

"'Tis dried up." Uncle knotted his fingers into the crocheted bedspread.

"What's that?"

"Shriveled."

Dr. Barnes sat beside Uncle, placed his hand between Uncle's shoulder blades. "I'm sorry to tell you, I don't have a remedy for a shriveled heart."

Resigned, Uncle blew a steady stream of air, sank deeper into the bed. "Good Doctor, I never supposed you did."

Later that night, Berta awoke to find Uncle's side of the bed empty, the sheets cold. Nighttime breezes danced across her face, and she left the bed, followed the trail of open doors. She found her husband outside in the garden wearing only his nightshirt. His bare feet were planted firmly in two trenches, feathery carrot tops growing in the row between his legs. His head was drooping backwards, mouth open. Above him, the sky was alive with the blazing of a million stars.

"Father," she whispered, her words spanning outwards. "Father."

She stepped closer.

"Father. Here's your boots." When she'd almost tripped over them in the porch, she plucked them up, clasped them to her chest.

He never turned, never spoke.

"Father. Is there something wrong? What did Dr. Barnes say today?"

Why did she repeat that word incessantly? Father. Mocking him over and over. His fatherless state.

"Did he tell you something?" Her voice now sounded as though it belonged to someone else. "Are you…are you dying?"

His head fell forward.

"I…I do believe I am, maid."

At once she began to cry. Tears bursting through the years of dryness, shaking her momentarily, before a hollow calm settled in. "I figured as much. These past months. I idn't blind."

"I…"

She sniffed. "I did love you, Father. In my way."

"Yes. I believes that."

"You never wanted."

"No."

"I done my best."

"I minds you did."

"Did you love me?"

Silence.

"Did you love me?" she repeated, a little louder. "Ever?"

A harder silence now.

A small cry from somewhere, from her own throat? Bitterness now seeping in, taking hold as she snarled, "I might have known."

She dropped the boots in the dusty earth, turned to walk back towards her house. She had already pictured the ending, but it was nothing like this wearying depletion. No, she assumed her change in status would be almost instant, and that she'd wear her newfound widowhood like a fashionable dress. She even considered that such an interruption in her marriage might even suit her complexion. But instead, she felt older, more worn than ever before. The girl that had always lived within her was long gone. *At least I was a good wife,* she thought. *I was that.*

The air was heavy the following morning, swollen with a dampness that bent the hay, curled the leaves, and distorted the line between ocean and air. Uncle tucked his undershirt and his loose plaid shirt into his trousers, tightened his suspenders. He felt a chill glide through him, and he appreciated it.

"Take your coat," Berta had hollered as Uncle rustled about in the porch. She lifted her hands, coated in sticky dough, leaned her head out though the door. "She'll cut you today. The wind."

Uncle took a cardigan from the hook, stretched from a summer of hanging, elbows still frayed. He walked down over the rocky slope lined with those painted beach rocks. Every time he passed by them now, they called out to be noticed, and it aggravated him. As he turned onto the lane, each step was a struggle. He had lost some sensation in his feet. His hands too were numb, so he kept them tucked into the front pockets of his sweater. Along the way, he paused many times.

He could smell the vinegary cabbage pickles as he walked up the weedy path to her home. The screen door was propped open with a junk of wood, and he watched her for a moment. Miss Cooke, Annabelle, was standing near a counter, her back to him, spooning the pickles from a large pot, steaming glass jars accepting them with a satisfying gulp. Then, even though he hadn't shifted his weight, the stoop creaked, announcing his presence.

She made no move to stop him when he eased through the door and walked in. He sat at her table, and waited for her to finish. Scraping the pot, she topped up the last jar, wiped each one with a damp cloth, and flipped up the glass lids, snapped them shut with the metal lever. Then she cleaned her hands, dried them in her apron, a black fabric, stark white flowers embroidered around the edges.

Still, she never spoke, and busied herself making tea. Uncle couldn't bring himself to look directly at her – only parts of her – the small puff on the shoulders of her dress, her narrow back, calves, unblemished shoes, and trim ankles. And then his mind spat up an image of his wife's ankles, almost splitting their seams, her kitchen shoes, so distended, bunion feet bulging.

She laid a cup of tea in front of him, and his hands went for it. There was something different in her face now, a hint of pity, and he did not find it unpleasant.

"What do you want here, Willard?"

"I don't know," he said. And he honestly didn't.

But he did know what had pointed the way. The event that had rudely driven him into foul discontentment. He knew. Precisely. Something so small, so insignificant, if he told her now, she would surely think him senile. In fact, he wondered about that himself, if he was slowly going mad.

It happened in the springtime when he was bringing in armloads of wood – Uncle noticed an enormous brown scale adhering to the underside of one junk. A cocoon of sorts, he thought, and he set the log aside. Every few days he would lift the log and peer at the brown fuzzy patch. Sometimes he would stroke the tough exterior with his finger, marveling at the level of protection the insect had created. He was curious what would emerge, and checked the progress frequently. But nothing happened.

Uncle knew something about the life cycle of the creatures sharing his farm, and he decided he had given the insect plenty of time to hatch. One afternoon, when he was alone, he bent down on his knees, took the log in his hands, and peeled away the cocoon. Larger than a thumbprint, he placed it on his palm, turned the fibrous bundle over and over. Ingenious, he thought, sealed completely shut, no escape route. Uncle tugged away the tough layers, felt a pang of disappointment when there was only a shelled creature inside, development arrested. Then, when he pinched the shell gently, it exploded, shooting liquid, the brilliant colour of spring grass, across his hand, up over his wrist, onto his chin. He threw the casing and the stringy casket as far as he could, swiped the watery remains of the insect on his pant legs.

That night he dreamt he was a young man again. He was naked, appeared fit, but his stomach began to convulse and threads spewed from his mouth, coiled his body in layer upon layer of dirty twine. Berta was beside him, smoothing the shell, whistling all the while, and once encased, he was relaxed, happy. But soon it soured. Confined and bathed in a jaundiced light, he sensed he was softening, felt his throat beginning to swallow an endlessly available liquid. Panic stabbed him, and he pressed against the sides of the casing, but could not budge. Soon he was gasping. Choking. And somewhere in the distance, above the faded whistling, he heard a sharp shovel wounding a plot of wet earth.

Uncle awoke, sweating, cramped legs wrapped in a sheet. He got up, dressed, and went for a drink from the jug in the kitchen. Glancing at the ceiling, the papered walls, he suddenly felt trapped, stunted, had the urge to strip off his clothes, peel off his skin, and flee. But he had simply stood, staring at the wrinkled cotton towel hanging near the stove, and wondering how to go back in time.

"Willard. Willard?" Firmness in her voice, a firmness he needed.

Uncle's cup and saucer rattled in his hand. She was the only person on the earth who called him by his name.

"You okay?"

He watched the steam from his cup rise straight up, ascending towards heaven.

"You're so pale. Would you like–"

"Don't," he whispered, then put his hands on his lap, leaned his chest into the table.

"Don't what?"

"Try."

"Try what, Willard?" Her back was straight now,

pressed against her seat. "You're sitting here in my home. At my table. I'm just trying to be hospitable."

"Don't. I don't deserve it."

"You're right. You don't deserve it." She took a long slurp of her tea. "It's all just foolishness, anyway. Utter foolishness. This life. Our tangled story – or lack of a story. I feel like a silly old woman, Willard. All these years." Her voice was an undercurrent, invisible, overtaking him. "What's wrong with me? How come I never stopped?"

"Stopped?"

"You know what I'm talking about. I should've moved on. There was certainly plenty of opportunity."

He closed his eyes. "Of course." There would have been.

"But I couldn't. I never stopped."

"Stopped."

She whispered now, body slumped. "Never stopped believing I was yours."

With these words, Uncle gathered himself up and pulled himself in. He squeezed his face, his shoulders, his behind, his legs and toes as hard as he could. A horrible tightness gripped every vein in his body, constricting the blood, constricting his heart, constricting the blast of emotion that throttled him. He was unable to speak, and stood up, stumbled from her home. Falling through the fields, the grass twined around his legs, claiming him.

He made it to the fence, their shared fence, and stopped at the gate. He had touched that gate untold times over the years, but never lifted the latch, never tested the metal hinges. With as deep a breath as he could muster, he pushed it open. The wood was nearly rotted, but it moved effortlessly, not a single squeak.

Bending over, he gripped his knees with his hands, tried

to calm himself. It was then that he noticed the hinges. So new-looking. Not a single speck of rust. He tilted closer, knocked them, then peered at the shimmer on his knuckles. A faint smell of grease tweaked his nose. Left alone, nature would have destroyed them. Instead, someone had been tending to those hinges all these years.

He sat down there, in the opening between the two properties, one bent leg leaning to the north towards Annabelle's, and one to the south towards his own home. Divided. Uncle leaned his head against the gatepost and allowed his lids to droop.

She came upon him like this, placed a pale hand on his bristly mottled cheek and began to weep. He never made it home.

chapter three

Even though Delia Abbott was on the tips of her toes, face pressed up against the window, she still could not see the beach. And to this day, it irritated her. Her husband owned a decent piece of land, and she could never understand why he chose to build their home where he did. While there had been many level areas, he had selected a small patch of struggling woods in the upper northeast corner. He cleared a path to the centre, felled the trees, then sawed them into logs and stacked them. The summer before they married, he and his father had built the saltbox home and the small shed beyond.

"Don't see why more don't do this," he had said after the work was completed. "Breaks up the wind for one thing, and 'tis a bit more grand, if you asks me. Living in a forest."

But Delia didn't agree.

Forest was a stretch. Grand was preposterous. Instead, they lived among a cluster of straggly spruce twigs that never flourished in the cold salty winds that tore through them. Underfoot, there was a never-ending supply of fallen needles, roots and knobs, and the ground was perpetually moist. To some extent, the trees did keep out the wind, but she also felt they somehow kept her in. She suspected that this was Percy's real wish – to protect her, hide her away from any peril that could walk, without care, right up to their doorstep.

Just once did she confess she didn't like it. Told him that only late afternoon sun could slant sufficiently to find its way to her windows. Said although her laundry did have a pleasant woodsy odour in summer, more often than not, it was graced with daubs of turpentine, a scattered whitish smear from overhead birds. And most importantly, she explained, she couldn't see when the ladies were strolling up and down the lane. There was no opportunity to invite someone in, have a moment to gossip, and she often wondered if her life was lonelier because of it.

She was about to suggest thinning out the trees, but Percy appeared so deflated with her complaints, and she immediately regretted saying anything. Then he stared at her with a curious expression, and it made her question if he thought she'd become somewhat spoiled since they were married. So, she let it go.

Percy was not only mistaken about those trees, he was mistaken on another account as well. Since the day they'd met, he'd treated her as though she were something far more fragile than she really was. Sometimes she felt like an enormous speckled porcelain spaniel, similar to the ones sitting so primly on her bedside table. In the fickle eyes of fate, that had surely been a blunder. Shielding her like he did. She didn't blame him, really, though she firmly believed that by tangling the trail, he had lured calamity towards her.

She began to feel ill a few years into their marriage. As she plucked weeds or kneaded bread, she noticed her arms weaker than they should have been. Throbbed after only a few minutes work. When she stood quickly, sometimes her knees would buckle, and she would fall, leaving oval bruises and a shock that resonated in her pelvis. More than once Percy had found her like that, and she lied to him. Said that she was such a devout Christian, occasionally the need for prayer simply brought her down. Then the stomach troubles, too embarrassing to mention to Percy. And the tedious weight loss. No matter how much she ate, she sensed her body was starving.

Over the years, Dr. Barnes would come and go, though he was never able to reach a diagnosis. Once, she heard him say to her husband under his breath, "She's a woman with a delicate constitution." She remembered Percy nodding pleasantly, as though Dr. Barnes were confirming an inkling he'd held all along. He liked to fix things, and it seemed to suit him better to be joined to someone broken.

Harrumph, she thought as she paced in front of the window and tried to find a crack of light amongst the clump of trees that had swallowed her. Even though her upper arm was not much bigger than her wrist, she still considered herself to be a tough old bird. Lesser women would have shriveled up, climbed so far inside themselves, never to be found again. What with James, her first child, and Emma, her second. Then all those hopeful starts and disastrous stops. The last time, she bled so heavily, she was convinced she saw the sinewy hands of long dead Great Aunt Enid reaching for her, and Percy swore he would never touch her again. He relented, of course, though only after much badgering, a handful of shaky assurances.

And then came Stella. Delia welcomed her with an open heart, even though the child was born from peculiar circumstances, to say the least. Delia hadn't questioned a thing, never asked Uncle for a single detail, just loved the child as though she were her own. Then, as if her hands weren't already full, within two months of Stella's arrival, she got word that her younger sister had passed away. The husband, who was the cook on a boat that carted loads of salt fish to Boston, was unable to take care of their three-year-old boy. The news came by way of a concise letter, something hinting at Delia's childless state, and the boy arrived shortly thereafter. A skinny child, he seemed lost in Sunday clothes, a brown wool sailor suit trimmed with pumpkin-coloured cord. Eyes of clear blue, and his nose and hollow cheeks were decorated with a smattering of freckles. His name was Amos Flood, and in the time it took her to take him by his sweaty hand, she had fallen in love once again.

As soon as Percy walked in for his lunch on the day Amos came to them, Delia said in a hush, "He idn't budged an inch. Been in the porch this last hour, staring at me. I don't want to force him."

Percy walked straight up to the child, bent slightly, hands to his knees. "Now, you don't look familiar. Not from around here, I'd say."

No response.

"Any chance you works over to the mill?"

He shook his head slightly.

"Didn't think so. I knows most men that works to the mill. Do you fish then?"

A slight nod.

Delia started to walk towards the child, but Percy jigged his hand for her to stay put.

"Well, now. A fisherman. I guess that means you're looking for a job. No self-respecting feller goes too long without a job. You idn't nothing if you idn't got work. Isn't that right?"

The child stuck his toe in the rug, wiggled his heel.

"I'll take that as a yes. You're after a bit of work, I'm betting. Well, wouldn't you know it, you're in luck."

The boy glanced at Percy now, and there was a faint twinkle of curiosity in his eyes.

"I'm betting too that you're a strong feller, with shoulders like that. And I needs a strong feller. But you got to eat a good meal. Keep up your strength and all that."

Amos toddled over, sat down in Delia's chair at the table. Then he spoke, his voice like a bird's chirp. "I's strong. My mommy says."

Said, Delia silently corrected, and the tense pinched her heart. It was difficult to reconcile her sister and the presence of this child. Delia had left home when Grace was only six weeks old, and in her mind, her sister was still only a newborn. She could hear her mother's warnings, *watch where you seats yourself*, as her sister was always tucked into the corner of the sofa or the back of a chair. Somehow it was easier for Delia to believe her sister was lost when she was an infant, perhaps someone did the unthinkable and plunked themselves down without consideration for the plump white pillow beneath them. This way, Grace had never lived a full life. She'd never skinned her knees or braided her hair, never felt her soul ache with love, the awe of conception, the bittersweet joy of severing the cord.

Yes, her sister Grace was long gone. But what to do with Amos? How could she squeeze him into this picture? Resolve his existence? There would never be any mention of her. Of Grace. A child his age would have the memory of a sieve, everything slipping through.

That evening, Delia was nearly reduced to tears as she sifted through the trunk – clothes hastily piled up, a book of nursery rhymes, embroidered handkerchiefs, a pair of shoes, a lot of empty space. An abundance of miniature outfits, nearly too small for the boy now. As though someone, an experienced seamstress, had created with feverish intensity, and then suddenly stopped. Those tiny overalls, pants, sweaters would hardly be worn by the intended owner. And at the time, she recalled, that saddened her more than anything else. That this small boy, so lost in the world, would barely get a chance to feel the affection in the stitches, the touch that still lingered in the fabric.

Delia stepped away from the window, wrapped a shawl around her shoulders, and sat down in the rocker. She wanted so badly to watch her family, watch her husband bend and lift in the cool October air, the children, cheeks flushed, pretend to labour diligently while they covertly played. She still hadn't gotten used to how enormous Percy became when the children arrived. His hands were dinner plates when he patted Amos's back, his thighs, like overnight logs, when he sat beside Stella on a bench.

She longed to compare them just now, but she could see nothing. Absolutely nothing, only a handful of old man's beard clinging to the trunks of those cursed trees. Next fine day, she would tear away as much of it as she could reach, burn every shred.

"You are a ridiculous woman," she said aloud as she pictured herself with both feet planted firmly against a trunk, two fists gripping the stringy moss, tree howling. "And now look. You're talking to yourself."

In the past five years her life had changed more than she ever would have imagined. The carefree existence between Percy and herself had vanished: the teasing, their special unspoken banter, the quiet dinners beside the stove when their toes would touch underneath the small table. With the arrival of Stella, and compounded by Amos, Percy had become deathly serious. He rarely smiled, and within six months of parenthood, his hair had morphed from the shiny black she adored to the peppered fur of a winter hare. Taking care of one had been pleasant, but three became overwhelming, and sucked the marrow from his bones.

Delia wandered around every inch of the kitchen, tapping her shoe in each corner, running her hand along every smooth surface. Caged inside her own home, and she was convinced this confinement contributed to her exhaustion. She sat upon the daybed again, breathing laboured due to her walking, and she listened intently. Gusts pushed at her home, twigs tickled the windows. Inside was glaringly still. She hated being alone.

"How long you going to be gone, Percy?" Delia had asked as they hauled on dusty boots, hats, sweaters.

"Not long," he'd replied. "We got work to do. Just because it's fall, don't mean things let up."

"I knows."

Delia was on the daybed, and as Percy unfurled a blanket, he nudged her backwards with his elbow. Unintentional, perhaps, but the gentle propelling riled her. Then he snapped the blanket in the air, tucked it around her, securely, intestine around the skinny sausage.

"God, Percy, I got to breathe."

"I would hope so."

"Are you going to be long?" Her voice echoed inside her head, the annoying repetition. A syrupy neediness that sickened her.

"You needn't worry yourself about that, maid."

"I idn't worried, just you knows I don't like to be by myself is all."

"Well, you're not alone. Why, there's... You got..." He looked around the room. "Stella can stay with you. Right, miss?"

"Noooo," Stella whined. The child's undersized sweater was tucked into oversized pants, and when she gripped Percy's forearm, dangled there, her silky belly was exposed, pants threatening to tumble. "I wants to work."

"And you needn't think I's staying in," Amos announced.

Delia turned, stung. Over the years, Percy had become the pleasure, while she was the painful punishment.

"Can't blame them for a wanting a bit of fresh air now, can you? Heh-heh."

"Wouldn't dream of it," she had murmured, hot iron pressing on her words.

Delia lay down on the daybed again, threw the blanket across her knees. Percy would be upset if he returned, found her traipsing about their house. Tomorrow was Sunday, everyone would be at church, and she needed to appear rested. Other than Dr. Barnes, no one really knew about her peculiar illness. Percy never told a soul, and neither did she – not that she really had a soul willing to listen. But silently, both of them had agreed. Sharing the story of her sickness, speaking of it in the open, would only change it into something real.

Last night's storm had torn away the mounds of seaweed that clung to the rocks, then thrashed them about, tossed them up on the beach. Percy and the children were down there now, crawling over the stones, collecting the slippery strings and shoving them into four enamel buckets. When the buckets were filled, Percy would cart them up over the road, onto his property, and dump the mess in small piles on his garden. After strewing it around, he would leave it, allow it to rot over the winter, creating a rich fertilizer for his potato plants in the spring.

As he tipped the fourth bucket from a load, Percy leaned his head in close to the pile, edges of the kelp already withered and blackened with the high October sun. He inhaled deeply, considered how it was an honest odour, the scent of hard work. His mother was jumbled up in that smell – along with his four brothers, a handful of squashed damsons – all part of the last pleasant family memory he held.

Every Sunday afternoon, when he and his brothers were boys, they were instructed to sit on the hard bench in the front room. The embroidered cushion was always laid aside, as their mother predictably announced, "Now's not the time to be thinking about comfort." The older three were told to read from a thick book of yellowed pages. Children's Bible stories. Percy, who was not yet big enough to read, was told instead to simply sit still and concentrate on something "holy."

Percy struggled with this, the concentrating bit. He tried, no doubt, but when he stirred his mind, a dirty stew of thoughts floated up, spoiled root vegetables bumping against the spoon. A dead chicken's head on a bloody stump. Blisters on his tongue after a fever. The queer excitement of watching his mother undress, the sheerness of her cotton slip. Nothing "holy" there. While he waited for something to arrive, he chewed and swallowed his fingernails, sucked the blood that often wept from torn skin.

"By the looks on your face, little Percy, your thoughts is a far cry from holy," John, the oldest, sniped. "Well, fellers," he continued, "if you asks me, I'll tell you something that idn't holy. Plunking our arses on this bench, when 'tis a fine day calling us. Surely God don't intend that."

Though Percy shivered at the thought of disobeying, he rose as the others rose, made his way out the front door with them and into what their father affectionately referred to as, "Mother's Newfangled Garden." A mess of sturdy sheep laurel, cornflowers, wild asters, and phlox. Other flowers now dead, tangles of sleepy plants beginning to wither.

They stole past a group of men in painted chairs, bellies like balls rising and falling as they dozed in the afternoon sun. "Holy dreams, I's betting," John whispered.

Down the path and across the log that made a greasy bridge over the brook, the brothers reached the backend of Widow Samson's yard. Her house was plunked in the very middle, blue clapboard, faded and crackled like a smashed robin's eggshell. Jumping her rickety fence, they crept through the dry grass until they reached the rough trunk of her damson tree. "Say it ten times fast, b'ys," John commanded, as the three younger boys whispered, "Samson's damsons, Samson's damsons, Samson's damsons" over and over again. "Louder," he cajoled. "Eyes like the hawk, but she's deaf as a boot." And louder they crooned, only falling silent when they shimmied up the tree, began the unlawful harvest.

Finding the branches heavy with sour fruit, they curled their backs into the elbows near the trunk, helped themselves, spit black slippery pits. The four of them gorged until their stomachs swelled, ached. "Shits tomorrow for the load of us," John announced, and the middle two sniggered while Percy blushed. Then they stuffed their pockets, snapped whole limbs, dropped like cats to the earth below. Carted the works home, twigs, leaves and all.

When they displayed their trappings on the kitchen table, their mother did not smile.

Her voice was like jelly, quivering with anger. "On a Sunday of all days. Thieving on the Sabbath."

"But–" John began.

"Don't utter a word! When your father catches wind of this, you'll all be lashed. And deservedly so."

As though coached, Percy, head hanging, eased himself forward and murmured through purple lips, "Why, they was for you. To make something nice. For our family."

She softened instantly, pinched his stained chin, said, "That's nice, my darling. But what do you expect? She'll be by for a drop of tea, and I'll serve her up a jam made from her own fruit? You don't suppose she'd be a mite bit suspicious?"

"Will you tell Father?" Percy's teary owl eyes were on her now, pleading.

"I could. And every one of you deserves to have your backsides reddened until they's raw, but I believes your intentions was nice, so I'll make you boys a deal. If you're up tomorrow before the crack of dawn and manage to surprise your father with the biggest load of kelp he's ever seen – well, that just might fasten my lips right tight. In the meantime, you can spend the remainder of the afternoon with your rumps stuck to that bench and thinking about how good your lives is."

Percy stepped back, marched straight to the bench and took his seat. As they moved past him, one brother knocked him, another yanked his ear, John struck him firmly on his crown with a fist, then grabbed his own backside, whispered, "Phew." There was pride blossoming inside Percy's small body. For once in his life, he was a hero.

The following night at supper, their father said, "'Twas a grand day. Never seen the boys work so hard, and now this lovely pudding. Was the widow by?"

Lifting the crumbly cake, Percy saw the illicit spiced fruit underneath.

"Mmm," she replied, and began to chirp on about her day: paying the widow a visit, helping her pluck the stubborn feathers from an old white hen that was no longer a giver. "Stuck tight, those feathers. Poor old widow, fingers on her, already seen their best days, could barely get a grip. I finished it up for her, lit a small stick in her stove, and burned off every last trace of hair. Wind came up, though. My good Lord, if it didn't coax every feather off the ground, into the air, scattering them hither and yon. Believe it or not, the widow wasn't the least bit undone about the mess. Sat back, watched them dance through the air. 'Twas like a glorious dream."

To the boys and their father, it barely mattered what she said. It was the lilt of her voice that captured them, made them chew slowly to prolong their meal. Her words were a harmony that filled every corner of their home. Making them forget the hardship of the day. She chirped about dipping candles, the secret ingredient in her steamed bread pudding, how she felt like a twirling child when she stared at the wonky lines of her log cabin quilt. She shared her life as a woman – a curiosity so beyond their world of muscle-work, it transformed even the most banal of her stories into something rich and exotic.

When she died in childbirth the following spring, a bitter stillness seeped into the home, uprooted every scrap of humour, of joy, and guarded the space with cold passion. At first the quiet was sharp and unbearable, but after a while the five of them grew accustomed to it. Over the years, they developed a system of nods and mumbles, and eventually, if a word was accidentally spoken, it was met with distain. Even the flowers fell silent, and Percy could no longer hear the buds bursting outside his window during a spring evening. He had imagined early on that they drooped and died because the gardener had abandoned them. Not until he fell in love did he consider that perhaps they were all so desperate for life, they had no choice but to choke each other out.

Percy's three older brothers left, first chance that presented itself. Married as soon as they were able to earn a living. But Percy lingered, bound somehow to that dour, soundless man who was his father.

He was nearly forty years old when he met Delia. Even though he remembered it very clearly, he rarely thought about their first acquaintance. Not because it was upsetting, just the opposite, actually. Bringing it out into bright light and replaying it gave him such pleasure, he only did so on special occasions. He feared wearing it out. Fondness enveloped their second meeting as well, but he was more carefree with this instance, would conjure her words frequently, and after all these years, still feel the scratch of his excited shyness. "You got to be the pastiest man I ever seen," she had said when they met on the road, day of drizzle. "Surely you've been living under a rock." Throat dry, but skin soaked, Percy nodded yes.

He remembered, too, the moment when he told his father that he too was getting married, leaving their home. His father had been hunched over his meal of boiled potatoes, boiled fish, shoveling the scalding food into his mouth. Conversation, Percy believed, kept the mouth alive, and it was clear to him as he watched steaming forkfuls enter that pinched oval in his father's face that the man's mouth was numbed, ignorant to any sort of pain. But Percy's was not, and he spoke clearly. He saw his father cringe at the sound of Percy's voice, but the old man did not look up, never met his eyes. Nothing but a sullen nod. And that was the end of that.

Delia waited at the front gate. As Percy walked towards her, he never glanced over his shoulder, never once looked back. And though he honestly wished it were different, through his shirt his spine could tell, there was no set of eyes gazing at him. No one was going to miss him. Even though some part of his father was still rattling around inside it, his childhood home was essentially dead.

Percy felt warmth spread out inside him, like hot jam filling a cold jar. This did not emerge from the memory of his father, but of Delia, waiting for him, in a navy dress, white piping around the pockets. She had been waving to him as he came around the corner, and in his mind, this was not so much a greeting, but a clearing of the air. Waving away his sadness, making room for hope.

Percy's reminiscing was interrupted by squawking, shrieks rising up from the beach. He could tell by the tone there was no danger, these were only the intermingled squeals of delight and irritation. He walked to the head of the cliff to watch his children.

With thumb and forefinger, Amos was snapping bubbles along a strand of seaweed. Beside him, Stella was attempting to do the same, and she puffed with effort, cheeks smoldering.

"Why can't I do it?" she cried, then dropped the seaweed, stomped on it. When her shoes smeared green paste over the rocks, she slipped and fell, knees crunching against cold stone.

"You're a girl, that's why."

"So?" Spite damming up the flow of tears.

"Girls'll never be as strong as men. No matter how hard they tries." A mocking tune in his words.

She lunged at Amos, arms swinging, while Amos danced left and right, easily avoiding her punches.

"Youngsters!" A few strides, boots dragging over the rocks, and he was between them. "Never fight amongst yourselves, you hear me?"

"It idn't fair. Boys can shave their heads if they wants, wear whatever they likes, do whatever they likes, and look at me?" She yanked her braids, hauled up the leg of her trousers to display lisle stockings. "Itching the legs right off me."

Percy's voice was firm. "Don't bemoan what you is, Stella. Some things you can't change."

She growled quietly, but complied. "Yes, Father."

"God knows girls is wonderful creatures."

"Yes, sir."

He squeezed Stella's skinny upper arm, then knocked her on the head, winked. "Besides, sometimes being strong got nothing to do with muscles. Do you understand me?"

She shrugged, and he said, "Someday you will, maid. It's all right in here." He tapped his chest. "Rolled up tight like a supper bun."

"Yes, Father."

"Now then," Percy said, clapping his callused hands together. "How's about one more load? Shouldn't take a minute with my two best workers."

"I'll fill my bucket first," Amos cried.

"That you won't," she hollered, and she was right. Fluttering hands scooped the slippery kelp, jammed it into her bucket. Task complete, she leaped up, arms in the air, brazen white belly exposed to the damp salt air.

Amos sniffed, said, "No fair," even though it was.

As Percy carted the buckets up over the hill, he turned to watch them once again, unflinching as the rusty metal handles cut into his palms. Together, they skittered across the beach, and the ocean seemed to mimic their glee, painting the stones grey-green as its wet fingers darted and poked, watery voice singing quietly.

For these children, that stretch of land contained a treasure trove of toys. They smashed empty sea-urchin shells, picked at the edges of a withered jellyfish, skimmed slender rocks across the rippling water. Crouching near a miniature salty pool, they discovered secret life tucked among the rocks. Percy watched their small faces, mesmerized expressions. He could not hear them exactly, but knew the words they were chanting as they held the tiny black coils close to their mouths. A childish threat of sorts:

"Snailie, snailie, come out of your hole
Or we'll beat your mother black as coal."

Percy laid the buckets at his feet and placed a hand over his heart. A tender spot had formed beneath his breastbone, likely caused by a perpetual emotion now residing within him. Though the onlooker might not guess, Percy was a man who was filled with joy. Cavernous holes, formed when he was a child, were now brimming. But instead of lifting his soul from his shoes, it stifled him, this unnatural sensation.

"Hey, Dad," Stella cried. She was standing on a wet rock that jutted out into the sea. "Look! The frog is rolling in."

He smiled inside, looked out on the horizon and saw the grim clouds creeping forward. When Stella was very young, she mistakenly used the word frog for fog. No one ever corrected her, and even though she now knew the difference, they still continued to use the word amongst themselves.

"Yes," he responded. "It's going to get froggy."

As contentment continued to settle, Percy choked on a silent fear. It was the fear of absence, of loss, and the pain he knew would rise up in its place. He sensed this progression was inevitable, braced himself against that morbid understanding. And as he watched his children play and once again reflected on the love for his wife, he cracked open the door to emotion. A gust of hollow bliss kissed his face, then damp terror, balled-up at the core, snuck up from behind and slapped him.

chapter four

Mrs. Delia Abbott, newest member of the First Ladies League, smoothed the starched gingham of her dress, checked the position of her collars, then opened the peeling gate that led to the clapboard church. Her shoes felt loose as she stepped onto the grounds, but when she glanced down, her laces were still snuggly tied. Just nervous, she decided, and her stomach was too: it bubbled and churned, panicked in shots of searing heat. Percy hadn't helped matters much – being so angry when she'd left. Telling her she was foolish to overdo it. Just because she had a thimbleful of energy these past few weeks, why waste it trying to please a gaggle of unpleasable women? After all, had they really asked her to join? He'd made her admit it in front of frowning Stella. No. They hadn't.

As she stepped onto the gravel path, Delia considered how she liked the grounds of the church much more than its hollow interior. Every Sunday, mind-numbing work was set aside, and people found a moment to exhale, the space to ponder their past. When they congregated in the church, their communal air was so sore with emotion – over dead babies, drowned husbands, blighted crops, and empty nets –

the damp wooden walls would almost weep. With all that despair billowing upwards, Delia imagined that one day, the entire roof might blow off.

Outside the church, though, there was a gentle calm. A well-tended graveyard bordered the walkway, and there was serenity in its neat rows of mounds and dips, lines of painted crosses. Pure and absolute peace.

Delia took a deep breath, tried to draw that sentiment into her lungs. Then she noticed a mangy crackie among the grave markers, snapping its jaws at blackflies overhead. Dancing and jumping, the dog was the picture of unfettered joy, and Delia smiled when she came closer. She could take a lesson or two from that dog. It didn't care that its matted fur clung to its ribs or that flies were not the meal it craved. A simple life, appreciating what was available, and that was enough. Maybe on her way home, she would try to lure it along. See what Percy would say. Shabby, yes, but she could tell it was full of boundless optimism, just by the way it waggled its behind mid-air trying to gain height.

Though when she passed by, the dog's demeanour changed. It froze stock-still, locked its shiny brown eyes on the air that surrounded her. She paused for a moment, held out her palm, offering a scratch behind the ears. "Here, puppy." But the dog backed into the shrubbery, fur puffed into a mane, a snarling show of yellow teeth. "Angry too?" she mused. "Were you talking to my husband?" And then she reached for the wooden railing, mounted the stairs in her uncertain stride.

"Well now, don't Mrs. Abbott look lovely," Mrs. Hickey announced when Delia entered through the open door.

"All ready for Sunday service," Mrs. Cable said tersely. "Though we's only cleaning today."

Delia reached up, touched the damp wire rollers

underneath the polka-dotted handkerchief that covered her head. Shame, a hidden spring of it, quickly broke through the surface and flooded her. Who washes her hair before cleaning a dust-riddled church? Who wears a good dress? Someone who doesn't know better, she decided. These were errors, and she now wished, in that moment of budding pride, she had not accepted when Reverend Hickey meekly suggested she join the church group. "Long overdue," he'd said. Oh, the glee in her voice when she blurted "yes," then how it drained away when she noticed the expression on the puffy face of Mrs. Hickey, the Reverend's wife. Her lips were pinched with displeasure, her wet eyes rolling, like two cloudy glass baubles floating in vinegar.

"Idn't going to get cleaned by gawking at it," Mrs. Hickey bellowed up towards the rafters.

"That's right," Mrs. George replied. "A good scrub before the Lord comes in. Lots of burden to lay down this week."

At once, Delia wanted to run back home, hide in the outhouse, lean her head against the splintery wall, and listen to the scratchy sound of spruce trees, intoxicated by summer sun. But instead, she began to collect worn prayer books, stack them on the rickety table near the back door. Slight dizziness had settled on her shoulders, and when looking downwards, she thought the floor appeared slanted, buckled in places. All the stress of the week, she decided, what with the fire.

"Could've been the lanterns," Mrs. Primmer said. "Something as simple as that."

"Got my doubts," Mrs. Hickey replied. "My bet's on that Johnny Bent. Smokes like a tilt, he do."

"Men just don't heed that sort of thing," said Mrs. Burden.

"Sure, a flick of ash on a bit of tinder. That's all it takes." Mrs. Wells now.

"A shame."

"A real shame."

"What about Fred Batten?"

"But he never smoked a day in his life, maid."

"Don't matter. He drinks like a fish. Every second day I sees him hauling up the lane, falling all over hisself."

"And the temper on him!"

"Hilda got no control over him. So drunk, he gets right wild every time."

"A decent woman wouldn't let him out through the door."

"A decent woman would never of let him in."

"Got no business bothering the men, he don't."

"And look what happens. No good."

"Burnt down to the dirt, it is."

"Gone."

Last Tuesday night, Delia and Percy had awoken simultaneously when the acrid stench of smoke began to ooze in around the window to their bedroom. She arose quickly, drew back the curtain, and witnessed a warm glow just beyond the trees.

So close, she thought. *Our home.*

Percy was silent for a moment. "No, 'tis too far off." Then, "The mill, by Christ. That's the mill. I'll bet you a damn."

Grabbing his trousers from the chair, Percy jammed one leg in, the other bounding after. As though by magic, Amos appeared behind him, both dashing from the house, suspenders flapping, buckets in either fist. Alongside his father, Amos was whippet-thin, but, Delia believed, what he lacked in bulk, he possessed in conviction.

Delia was suddenly alone, waiting in a cool creaky house, aware of measured time. Staring at the brightness through the trees, she saw it swell into a broad band of orange wisps, smoky ghosts circling. She had the urge to nudge Stella, tell her what was happening, but when she stood over her, Delia changed her mind.

In her sleep, Stella's plump face lightened, then smiled, giggled even, with an amusing dream. Delia felt a tinge of bitterness, as she knew that, when awake, Stella saved those expressions for her brother and father. In truth, she didn't blame her. Delia had barely been a mother to Stella, and a groove lived between them, liquid sourness coursing along. There had been occasions of lightness and giddy joy, but she could count those on one hand. And she rarely thought of them, never spoke of them, because the scarcity of those moments only made her sad.

Her illness might have been part of the cause. Throughout her childhood, Stella was required to nurse Delia and appease her. But Percy had never encouraged the child to openly love her. The choice was hers, and it was clear to Delia she chose not to. And, in turn, Delia held herself at such an aching distance, sometimes she could make Stella practically disappear.

Maybe, as Stella grew, Delia started to house a fiber of resentment towards the child. She would admit to just a hint, a wisp. A wispy wisp, at that. When Stella came into their home, the child had captivated Percy, and with each passing season, Delia faded more and more. Stella's health only made Delia aware of her continual shriveling. When Stella scampered about, boundless energy, overflowing promise, Delia chided her own frailty, her slight slump, curling shoulders. She hated when her husband chirped, "Stella, my star." But when he spoke to Delia, it was often instructional, "Now then, Del," voice like dough made with dead yeast.

She was blessed by Amos, though. Loving him was so comfortable, like dozing in sunshine, though she wasn't sure why. Perhaps it was because he was a boy, and by nature, boys were easier to love. Loving Stella hurt, in a way that was different and worse than being sick. And Delia's body was often so feeble, she needed to keep anguish away from her heart. If she were to survive at all.

Leaning in towards Stella, Delia smelled the woodsy-scent of her scalp, was reminded of the trees that surrounded them, the fire at the mill. She should check the progress from her bedroom window. But before she left, she touched the base of Stella's neck, felt moisture, and loosened the quilts that bound the girl, made the thin hair cling to her face. No matter the temperature, Stella had always been a damp child.

Just as the sun was pushing up behind the water, tipping the waves with pinkish froth, Amos dragged his body through the door. He looked smaller than when he left. Bleary eyes stared out from a soot-coated shell, and he went to his mother who was seated in the rocker. He knelt down, placed his head on her lap. Thinking he might crumble, she touched him gently at first, then snarled her hands in his dirty hair, shook it a little. *Not so easy, is it, my son? To be growed up. Like a man.* Exhausted, he sighed, then closed his eyes.

Percy arrived shortly thereafter, barreling in, fury and failure riding high on his back. He swiped cool water from the basin over his hands, smeared the soot on his face, and didn't heed the black water dripping from his elbows. His hands were fists, and they banged into each other as he paced.

He did not look at her for several minutes. *Destroyed,* was the only word he'd said.

"'Twas the lanterns," Mrs. Primmer clucked. "That's what my Bob says. Offering up only a pinch of light, they does. More trouble than they's worth."

"You said it, maid," Mrs. Wells replied. "Lost my best curtains three years ago. Just ordered them in from the catalog, not hung for a month, but up in flames."

"Well, now."

"Would've lost the house too. But I hauled them down, bunched them up, flames and all, tossed them right out the back door. Don't know what come over me."

"Good Lord was watching over you that evening."

"I allows." Mrs. Wells nodded vigorously. "A shame though."

"A real shame."

Delia tried to nod in time with the others. "Did you re-order, Mrs. Wells?" she ventured.

"Re-order?" Snorting. "My dear Mrs. Abbott, it took me half my lifetime to scrape together the few dollars for those. No, ma'am. I did not re-order. Nothing of the sort."

"Oh." Delia began to swipe the pews with a cloth doused in lemon oil. Dust rose up, tickled her nose, and she sneezed, saw a brilliant burst of colour behind her eyes. She sat down with force, and the sound of her elbows knocking the wood echoed throughout the church.

"Something wrong, Mrs. Abbott?"

"No, no."

"Well, we best carry on then. A lot to do, and I still got to peel all the vegetables for the crowd tomorrow."

"Can't work on the Sabbath."

"I swear, you'd think I hadn't fed them all week. Way

they goes at a Sunday meal."

"Georgina got mine all taken care of. God bless her."

"I needs time to iron those cloths for the service. But I expects I'll get them done by sundown."

"Well, I think I'll take a spell," Mrs. Primmer said. She sat on the step that led to the altar, shook her head. "Don't know what's to become of the men. What'll they do?"

"Doubts if the Fullers'll extend us either bit more credit," Mrs. Burden said. Her voice cracked, and she put her hand to her mouth. "Don't know how we'll make it through the winter. The girls'll have to come out of school. Work to get by."

"They don't deserve this. The men driving themselves into the ground. All for nothing."

"No need to be heading off to the camps this winter. There'd be nothing to do with the logs they cuts."

"The river'll be empty. Nar man out on the logs with his pickpole and peavey."

"Sure, that's no kind of life, anyways, if you asks me. Sleeping on those old bough beds. Eating old bologna, a scattered baked bean, gingersnaps if they's lucky."

"Surprised it's not the death of the load of them."

"Every year, John's a shadow of hisself when he comes out."

"And do you know what they does with all that wood?"

"No, maid."

"Ships it to the States, they does, where they uses it to make the insides of pianos. Can you fathom it? Our men near killing themselves so that some uppity rich youngsters can play their pianos."

"I never knowed."

"Mrs. May got a piano."

"Well, that's different."

Mrs. Burden whimpered, pressed her side into the wall by the door, knuckles in the mouth now.

"No point to belabour it," Mrs. Hickey chided. She was on her knees, both hands gripping a wooden brush. As she scrubbed, her backside, like two over-risen loaves of bread bound together, waggled. She sat back onto her calves. "Who amongst us is going to cast the first stone, hey? Like I always says, you can't unring the bell, ladies."

Curious about how it might feel to live inside such a grand body, Delia began to stare at Mrs. Hickey as she worked. A hint of jealousy bristled within Delia when she noticed Mrs. Hickey's body jiggling. Every few swipes of the scrubbing brush, the woman would pause, reach her soapy hand behind her and tug at the hem that was riding up over her backside, exposing her slip. Delia ran her lean hands down over the bodice of her dress, felt her ribs beneath the fabric. Skin pulled over bones, her body was nothing more than a series of emaciated racks. Mrs. Hickey, on the other hand, had surely managed to establish such a form by denying herself nothing. Plenty of lard, white sugar, heaps of dripping scrunchions. Her hefty skeleton was tucked deeply away, safe inside thick layers of fat, a good foot of room between her soul and the outside world. Delia wondered if she might be happier if she had Mrs. Hickey's hips, her doughy folds. And she had the sudden urge to put her arms around her, squeeze the softness, feel the warmth that such a pelt might offer.

Delia stood, daubed more lemon oil onto her cloth, and began to wipe down the pulpit. "It's good fortune that Percy makes furniture in the winter. He's guessing it'll tide us over until the mill is built up again."

"'Tis a pity we idn't all as fortunate," Mrs. Well said, words a caustic drip. Then, with smugness, "Doubts there'll be much sales, though, when nar man got a job."

"He thought of that. But he says most things he makes goes across the harbour anyways."

"Well, now." Mrs. Hickey hoisted herself to her feet, face mottled like beetroot smashed on white china. "I don't believe 'tis necessary to flaunt your prosperity amongst us regular folk, Mrs. Abbott."

"I certainly was not flaunting, then."

"Whatever name you choose. I would imagine the good Lord frowns upon such boasting."

"Come, Matilda. I was hardly flaunting or boasting, or any such thing. I was just trying to contribute to the discussion."

"Contributions like that we can do without, Mrs. Abbott. Now, if you don't mind, the Reverend would appreciate having a clean church. A little less tongue wagging and a lot more elbow grease might get us headed in that direction." Mrs. Hickey wobbled up the aisle, holding the back of each pew as she passed them. "If you've got no objection, Mrs. Abbott, you can carry on with those floors. As you well know, I have a touch of the arthritis in my knees, and today, they's right gone."

"Very well," Delia replied politely, and as they passed alongside each other, their eyes met. Mrs. Hickey's were dull, the colour of an old, but still tender, bruise. Though she tried not to acknowledge it, Delia knew Matilda Hickey despised her, even though they had never fought, a heated passage once, perhaps, but never an argument. After years of assessing the origin of the ill-will, Delia had decided it was deeply rooted in what she considered to be an informal exchange involving a marriage proposal and a reasonable man.

When she was sixteen, Delia had moved to Bended

Knee to help her mother's friend's littlest sister, a woman named Joanna Cable. Joanna's husband had drowned. He was lost along with three other men while clubbing seals when a sly blizzard engulfed what began as a fine day. Shortly after his death, Joanna gave birth to twin girls. Because she had been married only a short time when her husband died, she was very much alone in her new village, and Delia was sent to offer relief, to help smooth the rough patches.

Throughout that summer, the young minister came frequently to offer support to the new widow. Sipping tea in the front room, he always perched awkwardly at the edge of his seat, weight still on his thin legs. The embroidered cushion never felt a brush from his back. As he sat, his expression was frequently of the pained variety, reminded Delia of an uncle she had who suffered terribly whenever he consumed boiled cabbage. Conversation was often stilted, and his mind would constantly trip, mouth stuttering. He would blush when he spoke of Bod's Gook and when he told the women that he loved to hing symns. Delia wondered if four girls in one room made him nervous, and when he caught his slips, he would whinny like a jumpy foal.

Fall arrived, marked by the lonely smells of uprooted earth, burning leaves, irritated sea. Joanna told Delia she decided it was time for the Reverend to move on. During his next visit, she explained that she was getting by just fine, what with Delia and all. She gently suggested he might consider tending to others less blessed than herself. But he shook his head, hair tumbling into his eyes, and said, with some stammering, that grieving was an arduous process, being close at hand during trying times was the noblest part of his profession. How could she respond to that?

As the winter dragged on, Delia noticed the Reverend

spent less time ministering to Joanna's torn heart and more time staring longingly about the room. Perhaps the paisley wallpaper reminded him of a room in his deceased mother's home. Or, Delia wondered if he might like to stay there, if he envisioned himself sharing this simple family life that Joanna was creating. If he were to become a permanent fixture, and he very nearly was already, Delia would surely have to move on. She would never admit this to anyone, but she found the Reverend unattractive, thought his presence was like a gulp of cod liver oil – essential for good health, maybe, but with a rancid flavour that made her shiver.

Then, one summer afternoon, when she arrived home from the general store, small packet of sugar in her purse, she overheard a discussion that changed everything. The Reverend was in the front room (no doubt balancing on his particular chair), and talking to Joanna in hushed but furtive tones. Delia nodded to herself, confident he was confessing his adoration, and she stood just outside the door, eavesdropping. Keeping her hand in her purse, she felt the packet of sugar, lifted it, enjoyed the weight of it, the luxury of the pure white crystals. She would bake a pudding, maybe a cake even, for when Joanna announced her good news, and Delia took only shallow breaths so she could make out their exact words. But the air snagged in her throat when her own name was spoken, and the direction of the conversation became clear. "Delia is young and lovely," she heard the Reverend declare. "I won't deny she's caught my fancy." He coughed, then made a terrible noise, akin to a wet sneeze from a yawning cat. "I would like to ask her father for her hand."

Delia jumped, locked her fingers over her gaping mouth.

"My good man," Joanna responded. "That would be

quite impossible."

Imperceptible sigh from behind the door.

"Oh?"

"I'm surprised we never mentioned it. Some months back, we received a letter from her mother telling us they were moving farther eastward. If Delia wanted to join them, she best get on home. I told her I was in a good way now, but she decided to stay on, rather than dislodge herself again, I suppose. I figures she got a life started here, and she's a real self-reliant sort. So, I thinks you'd be hard-pressed to make the trek to see her father. 'Tis an awful good distance."

"Ohhh, that's too bad." Spirit twirling down the eddy.

"But I knowed her father pretty well, and he's always been a modern sort. I believes if you asked for Del's hand, he'd likely say you could have it."

Delia gasped, buckled over, then wrapped one leg around the other, squeezed to counteract the sudden impulse to rush to the outhouse.

"Then he'd probably laugh," Joanna continued, "good-natured like, and tell you he could give you her hand, but if you wants the rest of her, you best ask her yourself."

When Delia heard the Reverend's chair scrape, she quickly opened the door to the cellar, stepped down onto the top step, and waited in the musty darkness as he stumbled out. How wrong could she have been? He had not twisted his pity for Joanna into compassionate love. No. He lingered all those months, drinking tea, rubbing his hands through his hair, describing the virtue of Pod's Glan with another objective in mind. Now she realized it was all because of her.

Delia did her best to avoid him, feigned feminine discomfort and stayed in her room for two days. Thursday and Friday she managed to dart out the back door when she spied him strolling up the lane. But on the Saturday afternoon, when she was lost in thought as she shaved splits from a large junk of spruce, he was able to sneak up behind her.

"Walk with me," he said, and she had no choice but to do so. They strolled to an oak tree, a sturdy rope and wood swing dangling from one of its branches. She sat, idly swaying back and forth with a push of her toe. Leaning against the rough trunk, he pressed a glass of water and chipped ice Joanna must have given him to his forehead.

"Marry me," he said, without delay, and Delia had the immediate sense he chose the simple sentence so that any mix-up of consonants would go unnoticed.

She put her head down, stifling the inappropriate laughter taking hold of her diaphragm. Slowly at first, she began to swing, then climbed higher and higher, closing her eyes as the oak tree began to groan. How she despised herself, her immaturity, her conceit. She could not see past the pockmarks that traversed his face, crawled down over his neck. She could not ignore the clumps of gingery hair curling out over his collar, hinting at the vast rug beneath. She could not tolerate his moist hands when he touched her after a service, her yearning to rinse away the smell of his salt. She did not waver in her decision. She had to say no.

Just as that thought solidified in her mind, the tree issued a vulgar grunt and the rope buckled and snapped. Both swing and limb broken, Delia flew through the air, landed flat on the packed dirt of the path, skidding several feet. Rocks jabbed into her backside, tugging her skin, tearing the fabric of her dress. Body burning, eyes watery, she looked to the sky, puffy clouds floating with mocking laziness. *Your wrath is great, Lord, I feel it. But I just can't.*

In a flash he was leaning over her. "Are you hurt?"

"No," she announced through clenched teeth.

"Well, that's a relief."

"No." Tears ran from her eyes, pooled in her ears. "I mean, no."

"Oh," he replied, stepping back, freckled hand to his cheek. "Oh, oh. I thought you…oh."

She began to writhe now, rolling on her side, thin strips of wet earth peeling off the back of her torn dress, dropping away.

Joanna came running from the house, long skirt and apron lifted to her knees. "What happened?"

"I think I br-oh-oh-ke my ta-aye-ayel-bone." Sobbing now, as much from pain as from the embarrassment of her first proposal.

"For pity's sake, Reverend, don't just stare at her, help the poor child into the house."

He plucked Delia from her landing pad, and as she rode along in his arms, she stole a glance up at his eyes, his nostrils, saw a watery dejection beginning to run down. Letting her head loll back, she was thankful now for the pain that wracked her. Without it, her shame would have brought her to her knees. Her response was revealing, and she was stunned by the hollowness that existed within her. She could not close her eyes, marry in blindness, even though inside, the Reverend was good and kind and patient and strong.

Delia never would have disclosed the details of the debacle to another, but Joanna was a talker, and there was no end to the line of willing listeners. The Reverend's simmering affection. Delia's fall from the heavens. Her shocking refusal to become his bride. A bruised backside, an injured ego. All fodder for teatime. And the banter increased when, after only a fortnight, the Reverend's affection was transferred to a hard-nosed but eager girl named Matilda Button. She lived alone in a shack with her mother, her father having run off when she was a child. A scant six-week courtship, and the new couple married, first baby soon on the way. Though the gossip died down over time, Delia believed Matilda never quite got over it. That even though Matilda had wanted to marry the Reverend, perhaps somehow, Delia had bested her. Why would any girl have readily discarded the one thing Matilda was so eager to own?

Delia even recalled the wedding. When the Reverend and his bride exited the church, Delia was among the first to step forth, said with sincerity, "I wish you both every happiness."

The Reverend nodded, shyly, sadly, but Matilda gripped Delia's arm, pulled her close, had spat in her ear, "You'll rot in hell, don't think you won't. Being a pig to the Reverend." Delia had yanked her arm away, that side of her face flushed from the rage poured over it.

Kneeling now between the pews of Reverend Hickey's church, Delia took the scrub brush in her hand, but paused for a moment, touched her left ear. When she thought of it, she could still feel the heat of Matilda's spiteful words, like a curse on her skin. That nasty sentiment ricocheting about in her memory. Sometimes, she wondered about it, if her vanity had pushed her off course. Her life was so unlike her childhood predictions: fervent love, a dozen playful children, perpetually blooming goldenballs. There was goodness, yes, but Delia recognized her increased irritation as the years went by. Something vital was missing, within herself, with her relationships. Worst of all, she lacked the desire to investigate, as though a cavity within her was expanding, pressing out the desire for something more. And when Delia was exhausted (which she often was), stomach distended, foul-tasting gas repeating on her, she heard those words again. Maybe her entire life was marked by a gradual rotting. Maybe Matilda Hickey was right.

As she cleaned the church floor, she felt the disorientation return. Her hands, moving over the wet wooden planks were like a blur, and she slowed the rhythm until it almost stopped. She could hear the women, gossiping, and the formality of the conversation confused her. So many surnames, when on any other instance, they would be Anna and Ruth and Mary and, well, she wasn't quite sure. Delia tried to shake away the fuzziness, decided that this would be her last outing with the First, the First, the… She could not remember the name of the group. Sitting back on her calves, she stared at the material of her good dress, criss-crossing pattern lifting into three dimensions.

She held the brush in her lap, and it dripped onto her apron. As she watched the grimy water pool in a fold of fabric, a gauze wrapped itself around her mind. She wondered if someone owned that peppery little dog, yipping and jumping amongst the grave markers. But why had it growled so fiercely? Did it see that something was wrong with her? Or, about to be wrong? Here puppy, she whispered, reaching for the dog, but her hand never moved. Instead, Delia fell straight forward, nose smashing, warm blood spurting forth. Prostrate upon the cleanest section of the church floor, she began to shake violently.

Mrs. Primmer noticed first – two well-spaced legs jutting out between the pews, splayed feet jumping off the floor like water on a stoked stove.

"Oh my," Mrs. Primmer said, pointing. "Never seen no one clean like that before."

"Queer, don't you think?"

"I don't believe she's scrubbing."

"Mrs. Abbott? Is you all right?"

"Mrs. Abbott?"

No response, and while the other women squashed together slightly, Mrs. Hickey took charge. She marched through the church, grabbed Delia by the ankles, flipped her over with one twist, and yanked her out into the centre aisle. Delia's skirt slid up around her waist, and Mrs. Hickey jolted slightly when scarlet ribbons were revealed, each neatly knotted, attaching loose fitting hose to a garter belt.

The ladies clustered around.

"What's wrong with her?"

Mrs. Wells took a deep step backwards. "'Tis like the devil got hold to her."

"Don't be daft, woman," Mrs. Hickey hollered. "She's having a fit, is all."

"A fit?"

"Yes, a fit. Give her room. She'll come out of it. My mother used to...Oh, never mind."

Delia was still there, hiding somewhere within her own body. In the distance, the women were there, a handful of woodpeckers thumping their beaks against a weakened stump. The sound echoed within her, in time with her skull, as it vibrated upon the sudsy floor, striking it over and over again.

But the tapping soon grew dimmer, replaced by a pleasant silence. Quiet now, the birds must have tired of their pointless work, taken flight. She thought she felt the soft flutter of their wings upon her face. A watery darkness rose up among the gnarled roots, covering the forest floor where she lay. Floating, bobbing in the waves, she was with her father and mother now, resting on the floor of his dory, *Delia's Dream*. Her mother was balanced on a board that traversed the boat, a blood-red handkerchief covering her head and fastened underneath her dimpled chin. "What are you doing down there, little miss," her father said to her. "Old lazy bones." And she managed to kneel, the boat shaking her.

Leaning out over the edge of the boat, she felt the strain on her face, her mother behind her, yanking her hair, fashioning tight braids. She listened, her father grunting as he hauled in his net, hand over patient hand. And then she saw it, a boot, a bare foot, a child's calf, oozing up over the side of the boat. Her family, entangled in the brown wet mesh: Percy, Amos, Stella. She thought to embrace them, but her hands were pinned to her sides. *No rush,* her father said, *I idn't done yet.*

Someone else was in the netting, sliding up, the person's weight dragging the lip of the boat dangerously close to the vast sea. Who would it be? Percy's mother? A ghostly woman with light passing through. Amos's biological father? A faceless seaman, heavy jawed, and smirking. Perhaps that little dog, wanting to be with her after all? *Guess again,* her father said.

And then, she was there, standing amongst her family. Leaning, bewildered expression, jiggling vat for a torso, wet gauzy dress exposing a milk-laden chest. Miriam Seary. The fertile woman who had run from Uncle's house three days after Stella was born. They claimed she disappeared, leaving only the palpable threat of when she might return.

Pain pricked the muscles around Delia's eyes, making it practically unbearable to witness the lot of them, bobbing before her, together. Then, before she could turn away, vibration turned their edges to haze, and they melded into one.

"Get me water," Mrs. Hickey bawled.

"But we don't got no water."

"Only this." Pointing to the wash bucket.

"She can't drink that."

"God, no."

"Is you that daft, Patty?" Mrs. Hickey cried. "'Tis not to drink."

"What then?"

"Throw it in her face."

"What?"

"I can't do that."

"Look! She's moving across the floor."

"Like she's trying to get to the door."

"Remarkable."

"Should we stop her?" Mrs. Primmer questioned, sloshing bucket in her hands.

"She might leave."

"Don't be absurd."

"The water." Mrs. Hickey. "Quickly."

"I can't."

"Throw it."

"Is you sure?"

"Throw it!" No-nonsense screech.

And Mrs. Primmer did. Dirty water splashed across Delia's upper body, soaking her collar, pushing back the handkerchief that covered her head. Filth clung to her face, filled her nose, a tangled clump of hair caught in her eyelashes.

Inside the jittery boat, an iridescent bubble began to form, emerging from Stella's open mouth. It grew and grew, covered them all, except for Delia. She was trapped on the outside and began to panic, knowing that she had reached a point where everything might be lost. Pressing against the bubble with every ounce of her might, her face wet, body straining, straining, she felt an unearthly pressure against her own flesh. *I don't want this. I'm not finished yet. Where is that dog?* But the boat collapsed, bubble exploded, and her soul burst forth. A lifetime scattered like brilliant stardust upon the calm black sea.

"You see?" Mrs. Hickey said. "Right relaxed now, she is." Crouching down, she ran a slow hand along Delia's slender calf, quietly assessing the extravagance of the hosiery. "It worked."

The ladies leaned in, wanting to see her.

But Delia Abbott was already gone.

chapter five

"Start off with a scant cup of sugar," Matilda Hickey explained. "Then a few eggs, and give it a good beating."

Mrs. Hickey was beside Stella, a bowl and several ingredients on the table before them. Except for the Reverend, they were alone. Ever since Delia had died, Mrs. Hickey had been dropping by, "to ease the pain of the family," she said. But these engagements did nothing to dig out the misery that had urgently put down roots several weeks earlier. They only served to agitate everyone. Whenever Amos and Percy heard the shrill squeal of Mrs. Hickey's voice, they left through the back door. Before she arrived today, they were having a silent dinner, each pushing cold food around a plate. Then the breeze carried in the sound of clipping heels, news of some local scandal spilling from a wide mouth. Amos and Percy dropped their forks, scraped back their chairs, darted like wild animals in the echo of gunshot. Stella had no choice but to stay put, poke the plates of fish and boiled potatoes into a cupboard lest the Reverend and his wife suspect abandonment.

With each visit, Mrs. Hickey taught Stella to prepare a dessert that would never be eaten. Stella always insisted she take a bowlful or plate of whatever they made, but Mrs. Hickey wouldn't hear of it. Appetite was scarce, and so, after the squares or puddings or biscuits sat under a tea towel for several days, Stella would place them on the back stoop before going to bed. A stray mongrel, most likely, would wander by in the darkness, lick the platter clean.

While Mrs. Hickey explained measurements and sifting and folding in, the Reverend settled in a chair by the woodstove, Bible opened on his lap. Every now and again, he would pause his reading, spend a few moments describing the good Lord's healing power or His ultimate plan, but there were no listeners. Stella's ears were occupied with the incessant nattering of Mrs. Hickey, and there was no chance for the return of Amos or Percy. Amos was somewhere outside pacing up and down the laneway, and Percy was back among his thinning trees, hacking down every spruce within the swing of his axe. Lack of an audience did not hinder the Reverend, though, and he continued his mini-sermons unabated.

"Weeping may endure for a night, but joy cometh in the morning," he droned while flipping to another page. "Though it don't feel like that now, I knows."

"Don't knock the top off it, girl," Matilda said, huffing. "You cracks it like this." She knocked each egg on the side of the table, broke open the shells, raising her arms in grand gestures as the contents plopped into the bowl.

"Oh," Stella replied, taking the wooden spoon. Not trusting her tongue to be polite, Stella spoke very little. She didn't want Matilda Hickey there, her queer energy buzzing about inside the home, irritating its very walls. But Stella had no choice. The woman had made every effort to save her mother, and Stella was required to show her respect. "Let her try to teach you something," Amos had said. "It idn't going to mar you beyond repair." But Stella hated it. When Matilda moved, the wind that came off her smelled stale, like wet dog doused in rosewater. And her voice was torturous, sharp rocks knocking together, kik kik kik, kik kik kik, over and over again.

"Go on, girl." Mrs. Hickey nudged Stella. "Feels real good to give it a beating. Knock a bit of sense into those old eggs."

When Stella stirred vigorously, membrane slopped out onto the countertop. Mrs. Hickey tsk-tsked, then leaned in around her, and with practiced fingers, scooped up the egg white, tossed it back into the bowl. Licking sugar and slime from her thumb, she mumbled, "Bit of raw egg never hurt no one."

Reaching around for the stale bread, Mrs. Hickey brushed Stella with her full-larder-of-a-chest. She grabbed Stella by the shoulders, said, "Not much meat on you, girl. You'll fill out though, once you gets a bit older. You bet. Sure, take a gander at me." She pinched her rolls, smiled. "I was no thicker than a piece of shoestring when I was your age. 'Tis love that makes you fat. I believes that, I do," she said, looking over her shoulder at the Reverend. "True love makes you pack on the suet." Dark soggy laugh.

"All in Christ shall be made alive," the Reverend mumbled through his rust-coloured mustache.

Though Stella wasn't paying attention to his recitations, she could not help but stare at the Reverend from time to time. Judging solely by the top of his head, a mourner might take comfort in the purity of his downy white hair. But when the Reverend showed his face, that comfort would surely transform into uneasiness. His skin seemed to dislike the very bone beneath it, had fallen significantly, hung on either side of his jaw in fleshy dimpled jowls. Acne scars, a reminder of what once must have blighted his cheeks, had slid off his face, now colonizing his neck. His flesh reminded her of cold chicken broth, and it quivered when he spoke. Stella speculated on how he might have looked as a young man. Even with the pulling and tightening, the sunshine and bright hair her mind offered him, she determined that face still would have been mighty unpleasant.

Glancing up, he caught her staring, said, “That was Corinthians. If you wasn’t sure.”

“No,” she replied after a moment. “I wasn’t.”

There was something in his expression when he looked at her, as though he were steeling himself against her tacit criticism. It made her believe he knew what she was thinking, and he knew there were others who had thought the same thing before. Blushing, Stella turned back to the eggs, focused on Mrs. Hickey’s elbows, appearing and disappearing as she sawed through the bread.

“Yes, dear,” Mrs. Hickey replied, as she continued slicing. “Now a cup or so of cream or milk, then soak your old bread. Handful of raisins if you got them. Pay it no mind if you don’t. A grating of nutmeg, if it suits your fancy, or your daddy’s fancy.” The bread was tough. Mrs. Hickey began to sweat as her arm worked the knife, but she did not grow winded.

“’Tis hard work, but we mustn’t be wasteful. Only heathens is wasteful, if you asks me. Going ’round with the Reverend like we does, I sees all kinds of good food heaved out for the animals. Pigs never had it so good. Stuff folks could eat themselves, I allows. Back when I was girl, we was a might more sparing. No shame in being frugal, you knows. A lesson you should learn young, and I guarantees it’ll serve you well your whole entire life." She talked nonstop as her pudgy fingers pressed the bread beneath the cream, drowning each piece.

"Yes, Mrs. Hickey."

"And that's all there is in the making of it. Bread pudding. After that, you puts it into a Bane Mary and cooks it."

"What's a Bane Mary?"

"Nothing as highbrow as it sounds, girl. 'Tis French for a custard bath or a water bath or something. You puts the pan with your pudding into a thing of hot water. That way it don't come out all lumpy."

"How long do you bake it?"

"That's the same silly thing I used to ask when I was your age. My mama, God rest her soul, always used to say, you keeps it in 'til 'tis cooked, girl, and not a minute more. And I says that's sage counsel."

"All right."

"You're the woman of the house now," Mrs. Hickey said as she leaned over, placed the pudding in the oven. "Though I reckons you've been that way for a while now, considering the state of your poor mother."

"For the trumpet shall sound, and the dead will be raised imperishable and he shall be charged. I means we shall be changed. Changed. That's Corinthians too."

"Right, my darling. You knows just what to say." Mrs. Hickey wiped her hands in her apron, smoothed her faded frizzy hair. "We best be getting along, Reverend. Still got to stop in and see to the Vokeys." Then to Stella, "Next time, if you likes, I'll show you how to make a grunt. But you'll need to pick some berries."

Stella leaned against the counter, arms folded across her narrow chest. She was beginning to reconsider. Maybe this wasn't so horrible, Mrs. Hickey here, taking up space. Her commanding presence masked the gloom, and for a few hours, that colossal woman managed to push out the emptiness. Especially this room, for the kitchen was Stella's mother's room. This is where she had lived out most of her adult life.

Not that her mother had enjoyed it, Stella had long ago decided. And as the years went by, her mother made even less effort to hide her general displeasure. Even when she was asleep, the room snored with contention. There were rare occurrences when the conflict was playful, moments when Stella could imagine what life had once been like between her parents. But most often, she was tetchy, complaining about sunlight, the bland meal before her, the stain of squashberry jelly. Who had dared let it drip on her daybed quilt?

But since that Saturday morning when her mother had left to clean the church, the complaining had stopped. Shortly after, her mother had moved into the front room, placed in a temporary box, curtains tightly drawn. And while neighbours came, sat with Amos and Percy, Stella would not enter the room. "Disrespectful," Stella had heard her father say, but he did not force the issue.

When it came time to go to the funeral, her father pinned a black armband over the sleeve of her dress, and told her to lace up her shoes. He began to fold his black-bordered handkerchief, and while his back was turned, she had run from the house. At the back of the shed, she dragged out just enough flat stones piled against its base, and shimmied underneath. Tucked among cobwebs and scuttling mice, she watched her father's feet, stomping past her, his curse words drifting down, scalding her. She had never seen him so angry, and he had not spoken to her since.

No matter the consequences, she could not bear it. If Stella were to see her mother like that, in a state of perpetual stillness, she would be forced to accept that her mother was not coming back. Instead, she tricked herself into believing that her mother was still at the church, piling prayer books, dusting pews, poking at the intricate woodwork of the altar with a damp cloth over her finger.

But the kitchen, the very room, threatened to end the deception. When Stella walked from corner to corner, she confirmed that the proportions were identical, the furniture and cabinetry untouched. But something had changed. She sensed that the room was suffering. From absence. And if Stella acknowledged it, allowed the awareness to seep in around her young heart, she would surely suffer too.

"Yes, Mrs. Hickey," she murmured. "A grunt. That would be right nice."

Grief rolled up with waves of boundless energy. As soon as Delia was in the earth, Percy's muscles twitched relentlessly, and he started work on the hardest task he could fathom: clearing his land. Every twig, tree, and bush was severed, hacked into bits and stacked behind the shed. Roots were ripped away, and he followed their tangled paths, barely blinked as flecks of soil flew into his face, collected in the moist corners of his eyes. The remainder was gathered in a pile, burned, leaves and needles, sawdust, red boughs cackling as they melted into ash. By late summer, his land was transformed from a fairytale forest into a stark patch of dirt and stubble. Standing on the back stoop of his home, he surveyed his work, ignored the empty sense of conclusion clinging to the pit of his stomach.

She would be happy now, he thought, sunlight touching every plank of wood on their home. His home now. He sat down, looked around his clean yard, then rubbed his raw palms over his face. There was no work left to do, none of his precious trees left to destroy, and he feared what was coming next. The questions, no doubt, they arrived at lightening speed. What was happening to Delia? Did she miss them? Was she cold? Should he have put her wool sweater on over her dress? Was the coffin strong enough to keep out those nasty critters that wanted to consume her? If only he could have her back, just for a short while, he would tell her things. Lots of things. He couldn't think just now. But he would have taken better care of her. Such better care.

Percy went to the kitchen and sat in Delia's rocker. Stella was there, as she often was now, making something out of the flour and sugar from Fuller's General Store. Eggs from Miss Allan's, milk from Charlie Carrigan's cow. Nothing any of them would eat, and he resented the fact that the house smelled differently. Sweeter. More like a home. And that shouldn't be the case. Not when his wife had just died.

Stop it, he thought. *Quit your cooking. Your messing around.* But Stella didn't hear him, or else she ignored him, he couldn't be sure.

Sometimes he wondered about the girl's mother, what was she like? There was betrayal there, he knew, considering Miriam Seary in that fashion, but he couldn't help it. Delia's ailment had been too consuming for her to nurture a child. He should have recognized that, never proposed to take in the dense woman's baby. In hindsight, desperation drove him. He so badly wanted to be a good husband, to pacify her, soothe her itchy spirit. But instead of succeeding, instead of enriching her life, he likely greased the very planks on which his wife was teetering.

"I needs berries for the morning," Stella said. "But 'tis dusk. Should I go?"

Percy never responded, just stood, plucked the tin pail from a bent nail in the porch and walked out the door. As he made his way up the lane, facing the low sun, lines began to lengthen. He twisted around when he heard two children giggling behind him, shook his fist in the air when he saw that they were taking turns stomping on his shadow head. *Beggars.*

Early evening tossed a blanket of lavender haze over the cove. Percy ambled along. Though it felt aimless, his body knew where it was going. Without thought, he wound his way along the old road, up across the barrens, then off onto the cliffs where partridgeberries grew. Midway to the edge, he lay down atop a soft covering, ran his fingers over the moss and lichens, mountain laurel and Labrador tea. Squashed berries may have stained his clothing, but he gave it no mind. He had heard people complain they were scarce this year, anyway.

So soft in his mountain bed, and he wanted to rest, but the sandman avoided him, would not spare a speck of mysterious dust for his weary eyes. But that sandman hadn't hesitated with Delia. No. Reverend Hickey had explained to him that she was in a state of eternal rest. And who had put her there? The sandman. Dumped a whole load from his satchel in her pretty face. Percy knew the truth. This was not the gentle visitor he had told Stella and Amos about at bedtime when they were children. Not even close. The real sandman was a hunched crippled creature. When Percy was a child, he had no choice but to listen to the taunting of his brothers. In the pitch black of their room, they described a sinister old man who blinded drowsy folks then stole them away. Delia might be with him now, in his distorted nest, her nose transformed into owl's beak, speechless as he plucked out her bloodied eyes.

Percy filled with helpless anger, boxed the night sky with flailing fists. Grinding against the rock, his back and shoulders started to ache, and he melted into the mossy underbrush, breathing heavily. How he yearned to control his mind, impose a penalty for any weaving or wandering, and limit its ability to torture him. Looking up, he watched the dark clouds clumping, handfuls of damp wool sheared from the dirtiest sheep. Something pleasant, please God, he whispered, let me think of something pleasant.

And his prayer was answered. When that little drawer at the base of his brain slid open, the sweet memory of their first meeting emerged. She was a nameless girl then, crouched beside a tin tub in a backyard, rubbing laundry up and down a sudsy washboard. Her arms moved efficiently, water sloshing over her apron, and he wondered if she might catch a chill from the breeze that drifted off the ocean. But she showed no signs of distress as she snapped the clean clothes, tossed each piece over a line stretched between home and shed, fixed them with a jab of a clothespin.

Percy stood under an old dogberry tree, hidden in the shade. This was the first time he had ever spied on a girl, honest, and he wished he were wearing his brown shirt so that he might blend with the trunk of tree. When she nearly finished the laundry, Percy felt nervous, suddenly threatened by the solid walls of the saltbox home beside her. What if she disappeared behind them? Should he emerge, introduce himself? He had no idea if she would smile, turn away, or slap him in the face. Sometimes he wondered if he were actually invisible, and if she might not notice him at all.

While he watched, the occasional animal roamed past him. That was the way it was during spring and summer months. All animals in Bended Knee roamed freely, grazing wherever they chose. Small fences were constructed around vegetable gardens and work areas to keep animals out. And in the early fall, they were collected, sorted by the symbol branded on their rumps, and housed for the winter.

Percy sighed as he watched her, drove his hands deep in his pockets. From behind, one fat mother goat came up, bit on to the seat of his trousers, tugged. "Get," he murmured. "Get." As he turned, intending to knock the goat on its head, he lost sight of the girl, she had moved behind a layer of sheets. Percy pointed towards a set of tanned ankles, dusty slippers, then looked the goat in its gunk-encrusted eyes, said, "Now see what you've done."

With that, the goat released its hold on Percy, darted over near the girl, and started butting against the little fence that blocked its passage. Percy saw its full udder shaking each time it struck, as though it was filled with milk for a missing kid. Hole quickly accomplished, it scampered in, headed straight towards a piece of laundry, nipped it with its teeth, yanked, and bolted away. Zigzagging haphazardly towards Percy.

The girl screamed, "You little beast," and came bounding after.

At Percy's feet, the goat deposited a pair of damp cotton undergarments. He saw the strings that might tighten the bloomers around a delicate waist, the strips of ruffled lace that would encompass each slender calf. Percy wanted to run, but he was pinned to the tree, the goat ramming him with its steely head. Only when he bent to retrieve the garment did the goat relent, and by that time, the girl was beside him, slapping the animal on its backside.

"You little devil," she screeched, and the goat kicked up its back heels, missing her by a hair, and scampered up the lane.

Percy held it out to the flustered woman, the white ball of fabric, green grass stains from the goat's gnarled teeth, streaks of dirt where it had been dragged.

"Sorry," Percy managed.

"Is she yours?"

"Who?"

"That nanny goat."

"No, miss."

"Well, she deserves a good trouncing. Ruining my few bits of clothes."

"Yes, miss."

Then, as Percy held her underwear in his hands, he dared to think, *Seems she's trying to tell you something.*

The woman blushed immediately, grabbed it. *Yes. Brazen old goat.*

Her voice arrived inside his head, a flurry of tinkling bells; he had recognized it at once. And by the way she eyed him warily, he knew she had heard him as well. Then she turned on her heel, flounced home (he recorded every shift in weight), annoyance in her stride. Her head never wavered; she stole not a single peep back. But, for once in his life, Percy felt undaunted. Her coy voice, still flitting about in his mind, divulged that she was enticed. She wanted to know his name.

As Percy lay on the moss, the clouds cracked open, drifted off in different directions, and he reflected on those voices. Over the years, he and Delia, communicating effortlessly without words. Their secrets, so intimate, it was a blessing not to have to actually say them. But recently, those voices were hushed, and Percy could not think of when they stopped or why? It was not abrupt, so that either would notice, more of a subtle deterioration. Their connection slowly breaking down. Percy was reminded of an innocent leak that once gurgled at the bottom of his skiff, and before he knew it, the water was up over his boots.

In the early years of their marriage, he had worked to understand her, listening to every breath, working to see life from a woman's perspective. But her experience escaped him, she never appeared pleased, and as she got sicker and sicker, his efforts to relate to her grew trivial. Endurance was all that mattered. Her survival.

What Percy thought next nearly crushed him, as though a soaked log fell from the heavens, landed right on his chest. Rolling over onto his side, he spooned his torso around the cold tin bucket, began to shiver. How had he missed something so simple? Something that would have enriched his wife's life untold times over. And as this new consciousness flooded through him, he longed for his biblical brothers to appear on the rocks, deadly stones tucked inside their palms. Mete out justice for blatant neglect. While working so hard to take care of her, to keep his wife healthy, somewhere along the way, he'd forgotten to continue loving her. And with no love to keep her alive, how was that different than already being dead?

When the harvest moon clung to the sky, Percy arose, set about the task of picking a cupful of berries for his daughter. Squinting, he saw the berries glisten, and he crept sideways on hands and knees, plucking every one. Whether hard, overripe, white underbellies, or perfect, he tugged them from their healthy stems, listened as they clanked against the bottom of his bucket.

Almost full now, and he crouched for a moment, crammed a handful in his mouth, filled his cheeks. Chomping, he accepted the shudder that moved through him. How sugar could transform those tart little globes. But there was no sugar available, and he leaned to the side, spit them all out.

Percy was tired now, as he was often, as though his body suddenly realized just how old it was. But before starting the ramble home, he stood, leaned his head back, stared up at the night sky. He wasn't seeking anything in particular, was not so delirious as to believe Delia might make her presence known with a twinkling star or a dancing constellation. Nothing even close to that. From his height on the cliff, the view of heaven was stunning, and he simply wanted to witness every inch of it. He gazed out over the vast ocean, then scanned the high skies, but as he was viewing the horizon, he noticed a single wild cherry tree with its extensive network of fingerlike branches, growing out of solid rock. Percy could not see through it, and when he tried to shift his perspective, he forgot himself for a moment, took a single deep step backwards.

In that split second of descent, there were no scrambling limbs, no flashes of cold fear, no bloodcurdling screams. Instead, he remained silent, kept his body ramrod straight, arms pinned neatly to his sides. A soothing sense of relief enveloped him. Striking the rocks beneath, a kneecap popped, thigh bone splintered, and the brilliant red berries spilled over his face, in around the collar of his shirt. When the weight of his body crumbled in on itself, a sigh was forced from his lungs. The constant dread that had embraced him since he was married, since the children arrived, was beginning to ease.

"He's fine, he's fine. Don't worry, you."

A young man named Leander Edgecombe found Percy just after midnight. Whenever anyone or anything was missing, Leander was invariably the locator. A gimpy leg hindered his pace, but he had the tracking ability of a hound dog. People would always say to his mother, *Leander was born with something extraordinary*, and her eyes would automatically travel to that shriveled foot, even though she knew that's not what they meant.

"He's going to be fine, they's saying," Leander said to Stella. "Just beat up is all."

Stella turned her back towards him, stared at the water. The sea was blackness, and though she couldn't see a single ripple, she sensed it was moving. It always moved, never calm. Sometimes, when she was younger, she imagined it was giggling, one enormous delirious shoreline, but as she grew, its action felt more menacing. Standing there now, she considered that its steady bottomless seething was like torture. Enough to drive a person crazy, if they thought about it. And how could someone not think about it? Everyone was attracted to the sea.

"Looks like an accident," Leander continued. "That's what the men was saying. No one with either bit of sense would jump over with a bucket of berries in their hand. Though I reckons if you're going to jump, you got to be missing something upstairs anyways."

Tugging her shawl tighter around her shoulders, she drove her fingers in through the crocheted holes. She didn't understand this covering. *Don't keep the cold out or the warm in.* It really served no purpose. Maybe a little purpose in a garment was too much to expect.

"'Tis a good thing that ledge was there, else he'd been lost for sure." Shuffling sounds, then, "Sorry. Me running my mouth again. Guess you don't want to be thinking about that stuff."

Out of the corner of her eye, Stella watched Leander

jump a little in his place. Then he leaned hard to one side, his weight appeared unbalanced, as though he didn't trust his bad foot to keep him upright.

"No need to be worrying yourself. We all knows Mr. Abbott's as strong as a horse."

Her cheeks flushed, and she was surprised to detect shame among the tangle of emotions within her. So many times when she'd fought with Amos and lost, her father would take her aside, offer up his own definition of strength to her. Explaining that muscles were only a single element, true strength lived within a person, cradled inside his ribcage. *Amos is a good boy,* he'd say, *but 'tis only foolish to squabble like you does. You got to be strong for your mother, Stella, not be bickering with your brother.* And she would look up at him, see commitment in his sharp jaw line. How she strived to be like him. Even though his eyes reminded her of a stranded seal, she thought he was the strongest man in the world. But she was wrong.

It was late afternoon several weeks ago when Stella saw her father in his shed. She had been washing up the counter of bowls and cups and wooden spoons that always resulted from a visit with Mrs. Hickey. Above the sink there was a small window, and she stared out into the yard, counted the dandelions, heads bobbing as she rubbed the cloth round and round the inside of the pastry bowl. As the afternoon wore away, the backyard filled with shadows, cloaking the red shed where her father often built small pieces of furniture. But as the low sunlight crept along the wall of the shed, striking a window, at once the entire contents was illuminated. And there he was, leaning against the doorframe, his entire body clearly shaking, face distorted with pain. She could not stand to witness his anguish, focused instead on bits of dough still clinging to the hairs on her wrists, the murky water of the washbasin, and how her hands disappeared when she pressed them only inches beneath the surface. Seeing her father weeping that way, so weak, she felt disgrace, and even though it was terrible, she knew she would never feel quite the same towards him.

One of the men came up to Stella, said, "Best get on home now, maid. We don't need no more mishaps this evening."

Stella nodded. "Yes, Mr. Moore."

"That a girl." Then, to Leander he said, "Good job tonight, young man."

Leander lingered, stood behind Stella. "I found him, you know. I found him there."

"So," she replied. "Good for you." She recalled coming up behind the group, a handful of men clambering down over the rocks, shouts of *Lift fellers,* then, *Easy does it.* As soon as he was retrieved, the cluster of seekers headed home. Amos was among them, trotting alongside Clifford Arnold, a giant of a man who carried their father neatly folded in his arms. Stella noticed the awkward twisted knees and ankles, one arm looking much longer than it should. That was her father, broken beyond. When most everyone retreated, she stayed behind, sucking in the cool night air as fast as she could.

"I just thought you'd want to know, Stella."

When Leander spoke her name, the sound of it made her take a step forward. Closer to the sightless mass that undulated before her.

"Like Mr. Moore said, you best get a move on. We don't want you falling over too."

"I will when I wants." She paused. "Get a move on, I means."

"All right then," he replied over his shoulder as he walked away. "Suit yourself."

Stella stayed only a minute or two longer. She was too confused to linger, but too snarled to rush. Up until recently, she thought she understood everything that a ten-year old should understand. But in a matter of a month, everything she knew to be true had shifted. Even her own body. She had always considered it to be a solid structure, but now, when she lifted her arms above her head, she could hear the wind whistle right through her.

For some silly reason, Stella thought of the grunt Mrs. Hickey had intended to bake with her, and knelt in the near darkness, picked two cupfuls of berries, laid them in her lap. Before she stood, she gathered the fabric to create a pocket, held the hem of her skirt against her waist as she walked home. She trod lightly, so as not to crush the berries or blemish the cloth of her calico dress.

Along the path, she heard her steps return to her in an uneven echo, but when she glanced around, she could identify no one behind her. Except for the glow of diluted moonlight, there was no guiding light. She had to rely on the sounds of her shoes touching the earth, her own inner compass.

Just before Stella came to the pebbly trail that led to her doorstep, she stopped short, listened. There it was again. Scrape, clomp, scrape, clomp. She sighed, looked up at the lantern in her window, saw the people in her doorway. Now she knew who had been following her. At a mindful distance, Leander Edgecombe had walked her all the way home.

chapter six

"Hi, Nettie Rose."

"Hello, Amos."

Amos watched her climb the stairs to the church, body bouncing beneath a plain brown woolen coat. For three years, he had wanted to claim that bounce for his own, and he carefully scrutinized her every move for the receptive hints other boys had described: fluttering lashes, blushing and stammering, two-second gazes over the shoulder. "If she fancies you, she won't face you square on," Dennis Brown had explained. "She'll be looking at you from the side, pretending she idn't." When Amos had asked why, Dennis only said, "Girls is like that. That's just the way they is." But Nettie Rose had only flitted past, friendliness etched in her teeth, leaving Amos to continue in his secret state of despair – the backdrop to his life since he discovered that he loved her.

"I'm leaving tomorrow, Nettie Rose," he hollered after her.

She paused in the arched doorway, but did not turn. "Yes, Amos. You and everyone else that counts."

With those words, Amos felt a quick jolt move through

him. He wiggled his fingers inside his gloves, would have wiggled his toes too, but his boots were too snug. Did she mean that he counted? That perhaps she might prefer him to stay? There were no simple rules to explain such a statement, and he sighed with confusion. It made little difference now, anyway, as he had already signed up. If only she had given him some indication earlier, he would have remained by her side, in her shadow even. Rubbed salt in his eyes until they oozed, complained of chronic infection, and eliminated any expectation. But that choice was gone now. Tomorrow morning at sunrise, the men and boys were meeting on the docks where a boat would take them around to St. John's for basic training. And shortly after that, they were going to war.

"Nettie Rose," he called.

But she was already inside the church, and the only response he received was from the cluster of boys beside him. "Nettie Rose," they sneered, grabbing their chests as though to keep their hearts from splitting. "Oo-oo-oo, Nettie Rose, I loves you, I do. I do-oo-oo. I's leaving, Nettie Rose. Maaaaarry me now, maaaid."

Amos felt his cheeks burn, and he was grateful for the dark night, the gentle sifting of snowflakes that landed on his face, cooled him. He glanced over at Leander Edgecombe, leaning against a fence post. Amos saw him shrug, frown, drive his hands deep into the pockets of his coat. Nettie Rose was Leander's sister, one year his junior.

The mocking never lasted long. Within moments, they were clapping each other on the back, pumping clasped hands in manly fashion, saying, *You in? You in?* Plenty of *Yups, You bets. Better believe it, by Christ. We'll be the ones to finish this off.* Pride, courage, and biting unemployment had been the hooks, and they were united already, these newest members of the Newfoundland Regiment. As they talked about the future, their young fists formed in their knitted gloves, as though the battle were about to begin. They were a strong group. Some lied about their age, Amos included. Everyone knew, but no one dared to speak up. At such a sensitive time, there would be little tolerance for a weasel.

"Hey, Fuller," Dougie Arnold called over to the group of boys lingering beside snow-laden spruce trees. "Where's your mommy?"

"Letting you out tonight, is she?"

"Not even holding your hand."

"To hell with youse," a sulky Alistair Fuller replied. He kicked one of the trees, and a load of snow plopped down on his mottled rabbit fur hat. "Mother says your brains is going to be spread all over some field somewhere, while my brain stays right here." He knocked his hat off, punched himself in the side of his skull, then plucked his hat from the ground.

Alistair was among several boys who were struck from the rolls because their mothers had written letters, protesting their loved one's participation. *Dear Sirs, I respectfully request that my son...* These boys now skulked about, weaving amongst each other, a mixture of shame and anger hunching their backs, pushing their faces down behind their coat collars. They would be marked from here on in, the others knew. Trapped in the world of boyhood, pressed into a safe place by their mother's tongue.

"Can't wait to get out of this shithole." This was Hopper Johnson, a fifteen-year-old who had stretched himself to reach the five-foot-three height requirement. "Thumb stuck up my arse half the day, other half running around doing stuff for Nan. What kind of life is that for a growed man?"

"You's hardly growed, Hopper," his uncle joked as he strolled by, creaked open the gate to the church walkway. "Least I hopes not."

"I'd say they'll give you the job of stepladder," Dennis Brown said, stomping snow beneath his feet. "You's the perfect size."

"You can't bring me down," Hopper screeched. He clapped his gloves together, shook his rump, then hooted and hollered, head hanging back like a wolf under a full moon. "I got those nurses all over my mind," he sang. "All over it. Wanting to keep me in peak health, they is. Maybe I'll get some lessons in personal hygiene. Private lessons."

"You'll need it," Dennis replied. "The way you reeks some days."

"I'll submit myself to a daily exam," Hopper's brother announced. "Head to toe. I'll do my duty, if that's what it takes."

"You said it." Gus Smith now. "As long as she's blond and out to here." Hands jumping two feet away from his skinny teenaged ribcage.

Amos laughed, did not resist when Gus grabbed him, shoved his head into a mound of powdery snow. Hopper piled on, then Bobbie and Cliff and Dennis and the rest, until a great heap of young boys were tumbling around in the drift, punching each other, diving and screaming. They were light inside, and this allowed for higher leaps, softer landings.

"Time of our lives, fellers," Amos yelled, breathless. He sprang to his feet, brushed off his clothes. "Is you ready?"

"Good times await."

"The women loves the war, they does. Thinks it's right romantic."

On his way into the church, Fuller stopped beside the

boys, said through scowling lips, "Well, too bad it'll be rats you'll be kissing when you're stuck in some homemade sewer hole."

They pelted him with snow, bumped him until he fell, then forced handfuls of snow inside his jacket, down his pants, in his mouth and ears. Hopper grabbed Fuller's fur hat, stuffed it with salted slush, then forced it down over the boy's fat head.

Fuller squealed, like a child with a lobster pinching its backside. Freed, he shook and shook, ripped his hat off, and stomped it. "You's all a bunch of quiffs. Quiffs, you hear me?"

He stormed into the church, fiery cheeks, snow falling out from every crevice, and the boys roared, shook hands again.

Calmed now, Amos said, "Well, I heard we might see camels. Ride them, even."

"Long as they's girl-camels, and got two humps. Squat myself right down between them. Mmmm-mmm."

"That's right. I idn't no sort of one-hump man."

Amos noticed Leander staring down at his bad foot, a tightly laced miniature boot covering it. Leander cursed softly, crushed a hunk of dirt-crusted ice. Balance shifting, he skipped two steps in order to right himself.

"Look at you, Lee," Amos said, going over to put his arm around his good friend. "Face on you long as a loaf of bread."

"Sure, Leander, you've got the job of kings," Dennis called out. "Keeping all the girls happy while we's gone."

"Nar bit of real competition. You'll have your pick."

"Yes, and you better keep them away from Darcy over there."

"If we gets back and finds out Darce had his greasy little mitts on either of them, we'll thrash you."

They all turned in the direction of Darcy Norman, standing on the steps of the church, grinning widely at each female – child, girl, or woman – that passed alongside him. Though he met other requirements to join, he had been turned away because every tooth in his head was like a burnt stump, blackened with rot.

Leander grinned, danced a little on his uneven feet. Then Amos punched him in the arm, had to lunge to catch him as he began to topple.

"Sorry, buddy. Didn't mean it so hard."

"I knows," Leander replied as he began to scrape, clomp towards the church. "Come on."

"Yeah." Amos scooped the air. "Come on, fellers. I believes the show's about to start."

Inside the church, William Moore was setting up his newly acquired Magic Lantern. His cousin had sent one to him from England, a shiny metal contraption accompanied by a handful of slides in a box. Earlier that day, he had announced, with permission of Reverend Hickey, that he was putting on a show for the community. "A bit of a high time," he had said. "'Tis what we all needs."

Amos plunked down in the pew closest to the back door. Stella was beside him, and on Stella's other side was their father. Amos had pushed him to the church in a hard-backed chair, sleigh-runners attached to the base of each leg. If they had waited for him to shuffle with his two canes, they would have missed the entire show.

When the Abbott family was whole, they would never have dreamed of occupying this pew – one normally reserved for visitors, or reformed sinners who were trying to inch their way back into God's fold. When they were four, every Sunday the Abbott family marched proudly up to the third row from the front. This happened until the week before their mother died. Then, during her funeral, their father refused to walk up the middle aisle, sit with the mourners. He told Amos he didn't dare risk touching his shoe to the place where she took her last breath. Said that even though the church was holy, the air in there haunted him now, offered him no comfort at all. "If no one sees fit to complain about it," he told the Reverend, "we'll be taking the last pew, next to the door." He wanted to be close to the outside, he explained. The enormity of the open sky fuddled his brain, and there was relief in the fuddling.

"We have certain conventions here," the Reverend had said to them. His voice was soft, and he had nodded his head ever so slightly. "But I assure you, none of it applies to seating."

"You cold?" Stella whispered to Amos. "We could move up closer to the stove."

"Let's stay put. Too much fuss with Father."

"Guess so," Stella responded, put her mittens to her mouth, blew.

Amos was still, except for his knees. They rattled, jerked, the bound up energy seeping out. He kept his gaze firmly locked on the back of Nettie Rose's head, her beige tam tugged down over her curls. She was seated next to Gus Smith, and Amos's near-empty stomach wrung itself when he noticed their coat sleeves touching. People continued to mill about, blocking his view, and he craned his neck, willing everyone to be seated.

Up near the altar, Ned Wilkins opened the door to the stove, crammed in an armload of dry wood. "Good thing I brought that load of junks. She's crackling now."

"What a sweet little thing," Mrs. Hickey said when Mr. Moore pulled the Magic Lantern from its box. "What they won't think of next."

"Almost puts me in mind of a miniature pot-bellied stove," said Mrs. Primmer. "Got a tiny chimney and all."

"Do it give off much heat?" Ned said with a smile.

Mr. Moore cleared his throat, turned towards the congregation. "'Tis a mishmash of slides, I believes. I got no idea what's here. If it idn't no good, don't shoot the showman," he said, then gazed out at the young shiny faces, laughed nervously. Unclipping the side door, he lit the kerosene lamp. Projected warm light bathed the wall of the church.

"Before we starts," Mr. Moore announced, "I just wants to say this is our first show, and we'll wait until youse is all back for the next one. That way, we'll have something to look forward to." He hung his head for a moment, then looked up, offered a lopsided smile to his son. "May God watch over each and every one of you."

"Here she goes," he said, pushing the first slide through the slot at the front of the Magic Lantern. "For better or worse."

Collective air was pulled in as colour washed over the wooden wall, a brilliant scene of children swimming, a striped boat and a swan, a nude baby splashing in a puddle.

"Wouldn't that be a grand day," someone called out.

A winter scene next, snowballs flying, red and blue coats, ornate sleigh and a pair of horses, blanket of bells across their back.

"That's not so bad either, nar blizzard in sight."

Someone chuckled.

Mr. Moore pushed in another slide, a squirrel seated at a

wooden desk, feather pen poised in its paw. A duck playing the piano with bright orange webbed feet. Two lovebirds, dressed in party attire, standing in the glow of a fire.

"What they don't do when we's not looking."

More chuckling.

The following slide showed the image of a young boy, fancily dressed in high collar and knickers, sneaking one of his father's cigars. In the next image, he lay back in a grand chair, legs crossed, puffing away. Final frame, and a sour-faced girl glares righteously at the boy who is doubled-over in pain, face pinched, the cigar having worked its magic.

There was light laughter echoing in the church.

"Sick as a dog, he is."

"Serves the beggar right. Stealing from his father."

"These ones got to be slid over themselves," Mr. Moore said. "Bear with me."

The subsequent cluster displayed various types of naughtiness. One depicted a child hanging over a barrel of sugar, an angry shopkeeper paddling him. Next, an apple orchard, high pink brick wall, a boy dangling by the seat of his pants, apples spilling from the inside of his shirt. A man taunting a bull, then a frenzied chase. Children screeching because their drunken daddy won't be coming home.

"No shortage of trouble in this world." Tut-tutting.

"There's a series here," Mr. Moore said. "Ah, I'll give that a go."

One woman gasped when an ominous image flashed across the wall. An enormous beetle, black with a flat shiny shell, clinging to the edge of a sleeping man's bunk.

"Cuddle in, ladies," someone hollered.

In the absence of the slide, the light drove out the shadows, and Amos watched as Nettie Rose pressed in closer to Gus. The church was suddenly warm, and Amos unbuttoned his collar, tugged at his scarf.

"Let's try a different one," Mr. Moore said. "My cousin said this one's quite popular."

As he slid the slide through the Magic Lantern, onlookers saw a ghastly progression. A man was dozing, jaw opening and closing with reliable frequency. Along the floor boards a black rat crept closer and closer, growing larger and larger with each shifting slide. The image covered the entire wall, surrounding them.

"Lard. I reckons it idn't safe for a man to take a nap."

"That's utter filth," Mrs. Hickey said. "Borders on profanity if you asks me."

"With all due respect, that's what they considers art nowadays."

"'Tis all in good fun."

As Mr. Moore continued to feed the slide through, the rat crawled up over the side of the bed, the man's jaw opened wide, and in one mammoth gulp, the rat was gone.

"Talk about your free meal."

"Pure vulgarity. Crowd over there got nothing better to think of?"

"Well, I hopes it idn't a sign of things to come."

"Yes, now. We better get fed better than that."

"Don't count on it."

Mr. Moore pulled the slide from the Magic Lantern, shook his head. "We could go back to the first ones again?"

In the white light, Amos clearly saw Nettie Rose. Her face was turned and pressed into the thick arm of Gus, tam fallen back on her shoulder. He felt sick, sweaty, bolted upright, wooden pew sighing with relief. Through clenched teeth, he said, "C'mon, Stella. Let's get out of here."

"The once? What about Dad?"

"Someone'll see him home. You needn't worry."

Outside, the snow was falling heavily now, fat flakes driven. Amos thought the air had changed, the perfume of joviality had waned, pungent haste its replacement. But the air was still bright, even though it was nighttime. And when Amos looked straight up at the snowflakes, he imagined for a moment that he was moving through them. Moving away from Bended Knee. He could almost hear them brushing past him, like a thousand whispers. For an instant, he thought about their journey, the speed at which they could travel.

"You ready for tomorrow. Everything packed?"

"Oh, yeah," Amos replied, as he put a lit cigarette to his mouth, pinched it in his teeth. "My grand wardrobe. 'Twas a tough time poking it all in."

Amos struck a match on a hinge of the church door, inhaled deeply. Walking up the road, he locked his arm through Stella's. "What do you say, we goes over to the Devil's Hole? Haven't been there since I was a kid."

"I don't like that, Amos," Stella said. "Calling it the Devil's Hole. Why can't everyone just call it God's Mouth? Like 'twas meant to be."

Late one night, shortly before either of them was born, a colossal explosion woke the entire community. People came bounding out of their homes, some barefoot, hair ruffled, nightshirts and long gowns flailing in the wind. They rushed down over the bluffs to the beach, crept along the stones until they found the source of the noise. As they peered up at the rock face, the women held hands with their neighbours, while the men simply swayed in place. There in the rock was a perfect hole, a dark cave that had never been there before. While they were sleeping, a five-foot diameter chunk of rock had popped out from the face of a cliff, plunked down to the rocks below, seated there like a miniature table.

Stories abounded as to the force behind the creation. Each claim rooted in the events of the previous day. For one, the beloved Reverend Coates had been laid to rest, tucked inside a pine casket underneath a mound of gravelly dirt. The entire community was there, every face dampened with drizzle and tears. In life, the Reverend spoke often to his congregation of God's music. *God is everywhere,* he said, *playing for us, singing to us. Only we don't know how to listen proper.* But the crowd was listening now. When blustery gales passed over the gap, a whistle spun out into the night air. Someone said it sounded like angel song. About half agreed. And so, that group took to calling the cave God's mouth. Its formation was a divine act, a gift sent down by the Reverend as a permanent reminder of His holy presence.

Many others claimed dark forces were behind it. The whistling was evil, tempting and hypnotic. What had happened that very evening? The man who owned the general store, grandfather of young Alistair Fuller, had been killed. Nefarious circumstances. How else could he have been poked with a jagged-bladed hunting knife? When Elizabeth Crowley came upon the scene, she found him dead, head jammed into a half-filled flour sack, fabric bunched around his neck. His blood had tumbled out of the wound in his stomach, but was contained by a circle of flour sprinkled neatly on the floor, congealed into a thick reddish paste. Oddly enough, his few dollars were still there, his list outlining the credit he'd extended was unaltered. The only items stolen were cards and cards of buttons, silver ones, wooden ones, glass, and tortoiseshell. Two empty boxes crushed on the floor.

No one knew who the perpetrator was, but a story

linking the crime and the hole soon evolved. They said the devil must have come up from below to fetch whoever did it. Likely the bloke had escaped his grasp earlier in the day, landed in the cove by terrible chance. The devil chased the beggar as he bounded up and down the beach. Angered by the fellow's slipperiness, the devil slammed his fist into the cliff, a hunk of rock tumbling when he pulled his iron hand away. This is where the devil hid, they said, until the murderer, unaware of the alteration in the landscape, darted past for the last time. And so, it was labelled the Devil's Hole.

One fellow, by the name of Herber Mercer, said that although the fanatical theorizing was amusing, he was confident the fissure was a natural phenomenon. There must have been an air pocket in the rock, he explained, formed eons ago, and with the curious weather of the past summer, blazing heat one day, practically freezing the next, the gas just got cantankerous. Wanted to get out. No matter if that chunk of rock was in the way. He never came up with any sort of name, and people dismissed his ideas outright.

"How do you know if 'tis one or the other?" Amos asked.

"Because that devil story is utter foolishness if I ever heard the likes. And because it's a perfect circle. Almost perfect. The devil don't make things perfect."

"And why don't he?"

Stella ignored him. "Plus there's last summer. Little piss-a-beds growed in there, right out of the rock. Not a pinch of soil that I ever seen. And the devil don't grow flowers out of rock."

"Yes, then in the fall, I's betting those piss-a-beds rotted."

"Miracle they was there in the first place. That's the point. Nothing can live forever, Amos."

He fell silent for a moment, sighed and dropped his cigarette butt in the snow. "God's Mouth it is, then."

They ambled up the laneway, passing their house. "Wait here," Amos said, and he turned back, jaunted to the shed, plucked the lantern from the nail. Glow of light between them, they took the trail between Jenkins' and Smith's farms. Along the sides of the path, stubborn blades of grass that had been sticking up through the snow were beginning to bend now, giving up. As he walked, Amos turned to look behind him. He slumped inside his coat when he noticed that his footsteps were already disappearing.

Even though the snow continued to stumble from the sky, the beach was clean. Whenever a flake would settle, salt water would lick over every crevice and claim it. Amos and Stella picked their way over the polished stones until they came to the stone table. Across the top of it, there was a deep split, and when Amos held the lantern up, they could see the items children had poked down into it: marbles, a miniature cornhusk doll, a whittled piece of wood. Once prized possessions, now just beyond the reach of little fingers.

"Do you remember when we was little, and some of your friends weren't allowed to come out here? No picnics on the table?"

"Yes," Stella replied. "I remembers Lizzy Bugden's mom said it'd be like breaking bread with the devil hisself."

"I reckons if that were true, you'd have no trouble making a bit of toast." Amos smiled, nudged Stella.

"Nothing wrong with that."

Stella climbed up first, Amos beneath her, pushing up on her rump, until she was able to lean her torso over, slide herself into the hole. He clambered up next, jammed his feet into the cracks in the cliff face, perfectly placed.

"Like steps," she said. "Almost as if someone put them there."

He placed the lantern between them, then lay back, feet dangling over the edge. On the curved roof of the cave, going from its lip all the way back, someone had used the smoke from a flame to carefully write, *The hole is more worthy than the patch.*

"What do you suppose that means, Stell? Do you think they's talking about this here hole?"

"Maybe. In a sense. This is more fun that just a plain old flat cliff. Though they could be talking about a pair of trousers too."

"Yeah."

"Takes work to make a hole. Patching it up is easy."

"I don't believe that."

"Why do you say that for?" Stella glanced at her brother.

"Sometimes 'tis right easy to make a hole. A few cross words, and you've got a trench dug right through someone. Patching it up is the hardest thing of all."

"Never thought of it like that. But I doubts that's what they meant."

"Don't you think the patch is way more precious than the hole?"

Stella lay back next to Amos. Several minutes before she spoke. "I thinks there's some holes that don't never get patched. Can you imagine going around the rest of your days with a hole?"

"I reckons everyone got a hole, Stell. Whether 'tis a pinhole or a canyon is anyone's guess."

She leaned her head, stared at him. "Really? What size one do you got?"

Eyes focused on the roof of the cave, he replied firmly, "Never thought about it. And I idn't about to start now."

"Yeah, you're right. It's a dumb thing to even think about. Holes."

"I didn't say it was dumb. 'Tis something good to mind. But don't go getting undone about it."

"Yeah."

"I figures 'tis best to patch your holes before they grows too big."

"Or before it gets too late."

"Yeah. Too late."

Amos sighed, put his elbows up, gloves beneath his head. "I thinks I'll be back soon. Do you think?"

"Of course, Amos."

"Yeah. You best keep my supper warm."

Stella giggled. "All right. If 'tis going to be that swift."

"Yeah."

"What will you do after the war?"

"After the war. Few dollars in my pocket. Enough to make a go of something." Pinching his glove in his teeth, he yanked his hand free, scratched his forehead underneath the woolen band of his hat. It was surprisingly warm in the little space, both of them close together. He could smell his sister's breath, and it smelled sweet and milky, like innocent custard. "Though, to be honest, it don't got nothing to do with the money. No way. I just can't turn my back, Stell. I thought about it. I'd be a liar if I said I didn't. But I got to go."

"I knows."

"Got to stand up if you believes in something."

"If I weren't a girl, I'd be going too."

"Well, I's sure as hell happy you is a girl."

"Amos! The cussing."

"Ah, who gives a God damn?"

Stella started to laugh.

Amos began to snicker too, then added, "By Christ."

"You's wicked."

"Yes, I's a real little pisser."

"Amos!" she squealed, still giggling. "My ears is burning."

"All right," he said with another chuckle. "Let's see if I can keep my bloody trap shut."

"Dirty trap, more like it. Filthy. I should take you over to Mrs. Hickey's. She'd teach you."

"Bugger Mrs. Hickey. If Mother was here, she'd be jamming soap down my throat."

"Forget the soap. She'd go straight after the lye."

"Ha."

When the laughing petered out, Amos sat up, stared out at the snow, just flurries now. He lit another cigarette, rolled it slowly between thumb and forefinger. He wondered how far away a person could see the glimmer from a flick of burning ash.

"Lots of bad here, but 'tis pretty, idn't it?"

"Yeah." Stella sat up beside him.

"I likes the snow, even though it causes trouble. And I likes the water, even though you can get drowned."

"I knows."

"But she don't have to drown you, unless she wants to. She can give you a life instead. She's fickle, that old sea. You can never tell what's she's thinking. Fickle and rich. You can't never own her. And that's why every man loves her."

As they spoke, the flurries ended, the night cleared. And as though it knew they were talking about it, the sea balled up and rammed the beach proudly, jostling the helpless stones.

"Do you want to carry on with the fishing when you gets home?"

"Yeah. I didn't like working to the mill. Now Skipper Penny said he'd take me on with him."

"He took a real shine to you. Treats you like a son."

"Yeah, I loves to fish. For me, there's no pleasure in hacking down trees."

"No?"

"When you're out there jigging, and you heaves your hook and line overboard, and it disappears into the darkness. I don't know. There's some magic to it. There's chance. Sounds stupid, I suppose."

"No, it don't. Keep saying."

"Skipper Penny told me that. He says, 'Magic is blind. You don't need to see when you fishes, 'tis all in your hands, in your soul.' He says that I got to learn with my eyes closed, learn to feel the fish when they's swimming by, when they nibbles, when they bites. And I does that, I do. Out there with him, leaning over, eyes shut up right tight. And I tell you, something real wonderful moves through me when I knows there's a weight on my hook. Some wonderful magic."

"That sounds right lovely. Never had that myself."

"Don't want much, I don't. Don't want no uppity job at some store or nothing. When I gets home, I'll take up with Skipper. Then, when I gets a handle on things, I'll go off on my own. If she'll have me."

"Who's she?"

"The water, I means. I believes she's the only woman for me." Amos cleared his throat.

Stella put her elbows on her knees, leaned her chin into her mittens. "Sorry about Nettie."

"Ah, I put that out of my mind long ago. She's only a girl. There'll be plenty of those."

"She probably don't know what she's doing. Living in squalor all the time. All those sisters and brothers."

"That don't got nothing to do with me."

"Well, I can tell you. I idn't having no dozen kids."

"Me neither. Nope. No chance of that. No chance."

Amos stared out at the waves, pale watery fingers slithering through the rocks, reaching for him. Inside, he sensed his nerves were firing shots, shock running down through his legs, heart jolting, stomach flopping. He sighed again, then lay back, arm up, elbow covering his eyes.

"Do you ever think about dying, Stell?"

Silence for a moment, then a quiet, "I guess so."

"I mean, do you ever think about what it's actually like to die?"

"Sometimes. Yeah."

"And what do you think?"

"I don't know. You say first."

"Well, I thinks when you reach the point just before you dies, you won't be hurting no more or nothing. You'll feel good. But, it'll be dark, darker than it is now. Black like pitch. And you'll be somewhere on a cliff or something, high up, I imagines, and you'll know that one more step and there'll be nothing at all underneath your feet, only all the space in the world."

"And?"

"You'll feel good, I's thinking. And I reckons if you're going to die, it'll be your choice, no one nudges you or nothing like that. When you're at the edge, no one darts up behind and slams you. You makes up your own mind if you wants to go on. I bet you'll feel so good that you won't be able to resist it. You won't even think about it. Something else'll take over, putting your mind right at ease. And you'll have no doubt, real faith, I suppose, that when you lets yourself go into all that nothing, when you leaps and begins to fall, someone you love'll catch you right up. And that'll feel real good, I bet. Gathered in someone's arms."

"That sounds nice. I like that."

"I reckons it'll be."

"Only I thinks 'tis going to be cold."

"Really?"

"And dirty. Tons of dirt, so much you can't even move around in it. You'll be stuck. Like you're buried and covered, but can still breath."

"That sounds more like life to me, maid." Amos smirked in the flickering light of the lantern.

"Who do you think'll catch you?"

"My mother. My real mother."

"That'll be nice." Stella swung her legs, banged the heels of her shoes against the rock. "I bet she will too."

"I miss her, you know."

Amos heard her draw in her breath before she said, "I'm sorry. I really is."

"No need to be sorry, maid. Nothing you can do about it. Nothing you could've done. 'Tis just the way things is."

He saw her wipe her face with her mitten.

"Though," she said, "if nothing never happened to your mother, you wouldn't be here. And it may sound wonderful mean, but that would be worse than anything."

"Ah, maid," he said, and began to laugh, shoulder blades lifting off the stone. "Heaven forbid, you might have got a pinch of peace. Without me at you all the time. I'd torment the devil. Little bugger, I was."

"You was not."

"I allows I wasn't. I was worse kind. Bugs in your bed, in your clothes. Remember that time I trimmed your hair?"

"Trimmed? That weren't no trimming. You was using rusty old shears."

"Well, you let me."

"That's cause I knew what kind of trouble you'd get in.

'Twas worth more than my bit of hair."

"Oh, really?"

"Yeah." Giggling again.

"Ooo. Now that's cruel. I'm eyeing you in a whole new light."

"Though I never thought you were going to take so much off."

"Sure, the whole time I had you nipped between my knees, I was pretending you was a sheep."

"Yeah, you're right," she said, then punched his knee. "You're worse."

Amos took a deep breath, sat up again. Another cigarette, but he did not bring it to his mouth, let the curls of smoke trail over his knuckles before the wind found them, dragged them away. "Lots of times I tried to make you feel small, you know. Tried to make you think I was better."

"Nah."

"I don't know why I did that."

"That's what brothers does."

"Maybe I was angry, that you had your mother and mine was gone. Weren't even allowed to mention her name. Had to pretend she weren't even real. I thought you had everything."

"What? Is you codding me?" Stella blew air out through pursed lips. "If 'tis any comfort, I don't even think she could stand me."

"What?"

"Mother. I don't think she gave me much mind."

"Don't say that. 'Tis not true."

"Maybe it's not. But that's what I thinks sometimes. She never ever said."

"People don't need to say stuff. It's what they does that matters."

"Well, she never done nothing either. As far as I minds. Seems like she's been gone forever. Sometimes it seems like she was never there at all. Like I imagined her or something."

"Don't say that, Stella."

"All right." She leaned her head against the wall of the hole, sniffed hard to clear her nose. Several minutes passed.

"No. You can say it. I don't want you to stop talking. I don't like to hear myself breathe."

"Oh."

"Talk, Stella. Say whatever you wants."

"Can I tell you something?"

"That's what I've been asking you to do."

Stella pressed her mittens to her nose, mumbled, "I was scared of her."

"How do you mean?"

"I was afraid to touch her. Hug her. I wanted to sometimes though."

"Yeah."

"Thought I would hurt her. I used to dream over and over again I had big muscle arms and I squeezed her so tight. Damaged her right bad."

"Oh."

"And that she was dead."

"I don't think you could do that, Stell."

"Sometimes I got myself convinced that I was in the church with her, and somehow it was me. Me that done it."

"You weren't...you weren't even close."

"I don't know. I guess I was afraid to even love her. Had myself convinced she didn't even like me. To make it easier, I suppose."

"She loved you, Stell. I knows it."

"How do you know?"

Amos let the cigarette drop, saw it bounce, then die. "Because I used to watch her, that's how. Watch her watching you. She'd always be staring at you when you were doing something with a needle, or trying to knead bread with those skinny little arms. Sewing up the arse of Father's trousers. She'd watch you. And..."

"And what, Amos?"

"That was the only time she ever really looked content. Happy. She looked happy when she was watching you."

Stella rubbed her eyes, reddening them with the itchy wool. She yawned and shuddered. "I'm tired, Amos."

Amos moved the lantern back, illuminating the darkness behind them. "I knows," he said and shimmied out of his coat. "Lean here, maid. You can rest against me."

She laid her cheek against his shoulder, and he tucked his coat over her knees. "Thank you, Amos." Red mittens laid gently on his forearm, and he patted her hands. When he heard her breathing regulate into soft shallow puffs, he let his face fall, rest on her head. He could smell the salt air trapped in her hair, no sweeter scent in the entire world. Barely audible, he said, "I love you, Stella. I hope you knows you're my star too."

Amos never slept. He waited for morning, barely blinking, staring until he could distinguish the sea from the sky. Dead cold had stiffened him, numbed his fingers and neck. Beneath woolen clothes, his damp skin had shrunk against his body, and he felt smaller, wished he had just one more day to grow back to his regular size. But when the edge of the sky flushed pink, urged out the grey night, he understood his time was up. He nudged Stella, told her they needed to go home.

They traipsed over the beach and climbed the slippery hills that led to the pathway between the Jenkins' and Smith's farms. Stella tripped, clutched handfuls of long lifeless grass to pull herself up. And it held tight, saved her the fall.

As he watched her yank at that grass, Amos thought about the many elements of the earth, and decided they were female. The sea, the sky, the soil, the plants. All generous. So willing. And even though he viewed himself as being a decent man, he knew in the months ahead he was going to crawl over the earth and violate her. Abuse her nature. He thought of the war as noble havoc, played out upon the surface of a beautiful woman. Who really owned her anyway?

They reached home, and Amos entered to retrieve his things. His father was seated in the rocker, face so puffed with sadness, it pained Amos to look at him. But he went, stood before his father, took his hand and shook it firmly.

He mumbled something, but Amos never understood.

Sliding his hand out from the sandpaper grip, Amos said, "I'll be home before you knows it, Dad. After the war is done."

"That you will," his father replied.

Their eyes met briefly, and with that gaze, Amos asked his father one hundred questions, and every one was answered. And Amos was able to see the debilitating depth of his father's emotion, a continual pelting rain. Though he wanted to, Amos was unable to fathom a response, and so he stretched, tried to straighten his back. He nodded at his father, shook his hand once more, and walked out the door.

Stella waited at the front gate, leaning over the sharp pickets, eyes droopy. Gales peeled off the sea, snapped her scarf, and she covered her ears with her mittens.

Amos stopped when he reached her, said, "Do you want to see something?"

She stood. "All right."

Dropping his bag by the fence, he unbuttoned his left breast pocket and withdrew a scrap of fabric.

"Here." He handed her a clean white square of cotton, tatted border in a mix of navy and baby blue.

"That's real pretty. A handkerchief."

"My mother made it."

"Your real mother?"

"Yup. 'Twas in with the stuff I came with. That old trunk. I stole it, hid it away for myself, before everything was gotten rid of. Given to other families."

Stella unfolded it, laid it open on her mitten. "Oh. 'Tis lovely, Amos. Best put it back."

But as she reached her arm out to give it back, a bitter wind tore down the laneway, swiped the flimsy fabric from her open hand, and made away with it. Amos and Stella jumped to catch it, banging their chests together, but the wind lifted it higher and higher, forcing it to weave and dance as though it were enjoying itself. Towards rooftops, past smoldering chimneys, until it vanished against the cloudy sky.

"Oh God, Amos." Tears shot out from Stella's eyes, and she collapsed beside the fence. "I's so sorry. I hates myself, I do. How could you have someone so stupid for a sister? Now you don't got nothing left."

Amos crouched beside her, swallowed hard. "Don't cry, maid. That's not true at all. I got plenty left, don't you think no different. I got a ton of stuff in here." He thumped his chest, right at the unbuttoned pocket.

Stella wailed and wailed, buried her face in cold crisp folds of her skirt.

"Plenty of stuff. Who knows, I might have made it all up, but it still feels right real to me, and that's all that counts, right? Whatever feels real."

Rubbing her back, he whispered, "Say it, Stell."

He stayed beside her, holding her, waiting for the shaking to subside. But when he noticed a handful of shadowy figures skulking down the lane and out onto the road that led to the docks, he had to leave her, even though she was still shaking. He stood, unlatched the gate.

"Be good," he said, and let his fist fall gently on her head. "I'll be back before you knows it. Keep my supper warm."

Stella did not stand and turn towards her brother, could not watch him walking away. She listened though, and heard what she thought was the saddest sound. A pair of heavy tired feet, leaving home.

In the months to follow, she received several letters from Amos, but the one she treasured most was the following:

> *Dear Stella,*
>
> *I am listening to the rain, and it seems to fall much more softly here. Without guts, almost like it's scared to make too much of a noise. That sound makes me think of home, and the raucous rains that we gets. I miss that – rain with lots to say. And you, of course. You, with lots to say.*

Someday, after the war, I'd like to bring you here. The countryside is grand, and I bet you would like it. Parts are similar to home, like the fields, and the smell of bread when you walk by a farmhouse, herds of goats, but it's different too. You know that the loveliness is a bit of a trick. I won't try to describe it, I'm no good at that sort of thing. You will see, one day, when the horizon is more honest.

Even though I knows you might be, don't worry yourself about me, Stell. My spirits is good, and my legs is strong. Thanks to your knitting, my feet is wonderful warm. I could've sold my fine wool socks a dozen times over, but I never gave it a single thought. There is decent food and plenty of it. Too much, in fact. I'm not the same skinny feller that left you. Today, me and the men shared a jar of strawberry jam, and it tasted like heaven.

When I'm waiting, sometimes I dredges up the talk we had that night in God's Mouth. The patch is more precious than the hole. Do you remember? And I want you to know that I don't got neither hole to think of. Never did and never will, maid. That's the pure and utter truth. I listens to some of the other blokes' stories, and I knows I been blessed beyond. If you can do me a favour, when the time presents itself, please tell that to our father.

Remember me, until you see my old mug again.

Love, your brother,
Amos

P.S. Is you still keeping my supper warm?

Two weeks after this last letter, Stella and her father received word that Amos Abbott, aged 18, had been killed in the line of duty. With great honour, he died on the frontlines, shot by a near-mirror-image of himself. Stella did not weep, collapsed inside. *You lied,* she thought. *You lied to me.* She imagined his body, bloody, stuck face down in the icy muck of a trench. His last breath would smell like a rusty iron pan, and the air would emerge not through his mouth, but the holes in his torso. A riddle of holes. She could see them clearly. But knew no kind of patch in this cruel world would fix them.

chapter seven

Leander Edgecombe climbed the rickety ladder leaning against the side of the Abbott household. He had made this ladder especially for himself, the rungs very close together. That way, he could hop up with one good foot, rather than step with two.

He held tightly with his right hand, and hoisted a chair with his left. This chair was made from knotty pine, and the joints were seamless, edges smooth, spindles a lively mix of beads and grooves. With seafoam coloured paint, he had given the chair three thick coats. The legs were uneven, back shorter than front, as he wanted it to sit flat on the sloping roof that overhung the porch.

As he positioned the chair, Stella came out to watch him.

"If you asks me," she said, "'tis a waste of a lovely piece of furniture. All that colour will burn up, peel off like old skin."

"I don't heed one word you says," he replied, and smirked down at her. "Anyone who passes by'll know that a furniture maker lives here."

"Everyone knows now anyways, they don't need no

chair to tell them. But, suit yourself. Long as you sweeps up the flakes."

He laughed, pulled nails from his pocket and held them between pinched lips. Chair in place, he asked Stella to hand him up the hammer. He then nailed each leg firmly to the roof, shook the chair to ensure it couldn't budge. Satisfied, he clambered back down, stood back several feet to admire his handiwork.

"Come," he said, and Stella stood beside him. He wrapped his arm around her waist, squeezed her. "What do you think now?"

She smacked his chest. "I thinks the same as I did before, of course."

Leander looked at his wife, pressed his face into her hair, dampened by the heavy mist. They had been married two full years now, and Leander would say these years had been the easiest of his life. Getting there was a struggle though. He had asked her a dozen times to marry him, and she had always refused. But from very early on, he knew she was the girl for him, and he would never say this aloud, but his foot told him so.

Ever since he was born, his bad foot ached. A constant dull throbbing, as though blood were trying to push its way into hardened places, plump up withered flesh. Only when he was searching for someone or something did the ache lessen. And he was good at that, finding things. As he neared the misplaced item, his foot actually felt normal – not normal enough to walk on, but normal in that he might forget the discomfort.

By chance, he discovered that whenever he was close to Stella, he forgot about his foot. As though she was perpetually lost and wandering, and he was the one capable of finding her. And when he was with her and the pain disappeared, there was room for other emotions, room for laughing, love, singing a jaunty tune.

Even though he knew they were meant for each other, he was beginning to believe that convincing Stella was an impossible task. That changed though, one afternoon, almost nine years ago, when he saw her in her vegetable garden. She was crouched down among the cabbage leaves, still wet from morning dew. The plants were young and tender, and had yet to form a substantial head. Baby slugs were nibbling away, leaving telltale holes and tracks of slime. Stella was lifting and examining each leaf, picking off the freeloaders, dropping them in an enamel bucket.

"Dirty work," Leander said as he neared her.

"Yes, 'tis. And I idn't afraid of it." She looked up, squinted with the early sunlight, one eye closed.

Leander moved to block the rays, said, "I got something for you."

"Whatever you got, I don't want no part of it."

But he dropped it in her lap anyway, and he never could have anticipated her response. She stared at it for a moment, mouth agape, as though it had been a snake he'd tossed. Then, she snatched it up, pressed it over her face, and began to moan.

He stepped back, sunlight flooding her face again. "What is it, maid? Did I do something wrong?"

"Where did you get this?" Her voice was thin and face drawn. He could not decide whether she was angry or miserable or both.

"To be honest, I found it," he replied. "Few winters back. On the path out to the woodpile. I gave it to Mother, and she washed it and ironed it. Says the tatting is real fine work. Don't you like it?"

Stella never responded, jammed the clean white handkerchief with the baby blue lace edging into the pocket of her apron and strutted past him. The screen door of her house creaked open and slapped shut. Leander stood in the garden, confused beyond, then looked in the bucket, grimaced when he saw the seething bodies. Bucket in hand, he went to the shed, poked around until he found a wooden box of coarse salt, sprinkled a handful over the slugs. After an initial frenzy of curling and flipping, they began to burn. Leander laid the bucket on the step to the shed, walked away.

Four months passed before he mustered the courage to ask again. Christmas time, and he was mummering at the Abbott household. Sheer fabric over his face, woman's hat and dress, festive spirits coursing through his veins. He hauled Stella up from her chair, hopped around trying to dance, leaned hard on her shoulders.

"Well?" he whispered in her ear. "What do you say?"

"To what?"

"You knows, getting married."

She stepped back, eyed him with a sideways glance. "Now how can you expect a girl to marry a stranger? And one dressed like a woman at that."

He tore the veil from his face, knocking off the hat. "'Tis only me, maid."

When she smirked knowingly, he blushed, the heat making him wish for the veil again. But she teased no longer, nodded her head and had offered the few spoken sparks that exploded the revelry. "Yes, I believes I will, Leander Edgecombe. I believes I will."

"You best get in," he said as he looked at the churning sky just above his newly fixed chair. "Storm's a coming."

"You too," she said.

"Nah. I got stuff to do in the shed."

What was once Percy's miniature red shed was now a grand workshop. Leander and his two younger brothers had taken off the back, extended the structure up over the rocks, so that inside he had two work areas on different platforms. With beach stones and mortar, they had constructed a fireplace where Leander burned leftover scraps of wood, shavings and sawdust.

"All right."

"I'll light a small fire to cut through the damp. If you got mind to join me. Any thoughts on a cup of tea?"

"Oh, I've got plenty of thoughts," she replied.

"And?"

"You'll just have to wait and see."

She answered the same way every time. And he knew in a few minutes she would be tapping the door to the shed with her foot, holding a tray weighted with lassie bread, steaming pot with knitted cozy, two matching cups, hers with the tiniest chip on the rim. She would enter, lay down the tray on a sawdust-covered bench, prepare his tea. Then, she would sit on the only chair with a cushion, pick up the container that held the milk, and spend the next minutes fishing out flecks of yellowish cream with a small silver spoon, sucking it clean. She would watch him as he turned a length of wood, and every time he winced, she winced too. His hip ached as he pressed down on the pedal with his gimpy foot. No doubt from the stress of guiding something useless.

Finished with the cream, Stella would talk and talk. In her steady voice, she would tell Leander about her day, the community news, the supper simmering on the woodstove, the state of the vegetables, her favourite red hen, her father's health. And Leander would listen as he worked, turning her words into the wood, pressing harder with the chisel at the tense moments in her story, lighter when she spoke of someone's sadness. In the end, he would look at the spindle he had turned and see a wooden record of their afternoon together.

Sometimes he wondered about the emotions trapped in a chair after it was completed. Once he had formed the spindles for the back of a rocker in the weeks following the death of his younger sister's fourth child. Born hours after Nettie Rose had tumbled on the icy laneway. A daughter, the size of Stella's palm. She knew, because she had held it. Stella told Leander about the baby, the covering of downy hair, sealed baby bird eyes, wide lipless smile on a fat free face. She described the cool hollowness in the room, like a window was opened, though neither one was. He turned all of this into the spindles of the rocker. Laid it down in deep, sad grooves.

That summer, Effie Hussey waddled into his shop, buttoned cloth purse pinched in her fist. She was a weary woman with thickened joints and thinning hair, pale skin, a life of hardship and sorrow having washed much of her colour away. Glancing about, she immediately went for the rocker, plunked herself down, sighed.

Leander tried to dissuade her from purchasing the chair, but Effie had insisted. "It's a wonderful comfort," she had said, as she'd closed her eyes, rocked. "It feels like home."

"What are you making?" Stella was seated on the cushioned chair, one knee over the other, foot swinging.

"Kitchen dresser. Pine. For Mrs. Tilley."

"Oh yes, I'd forgotten."

"She gave me exact dimensions."

"Like she would."

"Fairly shallow, but right wide against the wall. Wants the rack to be yellow, base to be dark blue."

"Yellow? That's odd."

"Well. For eleven dollars, I'd paint it in stripes if that's what she wants."

He sanded the edge of a length of wood, blew the dust, held it up to his eye.

"Got some bones from your sister. Should be a nice soup."

"Loves soup, I do." Rubbed his ribs with his left hand. "Bones to warm your bones."

When the light began to drain from the room, Leander lit both lanterns, hung them on hooks where the ceiling slanted.

"These are my favourite days," Stella said. "Stormy days. Don't feel guilty for doing not much of anything."

A crack of thunder from overhead, and the droplets tumbled down, slowly at first, then a thousand thumbs drumming on the roof. Leander laid the length of wood on a bench, looked out the window. Rain criss-crossed it with driven madness, like streaks of translucent lightning.

"Will you look at that?" He was behind her, hands encircling her waist. "We might never get home."

"Stuck out here all night."

"Could be a flood. We'd float away."

"Just the two of us."

"Yes, my love."

"Wouldn't be so bad."

"Not bad at all."

"Wonder where we'd end up."

"Probably right where we belong."

"Here, you think?"

"Yes. We'd be lost anywhere else."

"Lost."

That night, they stayed in the work shed. They didn't have to, by any means, as the storm had mostly blown over, rain only tinkling above them. But they decided it could be a miniature adventure, an imaginary excusion, and they were still rather young, untethered, and equally foolish.

Around eight o'clock, Stella and Leander dashed into the house, returned with the pot of soup, bowls, bread, a rum bottle filled with cool milk, gingersnaps in a tin. They sat cross-legged, ate until they were warm and full, then snuggled in between layers of quilts piled on the dusty wooden floor. A few feet from their heads, the dying fire emitted the occasional half-hearted snap or pop.

Dreamy voice, Leander whispered, "Lard, if anyone could see us, they'd think us mad."

Stella opened one eye, peered out at her dozing husband, his forehead glimmering in the firelight. "Let them think," she whispered back. "'Tis an honest quality, if you asks me. A teeny bit of madness."

On her wedding night, Stella had been uncertain about what to expect in relation to romantic love. Several weeks earlier, when Nettie was visiting, Stella had hinted a question about the experience of it, but never asked outright. Nettie, slurping milky tea and shoving gooey date squares in her mouth, had rubbed her belly bump, said, "'Tis the only time I gets a proper rest. Gus don't paw me when I shows." This was followed by awkward high-pitched twittering, and Stella never pressed for additional information.

Mrs. Hickey had taken it upon herself to offer some advice. "Women idn't meant to be noisy creatures. Not like men is. We needs to keep ourselves prim. Modest." Stella must have looked confused, as Mrs. Hickey continued without abating. "Sometimes a married woman got to put up with a few things. Dirty business. Dirty habits." Stella nodded. "Don't make a big show, just accept that we woman don't stop toiling after the sun goes down."

After the wedding supper, Percy left the thin-walled house. He went to stay with a widowed uncle for an undetermined period of time, and he blushed, did not look Stella in the eye when he said, "You youngsters don't need me skulking around, casting shadows. Get your lives started. Good lives." His eyes fluttered, and he blinked hard. "Long lives. Stella. Leander."

On the counsel of Mrs. Hickey, Stella had ordered two silk slips, one white and one ecru, and a full-length cotton nightgown. Wearing the white slip, she sat on the edge of the bed, waiting for Leander to return from the outhouse. He had told her his stomach was queer, all the angst of the day catching up on him. After twenty minutes, she went to the porch, stared out into the breezy summer night. And with the light from a near-full moon, she could see Leander a good distance from the outhouse, pacing back and forth, hands bouncing as though he were talking, trying to cajole himself to come inside. Stella could clearly see he was nervous too, and his sudden timidity calmed her.

When he finally returned, his eyes widened when he saw her seated in the rocker.

"Thought you might've dozed off."

Stella smiled. "Thought you might've too." She moved the rocker slowly with her foot. "Tea?"

"All right," he said, and sighed, sat down.

With the metal handle, Stella lifted the largest burner from the stove and dropped in a handful of splits. Flames soon flicked up, and she replaced the burner, moved the kettle over top.

"How's your stomach?"

He put his fist underneath his ribs, said, "Worse, I believes."

"Oh?"

"Though I don't want you thinking it had something to do with the lovely food. Was beautiful, the meal. Right grand. Everyone thought so. 'Tis just I got a few things clouding up my mind."

"Anything you want to talk over?"

"No. Well, yes. Well, no. Well. Lard, I don't know." He rubbed his face with his hands.

"Just say it."

"'Tis old foolishness, is all."

"Sure, there's no one else listening."

"I knows."

"Well?"

"Well, I've been thinking about tonight a lot, well not a lot, not all the time or nothing, like someone crazed, but I've been thinking about it enough to know it should be a real special night for you, and I had my mind set on how I was going to be, a certain sort of way, all polished and stuff, but I don't know how to act like that, and now I'm outside traipsing around in the potato beds, which needs trenching up, by the way, and I'm thinking up stuff to say, and now none of it comes out, only this old garbage, and that's not near what you deserves, and if I was you, I wouldn't have nothing to do with me, kicked out before morning, the nerve, now, crawling back in here, half hoping that you're already fast asleep."

"My goodness." Kettle hissing on the stove, she moved it to a cooler place, spooned loose tea into a pot, added boiling water. "Well, that's a lot to be thinking so late at night."

Leander took the full cup she offered, set it on the table

before him, stared into the steam. "You looks real pretty, by the way."

"I do?"

"I thought so right when I came in."

"I ordered this from the catalogue. Mrs. Hickey told me to."

"Mrs. Hickey?"

"Yes."

For some unknown reason, the thought of this made both of them laugh, and they stared at each other's smiling shiny faces in the kind lantern light.

"Good old Mrs. Hickey. What would we do without her?" He unwrapped his hands from the teacup, pushed it away, then lifted the glass on the lantern, blew out the flame.

"No light?"

"Don't want to waste is all."

Stella considered that he might not want people in the village to see a glow radiating from the window. What might a newly married couple be doing in the kitchen at such an ungodly hour? Such a light might suggest to others that Stella and Leander were struggling, or else the very opposite. Neither conclusion was respectable.

"How about we goes on to bed," he said. "What do you say?"

Stella nodded, stood, shyly walked towards their room. As she moved through the darkened spaces, the home felt different with the absence of her father. Not empty like she'd thought it would be, just foreign. There was something exciting about that, having the whole place just for herself. Even though everything was identical, the ice box, the parlour chair, the picture with the frame of carved wooden shells, there was a sense of newness, as though she were experiencing it all for the first time. She wanted to tell

Leander, though she doubted he would understand.

As she moved, static built up in her slip, and she was mortified when she glanced down, saw it bunching and clinging, crawling up over her legs on its own. She tugged at it, worried that Leander might notice, might consider her (or her slip) too eager. She glimpsed over her shoulder, but Leander seemed oblivious, concentrating on shuffling down the hallway without bumping into anything.

Nestled in the bed, they both couldn't help rolling together into the middle dip, the mattress exerting its will. Then, as though he had read a procedural manual on the subject, Leander moved his hand in a prescribed but jilted manner, bent his knee as though it were a conscious act. That was, until Stella shifted in her fully charged slip. In the darkness under the sheet, the fabric emitted a shower of static sparks, and Leander creaked backwards on the bed, exclaimed, "That's all I needs. First night married, and my bride sets herself on fire."

They both giggled, and he pulled her close, hugged her and kissed the hollow near the base of her neck. In what Stella believed was an instant of bravery, he tugged at the silk slip, and another flicker of jagged sparks flashed as she slid one knee over the other. "That's a hazard if I ever seen one," he whispered, then slipped it off her shoulders, down over her hips, and tossed it to the end of the bed. "An honest hazard."

Stella felt as though she could lose herself in these moments. Her mind was no longer tethered, and she imagined a whetting stone pressing against an eager blade in a rhythmic slide. As Leander moved above her, she considered the pleasures of cutting cold meat with a newly sharpened edge. She thought of butter, how she liked to indulge herself, let a flick of it melt over her tongue. Coating the back of her throat. So sweet it was, satisfying some deep-rooted craving from a source she could not identify. Finally, she thought about Mrs. Hickey and her tangled suggestion that women need be in a perpetual state of readiness. Available for the dirty business that particular night might bring.

Lying side by side, Stella searched her mind for words, a witty phrase or some earnest comment on her emotion. But she could think of nothing to say, could not unscramble it all. Leander was silent as well, and she wondered if he was feeling her rush of exhilaration or if he was disappointed. But then, hand resting on his heart, he said, "Can you believe it? We got married. That's something, Stell. Really something. I won't ever forget that."

"That you got married?"

"No. You knows what I meant."

Stella smirked in the darkness.

"I'm going to grow old with you," he said through a yawn, wide like a trap door. "Love your face even when it looks like a, like a..." Yawned again.

Stella stayed awake long after she heard gentle puffs of air, intermittent snores from pursed lips. Their sides were touching, and he lay straight in the bed, arms and legs neatly arranged, never straying or kicking. She believed he would be a considerate sleeper. Stretching her leg, she ran the arch of her sole over his cold twisted foot, her mind already venturing forward to the following evening.

Though Leander worked with wood his entire life, he was not always a furniture maker. He had spent several years training to become a cooper. Mr. Jones, the local expert, had taught him the art of forming barrels and wooden buckets. After a very short time, Leander was able to fashion a barrel that did not leak, not even a drop. As he sawed and planed and sanded and shaved each individual piece, he had a sense when the angles were correct. A feeling of rightness in his stomach. And when he held the pieces together, knocked the hoops down over onto the wide section of the barrel, the joints closed, practically invisible to fingertip or eye.

"Jaysus," Mr. Jones had said. "No doubts you've done this before."

"Not really," Leander had replied, rubbing his hands over the wood. "Only learnt from you."

"Nope, you've done it before, my son. Maybe not in this lifetime, but you've done it before."

In no time, he mastered the trade, fashioning barrels for salt meat and liquor, used soft pine for barrels holding apples or grain, and casks for dried fish. His tubs and barrels were in demand. Practically everyone in Bended Knee owned one of his specially designed butter churns. He tried to incorporate a dash of art into each churn by turning the tops of the paddle handles with the lathe.

As a wedding gift, he used his keenly honed coopering knowledge, and made Stella a small wooden tub from various shades of wood. The inside of the tub was sanded and polished until it was so smooth and shiny, in bright sunlight it would offer up a distorted reflection. Like no other tub, the lip of this one curved slightly, perfect for resting working arms, or the most vulnerable neck. Just the right size for bathing a newborn child.

By its rope handle, Stella had hung it on a hook in the porch. At first she dusted it regularly, and sometimes Leander would arrive home for lunch and find her seated in the porch, tub in her lap, her hand running round and round the bottom of it. But as the months went on, the care of the unused tub waned. Leander noticed she stared at it less often, and after two years dissolved between them without a child, her eyes were no longer wistful. Now coats and sweaters often shared the hook, covering the tub, hiding the reminder of her perceived barrenness.

Stella was right to conceal it, let it hang there and warp with the changing seasons. What else could she do? He certainly didn't want her to focus on what was missing from her life instead of feeling the continual warmth of what was already there. So, he never said a word, never moved an article of clothing. But still, it hurt. He couldn't shake the connection that covering his best work was akin to giving up. Forgetting their plans for a large family. A large happy family. The satisfaction he derived from fashioning perfect barrels and seamless tubs began to wane. One leaked. A woman complained of splinters. It was time to move on to something else.

Once Stella and Leander were married, Percy visited every Saturday, slowly easing his way down over the hill from his widower's roost with his uncle. During warm summer afternoons, he and Leander would sit out in the front garden, two chairs crouched deep amid a tangle of lilac shrubs and unkempt grasses, lupines and goldenballs. Percy often slouched in his chair, knees a mile apart, dangling a strand of wild wheat nipped between his teeth. He'd grin when Stella brought out tall glasses of lemon crystals dissolved in water, ice chips.

Sometimes, when it was particularly warm, Percy and Leander would doze together, like father and almost son. Then they would eat an early supper, Stella languid on a quilt before them, cold meat and pickles, whole wheat bread, maybe a few caramel squares relaxing on a plate, liberating their brown sugary ooze.

Leander had always considered Percy to be a stern man. Stolid, even. Never had he seen his father-in-law smile, or nudge another in the ribs after a good joke. But in the years after Amos went off to war, Percy gradually emerged from his depression a looser man. Untroubled. Stella even dared to suggest content. She told Leander she believed his mind was "going soft," and Leander agreed. Losing practically everything could do that to a man.

Every Saturday, he would arrive in the kitchen, stare at Stella with glossy eyes and sing with unconcealed fondness, "How lucky, how lucky, how lucky is I. To see my star outside of the sky."

She always beamed and blushed, replied, "Now, Dad, don't be so foolish."

"If only he'd stay just like this," she'd said to Leander as they watched him make his way up the lane in an awkward cane-reliant skip. "I even seen him lollygagging over Miss Fuller. Wouldn't that be lovely? They gets on well, gets married, and perhaps she'll forgive us our credit."

"Folks says she idn't right in the head. A few rooms unpapered."

"I never noticed."

"And besides, that'd mean you'd have her son as a brother."

"Who? Alistair? He seems perfectly fine."

"That's because you don't know him like the men do."

"Well," she had replied, "I was only teasing anyways."

Percy spent hours in the red flaking shed with Leander, showing him how to turn a leg or sand in the direction of the grain. "You have to love the wood," Percy had said the very first time he'd taken Leander into his tiny workshop. "Respect it. Each tree yearns to be something, I always thought. But I weren't much good for figuring it out."

"I seen your work," Leander had replied. "'Twas fine. I minds you made a high chair once for Mother."

"I don't remember ever making no high chairs."

"Well, she said 'twas the most solid piece of furniture in the house." Leander picked up a length of wood, smelled it.

Scratching the peppery stubble on his neck, Percy said, "Put your tongue to it."

"What?" Frowning.

"Go on, my son," Percy pushed. "Don't be shy. Just put your tongue to it. Then try this one. You'll see. Each wood got a different smell to it. A different taste goes along with that. Some is sweet, and some is bitter."

"Yes, I sees," Percy replied after licking several lengths of wood. "Hmmm. Never would've guessed it."

"I'd hope not."

"Which wood do you like best?"

"Don't be daft now, Leander. There's good in all wood. You needs both kinds, of course. Both kinds to make up a strong forest. Makes more sense if they's together. Don't you think?"

"I do," Leander replied. "It makes great sense."

Percy smiled, nodded. "Now, sit down. There." He pointed to the bench, covered with the remnants of a previous project, long abandoned.

"What? On that pile?"

"My son," Leander said with a liberated roar of laughter, "if you wants to perch on a mound of sawdust for a spell, see if you can hatch something out of it, then who is I to question it."

"I just meant..." he said as he sat down.

Percy plunked down beside Leander, shoulder to shoulder, touching. "Now, hold this scrap of pine in your hand." Leander took it. "What do you think?"

"'Tis a bit damp."

"Of course 'tis damp, but anything come to mind?"

"What do you mean?"

"I means, what do you want to make?"

"I haven't a clue. Where do you start?"

"How in God's name do I know?" Percy winked at no one in particular. His silver hair stood up in patches and he ran his fingers through it, not to smooth, it appeared, but to ruffle it even more.

"Maybe a washstand? Feels like a leg."

Percy seized the length of wood from Leander, tossed it up in the air and caught it, then rapped it against the wall. "Yes, I believes there's a leg in there too. I can hear it plain as the nose on my face. Wanting to kick its way out."

"I was right?"

Percy didn't acknowledge the question. "Do you see that lathe?"

"Yes, sir."

"Let me tell you something classified."

"Classified?"

"That's what I said. Just because I been living in an outport my whole life don't mean I don't know a thing or two that's classified."

"I never meant..."

In a low voice, Percy whispered, "Once there was this feller who was a furniture maker who had a dog."

"A dog?"

"Did I say something other than a dog?"

"No, sir. You said dog."

"Then why, in God's name, is you asking me if I said dog?"

"Well, I don't rightly know. Just banter, I suppose."

Percy's mouth hung open, and he shook his lower jaw. "I idn't keen on banter, buddy boy. I'll tell you that right from the get go. I don't like banter, and I won't have banter. If you got mind to banter, you can go banter with some other feller down the road. If you wants to listen and learn, then plug it up, you hear me, you?"

Leander nodded, pulled his lips in over his teeth, pressed down.

"Well he had this dog. A dog. A good-sized d-o-g. And he had that dog trained to go in that drum there. See those steps inside, like a round-about ladder?"

Nodding again.

"He'd run on that. Power the whole contraption."

"Really?"

Percy cocked his head, stared at Leander through one eye. "You don't believe me?"

"No, no, that's not–"

"Smells like another whiff of that banter business." Percy ran his hands down over his thighs, held onto his knees, elbows locked.

"No, sir."

"Never could get a dog to do that myself. Though I tried. Time and time again. Not too many even knows about that. You'd have some business then, I allows."

"I'll bet."

Percy rubbed his hands in the pile of sawdust, then put his palms to his nose, inhaled deeply, and sighed. Looking up, he said, "Had a son once. Did you know that?"

"Of course. Amos. He was a good feller. My friend."

"Never much took to wood, you see."

"No?"

"Didn't like the solidness of it. What you see is what you gets."

"I minds he loved the water, though. Is that right?"

"Ah, the water." Percy stood and turned, swiped his forearm over the grimy window that offered a slender view of the sea. "You can't trust the water like you can a tree. Water is tangly."

"I never thought about that before."

"No. I doubts you would. Young folks don't think much, or else they thinks about all the wrong things. About saving the world. Water got nothing to do with that."

"You don't think?"

"I knows. You remember the flood?"

"What? No, sir. I don't recall no flood ever. No."

"You don't never read the Bible? Read about the great flood?"

"Oh yes, that one. That flood."

Percy rolled his eyes, rubbed the back of his neck. "Well, when I was a young one, we had to keep ourselves right still on a Sunday. Sit and read the Bible. And we was good boys. And that's what we did."

"Yes, sir."

"Tell me, what caused the flood?"

"What caused it?"

"Is you asking me or is me asking you?"

"Ah, the rains?"

"And what did the crowd do?"

"Built a big boat?"

"Exactly." Percy snapped his suspenders. "It's all there. The whole world saved by a few trees. Saved from the water by a few good trees."

"You got a point, Mr. Abbott."

"She took away my son."

"Who?"

"The sea, boy. Haven't you been listening?"

"But, Amos went off to–"

"Took him away, she did. With nar thought given to it. I never seen him again. I'll never forgive her for that."

Leander wasn't sure how to respond, so he said nothing, only nodded. Perhaps Percy was beginning to forget, could only recall seeing Amos leave in a boat surrounded by early morning mist. No question of where he was going. Leander decided it would be better for such a memory to dissolve.

Percy pulled the door wide open, brightness filling the musty room. "Must go on in, I reckon, and find my star. See if she can scare me up a drop of tea. Leave you to get started on your washbasin. Washstand. Whatever 'twas you said."

"Ah, yes, sir." Leander stood too, elbow against the window frame, wood held idly by his side. "Washbasin. I means washstand."

"And remember, Leander," he said as he stepped out into the day, "a tree is a noble creature. Each one is blessed by God above. Rooted down, good and reliable." He swiped his nose with his thumb. "The ocean, she'll cut you, if she sees fit. Run a hole right through you and leave you to drown. Stay with the trees, my son. And you'll live a fine life. Stay with the trees."

Percy clicked the door closed behind him, the pure light diminished to a shaft seeping in through the unused keyhole. Leander tugged open the small window, watched Percy hobble the short distance to the stoop, arms out at his sides and bouncing. When he reached the house, Percy hollered, "Where's you at, my star." Stella appeared, and he laughed, said, "Some feller up there got his gob stuck right tight onto a bit of wood. I'd steer clear if I was you. Steer clear." Tapped his noggin.

Leander slid back down to the bench, stared at all the dim corners in the shed. Spaces that clearly belonged to someone else. An axe, crosscut saw, chisels, drills, files, homemade tools for which he couldn't fathom names, let alone their function.

"I best get started," he said aloud, turning what now felt like a sacred piece of pine over and over again in his hand.

In three days, plenty of blisters and splinters, nipped fingertips, he had constructed his first piece of furniture. A little washstand that teetered on uneven legs and with a front door that wouldn't open. Leander wanted to destroy it, but Percy slammed back the door of the shed before he'd had the chance. And when Percy saw it, he clapped his hands together, picked it up with one hand, held it to his chest. Told Leander it was absolutely perfect.

chapter eight

In the week following that faded April day of the funeral, Stella saw a fat bird on the windowsill. It hopped along the wood, cocked its head as though it were staring through the glass at her. She put down the trousers she was mending, and went to the counter, slowly leaned in closer towards the window. The bird was familiar, with its shiny black eyes, and innocent eyebrows a solid ribbon of brilliant yellow. Weighting its face was an enormous bill the colour of weathered bone. She had seen this type of bird before, knew it liked to hide amongst the trees, bouncing on spruce branches or rubbing its wings against new pine needles. More than once, her father had said, "Do you see that, my star? How it plays with the trees? So free."

"Look, Leander," Stella said when he came in from the shop. "Over there."

"What?"

"That bird. On the ledge. It's been there all day."

"All day?"

"Off and on, I means."

"Must smell your cooking, maid."

"Do you think?"

"Maybe it's sick." Leander stood. "Here, I'll shoo it away."

Stella put her hand to his arm. "No, no. Don't do that. Leave it be."

Throughout supper, it sat on the ledge, then hopped from one side to the other. More than once, their conversation was silenced by the subtle riffling sound as the bird pushed its cone-shaped beak into the corners where the window pane met the frame.

"Must want at some bug or something," Leander suggested as he split a potato in half with his knife, then jabbed it, shoveled it up and into his mouth.

"Or else he wants to come in."

"Well, we don't want no bird in this house. You know what that means."

Stella swallowed hard, took a sip of her tea, and put her hand to the middle of her chest. "Dry," she managed to say. "The fish is right dry. I didn't mind it well enough while it was frying."

Reaching over, Leander held Stella's wrist, her fork still poised in her fingers. Though the backs of his hands were riddled with nicks and scrapes, dusty nails and rough knuckles, his palms were sand-papered to baby softness. "I's sorry, my love. 'Twas a thoughtless thing to say. Damned thoughtless."

Stella nodded, not because she was agreeing with Leander, she simply wasn't sure what to do with her head. Even though everyone was expecting it, when her father died, she was dazed. She had tricked herself into imagining that he was a permanent structure, a stable support. And when he vanished from her life, she felt exposed, uncomfortable, and peculiarly embarrassed by her reverberating grief.

At the funeral, he was laid out in a knotty pine box, every seam sanded smooth by Leander. He wore his black wool Sunday suit, and though no one would ever have noticed, every pocket was sewn shut. Stella knew this, as she had done the job herself – to honour one of her father's requests. He had made her promise to seal every pocket as he explained, "Dead men don't need them in heaven. No need to carry nothing, and I don't want no empty spaces." As she stitched the wool fabric, she thought of a hundred things to tuck inside those pockets. Useful earthly things. A coin, a button, a shiny nail. But she resisted, was tormented with thoughts of his vacant suit as he was laid in the newly thawed earth.

She could scarcely control herself during the service, during the burial. And though there was a hand on her constantly, an arm around her shoulder, it did nothing to ease the hollowness that was choking her. In a moment when her tears subsided and the sadness showed itself in only a shudder, Stella realized that the Smith sisters were staring at her, whispering just loudly enough to be heard.

"Not like 'tis a child," the older one snarked quietly.

"He was an old man."

"Gone soft at that."

"Had a good, long life."

"'Tis a sin to be so strickened over it, if you asks me," the older one replied, talking into the handkerchief covering her mouth.

Stella stared at the raw edges of the hole before her, then straightened her back, did her best to tuck away her tears, compress her emotion back into more private space. She glanced over her shoulder at the sisters, and they smiled sadly at her, then pursed their lips resolutely, and nodded. Maybe Stella had actually imagined their voices in her ear;

maybe those were her own words disguising themselves. Should she be feeling so distraught over the death of a gentle man who lived a good, decent life?

In the hours afterwards, when everyone ate and drank and chatted in post-burial cadence, Stella thought about this. Perhaps she might feel differently at another time, but right now she was convinced that deep sorrow was the correct emotion. Though she'd never be able to articulate it, she sensed that when Percy died, the whole world was somehow poorer for it. A portion of history was now unrecoverable, a million tiny branches perished. Was she mistaken to believe that the irreplaceable loss of a realized life outweighed the sketchy potential of a life unlived?

For several years, he had what Stella believed to be a joyful life. An untethered life. In summer, with hardwood cane in hand, he wandered the woods filling a bucket with berries or sawing birch trees and hauling them out a couple at a time. Most wintry afternoons, he could be found in the shed with Leander, spending quiet hours sanding the runners for a sleigh or planing a length of wood. As he meandered between Stella's and his late uncle's house, he could be seen standing on the cliffs that surrounded the harbour, gazing at the gulls as they dove into the sea, searching for food. From the window over the table, she watched him sometimes, cane dropped on the rock, hands to his chest, elbows out, head back, and she imagined he was mimicking their shrill cry.

During his last few months, his decline had been fast and furious, as though he had reached a crest, and plummeted. Leander found him collapsed in on the marshy bog near the river, and after that, both his body and mind began to give way like a long decayed stump. He moved back with Stella, took to resting on the daybed where Stella's mother Delia had spent countless days. So many times she looked at her father, fresh questions piled up on her tongue. But, in the increasingly rare moment when he was lucid, she hadn't the courage to ask them. Then, by the time she was certain of her words, he had grown silent and sullen, and rarely looked her in the eye.

As she sat beside the daybed, the burden of her ignorance gnawed away at her. She never really knew her father, never knew about his childhood, or his favourite meal, or how he learned to turn a piece of wood. She would never know if her mother had been the first girl he'd kissed or if her grandfather had ever told a good joke. It was her fault, this ignorance, as she hadn't taken the time to ask. With the daily life business of weeding and chopping wood and curing fish and knitting socks, these bits of knowledge had always seemed insignificant to her. Until she realized they were trapped. His life story wholly inaccessible.

One of their last sensible conversations, a riddle of words, replayed in her head, taunting her. It happened a few weeks before he collapsed, and in hindsight, she understood he was placing a soul door before her, and she hadn't the common sense to open it. They had been sitting on the back stoop, the two of them staring up at the same sky. She leaned into him, noticed his cardigan was mis-buttoned, one side of the collar jutted upwards, the other side tugged down. As she readjusted the sweater, she inhaled his smell, an old damp book, pages moulded together.

"Sometimes," he had said to her, "there's a moment in your life that shapes you. Shapes you up, tight like a supper bun."

"I'd imagine a million moments is shaping me, Dad. Dozens of supper buns." She slapped her well-nourished thigh, laughed lightly, but he never joined her.

"That's because you's lucky, my star. For others, though, there's an instant that puts them square on a path, and they got nar chance of stepping off."

At the time, she had listened casually, another part of her thinking about the stew on the stove. It was time to poke the chopped carrots in around the chunks of meat, whip together some dumplings. Leander had wanted a late supper.

But now, if she could replay it, she would ignore the stew, pay attention with both ears, and ask him if he was unlucky, if there was one moment in his life that changed its direction. She would ask him to describe the path he had been on. And in reflecting on everything, had it been a good path? How she dearly hoped it was.

"My grandfather once told me," he had continued, "that sometimes it takes more courage to stand by and watch. Takes more guts to do nothing. Do you know that?"

"Uh-huh," she replied, the stew still on her mind. In a moment, she would have to leave him and tend to it. Shifting logs could create a hot spot, and what a disaster it would be if the liquid had boiled off, meat stuck on.

"He said there's only room for so many fighters."

Stella cleared her throat. "Are you talking about Amos, Dad?"

"What? Ah, yes. Amos. He idn't alone. Not alone."

"No, Dad. He sure idn't." She reached over to hold her father's hand, his skin cool and dry, warmth retreated.

"'Tis a lovely evening. Can almost feel heaven pressing down on me."

She sighed. This talk of heaven again.

"And I got it in my mind," he continued, "that I'd right love another slice of that lassie bread."

"All right, Dad. Come. Sit to the table. I got to go in anyways."

They went indoors, and Stella cut him a thick slice of bread, the piece compressing with the freshness.

"Spare a drop of tea, my star?"

Kettle already warm on the back of the stove, she spooned loose tea into the pot, filled it.

He chewed slowly, ate every crumb, slurped from the cup. Plate clean, he leaned back in his chair, put his hands on his knees, said, "When they comes for me, I won't fight it."

"When who comes?"

"You knows."

"No, Dad, I don't." As she added more warm tea to his cup, she thought she saw suspicion in his eyes, as though he thought she might be mocking him.

"I's no fighter."

"Dad, you got no reason to fight."

"I's no fighter. Just wanted you to know is all."

"That's okay, Dad." She returned to the stove, lifted the lid, sampled the stew with the tip of a wooden spoon. Then, opening a cupboard, she said to herself, "Cloves. A whole clove. One little thing changes the entire flavour."

"One little thing," her father repeated.

Stella remembered looking at him and smiling, nodding when he said, "Makes everything different."

"Can you imagine? One clove." She had even held it up to him, pinched between thumb and forefinger. "Did I ever tell you that, Dad? 'Tis the secret in my stew."

Stella pushed her plate of overcooked fish away. If only she could shut off her mind and exist inside nothingness for a few hours. Their last real conversation re-played over and over again, even when she wasn't conscious of it. Just now, as she was having a supper with Leander, her face scrunched, and she realized she had come around to her comment about the cloves. Why hadn't she heeded her father? Surely he hadn't been talking about a spice, but making a clear attempt to share some crucial moment of his life. With her. His gift offered, and she had made no attempt to accept it. Instead, she had hidden away, tucked herself behind an aromatic bud.

She looked at Leander, a few feet away from her, as he slid a chunk of boiled potato around his plate, zigzagging through a puddle of brilliant beet juice. He was all that was left of her family, one man, a single set of arms. Her face scrunched again as she thought about it.

"Not hungry?" Leander asked.

"No."

He pushed his plate away too, said, "Me neither."

"That happens sometimes when you eats everything in sight."

Boyish smile. "I didn't eat that much, Stell. Watch. I won't have a single slice of that raisin pie this night. Not one bite of it."

She frowned. "And here I was hoping you'd eat the whole works."

Leander took their plates, carried them to the counter, then slid into the rocker by the stove. "Come," he said. "Sit with me."

She pinched herself between his legs, sat on his lap.

He put his hand into her hair, rubbed her scalp with the pads on his fingers. "It's okay to miss him, you know. You don't have to be strong for me."

Deep breaths.

"I misses him too. He was a good man, your father."

She sat up. "'Tis more than that, Leander."

"I knows."

"No, you don't."

"Well, then, tell me, maid. Explain to me and I'll listen

to you as best I can."

"'Tis. 'Tis. Oh hell, I don't even know." She stood up, paced the floor in front of him.

"Now, Stell."

"It's just, this is all there is." She put her arms out, palms up, fingers spread. "I'm not building nothing."

"You is, then. Building every day. Building. You can build whatever you wants. Just build."

"That's not true, Leander. I's just getting by, moving through."

"I knows you're sad, my love, but time–"

"Time? Don't even talk to me about time. Time is water. You can't hold it. Eventually, it all leaks out."

"All right."

"Everything is seeping away, Leander. My mother. Amos. Now Dad. And as far as I sees, nothing is clamouring to get in. Plain nothing."

Leander scratched his forehead, tugged on his right ear. "I'm listening as best I can, maid, but I got nar clue what you're trying to say."

"Me neither. I feels right mad in the head."

"Give it ti–. Go easy on yourself."

She clutched the back of a kitchen chair, squeezed. "Got so much going on inside me, I's betting I could haul a tree right up out of the earth. Hands and teeth."

Leander slapped his lap, chuckled. "Now that's something I don't want to see you trying."

"I won't," she said, and flopped back down into his lap. He rocked the chair slowly.

"Promise?"

She sighed. "Can't get his face out of my mind, Lee. Can't remember any of the other stuff, the nice times. His face gets in the way."

"Don't worry, Stell. It'll fade."

"He was so lost. Lying there on that bed. So lost."

Leander moved the rocker with his good foot, kept his arm snug around Stella's waist. "He weren't lost, Stell. I believes that, I do."

"But his eyes. Like he weren't even there."

"He might not've been with us. That I don't doubt. But wherever he was, he weren't lost."

She placed her head against Leander's shoulder.

He spoke softly now. "You knows how my foot aches when something is gone astray?"

"Yes."

"My foot, now, got some sense from beyond."

"I knows. 'Tis uncanny."

"Well, my foot never ached an ounce."

"What do you mean?"

"I can't explain it no better, maid. All that time when he was lying there, he weren't lost, my love. Wherever his mind was off to, he was right where he was supposed to be."

"You thinks?"

"Right down to my bones, maid. I won't ever claim to know much, but that I knows."

Lifting her head, she stretched up to kiss him, lightly, lightly. When she nestled back down, he exclaimed, "My Lard. Anything else I can say to get another one of those? Whatever you wants to hear, my dear, I'll utter it."

She nudged him in the ribs now, and as she did, she heard a small sound, like fingernails tapping on glass. Looking up, she noticed the bird was still at the window, wiry feet clutching the weathered wood. She got up, went to the cupboard.

"Don't take much to drive you away," he said with a gentle laugh.

She smiled, replied, “No. I just want to do something is all.”

In the bottom cupboard, she retrieved the cardboard container of salt, then went to the window and pulled it up. The bird fluttered backwards, lit on the painted handrail that surrounded the stoop. Leaning over the countertop, Stella tugged up the cover of the container and tipped a small pile of salt crystals into the corner of the windowsill. Wind would not touch it there, and the fat-beaked bird, a salt lover, might just be tempted to stay.

“Dear, dear Percy.”

“You got to sleep.”

“She’s right, you know, you got to sleep.”

He could hear the voices saying the same phrases over and over again. But he only frowned in response, kept his continually watery eyes open in a constant state of looking. He did not want to sleep. There was too much to tell this woman who stayed in the chair beside him. Too much he wanted to say.

He lay on a daybed in a kitchen, the grooves of the mattress familiar, the coolness coming off the nearby wall a comfort. The woman leaned in closer, and he tried to begin again. Untangling the snarl of threads clumped together inside his head. Pulling here and there, drawing out fragments of his life.

The words would not form on his lips and he used his free hand to convey everything. While one hand was tucked away under the blanket, the other rested on his chest and it moved accordingly as the stories came into his head. Back and forth, that five-legged pale spider, lifting and falling sometimes, occasionally picking away bits of wool from the blanket or conducting the air with swirls at the wrist. When he asked a silent question, his palm turned upwards, held there for a moment, then flopped back down.

Pillow behind his head, he stared at his hand, then stared up at the woman, into her sad eyes, close eyebrows. Every now and again, she would grab his gesticulating fingers, pinch them gently together, say, "Boy, seems parts of you got a whole lot to say." And his throat would tighten, old jaw quivering, and confusion would subdue the one-sided conversation. He could not understand why the woman didn't hear every word that rose up from his wrist on down.

Frustration turned that hand into a weak fist, and he could feel his thick fingernails, longer than they should be, pressing into the fleshy part of his palm. His mind was teeming with blurry ideas, like handfuls of flies in a laden web, buzzing, buzzing for freedom. But nothing came to him. Nothing pure.

There was a woman inside, somewhere, thin and struggling. Something about her face, lopsided smile, braid like a tarnished crown. Her mouth was open slightly, a tiny space between her two front teeth. Sprigs of pink and green flowers on her dress, belt encircling a waist of nothing, lily smell behind her ears. He strained, but no name arrived. No name to corral these parts, turn them into someone whole.

His hand clenched and relaxed, clenched and relaxed, as he thought about her. He wanted to reach inside his head, grab onto her image, polish it up, and see her clearly. But he was helpless to do so, breathed heavily as he willed the web to buckle in the breeze, obliterate her shadow and the anguish that walked beside it.

Behind her was a boy. And the boy was leaving him, would not return. His fingers wanting to extend, touch the hair. Soft like a child's. Too soft to be going away, wherever he was going. Left, an emptiness that was full of heat. Melted him. The soft clicking of a latch. A door closing a million times. Echoing like a drip of water falling from a great height, destroying his wits that lay below. Click. Click. Goodbye. Click. Why hadn't he been able to say goodbye? He wanted so badly to do that now. Say goodbye. His hand waved ever so slightly. Goodbye. To whomever it was. That boy.

The woman in the chair took his hand and held it. But he wiggled away, not wanting to be silenced. Palm up, who was that boy? Dying didn't make him a hero, the child with the soft hair, it only made him dead.

"I knows, Dad," she said. "I knows. Why won't you rest for a spell?"

He turned his face to the window over the table. The ocean was just beyond, he knew, but he couldn't see it. Brightness from the setting sun made the glass sparkle, and he squinted, was tempted to blink. Then, behind his eyes he sensed something flapping upwards, barely, barely, and yes, surfacing. Bridgette Connor. Bridgey. How odd that she was coming to him now, so compact, her memory, and even though he knew it would hurt him, he craved the realness of it, the solidity, and he stood up, walked towards her. Deep breaths, young muscles, a full head of hair on his thirteen-year-old head.

"What're you doing here?"

Bridgey giggled. A girlish giggle. "I got something to give you. Something you's going to love."

He gazed at her blond hair, her pudgy shoulders. Her feet were bare, even though the ground where they stood was still cool. She had just turned fourteen, and was full of bumps and curves that other girls her age still didn't have.

"Percy."

He glanced over his shoulder, no one else around, and he nodded.

"I got something to show you, I said. You wants it or not?"

They would tease him, he knew. About her offer, and his newfound desire to accept it. Once, they held him down, arms and legs pinned, jabs to the ribs, wet thumbs jammed in his ears until he admitted her name. The girl that he loved. And though he loved no one, he had to choose somebody, anybody, in order to be released. The name "Bridgette Connor" burst from his mouth, and she was the most unlikely of loves with her hefty body and her snug clothes, constantly running nose. She was a shy and uncertain girl, and whenever anyone asked her name, she always responded with a question. "I's Bridgette Connor?"

But as they teased relentlessly, "you wants to kiss her, you wants to rub her over good," they would not allow her to leave his mind. And in time, with that steady stream of reminders, his indifference bloomed into a tender crush.

"Well?"

"All right," he said, and he wasn't sure if he should hold out his hand.

"Follow me?"

Standing at the edge of the forest, spruce trees rose tall before them, offering up their shade and private places. He wiped his sweaty palms in his trousers and walked after her. The tattered pink ribbon securing her hair bounced as she moved, and the breeze made her ill-fitting sky blue dress flicker. He thought that dress might once have belonged to one of her older, more slender, sisters.

Running now, she dodged through the brush, zigzagging, looping. He followed closely as they danced through the woods, a couple, enchanted hunter chasing clever doe. Ahead of him, he watched her as her pale arms reached out and touched branches, slapped trunks. Chasing her now, panicking if she disappeared, his feet jumping on the spongy earth, pinecones collapsing beneath his shoes. All right, all right, he would admit it. He wanted to know if she might kiss him. Wanted to kiss her too. That was why he followed her into the forest as deeply as he did.

She stopped at a swollen river up behind the mill, spring thaw and downpours having pushed the water up over the banks. Sharp twig in hand, she stabbed pockets of turpentine from the bark of a tree, then crouched by the side of the river, dress sitting in the soft mud, and touched the tip of the twig to the water. The river grazed it, tugging away a trail of unbroken iridescence.

"Pretty. Don't you think?"

He agreed, but didn't say so. "What do you got to show me?" He didn't like being in the clearing so close to the water. Too close to the water.

She looked up and squinted at him, then stood, smiling nervously, tossed the twig aside. "Over there," she said, and dug her toes into the mud, feet turned inwards as though they were clubbed.

"I'm not going there." He folded his arms across his chest.

"Sure you is." She jumped now, spattering him with the mud. "If you wants what I got to give you."

"What is it?"

"You'll see soon enough." She patted her pocket. "All right?"

A log had fallen across the river, offering a slippery

bridge to the other side. She started across it, inching along, arms extended at the sides, dirty feet leaving a trail. A few steps across, and she turned to him. "See, 'tis easy as blueberry pie."

"Blueberry pie."

Water bullied the tree, frothed into the armpits of the branches, churned and spat up, slid over where it could. As she edged gingerly, he didn't take his eyes off her. Nothing bad ever happened when a person was looking, right? She was halfway, and the sun crept through the trees, and he blinked with the brightness. He hadn't meant to, but he blinked, yes, and she slipped, a leg twitching in the air, arms flailing, body folding backwards. Squeezing his eyes closed, then, heard her head striking, like the sound of the final thump of a frozen foot against a locked door.

Splash. And he stood, a human stone on the side of the river, peeking through the faintest slit formed by his eyelids. She was in the water, the tree trying to hold her, trying to save her, hooked into the neck of her dress, suspending her. Face beneath the surface, eyes open. Water continued to rush over her, hair and dress flattened against her, body like a writhing fish. Undulating. The current yanked and jerked, wanting her, until the branch snapped with the pressure, and she jetted away, coursing down the river. Another pretty iridescent trail of blue and blonde and pink. There one instant, and stolen the next.

He sunk down into the muck, much of the grass still creased and dirty yellow. Scanning the length of the river, he saw no sign of the girl he had followed. No sign. His eyes traced that muddy trail out to the middle of the log, and he waited for her to reappear, to glide up the river, unflip, and reposition herself. He waited. And waited. Rocked on his heels, sucked the back of his wrist, and waited some more. A bird swooped and dove over the spot, and he whimpered when he saw it. "I wants to fly, God," he whispered. "Please, God. Let me just fly away."

But he remained fixed by the river, stayed there until darkness turned the water black. Until a starless night made the world around him evaporate. Until men crunched through the woods behind him. Calling for Percy.

Someone lifted him, and he felt like air moving inside air. Scrawny body deflated with shame. A strong hand gripping the back of his head, pressing his crying face into a warm shirt that smelled like supper. And he was lulled by the cadence of a forest walk, stepping over roots and brave ferns, a rocking motion in the bed of someone's arms.

Truth drifting down onto him. "'Tis okay, boy. You're all right. They got her. Downstream. Caught up in the old dam. What's left of it anyways." Soft grass now beneath the man's feet, climbing up onto the lane. Closer to home, fog began to curl inwards, driving the scent of boiled vegetables from open windows closer to the ground. "You did the right thing, boy. Staying to the side."

"I don't swim," he whispered up into that bristly neck, bobbing adam's apple. "I didn't fight."

"Don't matter. Water was crazed. You could swim to beyond and back, wouldn't make one speck of difference." A few silent steps. "Besides, everyone idn't meant to be a fighter."

"I should've–"

"Should've nothing, boy." Deep breaths. "Don't go thinking too much about all this. Put it out of your mind."

"All right."

"Good boy. Some things got the power to change you. And your ways is too young to be set."

That summer, when the river had tempered, men came

to clear away the fallen tree, chopping up and burning the marker, the place where that poor girl had drowned. Once again, during late afternoons when chores were finished, boys and girls played around the stream. While the girls dallied on the banks, water up to their ankles, wetting the bottoms of their dresses, boys dove in, crab-crawled along the bottom, held each other under, bobbed up sputtering and choking.

Sometimes he walked to the edge of the forest, sat down on a mossy rock, and watched the children. But he never went near the water. No one ever asked him to come closer and no one taunted him anymore about the girl he had claimed to love. The girl he maybe thought he did love.

Mid-July and while he looked on, a boy with fiery hair and skin doused with burnt orange freckles, disappeared beneath the rippling surface, then rose up, shot a stream of water from his lips, and held up his hand. Pinched between thumb and forefinger was a perfect glass ball. "Look! A peppermint swirlie," the boy cried out. "Found it on the bottom. I's charmed today, fellers." Then the boy waded through the water, found his trousers amongst the several slung over a branch near the shore, and tucked the treasure into his pocket, buttoned the flap.

As he watched the boy, he remembered: Bridgette, on the tree trunk, patting her pocket. Not a kiss she was offering at all. Not a kiss for him. But a marble, carefully made with twirls of red and blue, moving together but never touching. Escaped during the fall, leaving her pockets empty, pressed against her body as she traveled beyond.

That was his marble, he knew. His peppermint swirlie now possessed by someone else. He never said a word, didn't want to own it, even though he knew it was a gem among boys. But, if she had of given it to him, if that had of happened, he would have held it in his palm, closed his fingers around it, cherished it. Her gift. He would have traded it for nothing.

"Dad?"

He heard her calling.

"Dad?"

And the river narrowed into a teardrop, trees that surrounded him shrank back into seeds. Scattered to the wind.

"Dad?"

Palm flipped upwards.

"I'm going to give you a little shave. Make you feel good."

Placing a towel across his chest, the woman massaged his cheeks and neck, scraped a warm blade across him. He lifted his chin, stretched his top lip, puffed out each cheek at the appropriate moments. While everything inside him was made of fog, he understood the motions for shaving, the correct way to lean, angle himself so that he escaped without a nick. Even though a nick was inconsequential, there was ridiculous pride in avoidance.

"All done." She swiped his skin with a towel, then held up a round mirror, dull metal frame. "Still as handsome as ever, Dad."

Was this his reflection? This man with yellowed skin and eyes nearly lost inside layers of wrinkles. Lips hidden, pulled in over gums. A strand of silver hair draped across his forehead. Each ear now so large, a bird might nest comfortably there. Who was this man? So disturbingly familiar. What's all this about?

He reached up to knock the mirror away, and she lay it on the shelf over his head.

The woman drew the blanket out from beneath his arm, then covered him up. Under the blanket, his hand continued to move, but she patted it, said, "Please, Dad, get some rest."

But he tried to resist, he had more to say. Why was she trying to quiet him? This woman, who reminded him of someone he once knew. An onion and a rabbit. A pair of pampooties. A lungful of cool night air. Wind rustling through the trees, carrying off the scent of pine. Through the canopy, a distant twinkling star. Yes, something there, and although he couldn't quite reach it, he felt it all around him.

Hand to his cheek.

"You're so cold, Dad. Leander, close the back door. Check the windows. More wood on the fire."

"Plenty warm in here, maid," Leander replied as he moved about, doing as she'd said.

"I don't want no drafts."

As she spoke, his lungs tightened, and his breathing moved to the very tip of his chest. He felt her fingers moving over his face, stroking his hair, and resting on the top of his head in the very spot where his bones had fused together as a baby. Inside, a newborn awe rinsed through him, and at the same time, he sensed a circle closing.

I'm going to fly now.

"I knows, Dad."

I can feel the bumps beneath my skin. Feathers poking through.

"I knows."

Can I fly?

Another quilt piled, and his hand was silenced by the weight. He gradually closed his eyes, began to doze, and felt warmth on his cheeks. An angel's voice whispered, "There you go. A long rest'll do you good." And he fell asleep, breeze fluttery against him, palm twisted upwards. A perpetual question.

In the months after Percy's death, Leander noticed that Stella had begun to act unusually. Several days in a row, he found her seated on a stool near the woodpile, axe in her hand and a mound of splits covering her feet. But she was not working, instead her top half was folded over her bottom half, and she was fast asleep. When he gently woke her, her face was a mess of reddened wrinkles, and he knew she had been dozing for a while.

On another occasion, he came in through the porch and found Stella on her knees, the lid of the salt pork bucket lifted, her head hanging inside, sniffing up lungfuls.

"Is there something in there?" he'd asked. "Something wrong with the bit of meat?"

"No," she replied, and her voice inside the near-empty barrel was oddly hollow. "'Tis fine."

"Is you counting what's left?"

"Nope."

"Then what's you doing, missus?"

She lifted her head, and her face was pale but pleasant. "'Tis the smell. The brine and the blood and the wet wood. I could stay here all day gulping down that air."

"Well, if that's all it is," he'd joked, nudging her in the backside, "then you best stick your head right back down into it, and carry on. Don't let me stop you."

Another time he found her seated at the kitchen table, bowl, flour, and starter before her, but no sign of any bread dough. She stared up at him, and there was a curious expression in her eyes. Something akin to guilt, but not quite. When he bent to kiss her, she coughed, powder exploding from her mouth. Her cheeks had been full of raw flour, and she was slowly swallowing it down.

"Couldn't help myself," she'd said, wiping the corners of her lips on her apron. She ran her fingers through the dust now coating the table. "'Twas all I could think about."

Early fall, and she took to wandering. When he walked to the top of the garden, he would see her trailing the edge of the cliff, stopping sometimes to look out over the water. Wind would tug at her dress and play with the helpless grass around her feet. Then she would find a path, and it always alarmed him, to see her descending, as though she were sinking straight into the sea.

Whenever he asked her where she went, she didn't have an answer. Only this most recent time, did she say, "Over to Devil's Hole."

"You mean that place where youngsters play?"

"Yes."

"God's Mouth."

"No one calls it that no more, Leander."

"Oh. What was you doing there?"

"Thinking."

"About me, I bet." He smiled, grabbed her hand.

"No. I don't think about you all the time, you know."

"Almost though, right?" His arms encircled her waist, and he twirled her around the kitchen.

"Yes, almost."

"Something on your mind?"

"Yes."

"Something bad?"

"No. Something good."

"Then why idn't you happy, maid?"

She hesitated, and her eyes watered. "Because good don't seem to last for me, Leander. Good don't never seem to last."

"That's not the least bit true, maid. You and me together have had years of good. Years of it."

"And I've gotten used to it."

"Like you should."

The next time he saw her walking, he watched her more closely. Her walk had changed, and she swayed from side to side ever so slightly as she meandered along the winding path. Each step was careful, as though a fear of tumbling over the edge had taken root. When she reached the point where she usually disappeared, she stopped, faced the sun, and lifted her arms up over her head. And that's when the wind helped him notice something he hadn't before. Gusts pushed and pulled at her loose dress, and Leander was surprised to see his usually thin wife had grown plump.

When he came in from the workshop for a lunch, the porch was a mess, sweaters and winter jackets mounded on the floor. His wife was seated in the kitchen, a bucket of warm sudsy water beside her. In her lap, she balanced the miniature tub.

"Lot of old dust," she said, all business.

"Oh," he replied, when he saw her cleaning the tub as gently as she might clean a baby. A jig played in his heart, and he began to dance. Even his bad foot couldn't contain itself. "Yes. Yes, yes. Old dust. We don't want none of that."

After the baby was born, Leander crafted a miniature cradle from pale birch wood, carved a delicate set of wings into the head-piece. Warm afternoons, Stella placed the cradle on the back stoop, wrapped her daughter and laid her in. Cool salty air held the child in a state of calm, and the naps went on for hours.

Once, while she was snipping young dandelion greens to have with dinner, she heard birdsong coming from the stoop. Not sweet and tranquil, but a hasty, hesitant warble. When she turned to look, perched on the base of the cradle was a familiar bird, with a yellow band over its eyes, white-tipped wings.

Stella sat back on the rise of rock, mound of greens in the lap of her apron, and watched the bird throw back its head and sing up towards heaven. She listened wholeheartedly as it chirped and sang, and before she knew it, the sky behind her was tinged with orange, the baby mewing, hungry for milk.

She put a hand to her face, and though she would never admit it to another living soul, she was nearly overcome with pride, pleased that the small feathered creature was witness to the life she'd created. The apprehension in its song did nothing to diminish it.

chapter nine

Sometimes, when the drizzle coated the windowpanes and the dampness slowed the rising of her bread, Stella thought of Amos. She wondered what life might be like if he had returned with the other boys. Would he have been empty and angry, or bursting with joy that he had survived? Would he have been happy when she married Leander, and was blessed with two children, Elise, now aged five, and Robert, one? Might he have married Nettie Rose after all, and had a sweet brood of his own? Of course these questions had no answer, but they chided her until her imagination felt raw and irritated. She missed Amos. Especially when it rained. How unfair it was to have a whole portion of her life lopped off, all those connections dangling now in a murky mess of nothingness.

Recently, in a rare moment when they were alone, Nettie Rose had asked Stella about Amos. What was he like for a brother? Stella was kind in her recollections, told Nettie of the innocent tomfoolery, the sensitivity behind his handsome face, how he was shy about the colour of his hair. He could knit with his fingers and a strand of yarn, loved poking through old junk. Never threw out a bent nail, or backed down from an argument. Said that Amos liked any kind of sweet, sticks of candy from the general store, cakes and puddings, bakeapple jam, brown sugar in his tea.

"I likes brown sugar in my tea, too," Nettie replied, a hint of wistfulness in her voice. "And I makes a wonderful rice pudding, sauce like silk." She smoothed her wrinkled skirt, scratched at a whitish stain, dried spit-up. "What did he think of me, Stella? Do you know?"

Stella couldn't stare into Nettie's round bland face when she explained that Amos had loved Nettie, had thought she was beautiful. Instead, she focused on Nettie's throat, the flesh rising and falling as Nettie kept swallowing something. Perhaps it was regret.

"Why?"

"What do you mean?"

"Well," Nettie pressed, "what did he think was beautiful about me?"

With this, Stella invented a few things, as Amos had never expressed appreciation for any particular feature of Nettie's. It was simply clear that he was besotted with her, overwhelmed with teenaged adoration. Love needed no visible reasons to seize a beating heart, render it into liquid.

Nettie reached up to plump her dull hair, then daubed wetness from her eyes with the edge of her sleeve. "I didn't know that," she said. "I didn't know he thought about me."

"You never knowed?"

"Not a clue, maid."

Stella knew Nettie was lying, and when Stella's lips betrayed a hint of her inner scowl, Nettie announced curtly, "Not like it makes nar bit of difference now. Things is the way they is."

Stella clamped her teeth together, angry at herself for participating in such nonsense. Even though Nettie was her sister-in-law and friend, this sort of airy discussion annoyed her. When her brother had been breathing, he'd been unable to charm her, though now that he was dead, Nettie furtively swooned over his ghost.

But when she reflected on her last visit with Nettie Rose, Stella understood. Nettie had married Gus Smith on a blustery day in January, only weeks after he'd returned from the war. Theirs was the sort of romance the community needed, young love, separated by forces beyond their control, amorous letters of devotion (read out by Nettie to every female willing to listen), then the homecoming, a spectacle of girlish squealing, macho smirks. They joined their hands in a gust, and within months, a baby on the way, this soon followed by another baby after another baby after another baby. The whole of Bended Knee felt it, this need to fill up the emptiness, replace the faces that were lost.

Then, after several years of rampant procreation, no one heeded them anymore. No one looked to plump and weary Nettie for an update on the bond between her and her husband. It was difficult to talk above the screeching children. At any given time, one would be yanking loose strands of her hair, or pinching her breasts, or trying to hide underneath her skirt. And no one mentioned the revelation that Gus had caught something over there – that something being a powerful thirst. Once married with umpteen children, his need to quench it overpowered him.

When Stella and Leander arrived last Saturday evening, Elise and Robert in tow, they could hear the racket from the front gate. Entering the porch, they came upon screaming twin girls in the corner crib, a toddler plunked in the middle of the floor, hand jammed down into his soiled cloth diaper, another boy picking a hole in his brother's wool sweater, clutched a string of yarn as the older one ran away from him. Two daughters chasing another boy with wooden spoons, a single quiet child tucked in beside the woodstove, darning a sock with a fat needle.

Nettie was at the counter, mashing a heaping mound of turnip in a wide bowl. She smiled wanly when they came in, hollered over the din, "Find a place for yourselves. Don't be fussy."

There was no sign of Gus. Leander held his cap in his hand, opened his mouth, and Nettie spewed, "Don't even ask. I got no idea where he's to. But isn't that lovely." She nodded towards Grace, the darning daughter. "Not yet nine and she does a better job than her weary old mother."

Stella went over to look, complimented Grace on her neat weave, and Grace maintained the placid lost expression that she consistently wore.

"What can I do?" Stella asked as she passed Robert, his black eyes like eclipsed moons, to Leander.

"Twins are teething. Daub some of that on those." Nettie jutted her chin in the direction of a jug, beside it two balls of fabric tied with a string.

Stella retrieved the rum, dipped her finger in, then touched it off the fabric.

"Not like that," Nettie said, wiped her hands in her apron, took the bottle from Stella and soaked each ball. Then she went to the twins, tugged their shiny fists from their chewing mouths, placed the dripping fabric on their gums, then pressed hard. They sputtered, fell back on their rumps, silent from the shock of the flavour. "There we go," Nettie said. Then to the other children (excepting the diapered one and the darning one), she yelled, "Get your arses out of doors this instant, or I'll give you all something to make noise over." On the back stoop, more bellowing, "Thomas! Harold! Mary! Get down here and mind your brothers and sisters."

"Elise," Stella said. "You too. Out of doors until I calls you for dinner."

Gus arrived in the exact moment a roasted chicken was placed on the table. Before even greeting them, he tore the crispy knob off the rump from the back of the bird, jammed it into his mouth, licked greasy fingers.

"I'll tell you one of my dreams, Stella, my love," he slurred between vigorous crunches. "Do you want to know one of my dreams?"

"Of course," Stella replied, hands folded in her lap. She could see the salt crystals around his mouth, drunken tongue darting out to retrieve them.

"A plate of pope's noses. A load of the little beggars. Before I dies, that's what I wants. To eat a whole plate of pope's noses."

Nettie snorted. "I allows. Keep dreaming."

"What? A fellow can't have a dream?" Gus leaned his chair back on two legs.

"You got your dream now, my son," Nettie replied. Bickering tone.

"What? Is you cracked?" he said as he peeled the entire skin off the back of the bird, balled it, then popped it into his mouth.

"That's not what you said all those years ago. When I was a girl." Hurt, now. "Just a girl."

"Get me a plate, missus."

Stella glanced into Nettie's faded eyes, and they reminded her of two steel-coloured beach stones, edges long gone. And she felt pity for Nettie, her friend, once so full of conviction and self-assurance, always a perfect ribbon pinned in her hair. She remembered Nettie boasting not so many years ago. How her and Gus, so deeply in love, even a whole world at war couldn't touch it. They were charmed, she said. A couple of charmed lovers who were going to do things right. Then, in only a dozen or so years, she had managed to recreate the home she had left behind. A husband who didn't understand his role. And so many children, she joked about having to search the outer limbs of the family tree to find enough names. Though perhaps Nettie never noticed the frenetic squalor, there was hardly time for observation.

"Well, now," Stella replied. "A plate of pope's noses. That's something." She tried to appear amused.

Throughout the meal, Leander nipped away at the rum, while Gus threw the drinks into his mouth, swishing it around his teeth as though trying to dislodge strands of chicken. He shook his glass over his open mouth, then winked at Stella, said, "Like the old woman who pissed in the sea says, Every drop counts."

Once the children were fed and the women started clearing, Leander hoisted the accordion on his lap, began to squeeze music from its stiff body. Not three notes in the air, and Gus was up from his chair, spinning his children around the room. One by one, each clung to his willowy trunk as their feet left the floor. They stared at Gus with absolute adoration, captivated, his boisterousness pressing at the walls of the warm room. The younger boys knocked their hair forward, a lock covering their eyes just like their father's. Older boys swaggered. After Mary and Grace and Lucy and Anne danced, they all blushed when he tapped his bristly cheek, said, "Give a kiss to your old father." Even Elise, suddenly shy, took a turn. "What do you think of your old Uncle Gus?" he said to her. "Lighter on my feet now than a seal on his flippers."

Nettie poured steaming water from the pot on the back of the stove into a washbasin. Dishes clanked harder than necessary as she dropped them in, scrubbing fiercely enough to damage the finish, water too hot for a sane person's hands. As Stella dried, she could hear Nettie mumbling to herself, inflection indicating endless questions.

But after each available child had been twirled around the kitchen dance floor, Gus came up behind Nettie, formed his body into her back. Instantly, the frown disappeared, and her face flushed when he held her waist, turned her around, and opened his hand towards the centre of the room. "Ma lady," he whispered, and she struck him gently on his shoulder, smiled, bitterness dissolving.

Leander slowed the pace of the music. Nettie and Gus began to waltz, his hand firmly on her lower back, her face resting on his shoulder, eyes closed. He danced her across the kitchen, into the porch, twirled her through the door and onto the back stoop. They swayed there in the evening glow of summer sun, and after several minutes, he danced her back again.

Stella glanced over at Leander, and he winked at her. They were thinking the same thing, this dip and climb of emotion was likely creating the simple foundation for yet another child.

Dance complete, and Nettie sat down, nudged Grace and Mary towards the sink.

Gus clapped his hands now, hollered, "Line up, you little beggars. Hop to it now. Show your father how it's done."

The children, Elise included, dodged and weaved, arranging themselves in order of height, backs straight, chests jutting out. Gus could have been at the head of the pack, his freckles and thick reddish hair making him look more like a brother than their father. But instead, he walked before them, dug his hand deep into his pocket, jingled his change, then plucked out a fistful of shiny nickels, placed one in the open palm of each. "Toffees for the load of you." Mouths open wide in disbelief, they stared at their coins, turned them over and over. Then, they stormed their father, squeezed him, squealed, "I loves you, Dad. You's the best father ever."

Nettie erupted from her chair. "That's what you don't then," she cried. Fog in hot sunlight, her afterglow from the moment of romance had burned off. "What do you think? Money grows on trees? Giving children the pittance we got to survive. What? You don't want to eat? Is you mad?"

Elise was the first one to fork it over, followed by the older ones. Nettie then pried the money from the sweaty hands of the younger children. Johnnie, though, would not relinquish his treasure, and she tugged at his hands until he flopped down on the floor, curled in a ball, hiding his money. Flurry of words: "But I loves toffees. Loves them, Mommy. I wants them. Wants them. Wants. Pleeeeease."

The accordion, which had slowed to a background melody, now choked on its bit of air, and everyone stared when Nettie hissed, "By Jaysus." She reached her hand underneath Johnnie's wild hair, tweaked the back of his neck. The veins in her forehead stood at attention, her heart pumping certain acrimony.

"I wants it," he cried, twisting on the floor. "Please, Mommy."

"That's what you don't then, you little bugger."

She freed his arm, bent back his wrist until he cried out in pain, the nickel dropping to the ground. "One gets it, they all wants it." Talking to herself now.

When he jumped to his feet, Nettie gripped his chin, spoke firmly, "That'll teach you to disobey your mother." And Johnnie, lips bunched up and ready, spit in her eye.

"Blood of a bitch," Nettie cried as she stepped backwards, stung. Her face looked like greased dough, and her mouth wrinkled as the anger dribbled off her, replaced by something different. Flouncing down on the pine floor, nickels rolling in every direction, she stared at Stella, began to whimper, "How is this fair? How is this fair? I cooks their oatmeal and washes their arses and scrubs their grimy clothes. Sews their trousers. Combs out their snarls. Daubs salve on their cuts. But they despises me. Despises me in spite of all I does. Spite of it. And that," nod towards drowsy Gus, "does not a thing but come home drunk, rile them up with his madness, fill them up with garbage thoughts. But they loves him. Loves HIM!"

Leander laid the accordion beside his chair and moved towards her. Placing a hand on her shoulder, he said, "Calm down, maid. You're frightening the young ones."

"I can't take it no more." Nettie began to cry. "Take him away, Lee, for the love of God. Take the bastard away."

Hasty retreats, and Stella and Nettie Rose were left alone. As Nettie tucked her head into her arms, folded on the kitchen table, Stella sent all of the children to bed. "Elise. Stay up there with your cousins until I comes and gets you." And without so much as a squeak, the pack of them slipped out of the room, tip-toed up over the narrow stairwell into the two large bedrooms above.

Stella went to the crib then, peered down at the three sleeping children, nestled together like bunnies, two of them doused in rum. Robert's mouth was slightly open, and she leaned in closer to check his upper gum. It was still swollen and she could see a blood blister forming, but no sign of the tooth.

"Goodness, those babes can sleep."

Nettie lifted her head, wiped her stained face in her apron. "'Tis shameful. The racket I made."

"They didn't seem to mind in the least. Never even stirred." Stella sat down at the table, placed her hand over Nettie's, her friend's skin chapped and cracked, yet moist at the same time. There was a strong odour of metal from the money that was once locked in Nettie's fist, and Stella had to resist checking her own hand, to see if that smell had transferred. "Is you going to be all right?"

"Fine, maid."

"Tea?"

"A dozen years of peace and quiet'd be better, but I'll take the tea, seeing as you're offering it."

When Stella placed the cup and saucer on the table, Nettie lifted both, winced when her jittery hands made them tinkle. She let the steam rise over her face, and when she blinked, Stella noticed her eyelids were so swollen, each lash had a generous amount of room.

"Don't know what come over me, maid," Nettie said.

"Happens to every one of us. We can't keep everything together all of the time."

"I knows."

"No sense in being hard on yourself."

"I don't think it had nothing to do with those nickels."

"No one even paid that any mind."

"Half of them gone now, anyway. Cracks in the floor."

"Oh, Johnnie'll root those out. You needn't worry."

"Not when I'm in the kitchen, I doubts. Sometimes he puts the devil right in me, he do."

"I knows."

"And I finds myself wishing time and time again, that when he's growed and has got his own, he gets it back. The misery he's caused me."

"'Tis always a gamble, maid. You never knows what type of child you'll get until it's sitting at your table with its mouth open."

Nettie laid the tea down, pressed her fingers into her cheeks. "I wonders where Gus is to."

"They's fine, my dear. Probably out tormenting someone else."

Nettie sighed. "I loves him," she said. "I really does. I loves my husband. Don't know that any other man could turn me right into a girl like he do. That being part of the trouble, mind you." She smiled wryly. "Yes, I loves him. But I hates him too. Hates his guts, like they was rotted through and through. Some days I believes I'd be better off if I'd married someone else."

"I knows, maid."

Nettie shook her head, as though she were answering her own question. "You'd think that would cancel itself out, wouldn't you? The love and the hate of him. Two of they would knock up against each other, and cancel themselves out. But somehow, I can't manage it. I prays for numbness every day, Stella. Prays for it, but God don't grant it."

"You don't want that, Nettie."

"No?"

"When all you feels is nothing, then your life is over."

Nettie slurped her tea, grimaced. "I burned my mouth."

"Drop of water?"

"No. I don't mind. Serves me right. Never could catch hold to an ounce of patience."

Stella patted Nettie's hand. "Well, God love you if that's your worst failing."

"You know what I even thought once or twice?"

"What's that?"

"To dump a boiling cup of tea down over myself."

"What? Down over yourself where?"

"You knows. Right into my lap. Spoil myself. Down below. Just to spite him."

"You didn't think that now." Stella shook her head, clicked her tongue.

"I did then. 'Tis a terrible sin."

Stella began to giggle. Nettie ground her polished nose into her face, and glared at Stella. "What's you laughing at? Is it that stupid?"

"No, maid," she said. "I's sorry. But I just couldn't help but think..."

"What?"

"That from what you've told me about your times with Gus, scalding yourself won't make nar bit of difference. He wouldn't bat an eye at that." Stella glanced over at Grace's work resting on the arm of a chair. "My dear, you'd be better off darning the whole works over."

Noise burst from Nettie's throat, and Stella held her breath for a second while she figured out what sort of noise it was. Ah, laughter, emerging with a force, as though it were snagged in the wretchedness, now suddenly released.

"You're terrible," Nettie hooted between snorts. "You're right, but you're terrible."

Stella snorting too. "And a good strong yarn at that."

"Double it over."

"What a start he'd get." Breathless with laughter, Stella, bent at the waist, eyes squinted, screeched, "Sorry, darling. We're closed for business."

Screaming, Nettie slapped her fat cheeks, was barely able to mouth, "For the next fifty years."

"Mother?" Grace was at the door to the kitchen, sheepishly staring in at the two women.

Nettie coughed, wiped both hands across her face, sucked in a lungful that was meant to calm. "Yes, my child."

"I just wondered if I could finish."

"Finish what?"

"On the sock. I was fixing the hole."

With this new mention of darning, Stella and Nettie locked eyes, then collapsed in a fresh fit of laughter. "The hole," Nettie squealed in a thin tinny voice, and this new level of secret girlish crassness forced tears from their eyes.

"Go ahead, Gracie," Nettie panted, once again wiping her face in her apron. "Fix that hole so it don't come undone for a good long time. Nothing would make your poor mother prouder."

Gus squinted in the evening sunlight, rubbed his hands over his face, then reached into his shirt pocket, retrieved a narrow tin. He and Leander were outside Fuller's general store, Leander seated on a picnic table bench, Gus perched atop the table itself. Just beyond them, the ocean lapped at the shore, waves arriving in perfect succession.

"I wonders will she ever stop?" Gus said. He opened the silver tin, plucked out a cigarette, and stuck it between his teeth.

"Nah, Nettie can go on forever."

"I was talking about the water." He cupped a hand over the lit match, brought it to his mouth. "Don't she get tired of licking the same rocks over and over again?"

"I got no idea about that."

"She's a lot like me, though, I finds."

"How's that?"

"'Tis too much trouble to tell you. But we both does–" Mid-sentence, Gus tossed his half-smoked cigarette, then reached into his mouth with two fingers, dug around. Fingers clear, he cast a sideways glance at Leander, said, "Ever get an itchy tongue?"

"Can't say that I've had the pleasure, Gus."

"Nah, no pleasure in the ailment, though there's some to be found in the cure." Gus smirked, sat on the table, let his legs dangle over the sides. He clicked his chin towards the store. "Don't suppose Fuller got a little something in there to wet the whistle, do you? You knows, on the credit?"

"I doubts it," Leander lied. "Nettie would lose her mind, and besides he's as chaste as a–"

Gus made a sucking sound. "I's awful dry, Lee. Could use a drop."

"Why don't we just sit tight? Enjoy the evening."

"Enjoy the evening, you says. There's no finer show to be had. Watching the sea. Look out there, just off from Quint's Island, I sees a woman in the waves. Look, look. She don't got a stitch on."

"I don't see a thing," Leander said, hand shielding his eyes from the low sun.

"She's lovely, even though she's blue." Gus craned his neck. "Now look, 'tis changing. Aw, Christ Almighty." Hands thrown up. "It done turned into a feller. What kind of cheating is that?"

Leander laughed. "Got some mind on you, I allows."

Gus tapped the cigarette tin on the table, turning it over and over. "Powerful thirst, I got."

"That'll pass."

"You wouldn't understand."

"Understand what?"

"The dryness. Me and the sea. The sea and me. I knows why she don't stop licking rocks. Can't stand the dryness."

"Well now, all right." Leander scratched the back of his head. "You might be right. I don't got no clue."

Gus then told Leander he'd come home from the war with this yearning, only he hadn't realized the strength of it until his eighth child was born. "I knows the reason why

I wanted so many babies. Yeah, I knows. Wanted to be surrounded by them, I did. Drowned in babies. Drowned in the life."

"That's a noble thing, sure, Gus."

"But things don't always work out."

"Well, you got your crowd. No doubting that."

"That I did." He lit a cigarette, tucked another behind his ear, then snapped the case closed. "But, I never counted on the racket. The constant squabble. Like they's mostly made up of mouth. Babies bawling over top of it all."

"Well now, Gus. That's part and parcel, I'd imagine. Nettie don't like what you're doing, I knows," Leander said, staring down at his bad foot. "She told Stella. She don't like the drink. Says she wants you good and sober."

Gus raked his fingers through his hair and laughed lightly. "I'll tell you a little known fact now, Leander. Women thinks 'tis the drop that makes you drunk, but if the truth be told, 'tis the drop that keeps you sober."

"That don't make nar bit of sense."

"Lucky you. That tells me you got nar reason to drink."

Once again, Leander glanced down at his bad foot, scraped it over the worn grass so that it rested neatly beside the other one. As he grew older, he was beginning to recognize that his body's imperfection was less a hindrance and more of an endowment. Having an impediment had kept him on a certain wobbly path, obliging him to slow down, be mindful of the ditches.

"Lee," Gus said. "Did you ever hear a man die before?"

"Hear?"

"Yes, listen to it. Listen to them." Gus's voice had lost its slur, his zeal degraded into dejection.

"No, Gus. Can't say that I have."

"When I was over there, you knows, all kinds of stuff

happened. You could do what you wanted, it made no difference."

Leander nodded.

"The feller next to me was shot, you knows. Shot somewhere, I got no idea. In his guts, I guessed. And I spent some time guessing. We was stuck there, right stuck, and I couldn't do nothing to help the beggar. And when he realized he was bleeding out, he wasn't all quiet, like you'd think him to be. Like you'd wish him to be. No, he started in talking, and talking, and talking. Non-stop. Then it turned to jabber. And he babbled and babbled until he was slurring, and I couldn't make a word out. Though I gave it an honest try, I swears to God I did. A few minutes of pure gibberish, and then he starts in with the bawling, gob hanging open, and the screeches coming right out of him. And those screeches petered out into whimpers. Then this sucking sound, awful, awful. And finally, he shut up. All his sounds was used. And then he was dead."

Leander blew a stream of air out through pursed lips. "Must've been right awful."

"Don't be talking."

Both nodded.

"I can't hear that ever again, Lee. And sometimes, up there in the house with your sister, I hears it all at once." Gus lit another cigarette, stuck it to his dry bottom lip, let it dangle as he spoke. "After a drink or ten, then I don't heed it no more. All I hears is the water. Shushing in my mind."

"I sees."

"No you don't."

"Maybe I don't, Gus."

"But you means well. That's one thing I've always known about you, you means well."

"Well." Leander didn't know what else to say.

"God damn, she's lovely."

"Who?"

"The sea. The beautiful sea." Gus leaped to his feet on top of the table, faced the ocean, and offered a crisp salute. "Sight of her makes me want to yowl."

"I wouldn't suggest it."

Gus leaned back his head, a hearty wail rising up from his bowels, spilling out of his mouth.

Within seconds, Fuller was out from the store, beside them now, shaking his fist at Gus. "Get yourself down from there. You hear me? Where do you think you is?"

Gus leapt from the table top, crumpled onto his knees, then bounced up. "Who's you talking to?"

"I's talking to you, Gus Smith."

"Listen up, fellers," Gus said, hauling up his trousers. He rolled his shoulders, then glanced side to side, as though he were expecting a crowd. "He's talking to me. This fat son of a bitch is talking to me."

"Now, now, Gus," Leander said. "We's just heading on in now, Fuller. Lovely night out."

Gus's voice continued to creep. "Was you to the war, Fuller? No sir. You couldn't fit your fat arse into the uniform. Or was you stuck too tight to your crazy mother's tit?"

Fuller's stern expression vanished, a curious mix of wounded rage taking its place. "I never touched my mother's tit," he cried.

With fists up, Gus ran towards Fuller, and Fuller raised his log-of-a-forearm, smashed Gus straight in the face. Gus toppled backwards, lay there like a splayed animal carcass. He didn't so much as flinch when blood began to trickle from his nostrils, glide around the crevice of his cheeks, producing a scarlet circus mustache.

Leander helped Gus to his feet, and Gus shook his head, stunned.

"I think we best be getting home," Leander said, once again.

Fuller grunted, folded his natural weapons across his cask-like chest.

Looking into his hot face, Leander thought that if steam could, it would now be seeping from those flared nostrils.

Blood continued to drip from Gus's nose, forming a matching goatee. "Well," he said, quite sober now. "Lovely evening, Fuller. Best to your mom."

And the two men turned away, Gus scuttling ahead, while Leander scrape-clomped behind him. Almost home, he noticed the sun dipping down into the water, those last fizzled rays ready to sink and die.

As Stella buttoned the neck on Elise's gingham nightdress, she thought to mention the turmoil at Nettie's house, but decided against it. There was no point in discussing adult business with a child, and besides, Elise had seemed oblivious to the friction. In fact, once Leander returned with Gus, Elise had wanted to stay with her cousins. "Good to be like her," Leander had said, rubbing his receding hairline. "Trouble rolls off her like water on this here oily scalp."

Drawing back the fresh sheets, Stella lifted her elbow so Elise could climb in under and up into the bed. Sheets down now, tucked around Elise. "Tight enough?" Stella asked.

"Almost."

Stella pretended to strain and grunt as she tugged at the sheets, and she then said, as she did every night, "I thinks that's snug enough, my dearie, else the bed'll swallow you up."

And every night, Elise giggled, flexed her body so that her legs and arms bounced upwards, freed from the cotton cocoon.

"What do you want to hear? Do you want Daddy to come in and read a few pages to you?" Stella adjusted the lantern on the night table, moved it an extra inch or two away from the wall.

"No," Elise replied. "Not tonight." Her eyes rolled upwards, and she chewed her lower lip. "Can you tell me about me, Mom? Not a book story tonight, but a story about me."

"If that's what you wants."

"I does."

Stella adjusted the white sheet, pulled it back up underneath Elise's arms, unfolded the crazy quilt made from odd scraps and tossed it over the child's feet.

"Well," Stella replied. "What do you want to hear? About the eggs you found in on the marsh or the time you lost Mrs. Rideout's wedding ring out on the beach? Or, when–"

"How about where you got me? I loves that story."

"Ah yes." Stella smoothed her daughter's tangled hair away from her face. "The cabbage patch."

Elise smiled. "Tell me all of it. Don't skip a scrap."

"Well," Stella began with a contented sigh. She sat on the stool beside the bed, hands folded in her lap. "Your father and I waited many, many years for you. Did you know that?"

"Yes. Until you'd almost given up all hope."

"That's right. All hope. Nearly gone."

"And what happened?"

"Early morning in the summer days, I'd go up to the garden, poke around a bit. Sometimes it'd be storming like you wouldn't believe, but I'd still go do my walk. Checking things here and there. When I'd get to the cabbages, I'd take it real slow, lifting up the big leaves and peering underneath. Hoping there might be something hidden there."

"What was you looking for?"

"I don't rightly know, to be honest. I never had the mind to ask my mother that, how she found me. So I guess I was looking for a flash of white, I suppose. A little toe."

"But nothing?"

"Not even a curly lock of hair."

"Was you sad?"

"Beyond sad. Forlorn."

"What do that mean?"

"Just really, really sad. Disappointed. Let down."

"Did you cry?"

"Sometimes."

"But not too often."

"I kept myself busy. Tried not to think about it too much."

"Then what happened?"

"Well, I was up in the cabbages, and the leaves was beginning to draw themselves in, and I knew the season for babies was almost coming to a close. We'd had a real warm summer, and there was extra big leaves, so I had to really take my time. And I minds it was a real quiet morning. It was cloudy too. I remembers that. Right overcast."

"How do you know?"

"Cause I minds seeing Eldred Wood sneaking down the lane. He don't come out much on a bright day."

"Sneaking?"

"Well, walking, I suppose. Though he walks in a particular way. Like he tiptoes. I shouldn't say sneaky, it don't sound nice. And he never done no harm to me."

"Oh. Did you find anything in the cabbages?"

"Not an ear, not a lip, not an ankle. Not one thing."

"And then what happened?"

"Well, I heard what I thought was a kitten."

"A kitten?"

"Yes, like one that was still blind. And I followed the sound, over to where the turnips was growing in the ground. Those bright leaves were wet from dew, and my skirt got drenched from all the dripping."

"And?"

"I went about looking for a furry little body, maybe black and white stripes or gingery like. But I didn't see nothing. Again. Not until I peered under this particularly large leaf. And guess what I found?"

Elise's eyes lit up. "I knows. I knows. I can tell it from here."

"Go ahead."

"Then you lifted up the great big old leaf, and there I was. A baby just for you."

"That's exactly right. A baby just for me. My heart nearly stopped."

"Really?"

"No, but I was real happy."

Elise bent her knees, white mountains in the bed. "What was I wearing?"

Laying her hand on top of the mountain, Stella said, "Do you want the truth?"

"Always the truth, Mommy."

"Well, to be honest, you weren't wearing much. Nothing at all, in fact."

"Really?" Her eyes widened. "I weren't cold?"

"I whipped you right up and brought you down to the house. Wrapped a blanket round you tighter than the skin on a fish."

"That's good." Rolling on to her side, Elise hugged her knees. "I always wonders something."

"What's that?"

"What if someone else found me?"

"No one would do that. 'Twas my turnip patch."

"What if that man got hold of me?"

"What man?"

"That one you said you seen sneaking down the lane."

"Oh, Eldred?"

Stella paused for a second, put a hand to her cheek. In her mind's eye, she had no trouble seeing the clothes that Eldred wore every day. Brown trousers, faded plaid shirt, collar and cuffs buttoned, black rubber boots. But his face, she was unable to recall it. Though she had seen him time and time again, his face eluded her. She remembered it was neither particularly youthful nor wrinkled with years. Not happy or sad. Never eager, and not at all indifferent. It just was. A simple face. Somehow unimportant. And she wondered if she'd ever really looked at him, or if she only looked about him, around him. Avoiding that simple face for uncomfortable reasons she could not comprehend.

She did recall that Eldred passed by the morning Elise was born, and their interaction was the same as usual. Whenever Eldred came around the bend in the lane, he would stop on the high point, stare at her house. Hairs would prickle on her arms, and if she was outside where he might see her, she would force a hand to lift and wave. Pull her lips back in the shape of a toothy smile. A good Christian was polite, especially to those less fortunate. And Eldred Wood, a broken-down man who was apparently terrified of his own shadow, was most definitely a less fortunate.

She had only ever spoken to him once, and this was at least two years before Elise was born, maybe three or four. She had believed he was mute, but learned that wasn't the case. Down by the gate, he stood waiting, drizzle driving his clothes against him. And as he stood there, he held the pickets, never lifted the latch to come in. Shawl wrapped around her shoulders, kitchen slippers still on, she went down to him.

"Baby here," he'd said, pointing a shaky finger at the house behind her.

"No, sir," she replied. "No babies."

"A girl. Was a baby girl."

She had the notion that perhaps he had second sight, and she put a hand to her abdomen. "How long ago?" she ventured.

"Years," he replied, eyes squinting as a thin rain spat at him. "Years and years and years. A baby girl."

She remembered smiling gently, thinking to touch his hand, still clasping the picket. "Well, that wouldn't be a baby no longer. Babies grows, Mr. Wood. But Leander is up in his shed, got it like an oven in there, if you wants to go dry off. Cup of tea?"

He hadn't responded, looked at her sideways, ambled away.

"Yes. He," Elise said. "Mr. Wood. That's who I was talking about."

"He's never come in on our property. He don't come in on folks' land."

"But he gawks."

"He looks. Probably looks at everyone. No harm in looking."

"But what was he doing out so early?"

"I got no idea. Maybe doing a chore for Berta – the woman who looks after him. Maybe the weather suited him."

"But what if he came in and stole me from under that leaf?"

"Well, life would be very different, wouldn't it?"

"Would you miss me?"

"What do you mean?"

"Would you miss me?" More serious now. "Would you cry?"

"Such funny questions."

Elise glowered, slid down in the bed.

Running her hand over the pillow, Stella plucked out several sharp points, errant feathers. "Well, I don't know. I don't think a person can miss what they never had. Miss what they never had the chance to love."

Elise pouted, twirled a finger around a few strands of hair, yanked.

"That's not like you," Stella said. "Now up on your pillow. The time for sleep is long past." She lifted the lantern, walked to the door.

"Mommy?"

Stella turned, held the lantern into the room, so she could clearly see her daughter's face. "Yes, dear."

"I asked Daddy, and he says I was born in the spring."

"Yes, you was."

"How come there was such big turnip leaves so early on in the spring?"

"Well, now. Maybe 'twas a warm spring. A real warm spring."

"Is that the truth?"

Stella let her arm down, lantern glowing near her thigh. "Yes, my baby."

"Mom?"

"Yes, maid."

Elise had rolled onto her side, her words bouncing off the wallpapered walls, reaching Stella indirectly. "I don't want that story no more, all right? I thinks I knows it by heart."

chapter ten

Harriet was a happy girl. Always upbeat. Leander had found her over a year ago during a spring rainstorm, half a mile into the woods. His foot had been throbbing, and nothing would ease the discomfort, unless he moved forward. Even though Stella thought he was foolish, this deep ache propelled him out into the foggy dusk, and he ambled straight into the forest, stumbling over roots and the litter of pine cones and needles and old leaves. After nearly an hour, he came to a spongy bog, stopped, and heard snuffling and whimpering. Leander clapped his leg, and something sprinted towards him, speed like rolling thunder. He closed his eyes, worried over what his foot might have discovered, and then felt wet warmth on his hand. A relieved tongue.

When he had found her, Harriet was not yet full grown, but no longer quite a pup. She had a broad long snout and large amber eyes. Her back looked like a curving shoreline, never-ending layers of furry white-tipped waves crashing in. Although he might have been mistaken, he had thought she looked very like a Newfoundland wolf.

But he knew there were no more left. Extinct. Perhaps this excited creature was a jovial relative, jumping now on the marshy bog, trying to lick the freckles from the back of his hand. He remembered his father telling him how gentle they were (even though they had a wily and vicious reputation), and how many years ago, when his own father was a young boy, there was a hefty bounty on the head of each wolf. Celebration when one was killed. How over the years, the ghostly howl had petered into silence.

Leander knelt down, placed his hands in her fur, shook away the water droplets that beaded in her coat. "Well, well, well," he said. "Where in God's name did you come from?" He was never able to answer that question, but the dog followed him out of the woods, over the laneway, and into the sweet orange glow of their kitchen.

At first Stella had been nervous for the children, their few chickens. "She looks like a wolf. She howls like a wolf. She certainly eats like a wolf." But after several months of yipping and dancing and making music with her curved nails on the wood floor, Stella told him, "Harriet Edgecombe is my easiest child."

Robert had big plans for Harriet. During the fall, Leander and he had built a sleigh, painted it apple red. "When I goes down Andrews' Hill, Harriet can haul me right back up again. I don't never need to get off." He tapped his chin, thinking. "Or I could charge a penny an hour and she could tug around someone else. I'll be right rich." But on their first official outing, boy and dog, Harriet chomped at the snow, leaped after drifting flakes, barreled towards Robert, knocked him clear off his perch. "So much for that," he said, shrugging his shoulders. "She hopped aboard, wouldn't budge. Had to haul *her* home."

Elise was the only family member who ignored the dog. In the beginning, she adored Harriet, but on Christmas morning, her tune changed to indifference. With feverish determination, Elise had set about knitting a bright red wool sweater for Harriet, and worked night and day to finish it, wrapped the mess of loose ends and gaping holes in brown paper, slid it underneath the spruce tree in the front room. In the morning, Harriet hauled out the package, tore it open, and Elise pinned the dog down, slipped the tangle of red over Harriet's head, tied some strands around the barrel chest. Harriet cocked her head, looked at Elise with wet uncertain eyes, absence of appreciation, then pawed to get out. Five minutes later, she returned, sweater missing, Elise in tears when she glared out the window, saw her gift clinging to a splintery fence post, like a streak of unwanted blood against the holiday snow.

For the most part, Harriet was Leander's dog. Wherever Leander went, Harriet went. She was so attached, she howled outside the church as soon as Leander disappeared inside. Her wailing during the Sunday service drowned out Reverend Hickey's raspy sermonizing, and they took to barring her in the workshop, lest the Reverend use his last breath to be heard over a dog. When Leander entered his shed, knelt in front of Harriet, she would bolt towards him, press her body against his, head on his shoulder, weeping like a lonely child.

While Leander sanded and sawed and hammered and turned in his workshop, Harriet was always near his feet. More than once, her paw was nipped when she stood too close to the treadle of the lathe. During the long weekdays, when evening shadows arrived early, they chatted the afternoons away, Leander asking questions, Harriet responding with various pitches, stressing different portions of her howl. Even though Stella fed Harriet left-over scraps and plucked burrs from her impressive fur, Harriet never had much to say to Stella, and Stella growled (half-jokingly), "If Harriet didn't go around on all fours, gob half open, I'd be some awful jealous."

Harriet garnered a fair bit of attention. Throughout the year, people dropped by to see the "almost wolf," for no one wanted to admit what she might actually be – the last of her kind. And whenever anyone questioned Leander about the dog, he replied, "I got no idea what she is. Other than our Miss Edgecombe. The household darling."

Robert would beam, Elise grimace, and Stella would always add, "Long as we all knows she's the family pet. To the best of my knowledge, the Lord above frowns on man taking up two wives."

"So sweet," a young schoolteacher said to her sister as they ambled down the lane. "Take a gander at them over there." She nodded out towards the wharf.

"Yes now," the sister replied. "Youngsters today don't play like they used to. Right refreshing to see them getting along. Working together instead of trying to knock each other down."

Though Elise and Robert Edgecombe were the subjects of the conversation, they didn't hear the women chatting. Instead, the children were dangling over the wharf, shoulders touching, blood filling their heads. Crabs, sculpins, connors, sea weed, they were hooking anything and everything that passed over their bent pins.

Birds cried overhead, flapping grey wings, faded feet spread, ready to pluck. One swooped down near them, and Elise twisted her head to look upwards, then shrieked, fell backwards on the wharf. It swooped again, stole a crushed snail, then ascended, beak full.

"You scared of a bird?" Robert said, his voice echoing beneath the wharf, rising up through the boards. "'Tis only a gull."

When she heard a muffled giggle, Elise put her fingers to her cheeks, pressed. "That's what you think."

"That's what I knows. Daddy told me. They's called gulls. Gulls starts with the letter 'G.' And they loves to eat old fish and garbage. Garbage starts with 'G' too."

"And little boys."

"What? That don't start with 'G.'"

"Them birds is right dangerous. Didn't Daddy tell you that?"

Robert slid back over the wood, sat up, eyes wide. He was light-headed, and his chest ached from the release of pressure. "Nope, he didn't say nothing about that."

"Didn't want to worry you, I's guessing. Seeing as you's still a baby."

"I idn't no baby."

"But you's a brat. And you don't know nothing about birds. Can cart you right away if they gets the mind to do it."

"What do you mean 'cart me away'?"

Elise picked at the nail on her biggest toe, replied nonchalantly, "A hoard of them can come upon you, drive their claws into whatever they can get ahold of, your shirt, your skin. They idn't fussy. And they'll fly right up, and you'll be gone."

"Gone where?" Voice a little wispy now.

"How should I know?" She flicked a curl of nail into the sea. "Off to their nests, I suppose. Maybe they'll feed you to their babies. Divide up the goods. Peel you up into bits."

"Bits?"

"Someday, Mother'll find your bones. When the old nests rots, and they falls out onto the ground. Skinny bones of a five-year-old."

"I's almost six." Puffing up his chest.

"Don't matter. And you knows what? I bet she wouldn't even cry, Robert Edgecombe. Not one single tear. Now if you were Harriet she might, but she don't care about you. She'll be looking at your bones, and all she'll be thinking about is what kind of soup she can make."

Robert sniffed hard, eyeballed his sister, then tried to spit into the ocean. He never leaned far enough and the bubbly gob landed on the rolled-up cuff of his trousers. "That's lies, Elise. All dirty lies."

"I's telling the truth."

"No, you idn't."

"Honest to God." She put her arms out, stared up at the sky. "Strike me down by lightning, oh Heavenly Father, if what I utters idn't the pure truth."

Glancing up. "You swears?"

"Right on Nanny Abbott's grave."

"I's going to ask Mommy."

"That you won't then, you little brat. Else I'll make sure those birds get you. Get you good, you little bugger. I knows what they likes, and you don't."

He stared at Elise, whimper suppressed, and when he saw the fat squawking birds circling above him, he wanted to run, push his face into his mother's skirt, into Harriet's protective fur. "Is I okay now?"

"Far as I can tell," she said with a smirk.

They were silent then as they leaned back over the wharf, watched the murky green water. Within moments, a mottled brown shadow drifted over Robert's makeshift hook, and he sucked in his breath. His hands were sweaty, but he didn't dare lessen his grip on the string. When the glimmer of his hook disappeared, he yanked with all the force he could muster. Up flew a flatfish, an impressive tethered arc, then smack onto the dried bleached wood of the wharf.

White belly up, Elise flipped it over with her toe, bare foot to steady it, and she tore out the pin. Kneeling down beside it, Robert watched as its fin began to slowly ooze, and he dug for the handkerchief in his back pocket, daubed the redness away.

"They don't feel nothing," Elise said. "You're wasting your time."

"How do you know?"

She picked up the pin, a fleck of fin still attached, and she jabbed it in the fish's stomach over and over again. "See? He didn't even budge."

"Huh. I guess you're right." And he smoothed the invisible holes with his finger, tried to pretend he hadn't seen her do that.

"Queer how a flatfish just sits, don't you think," she continued. "Don't barely put up no kind of fight."

"He did a bit."

"Well, he's not going nuts like some of them. Trying to get back to the water."

"Give him time." Robert stroked its cool damp back, touched its pair of neatly arranged eyes, pressed ever so slightly. "Maybe he's a skipper."

"Fish can't be skippers, stupid."

"Well, maybe he's an old-timer. That's what I meant."

"Old or not, he's not doing nothing. What kind of fish is that?" Foot drawn back, she offered up a swift kick, and the flatfish sailed out over the water, kissed the surface, and sank out of sight. Then, Elise strode off the wharf, and Robert grabbed his hook and string, skipped to catch up with her.

"Why'd you go and do that for?"

"Cause flatfishes is lame. That's why. Squids is funner. Squirting you square in the face." She laughed, then turned, held her finger up to Robert. A warning. "Don't you go hauling up no more of them dumb flatfish. Stupidest fish in the sea."

"You thinks?" Robert still had his handkerchief in one hand. He looked at the bloody streak in the cotton, put it to his nose, smelled pungent fishy metal. "Well, at least it worked."

"What worked?"

"He got back to the water. Never had to do so much as lift his tail, and he got back to the water." Robert balled up the handkerchief, jammed it into his back pocket. "Fooled you, he did."

Elise was swift now, jaunting over the lacquered beach stones, braids bouncing. Over her shoulder, she glared at Robert, eyes like slits. "That's dumb too," she yelled. "Dumb and stupid. Gulls don't like dumb and stupid, Robert. I'll tell you that. They don't like it. Not one teeny bit."

On the day of the garden party, Leander took a moment to appraise his creation. He held a weighty bowling pin, eyed its fat belly, slender neck, curving crown. He ran his fingers over the slick coat of black paint, the thick white strip, cunning sliver of red. The sides were flawlessly smooth, base with the precise amount of instability, this individual pin a near exact replica of its four brothers. When they clanked together time and time again (Robert being the pinboy), the sound of wood against wood was joyful.

"So, Harriet. What do you think of my handiwork?" A triumphant howl was the response.

Leander reached down, patted Harriet's head as she

nudged his leg encouragingly. Though he admired his work, it was with some sense of embarrassment, a tinge of shame over how perfect it was. He had a gift with wood, he knew, recognized the bowling pins as he and Harriet strolled through the forest, when the five were still locked inside the trunks of maple trees.

Gus would arrive any moment, and the two men would cart the works to the yard by the new schoolhouse. Leander had constructed two sets, turned the pins and balls on his lathe, built lanes complete with gutters. Prizes had been donated: a silvery thimble, small china dish, paper bag of trout flies, a miniature wooden jigsaw puzzle in the shape of a fish (Leander had made this as well), and a pair of tall glasses, ideal for beer.

"I'll be damned," Gus hollered as his shadow dimmed the doorway. His thin arms went up in exclamation, then settled on his oversized gut. "Got enough wood here to build a barn."

"'Tis not all for the bowling," Leander said, nodding towards the walls. "That's other stuff."

"By the looks of things, you're fashioning enough to supply the entire island. No arse gone chairless – I bets that's your motto."

"And a noble motto it is now, Gus." Leander grinned as he glanced about his workspace. There was little room to move now, every cranny was piled with unfinished pieces, legs and spindles, pine shelves, poor quality fir crates he'd gotten from the general store to use as backing. In the fall, he would assemble everything, and with the help of Skipper Johnson, they would deliver the furniture to communities dotting the coast.

"Well, we best get a move on," Gus said with conviction. "Don't want to be late. Give them all something else to complain about."

"Oh, I doubts we'll be hearing any grumbling today. 'Tis too fine."

Gus lowered his head, looked at Leander, bloodshot eyes in a yellowed face. "Has you forgotten I married Nettie? She's been whining since conception, my son."

The garden party was organized to celebrate the completion of the first schoolhouse. Up until then, the children who attended school to learn the "three r's" did so at the parish hall, taught by Miss Eleanor Hickey (daughter of the recently deceased Reverend). Only about half the children attended their elementary lessons, and if either one showed particular promise for academics, he was sent off to live with an aunt or uncle in a larger community that had better resources. But the families had had enough, and with a dodgy promise of government funding, like darkness in their back pockets, the men set about building a two-room clapboard school. Everyone had worked on it, wood donated from the mill, generous gift of a pot-bellied stove from Fuller's store, steady supply of warm lunches to the workers, a dozen desks from Leander, more to follow when he could afford the time. George Hiscock made a cement slab for the front steps, date of completion indented in the front. A day of pride for Bended Knee.

Once the final coat of maroon paint covered the structure, there was a communal desire to make merry. In the field next to the school, someone had hacked the grass down to its earthy scalp. A row of picnic tables were carted over, covered with clothes, laden with dinner rolls, dishes of butter, pickled beets, a mishmash of plates. The air was heavy with the deliciously offensive odour of boiled cabbage, turnip, salt meat. A separate table was laden with a proud display of late summer pies, partridgeberry, apple, and blueberry.

The men talked, drank, and bowled while the women

finished preparing the meal. Even with his unsteady gait, Leander was the best bowler. Every time he knocked over all five pins, Harriet would be up on her hind legs, yip and leap into the air, back twisting as though she was trying to achieve even greater heights. After winning two games, the other men, Gus included, began to protest lightheartedly.

"I believes you done something to the set. Something that we don't know about."

"'Tis in his foot. That skip."

"That's a hop skip, if I ever seen one."

"Bill, anyone knows the rules on a hop skip?"

"I reckons that's cheating, that kind of run up."

Third game over, and Harriet howled once again, stood on her hind legs, scratched the air with her forepaws.

"Or, 'tis the dog."

"Lucky charm."

"Is lucky charms allowed, Gus?"

Leander smirked. "'Tis only the practicing, fellers. A few rounds with my boy here." He pulled Robert to him, scuffled his sun-bleached hair.

"Well, enough is enough. Go wet your whistle while the rest of us has a go."

Leander stepped out of the play, accepted a single prize: a pair of cups and saucers, a string of pinkish flowers just below the lip. A gift for Stella. Where was she? He scanned the field, and saw her. She was with the women and older girls, bustling about, aprons snug around waists. They had begun to serve up heaping plates to the men, small bites to the children, stealing pinches for themselves. He noticed her face was flushed, hair slightly unkempt, and every now and again, she paused to slap at blackflies that nipped at her neck. He smiled to himself. She looked most beautiful when she was flustered, overheated.

Elise and Robert were yanking at his shirt, nudging him. In the far corner of the field, the younger members of First Ladies League were churning ice cream. Old Man Morris had offered up the last chunks of ice hidden under sawdust in his barn, and cream was collected from the many cow owners. A donation of sugar from Fuller's General Store, and ice cream was the result.

Leander dug into the pocket of his trousers, retrieved a nickel. "Here you go, you little beggars," he said with a smile. "Two each."

"What about the last penny?" Robert said. "I wants to keep it."

"I's the oldest," Elise squealed. "I gets it."

"Lardie," Leander said with a smirk. "You two sure don't need no schoolhouse. You got your rithmetic all figured out."

"Well?" they chorused.

"Weeeelllll, last one is for Harriet. A scoop for my youngest."

Elise cut her arms across her chest. "I'm not feeding no dog. Folks would laugh at me."

"And so what if they does?"

"I'll do it," Robert announced.

"Then you shall be in charge of the nickel."

Elise scowled. "You better not drop it in the grass, Robert. And lose it." They began to run towards the ice cream table, Elise taking the lead. Leander laughed at her annoyance when she yelled back at Robert, "And you needn't think I'll stand next to you. Not with you feeding that dog."

He went to find Stella, stood behind her as she took a break from serving. Wrapping his arms around his wife, he glanced out over the field, saw men bowling with perfect pins, children chasing each other, treats locked in sticky fists, neighbours eating food from their own fields, the smooth ocean in the distance, like God's looking glass. Leander put his mouth to her tiny ear, surprised by how his voice choked slightly. "Look around, maid. Can't you feel it? There's some magic here."

"Shush now," she replied. "Don't go jinxing it."

"I can't help myself. Our little part of the world. So far away from everything. But 'tis all here, my love. Every single thing we needs is right here."

Nearly forty years had passed since Uncle had crossed over. When he died, his devoted widow, Berta May, thought she wouldn't be long for this world. Wasn't that the way it often worked? One half of an eternally bound couple moved on, and within a ripple of time, dragged the other half with it? But that hadn't happened. Berta was still fully alive, and every morning when she awoke, glanced about the same wallpapered room, she placed a wrinkled hand on her chest and felt a jab of disappointment with the rhythmic thump beneath. Why hadn't she been called?

Though she would never admit this, her sourness was partly related to the well-respected midwife who once lived just north of her. Berta had heard all about Miss Cooke and her tangled history with Uncle. Though no one had mentioned it in decades, Berta had never forgotten it. In his youth, Uncle had been bound to another. He had sworn his undying love for Miss Cooke. How shocked everyone was when he took up with a fifteen-year-old (that being Berta) without as much as a goodbye to Miss Cooke. Then he married her no less (that still being Berta). Miss Cooke had been side-swiped, they said, and her heart never recovered. "Sure, they was like a pair of yoked oxen. Trussed up since they was running around with their arses hanging out."

Berta was already married when she learned this rather crucial tidbit of information. At the time, she'd pretended to brush it off, but to tell the truth, the knowledge that she was a haphazard selection, a second choice, had sliced the magic from her union like a sickle through spring grass. To make matters worse, Miss Cooke had given up the ghost only weeks after Uncle had moved on. At her funeral, the older folks were nodding towards Uncle's marker, the upturned dirt, healthy mound. Murmurs that Berta couldn't quite make out. All a slap in the face, the suggestion that the two close deaths were anything other than coincidence. Wasn't she the woman who had tended to that cantankerous goat for close to fifty years? Maybe a few more. She'd given up the count. "It weren't easy, believe you me," she whispered. "He weren't easy to live with." But no one was listening to her. And now, in his final statement, as he pulled his once-promised towards him, Berta May was left to suffer Uncle's last squirt of spite from beyond the grave.

Since Berta had turned the big one hundred, she rarely left her home anymore. While several ladies from the church had made her a fruitcake and brought her a lovely packet of fragrant white soap to mark that particular birthday, she feared they were secretly mocking her. So old now, dried up, and clearly unwanted. By the holy feller upstairs or anyone else. And she hustled them along. Never offered them a slice of the cake. Birthdays to follow were promptly ignored.

Many afternoons she sat in the chair near her bed, a worn afghan unfolded over her legs. She wasn't tired, and had no need for rest; she had simply run out of things to do with the ample hours in her day. As she sat there, she focused on the changing seasons in the garden beyond. She had told herself she would be gone by the time the goldenballs bloomed, then when they nodded in the salty air, she adjusted her expectations, and determined death would arrive before the oak tree turned fiery in the autumn. No such luck. Perhaps before the boats were hauled up on the shore, flipped, peeling bottoms exposed to icy November showers. *No. I'm here.* Before the final leaf was sucked away by the wind? She waited and waited, watching that withered leaf, teasing her. A bitter snowstorm, blocked her view, and when the sheet of white settled down over the yard, her death leaf was gone. And still, she wasn't.

Berta was now the oldest person in Bended Knee, and she needed no help to walk or cook or traipse out to the outhouse on a fine, clear day. In fact, since Uncle's passing, many of the discomforts she had complained about so frequently had left her. Her hips, gassy belly, ingrown toenails, watery hearing. She was confused, but this was not due to any trace of senility. She simply couldn't comprehend why she was lingering. Had she done something wrong? Did she need to make amends?

Whenever she considered the need for amends, her thoughts always circled around to that tiny baby who was born in her house. And lately, they circled often, as Berta, throttled with free time, continually replayed the birth, the aftermath. With knowledge that only a hundred plus years could offer, Berta now understood that she had stolen something from that baby. And the mother as well. A moment. That's all it was. A single moment. But at the time, it had meant so much to Berta, and she found the moment irresistible. Wanted so badly for it to belong to her. Now, she was certain that single act of thievery held her in a state of suspension, not moving forward, unable to move back.

Some days, while Eldred tapped out a harmony on the piano, Berta would go into that cramped bedroom and perch herself on the edge of the bed. Though the bed had not been used in decades, it was still neatly made, and Berta knew if she tore back the sheets, she could identify evidence of the birth. Sometimes she did this, just to make sure it really happened. And she viewed the faded earthy stains, a large mark in the centre, several smaller blots creeping down over the side of the mattress. That was how Miriam Seary, no more than a girl herself, had pushed the baby out, right at the very edge of the bed. One foot on the floor, another foot pressed squarely against Berta's hip.

No other child had ever entered the world in Berta's home. Stella Abbott, now Stella Edgecombe, was the first and only. While Berta and Uncle had had many children reside there over the years, helping out on the farm, minding the animals, the fleeting presence of this baby was different. When Berta had touched her for the first time, the baby was still streaked with blood, and dull white cream still resided in the crevices around her neck, under her arms. Once the cord had been severed, it was Berta who plucked up the child, swaddled her. Miss Cooke was occupied, massaging Miriam's fleshy near-empty abdomen in order to help finish the job, and Miriam was lying back, hands up and shaking in the air, crying. Without a word to either of them, Berta stood, cradled the baby, and crept away.

In the privacy of her own room, she sat on the bed and stared at the newborn. She marveled at the perfection of the pug nose, the ears like the tiniest clam shell, fringe of feathery hair. She felt certain that God was right there in the room, existing in the baby's expression of pure, blessed serenity. Berta reached out, nervously, touched a dry finger to one pink cheek. As soon as the finger grazed the skin, the baby's lips opened into an eager O, head knocking side to side, searching. Berta felt a sudden rush of elation within her chest. Before her mind could register, her hands were unbuttoning the front of her dress, exposing the purposeless contents. Released, her fat old breasts hung down, divided, as though they were at odds with one another, independent, unwilling and showing it. But Berta ignored their defiance, lifted and positioned, guided the baby's mouth onto a wizened nipple. Why should she be denied this one simple experience of womanhood? When she felt the certain pinch of suction, Berta leaned back against the headboard, closed her eyes, and pretended this was her holy child, a miracle, still warm from her own insides.

A flat knock on the door, and Berta jumped, unlatched the baby, hauled the flap of her dress over her chest. She pressed the baby against the buttons to disguise her nakedness. The knob slowly turned, door creaked open a foot or so, and there stood Miss Cooke, halfway in, halfway out. Berta could barely look at her, pin thin, righteous rigidity in her spine, all-knowing expression.

"You did a fine job, Miss Cooke," Berta said. She wanted to push her damp hair away from her face with her forearm, but didn't dare move her hands. "Don't know what we would've done without you."

Miss Cooke stared at Berta's chest, and Berta wondered if she was looking at the baby, or looking right through the baby at what was hidden just beneath. A shameful sign of Berta's foolishness. Evidence that a few nuts were missing their bolts. Surely, proof that Uncle had made a poor choice in wife. Berta held the child tighter, forced herself not to glance downwards.

"You should bring her to her mother."

"What?"

"Bring her to her mother."

"To Miriam? That I won't then."

Miss Cooke folded her arms, like two pieces of kindling, across her front. "'Tis only right that the woman should see her baby. Have some time to herself to say goodbye."

Berta turned her back to Miss Cooke, stared out the window. She spoke slowly, calmly. "I knows you means well, Miss Cooke, but I've been living with Miriam Seary for some time now. She got no idea about a baby. No idea at all. I doubts she even knowed what come out of her. She's as simple now as boiled cabbage."

"Be that as it may, she still got her rights."

A moment of silence followed, and Berta hoped that Miss Cooke had taken her leave. But no, her voice slit the air again.

"Look, 'tis your house and all, but I got to say my piece. Speak my mind. I've birthed all kinds of babies to all kinds of mothers in all kinds of conditions. Those mothers deserves their moment. 'Tis an honest shame for a woman not to look upon the face of her own child. If only for a minute."

Berta held her breath, then sighed as she heard clicking of shoes on the wooden floor, fading, fading. With her foot, she nudged the bedroom door, then laid the baby on her bed, straightened her clothes. In those minutes, Berta's exhilaration had leached away completely, replaced by an ever-handy sourness. She would forget this imprudence, never bring it to mind again. She would focus instead on getting the baby ready, handing it over once and for all to Uncle.

With warm water from the kitchen, soft scrap of fabric, Berta washed the baby, dressed her in a nightgown she had made, and tucked a miniature pair of leather slippers inside the swaddling blanket. Through the thin wall, she could hear Miriam crying, sound like a seal pup, alone, trapped on a shard of drifting ice. Berta convinced herself she was being kind to Miriam by taking the baby immediately, and that Miriam was only weeping due to discomfort. A woman like that won't miss what she never really had. The fact that the child had lived within her for months, had slid out in a rush of burning waves, Berta pushed those thoughts away.

When Berta awoke a few days later, she discovered that Miriam was gone. She knew Miriam must have enlisted the help of Jimmy Purchase, and he would have taken her around to Squinty Harbour in his trap skiff. In the weeks to follow, Berta never asked him, and he never offered any information. If Berta considered it, Miriam's disappearance was a relief. One less reminder. One less individual sulking around their house with uncertain intentions. The end of that story. Tattered book closed.

But Berta had been wrong about that tattered book. The story hadn't ended, and now that she was old beyond imagination, her actions tormented her. She had forced herself between mother and child, and Berta knew she had no place there. She remembered the late Reverend Hickey's sermon, that following Sunday. The words bore down upon her when he discussed spiritual connections within a family. Their strength, eternal. That divine mother love. She wondered if Reverend Hickey knew what she had done – instead of Miriam-Baby, it became Miriam-Berta-Baby. She was right in the middle of it. What would the world be like if someone had done the same to Mary and Jesus? Surely it was a sin beyond sins. And God was punishing her for it, keeping her tethered to an empty earth.

Sometimes Berta dreamed of telling Stella what she had done. Walking up to her, holding her pale sweet face, and telling her, Once, for a very short selfish while, *you were mine*. But that would only serve to destroy the foundations that Stella believed were real. She happened to look somewhat similar to Delia and Percy Abbott, so there was never a need to question. And besides, only a handful of people knew Miriam was in the family way, and this was never a subject for idle nattering. Weather, fine catch or bad, so and so's husband's sore back, yes. But an unwed mother, simpleton father, necessary arrangements, never.

And beyond that, the appropriate moment never seemed to present itself. In recent weeks, when Berta saw Stella and Leander walking on the lane, she noticed that they stopped often as he bent slightly at the waist, hacking. Stella would rub his back, and he'd straighten, take some deep breaths. Then they would move on, that mangy wild dog clipping along behind them.

Berta took it as a sign to leave well enough alone. That worked for her, as she was afraid of Leander's cough, afraid that the illness might transfer into her papery lungs. And the dog, that was another matter. If it bit her, sharp teeth in her withered flesh, surely she would bleed away to nothing.

Best to steer clear. While one part of her was waiting for the release death might offer, another mortal part of her wanted nothing more than to evade it. She was familiar with the loneliness she felt on her weed-riddled farm, like a damp and constant hitch in her heart. But she had no idea what awaited her. She didn't dare consider how sharp the loneliness would be when she crossed unaccompanied into the great hereafter.

"She's angry at me."

"No, she idn't. Don't be so foolish."

"Then where's she gone off to? Just like that."

Stella patted Leander's hand. They were seated side-by-side on the daybed. "She's scared. Don't want to see you with that awful bark. Harriet'll be back...when she's hungry."

He lowered his head. "You might be right."

"Feeling any better?"

"About the same. Don't want to go on about it though. Like it'll make a difference."

"Like they does with Gus?"

"That's right." His voice was sound and his words emerged with a weary slowness. "Talking about him turning yellow. Comparing colours to him. Pease pudding. Dandelions just after they bursts from their puckered casings. Yes, that's what someone said. Just terrible. What they all heard. Who was like it. Who got better. Who moved on. Well, it idn't going to make a lick of difference. All that yammering won't heal him."

"That's how people copes, I suppose. Thinking the more they goes on about it, the more they understands it, the less likely it'll do any harm."

"Well, his liver don't heed them. It's still rotting away inside him. Soused in liquor every day."

"Heaven help him."

"Yes, God help him. Nettie Rose'll be right lost."

"Lost." Stella shook her head, put the back of her hand to her mouth. She took a deep breath, said, "Want a cup of tea? Something to eat?"

"No, maid. Not now."

"What can I get for you? I needs to feel useful."

He coughed into his handkerchief, folded it in half, then rubbed his hands over his gaunt face. "Sitting with me is nice. I likes that."

"Is there nothing else?"

Coughing again, folding the cloth into quarters. "How about you tells me something I don't know. Something I could never imagine."

Stella never turned her head, though she knew he was looking at her. She shook her head again, tears welling. "You'll think I'm foolish."

"Over what?"

"What I tells you."

"Go on, maid. I'm asking to hear, idn't I?"

"Something I loves about you," she replied. "One thing."

"Only one thing? Is that all there is?" Bony joking shoulders rising up, dropping.

"No, you goose." She slapped his leg gently. "Do you want to hear or not?"

"Of course."

Stella looked down at her fingers, touched the dry skin cracked on her knuckles. "'Tis the sound of your walk."

"My walk?"

"Yes."

He chuckled, and when this morphed into a sputter, he held a fresh handkerchief to his mouth until the coughing subsided, crumpled it without peering inside. "You means my hobble. One foot always falling after the other. Clip clop. 'Tis pitiful."

"No it idn't. Nowhere near it. That sound walked me home when Father fell over the cliff. Do you remember that?"

"I remembers. No way I was ever leaving you."

"I felt so safe with that sound behind me. And now, whenever I hears you walking up the path to the back door, I stops what I'm doing and closes my eyes to listen."

"You does?"

"Yes. And you know what?"

"What?"

Turning to face him now, she ignored the streak of frothy red spittle on his chin. She gripped his hand, squeezed as hard as she could, then spoke with conviction that coated her fear. "Your walk that I loves. It sounds just like a heartbeat, you know. It sounds just like life."

chapter eleven

Stella was on her knees, once again scrubbing the plank floor with a sudsy brush. Back and forth, back and forth, long reaches that sent pain up through her hips, brought burning to her shoulders. But as hard as she worked, the stains would not release from the wood. "There are no stains," Elise had said to her so many times. Robert nodding, "No, Mom. There idn't." But Stella sensed something was there, something that begged to be cleaned. "Can't you see?"

As she scrubbed this evening in the shadowy light of a candle, she noticed the bite between her teeth and forced herself to relax her jaw. She remembered Elise asking her recently, "Why do your face always look like that?"

"Like what?"

"Flat. Like nothing. You don't never laugh no more. You don't get angry. I idn't never seen you sad since God only knows when."

Stella shook her head. "I don't got no answer for you, my dear. I don't know."

"Well, I hates it," Elise said. "Hates that dumb look."

Robert had been there, listening. He crunched his dog-eared Wonder Woman comic book in his fist, growled,

"Don't you go calling her dumb, Elise, or Mother won't have to knock you into next week. I'll do it for her."

"I never said she was dumb." She ruffled his hair. "Just her look."

He leaned sideways, away from her touch. "Well, watch your lip."

Whenever Robert spoke, Stella stopped and listened. He had developed broad shoulders, a solid chest made of heart and rib and muscle. Housed somewhere within this new body was a man's voice. It was so similar to Leander's that Stella often shuddered, and upon hearing it, she added this characteristic to her private list of "items I'll never get used to."

In the quiet of the early autumn evening, she sat back on her calves, laid down the brush, and touched her face. She was not one for gazing at her reflection, but at this moment, she wondered how she might appear to another. She felt the individual pieces of her face, united, eyebrows to forehead, nose to upper lip, cheek to ear. A flawless series of solid mortise and tendon joints. Secure and necessary. Did she look dumb? Well, if she did, there was no other option. She knew her expressionless face was a gateway, and she worked diligently to ensure the gate was latched. Wide open, and she feared wildness would emerge, sanity might come crashing through, pell-mell, taking gate and entire fence with it.

Just this afternoon, her fused face had been put to the test. Standing on the cliffs that lined the harbour, she had watched the MV *Christmas Seal* creep in. The retrofitted navy ship moved so slowly, Stella thought it looked like a dying whale being propelled towards shore. Impressive, no doubt, with all its promise, those hospital tools, that tinny music. But what good was it now? To her?

She could see the hoards of children and adults pressed together on the wharves, waving at the good ship, bidding it to glide closer, allow passage. When it docked, they formed a tight line, hopped aboard eagerly, stepped up for x-rays and a quick listen to heart and lungs, cursory nod from the doctor. No sign of tuberculosis. Dreaded TB. Excitement over the proclamation of good health, as though the staff of the *Easter Seal* had bestowed it instead of simply acknowledging it.

From that cliff far away from the crowd, she watched this scene, face flat. In her mouth, she detected the taste of overgrown greens, and she resisted the urge to spit. Was she so filled with bitterness that the emotion had oozed from her soul, invaded her taste buds? It seemed so, but she was justified. Where was this ship when Leander started pushing his food around his plate? When his fever spoke the loudest, frightened away his energy? Where was it when his relentless cough held his breath in a ruthless fist? But when Stella tried to force blame, she always came around to herself. *Where was this ship* was a shameful cover-up. Instead, the more telling query might be: *Where was she?*

Even though nine years had passed, Stella could not let this question fade. She had set the cot on the back stoop, helped Leander to lie down, rest while icy air drifted off the ocean. Healing air, she had thought. She didn't know what else to do. Dr. Wells said it would be good for Leander, good for his lungs. All that dust from the wood, sawdust clinging to the inside of his chest, had weakened them, made him more susceptible, the doctor had determined. "But he's still young, Mrs. Edgecombe. Good and strong. Yes, ma'am. There's plenty reason to hope."

But Stella could only hope when she didn't see Leander, couldn't hear that raspy death knock when he coughed. So, once he was settled in the cot, she left him there, went to

Nettie's for tea, raisin buns, and diversion. She remembered clearly the topic of conversation: Nettie's mother-in-law. On her last visit, the mother-in-law had scolded Nettie on the unkempt house, the grimy chins on the children. Stella giggled along as Nettie described the too-high pie incident. The mother-in-law had refused a slice of Nettie's freshly made rhubarb and wild-strawberry pie. In a voice like a pinprick, Nettie relayed her mother-in-law's words: "There idn't a fit surface to roll a crust, my dear. Far as I sees. This place is such a sty, heaven knows what I'd find tucked inside that pastry." More serious pinprick now. "'Tis an awful high pie, Nettie Rose. Awful high. Have you counted the children lately?" And Stella took on the voice of Nettie, replying: "Now, then, Mother Smith, I was wondering where young Milton was gone off to."

Conversation halted when clouds rolled in out of nowhere and the afternoon light was pinched black and blue. Tea still steaming, she left Nettie's, ran down the hill towards home, shoes slapping the mucky road. Icy water blankets falling from heaven, one layer after the other, and she found him, still in the cot, drenched, head cricked back, white mouth open. She threw herself across his frame, cried out into the storm, could not excise the loathing that rolled and tumbled inside her. Loathing reserved for herself. She had left him. In his darkest hour. Left him. And all except for faithful Harriet, slobbering his ghostly face, he had gone on alone.

So, yes, there was bitterness in her mouth when she watched that ship appear on the horizon. Bitterness was superior to sorrow. Sorrow impeded function, and she still had to take care of her children and her home and herself. But there was also abhorrence for her weakness. For her ability to snicker and mock with Nettie while someone she loved drifted away. She kept these thoughts close. Balled up inside her heart. Tight as a supper bun, her father might have once said. Others had suffered worse. She had to move on. There was nothing unique about her story.

Stella clasped the wet brush again, pressed down, continued invading the floor with bent bristles. Back and forth, back and forth. She shimmied sideways, dampened a fresh area. A smell of sweet forests wafted up to her nose, and in some way, it reminded her of fresh tobacco. Summer afternoons. Happy men sitting on the painted front steps, a leg bent perhaps, elbow resting calmly on a knee. Inside the house, she might have been mixing oats for a fruit cobbler or stirring flour and water into a rich seal gravy. She imagined Nettie, her best friend, in a floral dress beside her. And as they chirped away about nothing in particular, that smell of smoke would drift in through an open window, easy laughter not far behind it.

Those moments seemed a lifetime ago, and Stella wondered how she had let them all slip by, rarely slowing down long enough to appreciate them. She crinkled her body, and for a self-indulgent moment, laid her head against the floor. To spend a moment there, living inside the memory.

Eyes closed, and she heard thumping. Her own heart? No. The thumping turned into a stomping. Angry shoes rebuking the stony path. Someone charging towards her home. Annoyed by the tricky handle on the door. A dozen livid clicks. Whoosh.

Before Stella could budge, Elise burst through the porch, flounced into the kitchen.

"What in God's name is you doing?"

Stella bolted upright, gripped the brush. *Remembering,* was the first word that came to mind. But that would lead to explanation. "I's cleaning the floor, Elise. 'Tis long overdue." From the corner of her eye, she could see her daughter, tall with soft curves, hair falling forward like a rushing river in spring.

"Thought you was sleeping."

"Sleeping in the kitchen? What a thing to say."

"I wouldn't put it past you." Elise scraped out a chair, plunked herself down, knees jumping. "'Tis dark enough in here."

Without looking up, Stella made a few more swipes with her brush, dropped it into the bucket, then sopped up the splash with a rag.

"Why don't you ever listen to me?" Elise said, fury in her voice. "Why is that too much to ask?"

"What?"

"You knows what I's talking about. Every time I tries to talk to you, you just keeps on going, doing whatever it is you're doing."

Stella leaned back on her calves, stared at Elise. She started to say, "I'm listening," but instead, "Good God" popped from her lips. Her daughter's face was streaked with soot, triangles of clean skin where tears had flowed. Half of the sailor collar on her navy blouse was turned inside, dirty skirt wrinkled around her legs, her right knee, jutting out from underneath too short a hemline, was raw and bloody. Shoulders curled forward, and the certainty that always sat there was missing. "What happened to you, my child?"

"I got hurt."

"How? Did you fall down? Did you slip?"

Elise looked down. "Part that."

"Did you get burnt? At the fire?"

"Wasn't me."

"Someone got burnt?"

"Lewis did."

"Lewis Hickey?"

"Yes, he. And I was there. With him."

"What? What do you mean you was there? Weren't everyone there?"

"That's not what I means." She pulled the candle towards her, flicked her fingers slowly through the flame.

"What then, Elise? I don't understand you."

Elise peeled off a partially broken fingernail, lay it neatly beside the candle holder. "I needs a drop of tea, Mother. Can you do that for me?"

"Of course I can."

Stella stood, legs tingling, and she went to the stove, placed her hand on the curve of the kettle. Still warm, and she poured water into a teapot that was shaped like a small dog. Tea arriving through the outstretched paw, and when the cup was full, Stella sweetened it with a thin stream of molasses – white sugar still in short supply.

"Can you tell me what happened? Is young Lewis hurt bad?"

"He'll survive." Sardonic laugh, and Elise stirred her tea, round and round. "And he idn't that young no more."

"Well?"

"Well what?" Elise crossed her arms over her chest, hands gripping her shoulders.

"Tell me."

Shifting in her seat, eyes darting, she finally said, "A potato burst open, Mother."

"Potato?"

"Yes, that's what happened. A big fat stupid potato." As she spoke, composure receded, breaths hitched in her throat. "Burst out of the fire." Spitting words now. "Burst right out of the fire and ruined all my bloody plans." She began to shake, mouth drawn back in a scarecrow smile. High-pitched squeals, tight and shrill, as though air were escaping from a pinhole in her heart. When the tears were replaced by cumbersome hiccups, Elise confessed everything. Well, she tried, at least. Most fragments refused to be aired, dug their claws into the soggy caverns of her chest.

Earlier that night, in a corner where four farms met, a large mound of dried potato stalks burned. Handfuls of boys darted around the fire, prodding the mound with charred sticks, squealing, their faces stained with soot. Occasionally a blackened potato that had been tossed in earlier was re-discovered, knocked clear from the ashes. When it cooled just enough to handle, a boy would press it until the top split and steaming white flesh emerged. A moment later, he would ram it into his drooling mouth.

Elise and two girls, Bee and Marg, stood a few feet away, arms locked together at the elbows. They were too old now to race about, and instead, watched the older boys tend to the bonfire, layering on additional stalks, jabbing and lifting with larger sticks, tucking in fresh potatoes, rolling out cooked ones. One threw a brilliant red bough on the fire, and it crackled and raged when fire consumed it. As they watched the bough disintegrate, the girls pushed closer together, giggled as billowing smoke burned their eyes, clung to the large curls they'd worked so hard to create.

Elise, Bee, and Marg each wore near-matching woolen cardigans, blouses with peter pan collars, and skirts, heavy fabric cut on the bias. October breezes blew through their clothes, around their open necks, up their bare legs. Marg disentangled her arms from the other girls', tugged her skirt to the front, jammed the material between her legs and pinched it there. Through chattering teeth, she announced, "Mother said I'd catch my death if I goes out like this. Without no stockings."

Elise snorted. "Mine said the same thing. See if I cares."

"Don't do that, maid," Bee whispered, slapping Marg's thigh. "I sees James looking at you right this instant."

Grip on the fabric released, skirt freed and shifting in the easy wind, Marg raised a small hand, waved in such a way it appeared she was scratching the air. Like a kitten at a closed door, Elise imagined. A kitten, desperate to be let in. Desperate to be wanted. Elise smiled and nudged Marg's hip.

As the evening progressed, the banter continued. The three girls smoothed their hair and skirts, huddled and whispered, clutched their stomachs when laughter occasionally crippled them. Charred potatoes were offered by circling boys, and they accepted politely, nibbled gingerly. Anyone looking at the gaggle would think they were the best of friends. Matching both in outfits and demeanours. Yes, the best of friends. And from the perspective of Bee and Marg, that opinion would be wholly accurate. Though Elise, who kept several devilish deeds secret, knew otherwise.

Their paths had silently diverged three years ago. Each girl had turned fifteen, and tucked away inside the oven of Bee's attic, under a canopy of dried fish nailed to the rafters, Marg decided they should solemnly declare the names of the boys they loved. The ones they wanted to kiss. The boys they dreamed they might one day marry. "That way," Marg reasoned, "no feller will ever come between us. There'll be no confusion of who belongs to who. No cross-over affections, we'll say." Without hesitation, Bee proclaimed her eternal adoration for Chester Simms. After some high-pitched squeals and hand clasping, Marg calmed, ran her hands over her cheeks, and whispered, "James Gosse. He's so delicious," she cried, "I could eat the face right off him." More shrieks and mini-hugs, and then they turned their shiny faces to Elise. "Tell us," they hissed, "who you wants to marry, maid." And Elise stared for a moment, then smiled coyly, mouthed the first name that came to her mind. "George Winsor." All three howled and wailed then, fell back on the floorboards, kicking each other with stocking feet, bits of salt dropping onto them from the fish, until three thumps from the tip of a broomstick striking the ceiling below silenced them. "Beeeeeee!" Livid mother's tongue, sparks from a fire. "Get yourself down here this instant 'fore you comes through the floor."

Elise scampered home to finish her chores. She wrung out the wash waiting in a bucket on the stoop, squeezing and twisting until her rough palms ached. With split wooden pins, she nipped the laundry onto the lines, then once completed, she walked amongst the shivering shirts and sheets, let the damp fresh fabric cling to her bare arms, her cheeks. Cooling her. What exactly had happened this afternoon, she wasn't certain, but something had shifted. She recognized how different she was from Bee and Marg, and she hoped they hadn't noticed her lack of enthusiasm, her hesitation. For the truth was, she had not yet fallen in love. Not even close. Never imagined kissing a boy. Had never conjured the notion of being married. And when she pictured Marg and Bee, their souls pulsing with excitement, their passion flushing their cheeks, making their voices quaver in their very throats, Elise felt sore. Raw like a rope burn all up and down her insides. It wasn't her George Winsor lie that caused it. She understood. It was plain and simple jealousy.

Perhaps it was this bud of envy that made Elise stare at James Gosse during church service. Not that she found him particularly appealing, but when he turned in his pew and caught her eye, she never looked away. This went on for nearly a year, this brazen gawking through sermons and hymns, stolen glances during prayers. She took note of his disheveled hair and determined which side he'd slept on the night before. She eyed the collar of his shirt, envisioned his mother ironing his clothes. She watched him nudge his little sister when the Reverend sneezed or snorted during a sermon.

Whenever Marg would bend Elise's ear (which she did incessantly) about how fine a man James would be, Elise had no trouble to summon his image. So clearly, the jut of his chin, flatness of his freckled nose. His eyes reminded her of looking up through water. Down by the pond. When she lay on the slimy gravel bottom, facing upwards, and opened her eyes. Which she often did, alone, during summer afternoons.

"How can you do that?" James was standing by the edge of the water, waiting until she broke the surface.

"Do what?" she replied, catching her breath.

"Sink like that. Like you's made of stone."

Made of stone. She smirked, though she didn't mean it. *Made of stone.* "Maybe I is." And she knew when she said this, she would wonder about that appraisal long after her encounter with James was over.

She was almost sixteen when she let James reach up under her skirt, touch her backside, the very edges of her underwear. She was leaning against a birch tree, he pressed against her, gaping mouth wet on her neck, and for those few moments while his hands roamed, she peeled thin strips of bark from the trunk, scarring it, rendering a portion of the old tree naked.

After that, she rarely ever looked at James. Instead, her focus shifted to oafish Chester Simms with his pinched clothes, crowded teeth and unevenly trimmed black hair. These were traits that Bee adored, claimed he looked like a lost little boy, so innocent and sweet. Not so, Elise discovered. On a blustery afternoon behind the schoolhouse, Chester was stacking wood for the stove. Elise leaned against the pile, and he smirked at her, squinted his eyes in the reflected sunlight. "Well now," he said with a loud guffaw. "Don't want to be mistaking you for a junk."

Elise couldn't recall what she'd said or why he'd kissed her. She couldn't remember exactly how he'd unbuttoned her red wool coat, her sweater, then slipped his mittened hands inside and clutched her chest, several painful squeezes. When she sat to the table for an early supper that night, her mother simply frowned at her. Looking down, Elise saw that the front of her good blouse was marred with daubs of sticky turpentine, flecks of sawdust, strands of wool from her own sweater. "Carting wood," Elise managed. "For Miss Kilbride."

Her mother never blinked, responded, "That's an awful queer thing to look so sheepish over. So guilty in your eyes."

Elise thought about this as she watched James heap an armload of potato stalks on the fire. The dead plants writhed and curled, and in an instant, were swallowed by the flames. Her mother had been right, she did feel guilty. But, she also felt something else. When she stood alongside Marg and Bee, Elise felt absolute relief that the jealousy, like a troublesome ball of burrs, was now gone. Not that she wished unhappiness on her friends, Elise just wanted to have those secrets. Just wanted to know that Marg and Bee's rippling glee was an illusion, created in folly by a teenaged human heart. When her own heart had felt like a dried jellyfish, withered on the rocks, Elise had taken some solace in the knowledge that the objects of their love were flawed.

Perhaps because of her own actions, Elise no longer trusted Marg and Bee. She never admitted her indifference to George Winsor, accepted their condolences when he began courting Elise's cousin, Annie Smith. Even opened her arms to their hugs, shed a tear or two. Then, when her mind became preoccupied with Lewis Hickey, she never told a soul. She reasoned it was only like a fly bite, after all, and it would soon disappear. But her preoccupation developed from fly bite to full blown rash, and took over her mind. During the long summer days, she could think of nothing and no one else. And she was very careful, guarded that knowledge fervently.

Lewis was the grandson of the late Reverend Hickey. Everyone said he would be a minister himself, if given a little time to grow up. Elise believed this. There was a natural holiness about him. When she covertly watched him move about the fire, handing cooled cooked potatoes to the children, patting their heads, she thought he looked as though he were already practicing for the position on the church steps. Yes, there was definitely something godlike about Lewis, his soft curls, like a mound of wood shavings, eyes of a placid deer. She also noticed he had extraordinarily large hands, and she thought this was a heavenly feature as well. Bigger hands for holding, healing, helping. Godly hands. That seemed like Lewis. Though she barely knew him, she was certain he was someone who would have influence. Make her a better girl. Turn her into someone her mother might manage to love.

Lewis was within a few feet of her now, tossing raw potatoes into the ashes, covering them. He leaned in, nudged some stalks with his stick, and there was a sudden pop, then a yowl, and Lewis dropped to his knees, clawing his face. Several girls rushed, but Elise reached him first. He yanked at her skirt, drawing her closer, used the fabric to wipe away the clumps of steaming potato that clung to his cheeks, forehead and left eyelid.

Everyone stared as Elise put her arm around his waist, helped him to his feet. “Let’s get you home,” she said with an authority that surprised her. “Get that all fixed up.”

But as they left the bonfire, he never led her in the right direction. Holding her hand firmly in his, he walked towards a boarded up farmhouse a good distance from the fire. In the shadows, they picked their way across the abandoned property towards the well, and while Lewis propped himself against the stone surrounding, Elise lifted the wooden cover, lowered the bucket. Good shake of the rope, bucket sinking, and she drew up cool water. He splashed his face several times, then ran his damp hands over his hair.

“How do I look?” he asked, cocking his head, smirking. “Is I burnt beyond?”

Elise heard a giggle burst from her lips, even though she hadn’t given it permission to escape. “Not too bad,” she replied, gazing down at her hands. The brazenness she had felt with James and Chester no longer existed, and when she stole glances at Lewis, shyness altered her heartbeat, making her dizzy. “Does it hurt?”

“Nah. ’Twas only a small one. Good thing I weren’t that close.” He stood up, walked towards the house. Touching the weathered boards, he jammed his nails under cracks in the paint, and Elise watched as it flaked away, dropping, disappearing into darkness.

“Good thing,” she breathed.

He turned towards her. “You knows who lived here?”

“Uh-huh.” Elise stood beside him, but not too close. “Mrs. May and that feller.”

"Lard, she was an old one. Face on her like a cabbage left in the field all winter."

Elise giggled again. "I wonders why she lived so long."

"Grandmother told me once 'twas cause she had a cold heart. But don't tell no one I said that."

"I won't," Elise promised. She took his request seriously, sealed his words inside. "People'll think 'tis poor taste to speak ill of the dead."

As though testing the stability of the house, Lewis banged the walls with his fists. The sound echoed through the hollow home, and Elise thought she also heard desire mixed amongst the reverberation. A desire to be lived in. To be useful. She sighed.

"Do you think they was boyfriend and girlfriend?"

"Who?" Elise asked.

"Widow May and that queer old feller that was living there."

"Oh. Eldred Wood."

"That's he. Wood."

"I doubts it. I think he just stayed with her. Helped her out a bit. I believes he was a bit soft in the head."

Lewis plunked himself down on the cold ground between two dogberry bushes, dried leaves still clinging to the reddened twigs. Elise did the same, sitting a few feet away, legs bent, skirt tucked underneath her knees.

"Did you know," Lewis said, looking up at the sky, "that when my mother was young, folks used to come out here, listen to that feller play his piano? This was quite the spot for courting."

"A bit of entertainment, I suppose."

"He played and played, I heard, to get over a girl. She stole his heart right out of his chest, then took off with it."

Elise resisted the urge to bite away a hangnail she could

feel on her thumb. "I always had dreams about him."

"About who?"

"That feller. Eldred Wood."

Lewis puffed up his chest, grinned. "Now, is you trying to make me green-eyed, maid?"

"No, no," she said, shaking her head, hands clasped around her knees. "Terrible dreams, I means. I always hated the way he stared at me. Like he knowed me." She paused. "Like he owned some part of me."

Sliding closer, he wrapped an arm around her shoulder. "Well, he don't own no part of you, maid. That's for darn sure. You don't got to have no more of those old thoughts."

"I never told no one about that before, Lewis." She turned her face towards him, then crinkled her brow. "Do you want more water? Your eyes is a bit weepy."

He smiled. "That's cause I's right heartbroken."

Jolt of anger stabbed her stomach. "Over what? Over who?"

A quiet, "You, maid."

Heat in her cheeks that would ease a wrinkled shirt. "Me?"

"I seen you looking at me."

She was silent.

"But you don't never talk to me. And Lord knows, there's no chance of stealing a kiss off you."

"Ummm." She hesitated. "I wouldn't go saying that."

Her head throbbed when he leaned towards her, his eyes closing, tears glistening on his cheeks. Elise quickly shut her eyes as well, and in that instant while she waited, she remembered the potato, how its position had been just so, Lewis's face right where it needed to be. As though an authority from beyond had brought them together. Then, the courage in her own legs, how she marched up to him, forgot her promise to remain reserved, not entertain her heart. How she led him away. Gave him water to help his pain. And now, their first kiss was about to happen, and it would be over in an instant. If only she could control time, harness the stars, slow their drift. She would make these moments between her and Lewis last forever.

A moth striking her lips. That was how it felt. His mouth against hers. But before she could lean back, appreciate the fluttering sensation, he kissed her again, forcefully, hurting her. She resisted shoving him. After all, Lewis was the one she loved, and she would do her best to be obliging. "Ah, Elise," he murmured, pulling his face back several inches. She could feel his breath on her face, could smell the smoke on their skin, their hair. "You and me," he continued. "Can you imagine it? This worn house would suit us fine. We could fix it up."

These magic words registered in Elise's neck, and her head thrust forward, she kissing him this time, her hands in his hair. He clambered onto her, pressing her down into the overgrown grass, her head scraping against the clapboard of the house where they might one day live. "Lewis?" she said, and tried to shift out from underneath him. She wanted to hear him speak again, make certain the night air was witness to their future plans. But Lewis blocked her movement, pinned her with the weight of his chest, then reached one hand, one godly big hand up underneath her woolen skirt. The same style skirt worn by Marg and Bee. Cut on the bias.

"Lewis?"

He grunted, and her body stiffened as that hand pushed up the band of her skirt, gripped the top of her underwear.

"Lewis!" She tried to shift sideways, but he was a fallen tree, pinning her.

"Shhhh."

His mouth covering hers now, face pressed sideways, the flesh of his smoky cheek blocking her nostrils, smothering her. She turned her head, inhaled sharply, spit. "Don't you ever shush me, Lewis Hickey," she screeched into his ear. "Let's get that straight right from the start."

Meaty forearm over her mouth now, burnt tasting fabric touching her tongue, her teeth cutting into her own lips. A deep growl. "Shut your trap up, you good for nothing whore. Shut. Your. Trap. Up."

And she did. Shut her trap up. She lay still, never made a sound, even as he fumbled with her clothes, his clothes, kept the weight of his chest on hers, his eager feet slipping on the damp, dead grass, parts of her burning, parts of her freezing, salt water gliding out of her eyes, her right knee bloodied from scraping against the sharp edge of a rotting board over and over again. "Elise, Elise, Eeeleeeesssssssse." She stared at the sky as he hissed her name. She had gotten her wish. The million stars, glistening now, had stopped moving.

After what seemed like forever, he sprung away from her, jumped up and fixed his trousers, cleared his throat hard. Exposed, she sensed the night air on places that should have been covered, and hauled up some fabrics, yanked down others.

"Well, well," he said, hand cupped over his mouth, lighting a cigarette. "Talk about surprises."

Elise managed to mew, "I thought we would wait."

He took a long drag, then spit. "Wait? What's you talking about?"

"You knows." She stood, skirt scrambled at the back. Placing both hands on the wood of the house behind her, she considered that however unpleasant it had been, maybe this event between her and Lewis was only part of a bigger picture. Her palms searched for some assurance from the old house, but they discovered only coldness.

Lewis pitched his cigarette and started laughing, a throaty, happy chortle. Then he came up to her, held her face in his two grimy hands, kissed her full on the lips. "Oh, I loves it. You are such a card. Heard that, I did. Heard you was a good time."

Something burst within her, spread like infected heat throughout her core, traveled down her shaking limbs. Buzzing in her ears then, rising and falling, as though someone was holding two enormous conch shells there. Offering a dry ocean for her head. Just like that, in the moment it might take a burdened branch to snap, she had become a fool. And this ocean lolling about inside her head only taunted her, no opportunity for drowning.

"Elise, Elise," he said, nodding slowly. That reverential calmness had returned. Playfully, he repeated, almost singing, "Oh, Elise. Elise."

When he placed one of his hands on the crown of her head, began to stroke it, she jumped, leaving strands of her hair knotted in his fingers. "This don't got to–" he started, but before he could finish his self-preserving statement, she ran, leaping over decaying fences, flattened rows in longfallow fields, through shadowy shrubs and open patches of too bright moonlight, ran and ran and ran until her legs stumbled, and she fell, striking the hard-packed dirt on the edge of the laneway.

Far away from Lewis and Marg and Bee and James and Chester, she permitted herself to walk. On the hill behind her, she knew the fire was still smoldering, smoke and flames wavering up towards the inky sky. Distorted sounds of hooting and hollering stayed firmly on her back, pushing her away from the communal joy every other child was experiencing. While bits of her were bruised and burning.

Rounding the road, almost home, she stopped, exhausted. She hadn't the energy to lug herself another inch. Her arms were sealed to her body, legs, adhered to the earth beneath her feet. Through clenched teeth, she said aloud, "Why do I feel so heavy, God. How come I's so heavy? I'm sinking." She listened carefully. Heard the voice when it came into her head. *You is made of stone, my child. Don't you know that already? You is made of stone.*

There was nothing left to clean. She had run her brush so many times over that single spot, the wood was beginning to complain. Hand (or bare foot) appraising it, she could feel the layers lifting, surface damaged with the soaking and scrubbing.

She moved out of the kitchen and went to Elise's room, stood in the doorway. A lantern, sitting on the nightstand, offered up a weary light, and she could see Elise flopped diagonally on her bed wearing only an off-white quilted robe, skirt and cardigan crumpled in heap in the corner. Her face was turned towards the wall, head resting on folded arms.

"I knows you're there, Mother. I feels you watching me." Her voice was thick, as though she were pinching her nose.

Stella never stepped forward, and Elise made no invitation. "I weren't trying to hide."

Sniffing, Elise lifted her head, wiped her nose across her forearm. "Did I say you was?"

Stella glanced about the room, at the wallpaper, faded poppies on twisted vines. She eyed the hooked rug, the thinning bedspread, curtains that needed to be taken down and washed. Even though Stella had stood in the doorway many times over the past years, she had forgotten to look, forgotten how to see. What a pretty room she had created for her daughter. All so familiar, comfortable. She recalled making the choices with Leander shortly after Elise was born, remembered being delighted when he had an opinion.

"Elise? I'd like to say something to you."

...

"I'm leaving." Words smacked down. Flattened.

"What? At this ungodly hour?"

"No, tomorrow. First thing in the morning. I'm going to St. John's. To live."

"To live where? Who in God's name do you know in the city?" Stella sensed her body falling towards the doorframe. "And what with the state of the world? Can't you wait until it calms down a bit?"

"Grace. That's who."

"Nettie's Grace?"

"I got a letter from her. She told me to come on anytime I wants."

"You shouldn't let tonight play into such a big–"

"I idn't letting nothing play into nothing. He don't make no difference to me. Not one pinch. They got jobs for women, you knows."

"Jobs? What do you mean, jobs? What kind of jobs."

"There's stuff to do there. Really, Mother. They got stuff there that we don't. They thinks in ways we don't."

"Like what? How do you mean?" Upper arm pressing into the doorframe, hurting a little.

"I can do things, you know. Got no clue what it is, but I's betting I can do something. Aunt Nettie was always telling me I was a good helper."

Elise sat up now, swung her feet over the side of the

bed, bathrobe gaping. And Stella realized she hadn't looked at her daughter in a long time either. Hadn't noticed the legs and the breasts and the solid shoulders. Mouth pulled out in a pout that never seemed to go away.

Elise cocked her head, stared at her mother. "I wants to own a dress with shoulder pads."

"With what?" All of Stella's weight was now against the doorframe, and she wondered what her feet were standing on. "You knows we can't afford every whim."

"'Tis not a whim. 'Tis a small wish. A tiny wish. Almost nothing at all. Is that so wrong, Mother?"

Stella shook her head.

"Well?"

"I don't know what you want me to say, Elise. I was never much one for vanity. I always took what I had, tried not to want more."

"And that's where we's different." Feet squarely on the floor, tapping with her toes. "I wants more. Everything is changing, Mother. We don't got to stay in the house now. Strapped to the stove. Having all kinds of babies you don't really want. Women got more worth nowadays than they used to."

"Your worth don't got nothing to do with a shoulder pad, Elise."

Head back, sardonic laugh. "I's wasting my breath on you. You got no clue what I's trying to say."

"Just 'tis not good to want, Elise."

"Will you stop saying my name over and over again? I can't stand the sound of it. Like a bloody dirty word."

"All right, E–. All right."

Elise looked down at her feet, rubbed one with the other, said, "You says 'tis not good to want, but I knows you wants sometimes, Mother. Everybody wants."

Stella stood straight now, back of her head prickling as the conversation was turning in a spongy direction. "Not I, then. I haven't never wanted nothing I didn't already have."

"You're lying again."

"Lying? What a thing to say to your mother." She folded her arms across her chest.

"How can you live like that? Always telling lies. Is it right lovely grand inside that cocoon? I really hopes it is – you spent your life in there."

Stella stared at Elise, then closed her eyes. Since her children were born, she had tried to paint the best picture, the sweetest representation of a wholesome existence. Of course it might not have been entirely accurate, but how could she ever share her longings or her failures with Elise or Robert? Burdening them. Surely that wasn't the job of a mother.

And now, here was her only daughter, filled with contempt, accusing her. Part of Stella wanted to embrace Elise, while a deeper part wanted to slap her, tell her just enough to burn away her ignorance.

Stella glanced about the room again, and then at Elise. So unfamiliar, this cheeky girl, tucked inside this familiar room. The two no longer belonged together, that was painfully clear. Stella would not let it sadden her, this progression of life, and she kept her face strong and stable.

"We'll talk about it in the morning, Elise."

Elise flopped backwards, bare feet slapping the floor, knees spread. Stella lowered her head and closed her eyes once more. Then she turned, repeated, "Yes, in the morning, Elise," even though she knew they would speak not another word about it.

In the days after Elise left, Stella cleaned the room. Instead of pasting over the wallpaper, she stripped away every layer right down to the naked board. Folded up the bedspread, began in earnest to make a new hooked rug. The room remained blank for months, uninhabitable, and in springtime, Stella decided to replace it all in friendly shades of yellow.

Almost a year later, Robert could be found crouching between two pine trees. Fingers on the earth, he felt rotting humus, twigs, an earthy coolness moving up over his arms. In front of him was a mound of blueberry bushes, empty twigs where berries once resided. He hated this time of year, a time of constant weeping from a sky the colour of stone. A time when trees were still full of dead damp leaves, the weight buckling the branches. He no longer felt a sense of fullness when he stared across the fields. Once a lush green, shuddering in the breeze, they were now barren, only pockmarks remained where turnip and carrot had resided.

A shaft of moonlight illuminated the path directly in front of him, and so as not to be seen, he kept his head low, shoulders hunched. After dinner that evening, he had removed the white shirt he'd worn while working at Crane's Grocery, pulled on his navy wool sweater, made note of the dullness of his grey trousers. He would be invisible to someone strolling down the path towards home. But he needn't have worried. The person he was waiting for was not someone who would search the shadows.

Crunching. Confident steps approaching. And Robert's heart began beating, his eyes blurring. He knew who it was. Jaunting towards him, light on his feet. Lewis Hickey. Tomorrow Lewis would be leaving for St. John's to attend

Queen's College. When he returned, Lewis would be a Reverend, a man who would claim absolute respect in Bended Knee. The very thought of it made the salt fish and balled-up bread churn in Robert's stomach, press at the base of his throat.

Though he tried, Robert couldn't let it go. Only vaguely did he recall when Elise walked away from the smoldering mound of dried stalks about a year ago. Deafened by his own hooting and hollering, he barely realized that someone had been burnt by an exploding potato. He never thought to offer a hand.

And while he laughed, bit into burnt potato skin, spit it to the ground, his sister slipped away. He blamed himself, of course. He should have kept a closer eye on her. Protected her. Taken steps to ensure her name never emerged from the mouths of the local boys. But he hadn't. And the last time he saw her, her eyes were so swollen, they looked like winded sails. Her mouth was bruised, and when she lifted her hand from her knee, Robert saw the bloody mess beneath. She would barely look at him, and he could barely look away.

In the weeks that followed, Robert heard the snickering, the boasting. He witnessed the nudges, the appraising swipes of a sweaty palm across a soft-bristled chin when they spoke of her. He overheard one boy telling another that Easy Elise was "quick to get on her back." Someone said she did whatever was asked of her for a few cigarettes. A paper bag holding a handful of peanut butter kisses. She was stupid. And nothing was better than a stupid broad who didn't know if her skirt was meant to go up, down, or sideways. Too bad she had to up and leave. Ruin the good times before the rest of them could have a go.

Lies. All of it lies. He knew his sister well. She was not

perfect, no doubt, but she was not this person they described. She had her own way, and most folks wouldn't understand it. More than once, she only pretended to deposit her collection money in the wooden plate at church, and instead, bought him Captain Marvel adventures. At Christmas, she always encouraged him to gobble down his apple and then taunted him with her own, still shiny, red, untouched. But in the end, she would share. She always did. In the end.

When he thought about her, he imagined her as a sea urchin. Beautiful when he discovered one in the blue water, painful if he stepped on it, easy enough to injure if he turned it over and prodded. How could these boys, on the cusp of manhood, ridicule someone like that? Crushing her, heavy rubber boots, without even noticing how wonderful she could be. If she wanted.

As the months passed, even after the talk moved on to someone new, he could not erase the voices of those boys, their glassy excited eyes, the smug curling lips of the one who no longer needed to say a word. And his anger festered, in his arms, his shoulders. Hovering just over his heart.

When the yearly bonfire arrived again, Robert skulked about, a good distance from the shrieking girls, lurking boys, Farmer Johnson's pitchfork full of potato stalks ready for the throwing. He did not take his eyes off Lewis Hickey, the boy who had damaged his sister, driven her away. When he noticed Lewis wandering off, young Alice Stomp following behind, Robert's anger dropped down into his fists. He left the crackling, the burnt air, walked aimlessly along the beach, hurling stone after stone into the sea. But his anger would not be so easily mollified by punishing the waves. And so, the next evening, his feet had direction. He found a spot along the path on the inside of a curve, squat down, smoked three cigarettes in silence.

He was surprised at how easy it was to overtake Lewis. Bursting out from between the two pine trees, feet still in the barren blueberry bushes, Robert clutched Lewis's coat, shoved him backwards into the muck. Lewis tried to spring up, but Robert struck him in the stomach with his boot. Curling on his side, Lewis emitted a sharp squeal, wrapped his arms around his waist. Robert tumbled onto Lewis, his fists flailing, punching again and again, knuckles driving against cheeks, against lips, against bone, until strands of bloody spit flew from his fists like ballooning spiders. Sitting on his chest now, Robert pinned Lewis's upper arms with his knees. Air sputtering out of pressured lungs.

When Lewis began to weep, chant, "I's sorry. I's sorry," Robert eased himself off, shook his fists, then pressed them to his mouth, blew. He stared down at Lewis's face, witnessed the handiwork of his anger, the parts split open, other parts shocked closed.

"You good for nothing blood of a bitch. Dirty. Rotten. I should send you to hell where you belongs." And before leaving, he stomped on Lewis's right hand, the hand that had touched his sister, drove it down into the mud and buried it.

As he walked home, Robert whistled. He thought of the well-worn pages of his Captain Marvel comics, and he couldn't help but place a hand on his favourite navy wool sweater, envision the invisible lighting bolt that must be there. Justice done. "Shazam."

chapter twelve

Just a year after Elise married, Stella made her second trip to St. John's to visit her only daughter. She decided to journey there after receiving a telegram from Elise. There was no mention of an invitation, but based on the circumstances, Stella assumed she was wanted and needed. She used the phone in Crane's grocery, told her son-in-law she'd be arriving in two days. After all, Elise had just given birth to a baby, five pounds, seven ounces.

Stella packed a few items in her carpet bag, folded tissue paper around matching booties and sweater, and laid those on top. George Parsons took her across the harbour in his trap skiff, and from there she arranged for a taxi to bring her to the station. Several hours of jostling on the train, and when she stepped off in St. John's, Elise's husband, Joseph Lane, was waiting there, leaning on his shiny Morris Minor, dour expression constant.

"Hello, Mother."

"Joseph."

He opened the door for her, held her elbow as she eased herself in. "Thank you, Joseph, I'm fine," she said, perhaps too curtly. She had not yet reached the age when she felt an elbow hold or a hand hold or even a hesitant glance was required. Let alone from someone who looked nearly as old as she was. Joseph, although he was only in his early forties, had a full head of silver bristly hair, hollow cheeks, eroded eyes. His skin was wrinkle-free though, and Stella determined that was because he had never smiled. Not that she'd ever seen, anyway.

When she arrived at her daughter's home, the bungalow was dimly lit, damp, and surprisingly quiet.

"Elise is in bed."

"Of course she would be," Stella replied.

Joseph deposited her bag on the kitchen floor. "Can you fix yourself something?"

"I'm fine, Joseph."

"I have to get back." Joseph was manager of Tucker's Grocery at the end of their street. Even though it was only a stone's throw away, he refused to walk. Drove his buffed car the half-block, parked it directly to the left of the entrance, while the owner, whenever he was there, parked to the right.

"Don't worry about me."

"Goodbye, Mother."

"Goodbye, Joseph."

Stella remained standing just beyond the kitchen doorway even after she'd heard the car rumble and recede. Her new navy coat with the shoulder tucks remained on, purse still clutched in glove-covered hands. Joseph had been staring at her purse, and she couldn't help but picture how she might have looked to him, like an aged, slightly frumpish, uncertain woman. And after nearly a full day of traveling, that was mostly how she felt.

Now that she'd arrived, she didn't want to remove the coat that covered her back, had peculiar misgivings about laying down her purse. Already the linoleum flooring felt cold and foreign through her stockings. An unpleasant stickiness as she lifted her left foot, then her right. She wanted her slippers, those whimsical pink ones, knitted, with pompoms. Elise would grimace at the sight of them, Stella knew, and would suggest she buy something *suitable. Suitable slippers. A suitable hat. Suitable gloves and purse.* But when she tugged them on over her bony feet, she began to relax.

Stella went to her daughter's room, stopped at the threshold and peered in. Elise's eyes were closed, mouth parted. Instead of disturbing her, Stella returned to the living room, layered up torn paper, splits, dry junks in the fireplace, and struck a match. In the kitchen, she placed the kettle on the stove, listened until it just began to hiss. Second smallest beige canister had "TEA BAGS" written across it, and Stella pried open the tin lid, plucked one out. She couldn't get used to a tea bag. It was too convenient. The user, she thought, was deprived of the pride that accompanied a clean pour – a flurry of black flecks in the pot, not a single one in the cup.

Stella lifted the metal chair, orange vinyl seat, and seated herself, nibbled at lemon creams, slurped the tepid tea.

"Is that you, Mother?" Her daughter's voice was low and urgent.

"Yes, 'tis me."

"What are you eating? I can hear you all the way in here."

Stella laid down her biscuit, wiped crumbs from the moist corners of her mouth. "Just a lemon cream."

"Surely you could find something better than that."

She ran her fingers over the cold tea bag, then pinched it until it sat in a pool of auburn liquid. "I'm not much hungry."

Elise never responded, so Stella went to her daughter's room, sat in the wooden chair beside her bed.

"I made Joseph fill up the fridge, Mother. I don't want to see you acting like we're poor, without a bite in the house."

Stella slid back in the chair, pressed herself into the spindles, felt the beads in the wood against her spine. Leander had made it many years ago. And this sturdy chair offered up some comfort, when she sensed a childish homesickness beginning to curdle the very pit of her stomach.

"Well?" Elise continued. "Why don't you go make a decent sandwich? There's bologna and mustard. Good bread."

"The train."

"What? It couldn't have been that bad. I've been on it myself, remember, and I never minded it in the least."

On the train, there was a man seated across from Stella, his knees occasionally gracing hers when he shifted (which was often). She decided, perhaps inaccurately, that he was a pig farmer, partly from his rough hands and leather face, and partly from his smell. Although his hair appeared freshly washed and his clothes were unstained, there was a vile odour of butchery in the air surrounding him. Faint, but it made her think of clotted blood upon a sun-warmed barn floor, those dizzy moments before someone would sluice it away with buckets of water. Stella refused to cover her nose for fear of appearing impolite. The gentleman looked so pleasant after all, though it made Stella light-headed when he dandled his young son on his knee.

"My stomach isn't settled."

Elise frowned. Even though her colour was drained from the birth, Stella couldn't imagine any weakness within her. She had her own way of doing things and never deviated. As an adult, Elise had become the type of woman who never wore a scarf to church and scoffed at the notion of fixing herself up before her husband came home.

During Stella's last trip to St. John's, she had noticed that Elise rebelled in insignificant ways, insisting on using only cake mixes, driving the wrong way on a one-way street, smoking while sitting on the toilet (something Stella had seen quite by accident due to a partially open bathroom door). Her tendencies made little sense to Stella, but she tried her best not to comment. "I can see your eyes rolling," Elise would holler. Or, "Must you scowl at everything?" By the end of the two weeks, Stella was afraid to blink or twitch in front of her daughter, lest she be accused of being condemnatory.

"Can you hand me my cigarettes?" Elise asked. "In there."

Stella reached into the night table drawer, found the package amongst tubes of lotion, a handful of wrapped candy. She handed Elise a cigarette, laid the remainder next to a framed black and white picture of Joseph's car. "Do you need anything else?"

"No. Got matches under my pillow."

In the telegram, Elise had not made mention of the baby's name or even if it was a boy or a girl. In the two days before she left to visit, Stella avoided going outside. What if someone asked about her first grandchild, what would they think if Stella was unable to answer such simple questions? All Stella knew was that the baby was born with dark serious eyes at the stroke of midnight between September 21st and September 22nd.

Stella cleared her throat. "Where's the baby?" she ventured.

"In her room."

"Her?"

"Yes, Mother." Elise took deep drags from the cigarette, tipped the ashes in the green glass dish she held with her left hand.

"Oh."

"What else would she be?"

"You never mentioned it."

"I surely did, then."

"Perhaps, you did. I must have missed it." Stella tasted acidity on her tongue from over-steeped tea. "Did you name her yet?"

"Did I not mention that either?"

"Not that I minds."

"We've called her Summer Fall. Summer Fall Lane."

"What an odd name," Stella said, though she had tried to say "nice" or "lovely."

Elise responded curtly, "Not what you would've chosen, Mother, but now it's not your choice, is it?"

Stella opened her mouth to respond, but was unable to correct herself, unable to clarify the miscommunication. Instead, she replied, "It's just not a regular name."

"Who wants regular?"

"What's wrong with regular?"

"As always, you miss the point."

"I don't understand what you mean."

"My point exactly, Mother." She stubbed the cigarette in the overflowing plate.

"Do you want me to clean that?"

"No. I imagine I'll want another any second. Maybe sooner."

"Oh."

Elise picked up the butt, used it to crush each clump of ash, then she handed the mess to Stella.

"I would like to understand," Stella said slowly, as she laid the plate on the night table. "Can't you try to explain it a little better? About her name?"

"Summer is beauty, but it withers." A sigh that sounded like effort. "Pride cometh before the fall, and all that stuff."

"Oh."

"I want my daughter to be humble."

"Humble?" Stella shook her head. "I don't think you can make someone humble with a name. I don't think a name's got much to do with the way a person is."

Elise pressed her head into her pillow, further squishing her deflated beehive, and stared up at the ceiling. "You could be right. They named you Stella, and you're far from a twinkling light."

Stella sniffed now in an attempt to hide her confusion. How was it that every time she spoke with her daughter, her words were somehow twisted, as though they were falling from her mouth independent from her mind's direction? And in the rare moment when they emerged intact, they were warped by forces beyond.

Moaning, Elise lifted her elbows from her sides, said, "My chest feels like it's going to bust open."

"Cabbage leaves."

"What?"

"Put cabbage leaves in your brassiere. Works like a charm."

"Surely you're joking, Mother."

"We always done it. Back in the day."

"If you hadn't noticed, *the day* was a long time ago."

"Not that long." Stella examined her fingernails. Once smooth and even, now they were ridged, a little ragged. A few months back, Nettie had suggested she try some clear polish, and right now, it seemed like a good idea.

"That's all I needs, Joseph coming round, gets a whiff of me, thinking I've got a jig's dinner down my shirt."

"Suit yourself."

"I will."

Stella sighed. Did she have nothing of value to share? No piece of advice or tidbit of information to pass on? Sometimes she wondered how she'd gotten to this point in her relationship with her daughter. She was the annoying appendage, useless, but present nonetheless. An image of a limp foot came to mind, and Stella thought again of Leander.

"Your father would've wanted to be here, I bet."

"Yes." Elise closed her eyes.

"He would've been right proud."

Elise smiled, opened her eyes then, but didn't look at Stella. "Yes."

Stella continued the chatter, she preferred bickering to silence. "Such a curious time of birth."

"Curious?"

"You know. Being born like that."

"Like what? You say it like I had control over the whole thing. Like I planned it that way."

"Don't be silly, Elise."

"Silly, now, am I?"

"I minds being a bit sensitive after you and Robert was born."

Eyes turning toward heaven. "I'm hardly sensitive. I'm right fagged out, but hardly sensitive."

Stella folded her hands in her lap, pinched her own fingers. "I was just wondering when her birthday would be so I'd know when to...when to send a card or a little something."

"Well, I don't rightly know."

"What's that?"

"Joseph and I've decided to let her choose."

"Let her choose? Her own date of birth? Don't you got no certificate?"

"They put something down, but we don't heed that. 'Tis just a piece of paper."

"But surely, the doctor–"

"The doctor said it was my decision, based on the time she came out, but that seems unfair."

"You mean she's going to grow up not knowing what day she was born on?"

"She wasn't born on neither day. She was born between two days. Don't you understand? We'll just wait until she decides."

"But wouldn't it make more sense if you–"

"Really, Mom, I just had a baby three days ago. I'm exhausted, and you want to quibble about nothing. Do you think I should be the exact same parent as you were?"

Stella was about to speak, when Elise patted her hand, pacifying smile. "I really wasn't looking for an answer there."

Stella closed her mouth again, and as if on cue, a newborn mew came from a room down the hall.

"I'll go fetch her."

"Thank you, Mother. Now that would be a help. And if you could pass me my cigarettes again? I don't want to lean that far."

In the tiny room farthest from Elise's, Stella found Summer Fall Lane. She was in a painted wooden crib, dancing lamb on the headboard, sheep mobile clamped onto the white railing. She wore a pale pink sleeper, tiny mittens tied at her wrists. Stella noticed the mustard stains near her legs.

"Wait here one second, my little lover," Stella whispered, hand gently on the baby's belly. "I'll fix you right up."

Warm washcloths in hand, Stella plucked up Summer, and laid her on the change table. She thought of Elise as she cleaned the baby, thought of the endless questions she'd had in those first few days. Every hour or two, Leander ran to fetch his mother: "Stella is worried," and Mrs. Edgecombe would drop what she was doing, come huffing down the lane, sometimes bits of salt fish or pinches of dough still clinging to her hands.

While washing Summer's mottled bottom and swollen parts, Stella remembered why she'd been afraid when Elise was a baby. Liquid leaked from her tiny nipples. Her baby face had been covered in blemishes, blotchy rashes creeping into the folds of her neck. Her bony lower back was marred with what looked like bruises. "Witch's milk. Typical," Mrs. Edgecombe had said with a nod. Or, "Milk spots. All of mine had it." Or, "Not sure, maid. Thin skin, I allows. It'll fade."

Stella had been in St. John's over two hours now, and Elise had not asked her a single question. Not a single one – as though Elise was making an unmistakable point of rejecting her own mother. Rejecting Stella's ways. Her ideas.

Stella pinned the cloth diaper just underneath the blackened knob of cord, and wondered if she had done something wrong when raising Elise. But no, Stella told herself, she had been reliable and constant. Firm and loving. She had been the best mother she knew how to be, and it certainly wasn't her fault if it never took.

Seated now in a rocker, she nestled the baby in the crook of her elbow. Summer's arms flailed, mouth struggled to find something. Stella pressed the fist to the mouth, watched in amazement the intuitive suckling.

Looking into the baby's eyes, Stella understood why Elise had mentioned their colour. They were like the bottom of an untouched puddle, in the instant before the stomp. So clear, but at the same time, begging for disruption. Summer stared up at Stella, unapologetically, and Stella had to remind herself that this child, with her black doll's hair, was only three days old.

Summer Fall. Stella shook her head, clicked her tongue softly. How could someone who weighed not more than a good-sized bottle of beet be eternally wedged between two seasons? Surely an unkind place for a newborn baby. A nowhere sort of place. And even though Stella tried to assuage it, a damp sadness had caught in her throat, made her want to cry.

Stella returned home to days of impossible quiet. Visitors were few and far between. Many of the children who had plodded about, harping and throwing rocks and striking her fence with sticks, were now grown and gone away. She had long ago sold two parcels of her land, and the robin's egg blue saltbox constructed on the lot to the north housed an elderly couple who rarely emerged. To the south, a skeleton of a home stood, frame grey and warping in the salt air. On blustery days, the wind would whip through the boards, squeal and moan. But, since she came home, the wind never uttered a single sigh.

Stella had not received a letter from Robert in six months. After university, he had moved to Toronto, taken some sort of position in a bank that was never fully explained. When he first went away, he wrote every two weeks, then it slowed to once a month. And more recently, his letters had stopped altogether, only to be replaced by letters from his new wife. A woman named Jane, who with perfect script, wrote endless pages about the richness of their everyday: their adored pet cat, Elmer, who owned its own chair; a gnarly old peach tree in her yard that she'd coaxed into producing; imminent plans for a baby, her secret hope for a boy. Stella felt only hollowness when she read each letter. *Dear Mom, When are you coming to stay?*

During the past summer, Nettie Rose, Stella's best friend, also left Bended Knee. She had moved to a small apartment in St. John's, in order to be closer to her daughter Grace. In recent years, Nettie Rose struggled to take care of herself. She'd told Stella she didn't know what to do first. "Can't stand owning all this time," she'd said. "Carefree afternoons? You can have them for me." Her life had taken a shift towards simplicity. Most of her many children gone. Grandchildren distant. Husband no longer on the earth. Idleness caused rust to bloom from within, and Nettie became forgetful. After she had caused a small fire, a greasy pan, blackened fish, she decided to move. "Be where someone is apt to keep an eye on me. I needs that. There idn't nothing wrong with owning up to it."

During her time with Elise and Summer Fall, Stella had visited Nettie. But the meeting was awkward, strangely upsetting. In that stuffy place on a third floor, Stella complimented Nettie's matching plates, framed pictures of seashells and pink roses, yellow furniture set, polka-dot cushions. She told Nettie she adored her bright red upholstered rocker that looked soft, but really wasn't. When Nettie had sold her house, contents were included, and now, Stella's particular kitchen chair was no longer available. The kitchen table that she usually leaned upon was gone, replaced by plastic covered pressboard, cold metal legs. Nettie yammered on about a man named Milton Berle, how happy she was to have discovered him on her small television set. "Never laughed so hard in my life," she crowed. Stella nodded, though that comment jabbed her. She didn't finish her tea. It didn't taste the same when served in a heavy mug.

And now, with everyone gone, Bended Knee felt like a foreign village, bleak and somewhat uninviting. People continued to be helpful and generous, but she didn't appreciate it when Jo Taylor tucked a complimentary tub of candied fruit in among her purchases. Or when Skipper Johnson layered on an extra piece of dried cod, his wink and wide smile doing nothing to disguise the hint of pity in his eyes. And when Johnnie, one of Nettie's sons, still a bachelor, stacked a row of spruce logs by her back door, he wouldn't accept so much as a thimble of rum for payment. Such generosity embarrassed Stella, made her feel older and less competent than she was. The look on their weathered faces told Stella they believed she was a woman who hadn't had her fair share of luck.

When the few straggly trees separating the homes were stripped bare, the sight of the unfinished shell nearby bothered Stella more and more. But instead of drawing the curtains, she began to watch it, the way long shadows moved through it, the sun making rectangles and triangles dance upon the frosty earth. She sighed when birds rested in tight corners or when stray dogs hunkered beneath a lean-to of abandoned boards during rainstorms, drops like nails. Whenever she noticed a couple strolling up the lane, she would wait to see if they slowed, took interest. Perhaps they would be the owners. Ready to complete what they had started. But no creature, bird, dog, or person, ever lingered near the structure for any length of time. Like a joke, it was left standing there, a man's dream for home and family. Alone, against the sea, with empty eyes, holes instead of doors. A sad joke. Stella finally had to look away.

As fall gave way to winter, Stella rarely used her kerosene lamps. She took to eating an early meal, usually fish boiled on the stove, potatoes or bread, some sort of pickles. Occasionally she would make a grunt with a scoop of partridgeberries from the keg in the back porch. Afterwards, she would sit there in the dim light, missing the harvest moon. Some evenings she hummed softly to herself, but being alone, the humming echoed. Mostly, she quietly sipped her tea. Until darkness drove her to bed.

When winter's bitter hand gripped Bended Knee, Stella closed the door to the kitchen, caging the heat, and she took to sleeping on the daybed. She ate sitting near the stove in a hefty chair Leander had made. It was one of his last projects, thick wooden arms and back. On each side near the top, he had fastened what he called "a wooden ear," a piece of birch shaped and sanded into half a heart. Stella had wanted him to stop, to rest, but he pressed on. Told her, "No matter where I is, my dear, I'll hear you." And she had taunted, "I believes your ears is a mite bit smaller than that, now, Leander. Just how far do you reckon on going?"

Now, when she thought of those words, her smirk quickly turned into a frown.

Some nights, as she sat in the chair, she tried to talk to Leander. Tried to tell him about her day, her meal, how she'd burned her little finger on the iron. Sometimes she'd talk about the times they had when they'd just married. She told him about Johnnie, who would dig a trail to her back step after each storm, and fetch a few paper bagfuls of groceries from the shop. Mentioned how he was such a rabble-rouser as a boy, but had grown into a decent man. Leander would remember that, all the trouble that boy had caused. There were plenty of engaging stories.

She would keep her voice nice and light, imagining her words traveled from her mouth into those two cuplike wooden ears, then directly to Leander. But, her pleasantness always deteriorated, and instead, she found herself asking him, "Where have you gone off to? Where have you gone? What kind of cruelty is this? To leave me all alone." Darkness pushed her own voice back into her face, and her loneliness, out loud like that, only made things worse.

One afternoon, when blinding light bounced off the snow, penetrated her window, and made her small kitchen feel too close to heaven, Stella bundled in a blanket, sneaked into the coolness of the front room. It was quieter there, and Stella felt as though she were taking a break, away from the never-ending crackle of the fire and the relentless gales drilling the outside boards. Seated in a chair, soft cushion against her lower spine, she inhaled the odours of this space. There was history in those smells, damp books, woolen sweaters, four picture frames that hung behind her and perfumed the air with woody sweetness. Comforting, yet she sensed these smells didn't belong to her.

Glancing about, she identified her mother's blanket, the stump-like stool where her father would rest his feet, Leander's pieces of furniture, a forgotten pair of Elise's buttoned-up shoes side-by-side beneath a chair, Robert's navy sweater with the hole in the elbow that he'd left behind. All items belonging to others. The only thing she owned (other than the walls and the windows and the ceilings) was a tall cabinet made of pine. Leander had built it for her, designed to house her most precious possessions. It was sturdy, and the wood, aging gracefully, had developed a soft tawny colour. Leander had purchased green milky glass knobs, and she touched one now, but didn't open the drawer. She didn't want the additional reminder that nothing lay inside.

The following week, snow arrived and never let up. Gusts plucked up what had fallen, shaped it into heaps and drifts, blocking her door, coating her windows in a frozen crystalline mess. Clearing a path from her back stoop, she tied two lengths of rope – one from the railing to the outhouse, the other from the railing to Leander's shed. While the outhouse was practical, and the rope guided her when her eyes could not, there was no actual need to be connected to the shed. But in jacket and boots, she would journey there during the storms, pick through Leander's tools and swipe her hands in sawdust that always reappeared even after she'd cleaned. She couldn't bear the idea of being separated from the shed, and she spent countless hours, in blue winter light, poking through boxes and drawers of Leander's items, sorting nails, balling twine. Searching. She was certain there was something there. Something she was meant to find. Hiding from her. More than once, in her frustration, she plucked up a hammer or planer, let it drop, just to hear the dull thud when it struck the wooden floor.

After months of hollow days, rollicking blizzards, nights as black as pitch, the sounds of life that arrived with spring made Stella anxious. Icicles dripping, mud sucking at her boots, crows scraping at scattered bits of garbage, cawing. She removed the ropes that had linked her to the outside world, and coiled them, hung them over the railing to dry. For a moment, she sat on her step, clutched the frayed ends that dangled down. Somehow the winter had kept everything together, tight and clean, and now her world was thawing, coming undone. The snow was receding over the grass, stripping the rocks of their insulation, exposing the tree roots, moistening the soil. Blanket lifted, and Stella felt as though she were naked underneath. She lifted her face towards the sky, and when the wind entangled itself, she thought she could feel the sun, teasing her with hints of distant warmth.

Stella began to clean, swiping cobwebs from corners, airing quilts on the line. With damp cloth, she dusted every surface, but the blackish dust only seemed to shift locations. In the front room, the wallpaper had begun to bubble and let loose, and cracks could be seen near the ceiling. Her land was not much better. Flowerbeds, once overflowing with orderly blooms, were now riddled with the brown stems of nettles, heads long burst, seeds already scattered. Her shrubs were overgrown and spindly, and on her house, she saw flaking paint, several soft boards. When she pressed them, water beaded near the tips of her fingers. How had this happened? As though overnight, her house had stopped singing, starting complaining about aches in joints, weakness in the bones.

Inside the shed, she cracked open two windows, but struggled with the third. The thick coats of paint had bonded, and she used a bone-handled knife to cut through the layers. Heels of her hands pressed against the frame, she grunted and shoved until the window gave way, jumped upwards several inches. Lurching forward, she smacked her hip on the counter, and was forced to kneel, eyes watering from the pulsing pain. A deep breath, and she looked up, noticed a tiny cupboard tucked into a corner underneath the counter. She reached out, ran her fingers over the dented metal knobs.

She could not count the number of times she had looked at that cupboard but never opened it. During her winter visits, she had focused on the newer section Leander had built in the shed, ignoring the corner where her father's things were kept. Stella shimmied closer to the cupboard and tugged at the drawers. Years of neglect in the dampness, and the wood had swollen. Stella had to yank with both hands, then pry her fingers into the crack, and wrench each drawer open.

The first two drawers contained nothing of interest, but in the third, she found a cookbook, pages stained with berry juice and mildew. Stella moved out from underneath the counter, sat on a wooden stool, cookbook resting in her lap. Odd to find such an item in a woodworker's shed, and she realized it must have belonged to her mother so many years ago. Perhaps while her father was working, her mother would sit by the fire, maybe even upon the very stool where Stella now perched, and her mother would read through recipes, discuss dinners.

Stella shook her head. These images were difficult to reconcile. Her mother rarely cooked anything other than a hasty meal, and to the best of Stella's knowledge, never spent a moment perusing a cookbook. Delia Abbott was a woman who died with her own flesh withering on her fragile bones. There was no apparent interest in gastronomy. But then, how well did Stella really know her mother? Hardly at all. She barely remembered her. She had died when Stella was only a child. Should she be expected to remember her? Children remembered through their skin, by way of warmth and touch. Her mother had not been a woman who embraced easily, who bent her head just to smell her child's hair.

Opening the book, Stella shuffled the pages gently, and a dusting of flour sifted out onto her skirt. Her breathing slowed when she saw her own name, her maiden name, neatly printed on the inside cover. Miss Stella Abbott. Fingers shook as she turned the pages, read the miniscule notes written beside a multitude of recipes. Secrets. Hints. A record of mother's wisdom, meant to guide a young woman. "Don't handle the crust. Toughens it." "Treat dough like you would a baby. Gently, but firmly." "If late berries, cut sugar in half. Too sweet as is." "Dry pan on stove – or apt to rust." In the margins, she noticed the occasional silly doodling, a mouse, surprised expression, missing its tail, a fat blueberry staring upwards at its stately frilly crown.

With the palms of her hands, Stella pressed the pages together, held the book to her chest. There was discomfort there, inside her heart, and Stella took several deep breaths to ease it. Who was the woman who had written those words, sketched those whimsical images? She was the opposite of what Stella had conceived, what she held as fact. In life, her mother had been more than that distant cloud, a bruise on the sky, gradually drifting away from their home. The following realization came to Stella with startling fullness. That she was not, after all, born into the hands of an unhappy woman.

She sighed, closed her eyes, and let the joy spread through her. After wandering for years in dusky shadows, this cookbook felt like a passage, and there was warm milky comfort on the other side. Waiting there. For her to accept it.

Stella stood up, strode out of the shed. She never bothered to close the door.

One afternoon in mid-June, Stella stopped beside the window at the top of the stairs, stared out at the thin strip of sea on the horizon. Though the cobalt mass was calm, she knew beneath it all, there was a continual rumbling that would never cease. Creatures jostled in the currents, skittering fish, watery landscape altered. All these things changing, but the force behind them remained the same. She took solace in this one element of constancy. No matter the walls that surrounded her, no matter the earth beneath her feet, the ocean, her ocean, would never change.

As she stared at the water, she noticed a man standing in the laneway, black hair slicked backwards, hands on his hips, purpose in the spacing of his glossy shoes. Pretty wife beside him, bulbous belly, another child clinging to her skirt. "Go on," she said firmly and swatted the boy's backside. "Go on and look it over." He darted towards the skeleton house, climbed the splintery wood, bounced and grabbed and hung from the joists, testing the structure as only a child could. Husband and wife held hands, picked their way through the overgrown path. "I loves the smell," Stella heard the woman say. "Of building a home."

Stella thought about Nettie then. Content there in her small apartment, her space filled with items she had chosen. Smelly soaps and warm water from a tap. Kitty cookie jar overflowing with gingersnaps. Grandchildren jumping, jumping against the counter, knocking the kitten over, gorging on spilled treats. Then every Tuesday, reliably, Milton Berle. A man who made her laugh.

In her closet, Stella found her carpet bag, plucked it down from the shelf, laid it on her bed. She stared at it for just a minute, then unzipped, spread the mouth wide. And with no further hesitation, tucked the cookbook inside.

chapter thirteen

"I had a bad dream, Nanny."

"Oh, my baby." Stella rubbed Summer's warm head, tucked the blanket up around her neck. "Tell Nan about it. Sometimes that helps."

Summer's cheeks were flushed, and she rolled onto her side. "In my dream, it was right dark, and I got out of bed, and came to the kitchen and I looked outside. I could see the moon through the door. The door weren't there, that's why."

"Where was the door?"

"A man stealed it. I seen him running down the road. Door on his head."

"On his head?"

"Yes, Nan. On his head."

"That's really something. I'd imagine that'd be real tough. Balance a big door and run."

"Was only a dream, Nanny. It's not real."

"Oh, yes."

"I weren't scared. A door is just a good thing to have."

"That it is."

"Should I chased him?"

"What? Gone after him?"

"To get the door back." Summer wound her fingers through Stella's, palms touching.

"I wouldn't even think of it."

"What about the wind? Do you think it'd get in?"

"No, my maid. The wind I knows don't like the indoors."

"You're right, Nanny."

Elise was leaning against the doorframe to the living room, a tumbler of clear liquid and ice in hand. "Quite the philosopher, isn't she?"

"Yes, she is."

"Fever don't seem to affect her tongue."

"You was like that," Stella said. "Talked your way through any kind of illness."

"Don't go filling her head with no old garbage, now."

"What? I wouldn't do that." Lips crimped.

"That you wouldn't," Elise grunted, then turned and went back to the kitchen.

After a moment, Stella whispered, "Are you feeling any better?"

"My head still hurts."

"How does it hurt?"

"I don't know. It feels kind of like an echo."

"Maybe another pillow will help." Stella lifted Summer, placed an embroidered cushion underneath her head.

"Thank you, Nan."

"God bless you, my little doll." Kiss on the freckled bridge of her nose. "God bless you."

Summer sucked on a length of her black hair, stared at Stella. "Nan, what's God?"

"Ummmm. Well, that's a very tough question."

"Why?"

"Ah, because God is everything."

"Everything?" Feverish eyes widened. "Is God a sandwich?"

"I guess so." No old garbage now.

"I bet God is in the phone. How else would phones work?"

"You might be right."

"He's in a rainbow for sure."

"Yes, for sure."

She took the wet hair from her mouth, drew lines across her chin. "Is He in me?"

"Of course. Without a doubt, my little lover."

"Where to?" She touched her nose, poked her pinky in her bellybutton.

"Well, there is a part inside of you that's sweetness, right? Somewhere in there." Stella placed a hand on Summer's chest. "You feel happiness. Or love. Well, that's God. That's what I reckons anyway. Other folks might think different."

Summer pinched her upper arm, ran her fingers over her ribs. "I don't feel God. I think that's bones, Nanny. It's like rock."

Stella laughed, touched Summer's cheek.

"I want to meet Him. Can we call Him?"

"God?" Stella frowned thoughtfully. "What would you like to ask Him?"

"I'd ask Him to change this monkey on my pajamas into a bunny rabbit."

"I'm not sure He could do that. Or if He'd want to."

"Why not? I don't like monkeys. I bet He'd have green skin. And I'd be scared to see him, and He'd be a bit scared too."

"Maybe, sweetie. I'm not sure about all that. But I do know one thing."

"What's that, Nan?"

"That He really loves you. No matter what you do in your life, He'll always love you."

"Like you love me?"

"Yes, my baby."

"And like you loved Pop before he died?"

"Yes, my baby."

Summer sat up a little on her elbows, took a drink of apple juice that Stella offered, then lay back, started tying the floppy ears of her bunny into knots.

"Nanny?"

"Yes?"

"Did you ever have another boyfriend after Pop?"

Shifting in her seat, Stella glanced towards the door to the kitchen. "Not a one."

"Never wanted to smooch someone else?"

"Never."

"Never wanted to get married again?"

"Hardly." A laughing word.

"Don't lie to the child." Elise was at the door again, tumbler still full, or refilled. Stella could only guess. "Tell her the truth."

"What truth?"

"You know."

"That I don't."

"Yes, you do. You bloody well know."

Thick silence for a moment then, "That idn't no one's business but my own."

"Don't be stupid, Mother." Trace of a slur. "You don't live your life detached from everyone else. We're all like a bunch of damn scales on the same godforsaken fish. You move down by the tail, and I still feels it up by the head."

"Aren't we getting poetic."

Big gulp. "No one owns their own life. Not even you."

Stella pursed her lips, pressed her toes down farther into her slippers. Elise was being unfair. Dragging that matter up, polluting the very air with her sentences. All this in front of a five-year-old.

What was the point of it? Stella decided long ago, if she were ever to tell her story, this would be the part she would leave out. Omit entirely with razor incisions. In her opinion, it added no value, offered no insight into her character. And doesn't everyone deserve to skip a chapter? A few pages at the very least.

Summer pouted, then said in a scratchy voice, "Why'd you go and do that for? Upsetting Nan."

To which Elise replied, "Don't you be fooled, child, nothing don't upset that one."

Stella patted Summer's hand, said, "Your mother's right. Nothing don't upset this old goat."

Summer giggled. "Why don't you tell me then? About Pop number two."

"Oh. Oh, oh. I couldn't do that, darling. There's nothing worth telling. There was no Pop number two."

"Well, then, make something up."

"I'm afraid I'm not very good at that either." Stella reached for the nearest book, pushed up her glasses and held it at arm's length. "How about I read to you instead. Henry Huggins?"

"Good," Summer replied. "That's my favourite. I love Ribsy so much."

"All right." Stella nestled herself on the couch near Summer's head, and the child closed her eyes, sucked her thumb. Stella was tempted to nudge that wet digit away, but didn't. Instead, she stroked Summer's forehead, smooth with youth, and started reading on page one.

"Henry Huggins was in third grade. His hair looked like a scrubbing brush and..."

As the front part of her brain registered the words and spoke them, a deeper part couldn't help but tickle the sleeping memories. And they awakened, much to Stella's dismay, with startling vividness. Yes, she was married the second time in the legal sense. But her heart never gave into it. Never gave into it at all. He never gave her heart the chance.

Just before Christmas when Elise was fourteen and Robert was nine, the harbour filled with great chunks of ice. Stella could still remember the sound, like dishes breaking, when the pans crowded in. They seemed livid, she had thought, crashing into one another, some buckling sideways, jutting up out of the black water. In the winter sun, it burned her eyes just to look at it.

Everyone thought the ice would last a week, maybe two, and then depart overnight, a crafty visitor who doesn't say goodbye. They would once again relish the sight of the water, choppy with the bitter winter winds. But, this never happened. The ice stayed on, well beyond its welcome. Morning after morning Stella would awake to a brilliant white harbour, nothing more than a seething blanket, a floating trap.

People shook their heads, talked relentlessly about the ice, first praising its beauty, then condemning its cruelty. Can you imagine, they joked and laughed, if the ice were there to stay? What would happen to them all? Stella could not bring herself to mention it. Silliness, she knew, but she worried the ice might find all the attention attractive.

As the weeks continued to creep by, the geniality expired, and people became antsy, snapped at one another. For Stella, the incessant noise began to torture her. Sometimes, she thought it might actually be alive, the ice, calling to her with a cold creaky moan that sent shivers down her spine.

Dried goods were dwindling. Ships carrying supplies and mail were unable to break through, and in late spring, the general store closed. No one banged on Mrs. Fuller's wooden door unless they wanted a wooden spool of thread or a scrap of fabric. Money or credit made no difference as the molasses barrels were empty, flour sacks were flattened, every glass jar of stick candy was void of even a sugar granule.

Stella's pantry was bare. At first, people dropped off the occasional bit of fresh meat, a few rabbits. But the harbour remained bound up, and when people began to worry about their own survival, they were less generous. Stella didn't blame them, she would have done the same if she had only a handful of chickens, diminishing supply of crabapple jelly, a pat or two of butter from a cow who refused to give more. She and the children survived mostly on salt fish and the potatoes they had not planted, cutting away the sprouted eyes.

With the cold breath coming off the ice, the vegetable harvest was poor. Everything was miniature in size, turnip, beet, stubby flavourless carrots. Elise and Robert whined and cried with hunger, grumped over the similarity of every meal. But Stella had little to offer them.

People panicked. A group gathered outside the general store, fists formed, claiming Fuller, who was as robust as ever, and his mother were holding back. Reverend Hickey arrived to calm them, sent them home. On their way, a whippet-thin man named Cornelius Greene went out onto the ice, leaping from pan to pan. Neighbours gathered to watch him, hollered at him, but he kept hopping until he was only a silver dot. A sparkle. Then nothing.

Stella, too, could sense madness in her desperation. Late one night, under a full moon, she slipped down over the icy hill that led to the beach, and with an axe in hand, smashed at the hulking shards. Water rinsed up over her boots, numbed her feet, and she raised that axe over and over again until she was unable to lift her arms above her head. With frustration fueling her last bit of strength, she tossed the axe out onto the ice with as much force as she could muster. In an instant, the layer of white rippled, and the axe slid off, swallowed without as much as a burp.

Stella sat on the rocks, water washing in, trying to steal the hem of her skirt. Her hands were lead at her sides, and when she pounded the rocks, she didn't feel a thing. Head upon her bony knees, she began to cry. She knew when she returned home, she would not sleep. Only listen to the restless whines of her children as they tossed and turned, bellies filled with damp air.

She stood, clothes sticking to her skin, and began to lumber home. Empty hands, and she felt a flash of anger over her own stupidity. She had lost their axe. She thought of the few axes hanging on the wall of the general store, each held up by two nails, and she glanced over at the building. In a window on the upper floor, a thick shadow nearly obliterated an orange glow behind it. Someone was watching her.

The next morning, a small jug of molasses appeared on her back stoop, along with three rabbits, a braid of onions, raisins, paper packet of salt. Whoops and squeals of childish joy. Noontime dinner fit for a king. Her children loved her that afternoon, shrunken bellies once again stuffed beyond.

When Christmas re-appeared, and the ice showed no sign of departing, Alistair Fuller said he wanted to be married. Have a life away from his mother. Hunger turned her into a repeat bride, hunger and a secret desire for a companion. Plus, there were her two excited children, who didn't notice his empty eyes, yelped instead at the sight of sugar crystals on the corners of his mouth.

As though on cue, shortly after she had said "I do," the ice departed, leaving a gentle lapping quiet.

"Nanny?" Thumb like a bleached prune.

Stella put down the book, removed her glasses and let them sit on her chest, thin chain holding them. "I thought you was gone to sleep."

"Then why was you reading?"

"Was I?"

Summer cocked her head, stared at Stella through doubtful glassy eyes. "Do you like Ribsy?"

"Well, yes. He seems like a perfectly lovely animal."

"When I get a dog someday, I'm going to call him Ribsy."

"That's a nice name."

Fists underneath her chin, squeezing. "I love him too much, Nanny. More than Henry Huggins do."

"I see why. Dogs can be very, very special, Summer. Part of your family."

Whispering now, "Nan?"

"Yes?"

"Is God in Ribsy?"

Stella sighed, rubbed her chin, pinched at the whisker or two that had appeared there in recent years. Quick peek at the door, all clear, and she whispered back, "If that's what you feel, my duck, then God's most assuredly in that dog. I wouldn't be surprised in the least."

"That's just what I was thinking too, Nanny." Thumb in again, talking through her cheek, Summer said. "You can read some more."

Stella never knew such a man could even exist. Filled with "piss and vinegar" didn't begin to describe him. He had not wanted his mother to attend the small service, had an enormous argument with her on the steps of the church. A yawning rift developed between mother and son. Sulking ensued, and years of swallowed ire started seeping out. The only time he calmed was when Elise sassed him with appalling flirtatiousness, or when Robert cajoled him, drove his small hands into Fuller's coat pockets in search of something sweet.

His first act of violence was against Leander's chair that had been nailed to the sloping roof above the porch. Fuller had heard the rumours, people saying that in a wispy fog, they could often see Leander's ghost perched there. Sometimes, they said, he'd nod cordially as a guest entered his home, reach a chalky hand out to welcome them. Since his death, he was seated above, watching over Stella and the youngsters like a good spirit would. But when Fuller moved in, the sightings changed. Leander was described as being on the edge of the chair, appeared ready to spring forward.

One evening, after he'd returned from working silently beside his mother at the general store, Fuller took Leander's ladder, and without a word, leaned it against the side of the house, hobbled up. Hammer in hand, he slammed the chair until it splintered, icicles exploded, legs and spindles rolled down off the roof, jabbing the snow drift below. Back and base cracked against a bent knee, jammed into the woodstove.

"This is the house of a shopkeeper now. No furniture maker lives here."

Stella wouldn't permit her mind to dawdle on every slight, every aggression. What would be the point? She already hated that part of herself, hated that she had let him in, and hated that she hadn't the courage to force him out. During those months of marriage, she went entirely limp, shocked into submission.

But there was one act that she had solidly locked in her memory. One unforgettable act. Whenever her mind spat up the secret end to their story, she used it as justification for her lack of action. Sometimes she wished she could bring herself to explain to Elise, but the words would never come. How could she tell her only daughter that she had stood idle while he died because of love for a dog? Justice for a dog.

Thumb out again. "I really want a dog, Nanny. Can you ask Mommy?"

"No, my treasure. I can't do that."

"Why not?"

"It would be better if you asked."

"I already did."

"And what did she say?"

"Keep dreaming. That's what she said."

"Oh."

"She said she had one when she was young, and it ran off. And I told her if I got my Ribsy, it won't never run off because I'll love it."

"And what did she say to that?"

"She said it don't make no difference. Dogs is dogs. And sometimes things run off. Even if you loves them. And she said that idn't nothing a youngster should know about."

"Oh." Stella marked her page with a finger, ran the other hand over her forehead.

"Did she have a dog?"

"Yes, we did. Once."

"Did it run off?"

"Ah." Stella swallowed, glanced at the doorway again. "That was a long, long time ago. Do you want me to read on?"

"Uh-huh. But can you tell the story like it's about me? Me and my dog Ribsy?"

The first time it happened was on her wedding night. As soon as she slipped into bed, Fuller rolled over on top of her, began to twitch his hips in a tormented manner. Immediately following, Harriet howled and banged her body against the bedroom door. Perhaps it was the sounds that came from Fuller's phlegmy throat or the stressed joints on the headboard. Whatever the reason, Harriet scratched and growled and knocked until Fuller tore out of the bedroom, long underwear still unbuttoned at the front, grabbed the dog by the fur between its shoulders, and kicked her out into a vicious sleet storm, gale force winds.

From that moment, Fuller developed instant hate for Leander's loyal sidekick. When Harriet came around the following morning, icy clumps dangling from her belly, Fuller looped dirty rope around her neck, secured her to the door handle on the shed. "That'll learn you." First sign of spring, and he built a wood and wire enclosure, lured Harriet in by dangling a scrap of meat, then latched the door with a quadruple knot, meat still in his fist. After a few weeks, Harriet had worn a three-inch groove in the dirt. Stella watched from the porch window. And for some uncomfortable reason, that continual pacing reminded her of her mother.

The growling and moaning were relentless, but only during the act. Sometimes, Stella would find herself coated in Fuller's aggravated sweat, and he would curse such a streak that she wished herself deaf. Moon or no moon, it was irrelevant. That dog knew what was happening inside the house, and needed to complain bitterly to heaven above.

Perhaps Fuller viewed this as a confrontation, Stella never knew. But one night during mid-summer, Harriet snarled nonstop, her growl like hailstones tumbling into the ocean. With alarming calmness, Fuller went to the porch and clutched the stabber. Earlier that day, Robert had fashioned the tool, several long nails driven through an old broom handle, and used it to kill flatfish down by the wharf. Fuller balanced the stabber, coated in slime and fish guts, on his shoulder and stepped lightly out to the wire enclosure. Peeling the roof off the structure, he reached his arm in, and stabber poised, whispering, "Come here, puppy." Fuller struck that dog over and over and over again. Noises that Stella couldn't even bear to conjure, cries that might erupt from a scalded child.

From that night on, Stella could only evoke partial images of Harriet. The thick fur of her legs, a pleasant curl in her tail, stripe of impossible white on her underbelly. But all memories of her head disintegrated. Whenever she thought of the dog, chasing gulls up and down the beach, racing beside Leander, licking Robert's sticky face, there was only a bobbing shadow where her head might have been. Layer upon layer, she had gradually willed it away. The crimson spatter, dislodged eye, blue jutting tongue, protective paw up. Gone. All washed clean. Harriet Edgecombe was no more.

Stella dug the grave herself, hid it from the children. When they returned from a night with Nettie and the cousins, she told them their father's dog had run away. Likely she was old, and ready to die. Yes. It wasn't fair. But sometimes dogs do that. Run off without warning.

They asked none of the obvious questions. Instead, Robert eyed his mother in a sideways glare, kicked the dirt, and wandered down towards the wharf. Elise darted over to Fuller, who was seated on the step of the stoop, his forehead like a storm at sea. She buried her face in the soft cotton of his shirt, steadied herself on his plump lap, arms looped around his neck. He placed one arm around her girlish waist, and through her tears, she smiled when he pressed a warm peanut butter kiss into her mouth.

"Mother?"

Stella looked up from the book.

"She's asleep. You can stop reading."

"If you don't mind, I think I'll finish."

"And why on earth would you do that?"

"I was enjoying the story."

"I can give you something better than a book about some kid and his stupid dog." Elise rolled her eyes. "You know, the older you get, the queerer you get. When will it end?"

The conclusion to their relationship was on the horizon. November 17, to be precise. They were not yet married a year.

Stella had been visiting Nettie when a wind rose up, hefty flakes patting the windows, tumbling down to the sill. By the time she was halfway home, she was practically blinded, moving through a million icy veils. Stopping just outside her gate, Stella looked upwards, eyes closed. The world made a slishing sound, as though a pair of unearthly scissors were cutting the sky away. She sensed the weight of the snow on her lashes, and for a romantic moment, she longed to stay there, gobbled up by the blizzard. But she could not give in to desire, plodded up the icy sheet of rock towards home.

When she reached the storm door with its wooden Z, her entire body looked as though she'd been rolled in flour. Behind her, the harbour had disappeared, Nettie's golden yellow house no longer glowed on the hill. Everything, save her small home, was gone, lost inside the storm.

Snow caked her coat and scarf, and dropped in mushy puddles around her feet when she stomped in the porch. Out of her boots, her feet felt naked and cold. She glanced about for her slippers. They were not by the woodstove, and she remembered placing them beside her dresser earlier as she'd tugged on a pair of woolen stockings. Stella rubbed stiffness from her neck, went to the hallway, but stopped short when she saw Elise rapping at her bedroom door.

"I wants to come in," Elise whispered, shoulder and head leaning against the frame.

Stella could not hear the response.

"Please?" Elise rolled ninety degrees so that her entire front was pressed against the door. Mumbling, then a giggle, and, "She won't. I knows she won't."

When Elise noticed Stella, she skittered across to her own room, quietly closed the door. Stella tore down the hall, rapped her fist against Elise's door, cried, "Don't you come out of there, miss. Don't you come out." Then she burst into her own room to find Fuller, squat overtop of a bucket, brown trousers around his ankles, suspenders draped across his thighs. As her reluctant eyes moved over him, she caught sight of his backside, the colour of death, and realized he was using the miniature wooden bathtub that Leander had made as an oversized chamber pot.

"What are you doing?" Her voice vibrated in her throat.

Twisted his neck around, shoulders still square. "What do it look like, maid? My business."

"But, that's a wash basin. For a baby."

"Don't see no babies 'round here. You got some stashed away or something?" He pulled his bottom lip in over his teeth. "What is you staring at?"

"My tub."

"For the love of Jaysus, I could get lost out there. Is that what you wants? Who in God's name would take care of the load of you?"

"I managed."

He chuckled now, and his backside pressed deeper into the tub, pair of fat dinner rolls squeezed. "We all seen how you managed. Acting like a mad woman down to the harbour trying to bust up the ice with a dull axe. Never seen such a sight in my life."

Stella could feel her heart beating behind her eyes, inside her jaw. "Elise. What did she want?"

"She's at me. At me all the time. I don't know what she wants. Ask her yourself."

Stella whipped up her slippers, clutched them to her chest. Face crinkled with the sour stench, and she strode to the door.

"Hey."

She stopped. Hand still on the doorknob.

"What."

"Arn Tuck brought in some steak to the store. Killed his cow. Made good on his credit."

"Oh."

"Cook it up right. I don't want to see no pink. If I sees pink, you'll be doing it again."

"I knows how to cook it."

"Pink meat'll kill you, you knows."

"Pink meat'll kill you," she repeated.

On the kitchen table Stella found a beige bowl, crackled glaze, chipped white plate over the top. Inside was a thick slab of meat, two-inch border of membrane and fat, pool of watery blood. She opened the door to the cellar stairs, retrieved the frying pan from the hook on the wall, an onion from the braided bundle dangling beside it.

Deep even breaths as she chopped the onion, leaned her eyes over top of it as excuse for a few tears. How had this happened? She knew, she knew, she knew. But it was so tough, insufferably tough to admit. She was afraid of Fuller. Right down to the inside of her bones. She was afraid of him.

Growing up with Percy and Amos, being married to Leander, they all allowed her to be strong and opinionated, encouraged her to fight back. Something of a luxury, this was now clear to her, as a single slap, a single fist pounding upon a table might have turned her inwards. But they often seemed amused with her snarkiness, came to expect it, even though it was all a ruse, a childish mask that covered her insecurity. Gradually, though, her insides were growing, fusing with that crisp outer shell of resilience. The woman she was had begun to transform into the woman she wore. All this, before she married Fuller. When the rules changed.

During that first night, she fought over the dog. Fought hard. But banging against him, she was nothing more than a bird striking a sunlit window. He never budged. Wouldn't listen. Her anger soon tempered into alarm when she looked in his eyes, something there, long fermenting, finally uncorked. Lips curling, teeth clenched, hand like a rake driving into her shoulder, he said slowly, as though to ensure proper communication, "I's the man of this house now. Don't. You. Ever. Cross. Me. You got no idea what I can do. No idea at all." And with those few words, he had plucked that mask from her reddened cheeks, exposed the frailty that lay beneath.

One Sunday after church, she had hinted to old Mrs. Hickey about the dire circumstances of the marriage. The farce of it. The continual undertone of aggression. (She would never admit that she was frightened.) But Mrs. Hickey dismissed her concerns, said tritely, "Contrary to popular belief, no union is picture perfect. Everyone's got their faults. You make your bed, then you lie in it." She stared down at the opal brooch pinned to her left lapel, ran her hands over her chest. "Besides, we all knows that poor man was under the thumb of his mother from the day he was born. A wife might expect a bit of belligerence, if you asks me. It'll die down."

"Die down?" Stella replied.

"Or die out. Whatever you says nowadays." Mrs. Hickey had unclipped the brooch, moved it to her right lapel, then hunched a little less, shook her gullet. "Now," she had said, eyes on Stella. "Don't that look better? 'Twas bothering me all service."

Stella stood in front of the stove, waited until a slice of fat pork sizzled, coating the pan in a thin layer of grease. Generous sprinkle of salt, and she laid the steak in the pan, fried and flipped, fried and flipped, until the meat was as tough as hardtack. Onion strewn over top of the meat, a final turn for good luck, and she dumped the entire works on a plate. Large glass of crimson Purity syrup and water beside it.

As always, Fuller pinched himself in around the back side of the table, chair pressed against the wall. He said eating made him hot, and he liked the coolness from the draft that came in around the window. Table pulled in just underneath his breasts, and Stella had to move the armchair around to the front of the table so that she could serve him his meal.

In the meager times that had descended upon the whole community, a steak was a rarity. Stella thought he might savour it, but he sawed enormous morsels, jammed them in his mouth, his cheeks. Talked around the ball of meat, even while his tongue floated in syrup. "I minds my mother saying to me, *I loves to see you eat.* Was one of her pleasures, I believes. Watching me poke food into my face. When she used to feed me as a youngster, she'd nearly throttle me though. Did I ever tell you that?"

Flat, "No."

"Well she did. Used to clap her hands together when I managed to swallow."

"Oh." Stella sat on the very edge of the daybed, hands folded on her lap. She had sewn her skirt from an old pair of Leander's tweed wool pants, and this gave her some sly pleasure, to know that Leander was covering her now.

"Fed me for years, she did. Years."

She stared at Fuller as he plowed through the plate-sized slab of meat, then looked away. How could he talk so cordially like that? Sharing quaint stories about his life as though the two of them were friends. Instead of corralled enemies. Stella never gave it much thought, only recognized that it was his unpredictability that made him dangerous. One moment, he was a lamb, next, a mammoth boar, trapped in an undersized pen. She did not care what pain was behind it all.

A sound from the table, a gasp of sorts, sudden suction, and she looked up at Fuller. His hands were coiled around his throat, temperature rising in his face. Eyes bulging, he reached for his drink, chugged a mouthful, but the candy red liquid shot out his nose, spattered on the cream-coloured tablecloth. He stomped his feet, shook his fists at her, then whacked the steak from its plate. Alistair Fuller was choking.

Up, he tried to rise. But he was squeezed in so tightly, he lifted two legs of the heavy table off the floor, and it knocked him backwards. He tried again, but in his panic, he was unable to free himself, and then he gripped the edges of the table, rolled his head, shook his head, banged his head against the window behind him. Threatened the glass.

Stella plugged her ears, sealed her eyes. In her mind, she tried to see and name every colour that she had ever seen. They flashed in rapid, vibrant succession. "Pink, rose, red, green grass, periwinkle, lavender, honey, honeycomb, white, white, pink, white, lilies, black, of course, can't forget black, pink, pink, blue, pink, pink. No more pink. Please, God, no more pink. I'll have to do it all over again." She shook, bent over at the waist, nose trying to catch any of the long lost scent of Leander in the fabric of her skirt. Nothing but fried fat and onion. Any moment, she thought she would feel fists on her, his roar in her ears. "Just go," she whispered. "Leave. Please, God. Make him leave." And that was all she had to say. After eternity, the banging stopped. The marriage bond dissolved. Only dead quiet in the kitchen.

Stella opened her eyes. Mound slumped on the kitchen table, hair like tufts of grass trying to escape the earth. Shards of broken plate scattered everywhere. Strings of onion stuck to the wall and rocking chair. She stood, tiptoed a few feet forward, bent down on a single knee. Resting on the worn floor in front of the sink was the steak. Motionless. True, at that moment, she had expected it to move. She watched as her white hand, strangely calm, reached out and lifted it. Then, with her other hand, she ran her fingers over the mark where grease had blemished the wood. And she stared at the shiny stain, this reminder, and knew it would never lift. Knew her floor was changed forever. It would never be clean again.

"Mother?"

Stella couldn't avert her eyes from the tall trees outside the window, the wind blowing through them, lifting whole heavy branches, letting them drop. They swayed and shuddered, moving towards her, then drawing back. She was certain the wind was searching for a voice, using the leaves for vibration, creating a set of organic vocal chords.

She didn't want to hear what it had to say. She would not listen. There were no words. Of any consequence.

"Mother?"

"Yes, dear."

"What were you doing, gone off into space like that? Looked like you was having a stroke or something." Fists jabbing her hips. "Well, not on my watch you won't. You can save that for when you visit Robert."

chapter fourteen

As she was driving her Rambler over the smooth pavement, Summer Fall Lane glanced at her watch. Mickey Mouse glanced back at her, his head cocked, skinny arms and fat white gloves locked in a five-after-one sideways cheer. Hurrah! The watch was a gift from her father, who now resided in Florida with his wife and her two daughters. His second wife. A woman he'd met at some sort of convention for the service industry. With little effort, she had stolen Summer's father away with the promise of fatter oranges, winters without dampness, a pancake breakfast any time of day or night. It didn't take much for him to transplant himself. A few words, some papers, a worn leather suitcase. A breath or two, and he was gone.

When Summer summoned an image of his face that last night, she could not recall the slightest hint of pain in his eyes or chin or forehead. She remembered the weather too, greedy winds, sheets of rain that distorted the headlights of his car as he backed down the drive. She thought the ferry might not leave port. Thought he might come back. But he never did, and she'd felt ashamed of herself for hoping, ashamed of waiting up just in case.

Out of habit, Summer shook her wrist, stared down at Mickey. The watch was broken, had been for a considerable while. But she never took it off. Even though she derived no pleasure from wearing it, she liked to believe she never dwelled on it either. That watch was just a habit. Nothing more.

Hand over hand, she turned her car (nicknamed Betty Blue) up a street, noticed a loose string hanging from the sleeve of her peasant blouse. Leaning forward, she caught the thread in her mouth, severed it with her teeth, spit it to the side. Her blouse was worn, practically falling apart, and this matched her brown corduroys, knees and backside about as strong as tissue paper. Her pants were held onto her skinny frame with a leather belt, so old and stretched that when it lay flat, it grinned. Though she wore these items frequently, her favourite article of clothes rested on the seat beside her: a crumpled navy pullover she had pilfered from a box at her grandmother's. It had once belonged to her Uncle Robert, she was told, and even though the elbows were nearing disintegration, she wouldn't think of giving it up. She sensed there was righteousness trapped inside the wool (righteousness being in short supply these days), and besides, wearing it made her feel invisible.

Though Summer was quite comfortable with her worn look, her mother never tired of complaining about it. "Couldn't you please, just this once, wear something decent?" "You look like a streel." "Who do you belong to? Surely to God 'tis not me." Whenever her mother's friends dropped by, Summer was shooed out the back door or down into her basement room. Occasionally Summer would sit on the top step, listen to the drivel, and close her eyes as she felt their superficiality drift past her. "Elise, darling, where is that curious daughter of yours?" "Oh,

Elise, darling, couldn't you coax her into trying on a little colour?" "So pale. My Jessie says she saw your Summer last week, and she was, well, looking more like winter thaw." They spoke of her as though her clothes and her clean white face were all that she was. All that she'd ever be.

Summer took one hand off·the wheel and held the end of her braid, felt the bound mass of split ends prick against her palm. How different they were, she and her mother. Difficult to believe they had once been joined together by a tough cord. While her mother struggled to isolate herself from any hint of blandness, Summer wanted nothing more than to twirl downwards, root herself, like a hardy tree. Her mother never seemed to crave attachment, while Summer lived with a nagging feeling that she was constantly soaring in someone's uncertain hands. And, at any given moment, that someone was going to let her go. Drop her. And she was going to fall, fall, fall, her life forever changed. She told her mother about feeling dizzy in the darkness, and her mother had curtly replied, "Nothing that fresh air won't cure. Why don't you try poking some of that into your lungs for a change?"

Summer pulled up in front of Sunray Towers, the apartment building where her grandmother lived. It was a brick structure, tall and sharp and boring, and her grandmother always called it Sardine Towers. "Because everyone lives on top of everyone else," she said.

One afternoon, when Summer had been high, she'd replied, "More like Celibate Towers. They might live on top of one another, but they don't do nothing."

And her grandmother had twittered, nudged her and replied, "You'd be surprised now. I sees all kinds of ladies coming and going to 316. A widower lives there."

Summer had stepped back, fingers to her chin. "I'm surprised you even know what that means, Nan."

"I haven't quite been around the block," her grandmother had whispered, glancing sideways, "but maybe I ventured out for a stroll once or twice."

Her grandmother shifted her feet in her thick-soled shoes, and that gave her away. She was embellishing, as she sometimes did for comic effect. And Summer loved her for it. Loved her more than any other person. "Christ, Nan. That would shock the ass off Mother. She'd have you whipped out of there, put in an all girls' old-age-home in jig time."

Summer's grandmother was a woman who surprised her frequently – with her openness, her quirky humour, her soft cool hands. Summer had often heard her mother say how frigid her grandmother was. Distant. Detached. Perpetually distracted. But, from Summer's perspective, nothing could be further from the truth. Many times Summer imagined that instead of sliding forth from her mother's womb, she had budded off the side of her grandmother. A human hydra. Taken a neater route from dark oblivion into life.

Inside the building, Summer pressed the back of her hand against her nose. Every Sunday, the hallways smelled the same – cabbage and boiled salt meat. Perhaps this heavy stench was a daily occurrence, but she was mostly there on Sundays. She tapped lightly on door 310, and as she listened for the sound of slippers shuffling over linoleum, she chewed on the end of her braid, touched the damp hair against her neck.

Stella Edgecombe grunted as she pulled open the door. She was dressed in black polyester pants, crisp white blouse, a necklace of unreasonably large glossy orange beads. "I swears," she whispered, "this door is getting heavier and heavier every day."

"It's a conspiracy, Nan," Summer whispered, leaning her bony backside against the door. "Every night they spray it with weighted paint. Just enough to make you question your own strength. Don't you be fooled now."

"I wouldn't be surprised in the least." Stella lifted her arm, sleeve moving upwards, stringy tendons in her wrist showing. "Time to come in? Something to eat?"

Summer's foot tapped and she ground the wet end of her braid in her fingers. "Nah. I got to stop off somewhere first. Shouldn't take more than a few minutes. And you know how your firstborn frowns on tardiness."

"All right, my dear. Let me get my coat."

Summer bowed. "Your chariot awaits, Nanny E."

On their way towards the still-sputtering car, Summer stopped, said, "Look at those flowers, Nan. I can't believe it. Already."

"I knows," she replied. "'Tis terrible. I can't even bear it. Frost is going to get them any night now. A touch of it'll kill a marigold. Don't they know that? 'Tis a sin, if you asks me. And an awful waste."

"Then why do they plant so early?"

"Well, folks is... Well, most don't buy green bananas, if you gets what I means. And as soon as the ground is soft, they wants a few flowers put in. They reckons they might be the last they ever sees." Stella shook her head, tut-tutted. "All I can do is think about them, half froze, waiting for some late shock of snow to finish them off. Queer, but it makes me right upset."

Summer yanked open Betty Blue's passenger door for Stella, helped her slide into the seat. Then she went around to the driver's side, put the car in gear, and drove down the second half of the semi-circle driveway. As she passed the raised beds, she considered the fate of the flowers and how they would look most striking when suspended in frost. A single moment of absolute sanctity. They would have that, at least. But when sunlight touched them, they would wither almost instantly. She decided against mentioning this to her grandmother.

They drove several minutes in silence, Summer humming along with the scratchy radio, her grandmother staring out the window. Bands of sunlight bent through the windshield, making the two women squint. "Days are getting longer," Summer said as she flicked down her visor.

"That they is. 'Tis awful welcome after that winter we had."

"Some bright, the sun. That colour."

"You don't like that colour? Do you think this necklace is all right? Jane sent it to me. I reckoned I should wear it at least once. Get some use out of it."

"No, no." Summer glanced over. "It's fine."

"All right. I weren't sure. Maybe it's too young for me. Too shiny. I should give it to you."

Summer laughed. "Sure, Nan, you're still plenty young. Got lots of spark. Sparks coming off you left and right."

"That I allows."

Summer drove out of the city, onto beaten roads where the pavement fell away from the sides in chunks. "We're going to be late," she said. "But not by much, if I hurry." Foot hovering above the brake, Summer eased Betty down a steep hill, wall of solid rock on one side, drop to nothingness on the other. Around a final turn, and they came upon a small community, pink and blue and yellow box homes, every window reflecting the sun as it dipped into the ocean. Dust billowed up around the car, crept in through unseen holes.

"Almost there," Summer said, quick cough, and she turned into the driveway beside a darkened house. "You okay to wait?"

"I...I guess so, maid."

"You can listen to whatever you want," she said, motioning towards the radio. "Just press those buttons. Don't go nowhere and don't talk to no strangers." Summer laughed lightly, then stepped out, and slammed the door. As she walked past a chained dog, in a frenzy now of yips and squeals, she paused, clapped her thigh, called, "Hi Precious. I know, my puppy, you want to be free. Don't we all."

Instead of going to the front of the house, knocking at the dented screen door, Summer strode around the back, towards a shed with peeling paint, a flat roof, hazy light over a black door. How many times had she been here since she'd met James and Scott? Summer couldn't count, and she would never admit to another the reason why she kept coming back. James and Scott were not friends, instead she viewed them as leeches. Draining her.

After the let-down of her conversation with her mother, she had told her grandmother about the vertigo, her fear of plunging downwards. Confided about her sensation of being suspended, thick hands gripping her waist, twisting and turning her as though she were a human airplane. And how Summer was teetering there, uncertain. "You won't let that happen, will you, Nan? Won't let me strike – strike bottom?" She had expected her grandmother to reassure her, as she often did when Summer was a child. Say something along the lines of, "Of course not, honey. I'd catch you right up." But, instead, she was quiet for a while, stared at nothing, then replied solidly, "Sometimes you just got to let yourself go."

She took her grandmother's words to heart. Spending time in this shed with James and Scott, she was slowly descending downwards, easing her body through an ocean of broken promises, feeling the edges of wasted potential. Letting herself go in the only way she knew how. And it was comfortable there, scraping away at the bottom, picking at all of her loose threads. Keeping herself on the floor, she felt safe. There was nowhere to go. Nowhere to fall. In this place that smelled of rot, thick with blue smoke and roaming hands, her emptiness was verified and coated, and what blood she had left had no other purpose than to move in a circle, holding her steady. Holding her still.

Telling herself she would only stay a moment, she lifted the latch, and disappeared inside.

Stella angled her watch towards the dim light, squinted at it. A thin silver band, delicate face, single diamond below the twelve like a twinkling third eye. The watch had been one of the less practical but more appreciated gifts from her daughter-in-law Jane. In recent years, the "tone" of her Christmas parcels from Toronto had changed. Blouses and smart shoes had turned into pajamas and bathrobes. Scented salts replaced bath oil. Without fail, each box contained a fresh package of no-slip flower stickers that were to cover the bottom of her tub. One year, Stella had adored a lovely pair of slippers, cream coloured with criss-crossing golden thread, but the accompanying note, heralding their no-slip rubber soles, had tarnished them completely.

The light was scant, and with the miniscule numbers, Stella couldn't tell the time. She wasn't certain how long she'd been waiting, though it felt like a good hour or more. Sunlight had evaporated, and the bit of glow from the shed cast long lonely shadows. She could hear passersby, their crunching footsteps in the road behind the car, but when she twisted to see, no one was there.

Stella glanced about. In the driveway, there were potholes in the earth large enough to hide a wheel. The fence was half falling down, and every third or fourth picket missing. The skinny dog that had recognized Summer now stood motionless on the porch, hackles raised, staring at Stella, and before the light had evaporated, she'd noticed the grimy rope holding it was unraveling. From that point on, she gripped the door handle, fearing the door might fall open if she let go. Inadvertently offering "Precious" an invitation to a meal of porous bones.

After what felt like hours, the dog lay down. Cars passed up and down the lane in front of the house, but the dog didn't budge, never even lifted an ear. Stella unhooked her fingers from the door handle, rubbed her palm over the glass face of her watch. She would have to go and find the child. Go to that shed and enter through the dimness beneath the crooked awning. Walk in the muck in her Sunday shoes. Straight past that dog.

She eased open the door of the car, but the shriek of dry metal hinges alerted the dog, and he was up again, waiting. Harriet came to mind then. Harriet and her thick fur disguising a trim body, her sharp teeth, claws like talons. An imposing figure she cut, but Harriet was a baby. Perhaps Precious was the same. Sometimes appearances were deceiving.

Slowly, Stella moved up the driveway without looking sideways at the dog. And it never budged, never burst free from its rope, galloping towards her, taking her thin ankle into its mouth. As was so often the case, her fears weren't warranted, and she felt that increasingly frequent wave of foolishness drape over her shoulders. She reached the side of the house. Precious was about to disappear from view, and when Stella turned, a light came on over the front porch and she was able to see the dog from another angle. One that revealed a taut abdomen, fur pulled over flaring ribs. Her fear transformed into pity, and she dug her hand into her purse, retrieved a Cherry Blossom bar, tore off the wrapper and tossed it within the dog's reach. He was on top of it in an instant, and the chocolate was gone.

As Stella moved down the slight incline towards the shed, her shoes sank into the mud, each step making a sucking sound. The air smelled of decomposing garbage. Springtime had taken over, was making short work of the trash discarded during the winter months, and the wind was reluctant to pick up the odour and move it. When she reached the shed, her heart began to beat, and for a moment, she placed her hand against the wooden door, felt the dampness in her palm.

She knocked. "Summer, you in there? Summer?" Music moved out through the walls, and she could hear voices, a mixture of high and low, slow cadences. "Summer? It's your Nan."

At once, Stella felt silly again. 'Tis only young folks courting, she thought, and she pushed the door open, stepped inside without hesitation. Her breath caught, and she stared from one confusing corner to the next. She tried to find her granddaughter in the heavy air, but it was like searching for a beloved animal in a slaughter house.

From the ceiling, a lone flickering bulb hung, inconsistent electricity surging through the wires. The walls were covered with posters. One depicted a man with a bare upper body, skinny arms outstretched. Another showed a dark-skinned man, hugging a guitar, hair like a halo of chaos around his distorted face. A back door was propped open with a thick stick, and on the stoop outside, a hibachi smoked, pieces of burnt meat feeding a steady stream of dead air into the shed. Unlit candles jammed into wax-coated bottles stood on uneven shelves. High-pitched laughter erupted from two skinny girls, clutching each other in a corner, while two skinny boys (she couldn't fathom that they might be men) moved around them like feral creatures. On the opposite side, near the back door, another girl, leaning against a wall, rolled her body one way, then rolled back again, wailing or singing, Stella couldn't tell. In the middle of the room, a boy lay next to a hole in the floor, piece of soggy pressboard moved aside, what looked like vomit gliding out of his jerking body.

"Summer Lane?" Her granddaughter's very name did not belong in this place, let alone the girl herself.

Music moved through the smoke, sharp and jagged, in a tune Stella could not describe, though the very sounds made her feel as though there was something wrong with her heart muscle, the tendons in her thighs. "Summer?" Louder, this time, and Stella's dry voice cracked.

Squinting, she saw her. Recognized her shape, her shoulders. Against the back wall, Summer was sprawled on a collapsing chesterfield, torn piece of blanket beneath her dozing head. Upon seeing Stella, a boy seated next to her removed his hand from her upper leg, then reached up with a bare foot and tried to twist the volume of the stereo down with his toes. Music diminished, and he nudged Summer, then lay his head back, closed his eyes.

"Huh?"

"Summer," Stella yelled.

Summer stumbled across the room, fell into her grandmother, then righted herself.

"Summer, I've been waiting this long while."

Summer looked up at Stella, then held out her bent arm, looked at her wrist. "Sure, I haven't been not more than a minute. Look. Not a minute passed. Look." She showed Stella her Mickey watch. "Are you sure you're not talking about another time, Nan? Waiting for someone else?"

"No, honey. Are you ready? I'm–" Words cut short when she noticed the boy on the floor moving, his hand reaching out, fingers crawling closer to Summer's shoe.

"Summer, mind your foot. Is he okay?"

"Couldn't be better," she said, kicked his hand away. "Ran out of seats, is all."

"Ah, ladieth," he slurred. Up on his knees, then on his feet, he swayed once, twice, then stepped towards Stella, rubbed his hands up and down his dirty shirt, fabric a repeat of whimsical cowboys with miniature guns. Bang, bang. "Wanna a drink, Dolly?"

"No thank you, sir." Stella's arms locked across her chest. "I's quite fine."

"C'mon, Dolly. Danth wit me." His eyes were slits in raw goose skin, front teeth missing.

He leaned in, breath like bitter tea and curdled milk, and grabbed her around the waist, transferring his unsteadiness onto Stella's sore left hip. Stella twisted, and her arm jolted, thumb catching in her necklace, thread breaking on her beads, orange baubles dancing everywhere.

"Ah, shit," Summer said. "Shitity shit. Look, you fucker, look what you did." She shoved him, and he fell backwards, rolled on his side, holding his stomach and giggling.

"Ah c'mon ladieth. Danth. Love me." Flat on his back now, he lifted his hips off the floor, once, twice, moaned, slurred, "Fff-uh-uh-uh-uck." Then, with blackened nails, he scraped one of the bright beads off the grimy floor, shoved it into his mouth, crunched down hard as though it were a jawbreaker. Within seconds he spat the bead out, and it bounced against Stella's calf, rolled away. "My tooth," he cried, laughed, cried, "My ff-uh-uh-cking tooth."

Summer moved closer to him, but Stella clutched her elbow, said, "Never mind, never mind. Let's just go."

On their way back to the car, Summer lurched, caught herself, then lurched again. Stella picked her way slowly through the muck and the pebbles, eyes locked on the car, but when she came around the corner, she glanced at Precious. Curled in a ball and sleeping. Poor dog. No wonder it's as surly as it is.

"I'm gonna get you new beads, Nan. I'm gonna do that for you. I'm gonna, I swears. If I got to thumb it all the way to Toronto to get 'em."

"That's the last thing I wants now, is new beads. Believe you me. The very last thing."

When Summer stopped to look at her, Stella had to avert her eyes, would not be able to disguise her dismay. Summer swayed again. And this time, as she watched her granddaughter in her peripheral vision, she reminded Stella of someone. Not so much the balance dance, but it was something else. Perhaps the tottering of the head. Or her arms, maybe, elbows bent, hands, fingers slightly curled. It was the way they were held out in front of her, as though she was reaching for something. Something that kept moving away as her granddaughter walked towards it.

"What was you doing in there? All that time."

Weakly, "Talking."

"Talking?"

"Yes, Nan."

"About what, for God's sakes? Lordy, Lordy. Whatever happened to a cup of tea at a proper table?"

Summer backed Betty Blue down the driveway, narrowly missing a gate that swung slightly on its hinges, even though there was no breeze. Stella stared at the house as it receded, and it did not look happy. Clusters of shadows, grey patches emerging underneath peeling pinkish paint. Even though it was inhabited, the house appeared empty, lonely, troubled, no doubt, by activities taking place within its walls. When they converged in her view, the fence pickets looked like thin rotten teeth. A final peek at the house, and the windows were now black. Stella wondered if someone were standing there, disguised by darkness, watching them leave.

Once they reached the high road, Stella sighed. Though she didn't enjoy traveling in a car, she was glad to be moving away from that community into which they'd descended. Summer was speeding and swerving on the road, and when Stella noticed the sharp drop just outside her window, she said, "Do you want to pull over?"

"No," Summer replied. "Not now. I'm good."

"We'll both be good if we goes over the edge. We can say that to Saint Peter when he asks us."

Summer braked slightly, leaned forward, squinting when headlights came upon her, horns blaring. As they reached the outskirts of St. John's, she relaxed in her seat, turned up the radio. Jammed her forefinger on the tabs, channels hiccupping, music finding its way. A voice arrived in the car, and he sang words that made Stella's lips turn downwards. "Ooooh, the time to hesitate is through, there's no time to wallow in the mire..."

"I like the Doors," Summer said flatly. "I like his voice."

"Sounds like his head is stuck inside a fishing cask, if you asks me."

Summer giggled quietly. "Oh, Nan."

"Who on earth would want to sing something like that? Or who would want to listen to it?"

"It's hard to explain why. It just...it just pushes my soul closer to the surface."

"Well, my soul can stay right where it is." Stella reached up and flicked the volume button counterclockwise. "My soul idn't in no rush to be pushed."

Summer giggled again. "Woman, how did you get to be such a card?"

Outside the window, Stella noted the return of the rows of houses, the sidewalks, the occasional burst of forsythia illuminated by a streetlight. Though Bended Knee never looked like this, she had grown used to the square order of the city, and took great comfort in it. Everything had its proper place.

"Why," Stella said, putting her fingers up to touch her side window. "Why on earth would you ever go to such a place?"

"I don't know, Nan. It's no good, you don't have to tell me. I know that's what you're thinking."

"Beyond that, honey. I've seen a lot of stuff in my day. I've lived through two wars. I've known good men to destroy themselves with the drink and God only knows what else." Her voice trailed off. "Ah," she half-snarled, "I'm not one to preach. Never was, and I don't mind to start now."

Summer never spoke for several minutes. Then, she said, "It makes me feel better."

Gently, "Better than what, honey?"

"Better than I do."

"How do you feel then?"

"Like a book with all its pages torn out. Two covers." Gulping sound. "Hollow."

Stella looked over at Summer as she slowed the car at

a stop sign. Robert's old sweater hung off her arms, and her shoulders were thin like sickles. Stella remembered holding her, that first time in the nursery. Something blocked the light from entering the window, thick spruce growing outside, maybe bulky curtains inside. She couldn't recall, though she did have a clear memory that the room was poorly lit. Full of shadows. And that Summer was nearly weightless in the heaviness of the room. Swallowing her. Stella remembered how, with no concrete reason, a sadness had crept into her heart. To this day, it lingered still whenever she looked upon her granddaughter.

"Do you want to stop somewhere for an ice cream?"

"Oh, Nan," Summer replied, reaching up to hold her braid. "I don't know whether to laugh or cry at you half the time. I swear you think ice cream is a cure-all."

"It usually goes with happy times." Her brother Amos arrived in her mind then, how he'd brought her to Old Man Morgan's back step, handful of children already there, waiting for a spoonful of ice cream made from the last chunk of ice found in the sawdust. Stella looked down at her hands, blinked.

"Maybe another time, all right?" Then, as they neared the turn-off for Elise's house, Summer moaned, "I don't think I can do that tonight either. Do you want me to drop you?"

"Drop me off?"

"Yeah. I just can't listen to it tonight. Yammering on about petty bullshit. Hair dye and bottled moose."

"They'll probably miss us."

"Mother and her friends? They'll miss me now, like they'd miss a wart on their backsides. Only something to complain about. And you? No offense, Nanny E, but you are just a required invitee."

A short unintended “Hm” darted from her throat. Stella coughed lightly, said, “Well, I guess there’s no harm in it. Us carrying on like we is.”

Summer pressed down on the gas, looking at Stella now, shaking her head. “How come I knew you were going to say that?”

“Watch the road, honey,” Stella said, wagging her finger at the windshield.

“We’re just so damn alike, Nan. Believe it or not. Twins born fifty-odd years apart.”

“Now, now. You’re way too young to be old like me.”

“You’re not old in your head, Nan.”

Images of the scene inside that shed burst onto Stella’s inner eye, and she winced at her own discomfort, said, “Oh, I believes I’m plenty old in the head. Old-fashioned.”

After criss-crossing streets aimlessly for an hour, Summer made her way down along the water. Stella watched the men walking away from the hulking boats, foreign words printed across great rusting hulls. On the opposite side of street, two women traipsed up and down the sidewalk, wobbly heels, skirts too short for the damp spring weather. Summer turned up a steep side street, past a handful of houses clinging to sheer rock, and then began the lazy ascent up Signal Hill. She parked at the very edge of the lot, away from the handful of other cars with chugging motors, steamy windows.

“Do you want to take a walk?”

“I suppose,” Stella said, as she hoisted herself from the seat. “Not too far though. I don’t trust my legs on wet grass. Especially so when cliffs and waves is involved.”

They made their way along a well-worn path, stopped near the end of a low rock wall, sat down side-by-side facing the ocean. Summer stretched, removed the bands securing her hair, and undid her braids. Watching her, Stella reached up to touch her own curls. Earlier fluffed with a plastic pick, they had now returned to their orderly sausage rows. Dampness would do that to a style. And dampness was readily available. Moss-covered rocks and earth beneath her felt almost swollen with moisture, and wisps of fog crept inwards, splaying and scattering distant lights. Lonely horns, begging for a dry day, cried out to anyone who might listen.

"It's all so sad," Summer announced.

"What's that, honey?" Stella crossed her feet at the ankle.

"Life. So sad."

"There's good times too. Got to think of those."

"Don't you find everyone is desperate? Even those horns sound desperate. Don't you think, Nan?"

Stella nodded slightly, shivered as the rock released some of its cold agony up through her sloping spine. "I do. Sometimes I do too. Think that."

"Why is it? Why does everyone bang up against each other, then act like they don't even feel it?"

"I don't know, honey. I wish I could tell you, but I don't."

Simple laughter. "That's one thing I know about you, Nan E. You won't lie to me, even when it's harder to tell the truth."

"I try. With you. Though I'm not very good at it."

"Well, you're better than any other person I know. Lots better."

Stella pursed her lips slightly, not sure whether to frown or smile.

"What do you think they're doing now?"

"Who?"

"Mother and her friends?"

"Oh, I don't know. Eating dinner?"

"Ah, c'mon. Something better than that. Guess."

"I'm not much one for guessing."

"Well, I bet they're talking about me. What a waste I am. How Margo's daughter's about to become a teacher. Probably win some stupid awards. Impact the future generation of our province and all that shit. Poor kids."

"I doubts that, honey. Your mom wouldn't do that."

"Pouff." Summer shot air from her mouth, knotted her fingers together. "I reckons you stayed in that shack a little too long, Nanny E."

Stella reached around and put her hand on Summer's shoulder. The entirety of Summer's shoulder bones could be cupped in Stella's hand. "At least I likes to think she wouldn't. You two are black and white."

"That's an understatement."

"Well."

"I think about Mom sometimes, you know. How could she be the way she is when she had a mother like you?"

"I don't know, maid. We all lives our own lives."

"You know, she never tells me a single thing. I ask her about stuff, and she says it's none of my concern."

"She might some day."

"I doubt it. She's all sealed off."

"I'm sure she don't mean to be. I know she cares about you."

"I think she got secrets, Nan. Lots of them."

"Most folks do."

"I think she's a bee box."

Stella fastened the top button of her coat, shivered. "What's that?"

"A bee box. I was reading this poem this woman wrote,

talking about how she ordered herself up a bee box. A box filled with bees, buzzing up a storm."

"Now that's a bit queer. Never saw nothing like that in the catalogue. What sort would ever want such a thing?"

"I don't think it's real. I think she was talking about all the bees that live inside her. All locked up tight inside this lovely perfect box. So nice on the outside, but swarming on the inside. She thinks an awful lot about her bees, and she's trying to convince herself of stuff, and she's going to let them out, even though they'll probably sting her real bad. I don't think she's got much choice about it. Or else the sound'll torture her."

"Hmmm. I don't go in much for poetry, I'm afraid."

"Ah, neither do I, Nan. I might've read it all wrong. I just wonder about her sometimes."

"And I reckons she wonders about you too, honey."

"I doubt that."

After several moments, Stella replied, "Sometimes a mother might find it hard to love someone who is so different from herself. Love them out in the open. Love them like the other one needs to be loved." She waited for a moment for Summer to react, but Summer never did. And Stella wondered if she'd actually said those words out loud, or if only her mind had spoken. "It idn't easy."

"Why did you leave?"

"Leave where?"

"Bended Knee. Why did you leave your home? All those memories?"

"Seemed like a good idea at the time. And Nettie's here."

"I picture it, you know, and it all seems so quaint. That life that you had. Knitting and gardening. Puttering around. Making bread. Two small children."

"It wasn't always so lovely. There was hard times too. Plenty of them."

"Even being widowed. Working to raise your family. There's charm in that."

Stella stifled a laugh. "If only I had of known that then. Might have made things easier."

"Oh, Nan. I didn't mean no offence. It's just like something out of a book. Nothing like I know."

"Well, you growed up without a father, too, in some ways."

"It's different though. Mom gets her cheque the first of every month."

"There's still struggle. Maybe not so obvious."

"Hey, remember that first time I ran away from home?"

"And I found you."

"And you asked me if I was coming home, plain and simple, and I said, 'No. I'm going to live here forever.'"

"Yes, you had your mind set. Living in a swamp. Why did you run away again?"

"I haven't a clue. Only thing I remember is the feeling of the warm muck on my bare feet. You told me I looked like a motherless kitten kneading a blanket with my toes."

"Did I say that? Lord, you've got a mind like a steel trap."

"Yup. I never forgot it. 'Cause I felt motherless a lot of the time. And somehow you knew it. You saw it. Like it was written on me or something."

"Ah. I was probably just trying to lure you back is all. Perhaps I should've offered cookies."

"Mmm. The mind job was all right too."

"Oh, honey," Stella said. "Try to think about sweet things."

"Sweet things."

"Not things that are going to tangle you up inside. Taking God-only-knows how long to straighten out."

"I guess you're right, Nan. No point dwelling on that."

"That's the spirit."

"Too much other stuff to dwell on." Summer jumped up, shoulders hunched. "Do you want to go back to the car?"

Stella eased off the rock, and her body felt as though the rock were reluctant to let her go. Bones and joints and muscles stiff. "If I can make it."

They back-tracked to the car, and Summer gripped Stella's arm to guide her in the pitch black that coated them.

"Nan, you're like a chunk of ice. Should we go get some chips and gravy?"

"Cup of hot tea?"

"Chips and gravy and hot tea. It's a date."

They reached the car, and Summer twisted the key, patted the dashboard when the sputtering settled into a gentle hacking. "Good old Betty Blue. Knows when to kick up a stink. Knows when to come through." Summer adjusted the volume on the radio, pressed buttons, said, "Ooo, I love this one too. Bob Dylan."

"Oh my." Stella put her hand to her cheek. "Sounds like a rusty screen door."

Summer looked over at Stella, said, "One thing, Nan. Before we leave."

"Go ahead."

Summer got out of the car, came around to Stella's side, and opened the door. She held out her hands. "Will you dance with me?"

Stella laughed, shook her head. "My Lord. Second invite tonight."

"Well?"

"No, no, my dearie. I'm far too old to dance. I haven't danced a step since I was your age."

"Please, Nanny? I swear I won't make fun."

After a moment, "Do you promise to stop tormenting yourself over nothing?"

"I can only say I'll try," Summer replied, and helped Stella out of the car.

"All right then, but none of that old funny stuff. Just something slow and respectable."

Dome light spilling out onto the wet pavement, Summer took Stella's dry hand in hers, hugged her, and guided Stella around in gentle circles. "I'm sleepy and there is no place I'm going to."

"Take it easy, maid. Not too fast with me."

"Then take me disappearin' through the smoke rings... foggy ruins of time..." Humming now.

"Oh my, honey. Folks'll think we belongs in a mental institution."

"Who gives a rat's ass?"

"Well, now. I don't suppose no one does."

"Nanny E, can you promise me something?"

"If I can, sweetie."

Summer rested her head on Stella's shoulder, the crisp fabric of Stella's coat creasing Summer's face. "Don't ever die, all right? Don't ever leave me."

"I'll do my best, Summer. My best is all I can do."

And as they turned, Bob crooned, "...in the jingle jangle morning I'll come followin' you."

Her friends had left, plates and glasses were washed, and the leftover chicken tomato casserole was completely cold. Quite late, that was all she knew, though Elise wasn't certain of the time. On the wall behind the dining table was a large gold-coloured sun, pointed rays, gently ticking clock for a face. But, the shaft of light from the street lamp fell just below the numbers, and in the dimness, she couldn't make out the hands. For some reason, she did not want to rise from her spot, perched on the slender arm of a high-back chair, and look.

Most days, Elise tried to avoid thinking about Summer. Thinking about all the ways she had gone wrong with her daughter. Thinking about how different they were. But tonight, she couldn't sleep, and even though she'd had three ounces of cognac, the thoughts could not be kept at bay.

To begin with, she had rushed into marriage. There was no doubt about that. After leaving Bended Knee, life in St. John's wasn't how she'd imagined it at all. Grace, Nettie's daughter, was about as exciting as three-bean-salad, though she did help Elise get a job as a maid. Room and board and light meals were included, but the extra money was not enough to afford the hairclips and the dresses and the burgundy round-toed shoes that she craved. Still, she managed to fritter away her monthly allowance on what Grace curtly called "non-essentials." And after several years of going nowhere, Elise turned her attention to her employer's unmarried eldest son. Joseph was shy and stern, but it took only a month of working her charms. Then, they were caught by Mrs. Lane in a compromising situation involving her perennial garden, pink phlox, a mound of crushed goldenballs that had been in full bloom. She encouraged her son to marry posthaste. "For decency's sake."

At first Elise was proud of her small bungalow, proud to be the wife of a supermarket manager, proud of strolling with her daughter. Early on, Joseph had given her permission to purchase a pair of red shoes, but they scuffed easily, and the heels wore down with her walking. He told her to make do. Make do with the shoes. Make do with the table set. Make do with her wardrobe of outdated clothes. Gradually she felt bored by it. Yes, bored. And she became acutely aware of everyone else around her: the women who had more, and nicer, and the men who held the door for her, smiled. She knew those men sensed her ability to stray before she even acknowledged it. She wondered if there was a smell to it, clinging to her. A wanton smell, rising up from dissatisfaction.

The garden hose finally did her in. Of course that might sound silly, but it was the truth. She had been planting marigolds in the backyard, needed to water her orderly bed, and she picked up the hose with one hand, twisted the spigot with the other. On her palm, she felt the water rushing through, one amazing pulse, a sputter, another amazing pulse. The entire green snake coming alive right in her hand. With that, she felt such an overwhelming sense of arousal that she dropped the hose, water still gushing, and started walking towards Tucker's Grocery. She pretended to herself that she would wait for Joseph in his cramped office, but now she could admit that she knew Joseph would not be there. Instead, she marched straight into the stockroom, leaned her back against the door, reached her hands up behind her and flicked the lock. Six months before, Mr. Tucker had hired the blond-headed teenaged son of a friend to organize the shelves, and the boy always winked at Elise as she tossed the cans in her cart from one hand to the other, and up onto the checkout table. In the storeroom, Elise could smell cardboard and dust. She could hear her own breathing. And she could hear the promise of a blond boy rustling packages behind a dimly lit shelf.

That had been a mistake. Elise knew it. Her A-line skirt hiked up around her waist, back pressed against a splintery shelf, canned goods tumbling, rolling across the floor. It was heady business for several passionate moments, but the boy stomped out any afterglow when he smirked at her, uttered, "Christ, man, you're old enough to be my freaking mother."

In some divine form of intervention, Mr. Tucker, a bachelor, died shortly thereafter, and left that store (and four others) to Joseph. Their lives became more comfortable, and Elise learned to be much more discreet in her dalliances. When Joseph came to her one drizzly November evening, told her he was selling the stores, moving to Florida, she felt betrayed. Cheated upon. How dare he? Abandon her and her daughter. He stared at her, eyes like a dead fish's, and said, "Don't be dramatic. You abandoned us years ago." He had wanted to take Summer, begged for the child, but Elise had refused. Wanted to hurt him. No court would ever listen, she assured him of that, and he exited her life as quietly as he had come into it.

Elise was the only one of her friends who was divorced. They pretended to envy her when they came by for coffee, the freedom of choice that was now available, but still, Elise knew, they would never switch places. There were plenty of romances over the years – shallow encounters, a few months or even a year of meaningful dates – but in the end, they never progressed past a certain point. Two men had wanted to marry her, but she couldn't manage it. Discovered that being alone, being untethered, suited her just fine.

Elise smiled sardonically at herself. How come she had started out thinking about her daughter, and ended up thinking about herself? What does that say about a mother? "It doesn't say very much." Elise's voice sounded hollow in the darkness. She didn't want to concede that such a pattern of thought was the standard.

Elise pulled across the sheer in the window, pinched the fabric behind the bend in her knee, and watched the road. Where were they? The two of them, grandmother and granddaughter. Out having a good time. Having a good laugh at Elise's expense, no doubt. Their bond seemed so easy, and witnessing it made Elise almost nauseated with envy. Though when she saw them next, she would not let on that she was even bothered by their absence. By the snub.

She let the sheer fall away, once again covering the window. Early morning light was beginning to open the room, and Elise stood abruptly, knocked over the cigarette stand. The green glass tray tumbled out of its holder, and ashes and butts spilled across the cream-coloured carpet. She stared at the mess for a whole minute, decided to clean it in the morning. Without glancing out the window again, Elise turned and walked towards her bedroom. The clock on the wall was illuminated. But she did not look to see the time. She didn't want to know.

Eldred Wood. That was who.

The name came to Stella when she was making her way along Water Street, on a slow stroll with Nettie Rose. They stopped for a moment in front of F. J. Hines Piano Shop, and Stella was reminded of that old man who would play piano when she was a young woman in Bended Knee. She remembered how he would wander up and down the laneway, tripping over his feet, hands awkwardly positioned in front of him, fingers bent over eighty-eight invisible keys.

Stella shook her head. How strange to see a connection between two completely unrelated people.

"Did you want a cup of tea?" Nettie asked. "We could rest a spell, have a cup of tea."

"We just had one," Stella replied. "Not ten minutes past. I can still taste it on my tongue."

Nettie smacked her lips. "Oh."

Stella glanced up at the sky. Above the buildings, a clump of birds in flight wavered this way and that. Gusts of wind coming off the harbour, trying to force them apart, and they struggled to keep together. Keep their formation.

She took Nettie's hands in hers. "All right then. A cup of tea."

"Yes," Nettie replied. "That's just what I was thinking."

"No harm in having another, maid. Have another drop, and talk about things long past."

chapter fifteen

These days, Stella wondered if her friend could even hear her. If she understood the stories, the descriptions of life outside the home, the one-sided banter. Nettie Rose's only response, in the form of an occasional deep swallowing, came whenever Stella mentioned Bended Knee. And Stella liked to believe that Nettie was truly listening, that the swallowing was a sign of happy emotions welling up, nearly throttling her.

Two and a half years ago, Nettie moved out of Sunray Towers and became a permanent resident of Pine Ridge Retirement Home. At first, when Stella visited, they participated in the summer-camp-type crafts together, or sang happy songs during piano time. Gradually though, Nettie stopped interacting, and she and Stella would pass a visit by sitting and watching two episodes of *Three's Company*. Nettie squeezed Stella's hand, her eyes glowing, whenever Jack came flitting across the screen.

After nine months or so, Nettie no longer sat next to Stella during television time, and instead, she snuggled into a heavily wrinkled fellow resident, a man whose face and fingers were yellowed from cigarettes. While Stella looked on, Nettie rubbed the man's bony knee, patted the ducktail of hair at the back of his scalp, and called him Amos. Occasionally, Stella tried to separate them, have a proper visit with Nettie, but she was met with irritated rejection. "Like two peas in a pod," one nurse had commented. "Can't keep those two lovebirds apart. That happens. Amos was her husband, I take it?" Before responding, Stella had to clear the bitterness suddenly lodged in her throat. "Yes," she'd said. "Yes, he was." The lie grated at her. Such a silly effort to preserve Nettie's dignity. So that the staff at Pine Ridge wouldn't label her lifelong friend as an over-the-hill tart.

Though Stella had the good intentions of visiting frequently, her trips to Pine Ridge soon became sporadic. Nettie no longer seemed to recognize her, no longer seemed even to want her there. Weeks went by, and Stella tried to tell herself that her presence made no difference. The Nettie that she knew was already gone. The Nettie that now existed preferred to rest her head on the shoulder of a stranger who felt familiar only because the mass of wires housed within the thin bones of her skull were snarled beyond.

In recent weeks, Nettie was bedridden, sharing a rectangular room with another woman nearly every hour of the day and night. Other than the occupants, everything about the two women's living space was identical. Same sheets, same Hudson Bay striped wool blanket, same convenient rollaway table for the now uneaten meals, card games that never happened. Above their beds, each had a corkboard covered in thumb-tacked snapshots, fat-cheeked baby portraits, daughters and sons, black-and-white of the late husband. For some time Stella pondered the significance of that corkboard. Placed in such a position that even the most youthful and agile of necks would be unable to twist and view the contents. Perhaps, Stella reasoned, the corkboard was not there for the sick. Instead, it served as a pictorial reminder to staff and visitors that these women were so much more than a wrinkle in the bed. They were part of a family. They were loved by all the smiling shiny faces captured there.

Pine Ridge was spotless. Not a hair in the corners, floors gleamed, and if Stella chose to, which she did not, she could have seen her reflection in the fingerprint-free windows that faced the parking lot. A good place for Nettie. She was being taken care of. That's what Stella told Nettie's children, scattered hither and yon, when one occasionally called long distance for an update. Voice cheerful, she would slightly over-exclaim, "Your mother couldn't be in better hands. Grace says the same, I'm sure."

Though whenever Stella glanced about the sterility of the room, doubt crawled over her stomach, tickled her. The entire place made her nervous, made her aware of the slight flutter in her heart. She spent a good deal of her visit watching the door, making certain it remained open. Sometimes the door jam would slowly slip, or some unnatural breeze in the hallway, an ethereal whisper, would bid it to close. Halfway, and Stella was up, pushing it open, kicking the piece of rubber underneath the door with her neat black shoe. It was important for that door to stay open. For Stella to know that even though these four putty-coloured walls were the last things Nettie would ever see, Stella was capable of leaving. Capable of getting up and walking through that door, down the elevator to the entryway, and into a car filled with stale smoke, plush burgundy velvet seats scarred with cigarette burns, and a sign reading "ABC Taxi" strapped to the roof.

"Hello, Nettie," Stella whispered. "Hello, my old friend."

No response. Not that Stella expected one.

"How are you feeling today? Do you want me to draw the curtains? Are you warm enough?" She kept her voice light and chipper, unnaturally so.

Stella leaned in to kiss Nettie's cheek and shuddered at something she'd noticed only recently. A new smell clinging to Nettie. A smell very much like a completely read newspaper. It was a dry, slightly chemical odour, what Stella would define as the scent of something used up. Even though the workers in the home tried to disguise it with lilac soaps and powders, it lingered. And after breathing it in, Stella couldn't help holding her breath for a moment, considering that someone had already perused the entire life of Nettie Rose, and was just waiting for the bag to be full before dropping her down the garbage chute.

"Did I tell you Summer's been trying to have a baby?" Stella said as Nettie peered out through chalky eyes. Somehow, even beneath that sheer jaundice veil, Nettie's eyes appeared darker, harder. Stella found it difficult to hold Nettie's stern gaze. Sometimes Stella had the very secret thought that Nettie knew exactly what was going on, and that she despised Stella. Jealous that she was trapped, laid out on a mattress, while Stella was free. Stella could hear her own voice in her ears, crackling out of her mouth, an octave higher. "She's had a devil of a time of it. Her and Tim."

Nettie made no movement, except for a pale tongue touching the corners of her mouth over and over again. One side, then the other. Assuming she was hungry, Stella lifted a spoonful of the tapioca snack towards Nettie's mouth, touched it off her dry lips. Mouth clamped shut. This was the second week like that – eating nothing. Even though no one acknowledged that Nettie was able to make a decision, here she was, choosing not to eat.

Stella placed the snack back on the rolling tray. "Did I ever tell you how Tim and her met? I supposes I did. Apt to have done it more than once."

"Make no mind, maid." Clear voice from the opposite side of the room. "Go on with you. Never knowed you knew my grandson, Jim. Fancy that."

That was Bed 216. Mrs. Jenkins. Soft upstairs, but the senility had done nothing to sedate her mouth. Mostly bald, Mrs. Jenkins had gradually plucked out the majority of her hair, until the staff, with permission of her family, shaved the remaining halo of white curls to an ungraspable stubble.

"Jim don't come see me no more. He's all tangled up. Tangled up."

"Tangled up in what, Mrs. Jenkins?"

"Tangled up, maid. Biggest kind of snarl. Got police looking for him. Stole all my money. Robbed banks. He owes four dollars, he do. Four dollars and forty-two cents. Shocking."

"Shocking, indeed, missus."

"Gave him a crisp five-dollar bill, I did, told him to buy me a bar and a drink. Never saw hide nor hair of it. He, coming back now, face on him like a sunset. And I says to him, Where's my drink? Was that my orange pop?"

"Drank it down, did he?"

Mrs. Jenkins sat on the very edge of her bed, one hand on the black pressboard nightstand, one hand gripping the lowered metal railing of her bed. "Police came in here looking for him, they did." She leaned forward, then sloped backwards with a sigh, as though she were letting herself know she could move if she wanted, but was choosing the comfort of staying put.

"The police?"

"Yes, now. Looking for Jim. Jimmy Jenkins, my grandson."

"Over the bit of money?"

"I lied to the feller, looked he straight in the eyes, and told him I had no idea about none of it. And if he comes in here again, looking as dapper as that, he won't be getting back out." Throaty laugh, and she shook her fist.

"Yes, missus. We're not over the hill yet," Stella replied, patted Nettie's hand.

Even though Stella knew it was all nonsense, she found relief listening to Mrs. Jenkins. The back and forth. The normality of it. She also felt guilty, as though these visits with Nettie should be hard, should be uncomfortable, and that Stella should not be seeking out ways to relieve her own uneasiness by chatting with a total stranger. Nettie deserved more.

"Well, I suppose you don't mind hearing it again," Stella said, pulling her chair closer to Nettie's bed. "'Tis a charming story, if you asks me. She just got back from some trip – spent a few months teaching some kids somewhere where the folks had less than nothing. Makes our living look like we's royalty. Awful poverty. Burn you almost. I seen the photos. Lucky to have a garbage bag for a raincoat. Anyways, there was some big barbecue at Elise's – I reckons she was relieved to have Summer back on our soil. As hard as the two of them goes at each other sometimes, Elise cares for that girl. In her way. I knows she does.

"Anyways, Summer left in her car and was driving down by The Boulevard and there was this string of ducklings crossing over, the mother up in front. Now, we all knows Summer, and what does she do? Puts herself right into the ditch trying to avoid the babies. Does a real number on her car. Knocks herself clear out on the steering wheel.

"First person she sees when she opens her eyes is this Tim feller. I told her, 'tis almost like he was sent right there for her. Helped her out. Waited for the ambulance with her. And they has been together ever since.

"I'm right glad of that, you know. She needed someone, and he's a wonderful fine young man. Teaches physics at some high school. And he's a writer, too. Had a verse published in a magazine. Summer rhymed it off to me a couple of times. Some poem about a tomato and its seeds. I'm sure it was right smart, but I got no mind for that sort of thing.

"How long ago was that, now, I wonder? Five years? Or maybe three. I idn't sure. I got no sense of time these days. Seems like practically every time I wakes up, 'tis Christmas."

Stella looked down at her hands, neatly folded in her lap, fingers crossing over the permanent crease of her polyester pants.

"What's it doing out?" Mrs. Jenkins again.

"Blustery. Not nice at all."

"I idn't one bit surprised. When I was your age, the weather was lovely. Not a blade of snow this time of year. I swears it's all gone right to the dogs since we went into Confederation. Weather hasn't been the same. I hears people say that all the time, and I tends to agree."

"Well, now. I never gave it much mind."

"You young folks don't care about that old muck. I knows all about what's going on."

Stella smiled to herself. "No, we don't."

"Do you know what's for supper? I wish they'd bring supper around. I don't know how they expects us to survive on air."

"Lunch was only an hour or so ago, Mrs. Jenkins." Then, to Nettie, "I decided I won't be going to visit Robert and Jane no more. Getting too old for all that traveling. Can't take the heat in Toronto. Too hot to go outside. Jane took the lot of us strawberry picking one afternoon beginning of July, and I thought I'd just about die with the heat.

"They keeps their house all closed up – to keep it cool. But it's awful damp, I finds. And dark, with the curtains always drawn. And Robert's son, Michael, now he's got those two young boys. They's a real handful. And, I don't got the wherewithal for it nowadays. Don't know what to be doing to entertain the young ones. It's like they got too much of everything, and idn't able to settle down to nothing for any length of time. Spin tops, I says. All that sugar they eats.

"Do you remember those days, Nettie? When we had our own young ones? We both thought we'd never have a peaceful moment again." Pausing, Stella listened to all the muted sounds of the elderly residents, the nurses, the shuffling feet. "And now we got more than enough quiet. More than enough." Voice trailing off.

"Do Grace come around much? I haven't seen her in ages, though I did come across some of her handiwork down to NONIA. I was thinking about buying a sweater there with a big Newfoundland dog on the front for one of Michael's boys." Chuckling now. "And there one was. I was some surprised to see Grace knitting any kind of dog onto anything."

"Why is that now?" Mrs. Jenkins.

"Well, it puts me in mind of the day Grace was married in Bended Knee." Stella heard Nettie's swallowing, and she squeezed Nettie's hand. "This is a story you can only smile about after years have gone by. Isn't that right, Nettie Rose?

"Grace was getting married. Some young man from Culver's Cove. Everyone was there – all the folks from

Bended Knee and a good-sized crowd from up along. Even a few folks in from St. John's. Everyone dollied up in their Sunday best. Do you remember, Nettie?

"Back then, there was always old dogs roaming around. They belonged to someone, no doubt, but no one heeded them much. Well, the service was about to start, and these two dogs come tearing into the church. Got into some dead seal washed up on the beach. Tore through the aisles, rubbing up against everything, and then right up to the pulpit, back down again, and barreled through the door where poor young Grace was waiting for the organ to start up. I swears they knew she was the one getting married, and they rubbed right up against her, like they was trying to scrape the stink off themselves. She, now, screaming something awful. I believes Ned Piercey got them out. In fact, I believes they was his dogs. The service went ahead. What are you going to do? But we all reeked to the high heavens. Bit of dead seal can go a long way."

Nettie's expression remained unchanged, and Stella regretted bringing the story out into the light. She stared at Nettie for a moment, then at the bowlful of tapioca on the tray, edges dry, plump fish eyes beginning to shrink.

Even though Stella knew her aggravation was unwarranted, petty even, sometimes she resented Nettie. Resented the fact that Nettie offered nothing in return, no clues on where to go, on what to say. But there was always an expectation hanging in the air, though Stella was unable to define that expectation. She generally tried to keep the chatter easy and humorous, to offer up stories that might float in through Nettie's ears, and make some hidden part of her smile. But how was Stella to know if this was what Nettie wanted? And when Stella sat in silence, Nettie would stare at her, blinking. Stella thought that if Nettie's eyes could make a sound, that sound would be shrill.

Perhaps Nettie preferred that Stella talk about the greater meaning of everything. She had tried that, but it always sounded too personal, especially when Mrs. Jenkins or the nurses were listening. No. That was a lie. It always sounded too final. Reflection did not involve moving forward, only looking back. Stella did not want to look back. And think. There was too much that didn't make sense. By surveying, she was likely to discover too many strands in her life that were unfair. Growing old was one thing. Old and bitter, something entirely different.

Stella stood, unfolded the quilt draped over Nettie's footboard, and laid it across Nettie's folded knees. As she did every time, Stella touched Nettie's face, pressed slightly at the corners of each eye, daubed both sides of Nettie's mouth. Paper-thin skin, sunken and nearly mummified, Stella's gentle touch adjusted her best friend's expression. It's a harmless thing to do, Stella told herself. Who would ever know? At the end of every visit, Stella kissed Nettie's forehead, and Nettie stared back with a fixed, but pleasant smile.

On her way down the hallway, Stella stopped at the door with the brass cowbell decoration. Her visits with this hapless elderly woman began as a favour, but had turned into a habit. And now she was unable to leave Pine Ridge without at least saying "Hello" to Miss Miriam Seary.

Some months ago, a nurse had approached Stella about another resident of the home who had spent a short time in Bended Knee.

"Well, travel's a lot easier these days," Stella had replied.

"No, no. I believe 'twas when she was much younger. A young woman. She doesn't talk much, but when she does, she always goes on about Bended Knee." The nurse leaned closer to Stella. "I minds she says she fell in love there."

Stella was curious now. "P'raps I knows her?"

"You could, my dear, though she's quite a bit older. Miss Seary's her name. Miriam. Oldest woman on the floor. Lived here for ages. Before I came on to work, even, and I won't tell you how long I've been here." The nurse reached out, touched Stella's elbow. "Don't suppose you got the time to spend a few minutes with her?"

"Ah..." Stella stepped back slightly, glanced up and down the hallway. Close by, she noticed a woman with a liver-spotted scalp in a reclining wheelchair, staring at a framed print on the wall. *Why do they hang such dull artwork?* Stella wondered. *Why would someone whose sense is lost want to stare at a bird flying into a forest?*

"I knows, 'tis a lot to ask. But Miss Seary's a lovely woman, and as far as we knows, she don't belong to no one. Never had a single visitor since she came to us. Not a one. Not even a card or a call. We all says she come out of nowhere. Got no line. No line to speak of." The nurse hesitated. "Plus, Mrs. Smith used to enjoy spending a bit of time with her. Before, well, she took to her bed and all."

"Well, I suppose."

"You never knows, you might end up related." The nurse had nodded. "There's always some connection, isn't there?"

Stella found that notion highly doubtful. She had never heard of anyone in Bended Knee with the last name of Seary. This woman was likely someone who'd spent a summer there, or maybe worked for a year or two as a mother's helper.

Placing her hand on the door, she stopped for a moment, wondered what type of person she was going to find behind it. A person who belonged to absolutely no one. What might that be like? No parents or aunts or uncles rooting her with stories and tradition, no children or grandchildren, making her light with their silly antics, unwavering love. How empty must that feel? To have no line. No line to speak of.

As the nurse looked on intently, Stella shuddered slightly, pushed open the Seary woman's door, secured it in place with the rubber doorstopper and stepped inside. She had intended to visit that one time, but was surprised to discover she found Miriam Seary's childlike company comforting. Familiar. There was something filling about it. Reminded her of warm bread, ready to eat, thick layer of butter melted down through.

When Stella entered the room after visiting Nettie, Miriam Seary was seated in the worn chair next to her bed. Her head was angled towards the window, likely tilted to watch the blustery wind hurtling hard flecks of snow against the glass. Light arriving through the snow was clear and bluish, and the room was cast in soothing tones. Stella slipped into the second chair, its burlap textured fabric weathered, and though she was tempted, she resisted picking away at loose strands, bits of exposed yellowed foam.

Settled beside Miriam, Stella felt incredibly slight. Miriam was a woman of grand proportions, her girth was made worse by the clothing she wore – large print polyester dresses, usually a combination of brown, dull green, a smattering of white. In her current dress, her trunk was a human landscape, rolling field, earth turned, dead vegetation turned inwards, first snowfall hiding in dips and folds. Her cheeks appeared greasy, and her shiny cleft chin, resting on the loose skin of her chest, was nearly lost among the layers of soft fat. Though Miriam was certainly clean, Stella found that she still smelled very much like a baby who had not been bathed, as though drops of creamy milk, trapped behind her fleshy ears, were fermenting. Stella did not find this offensive at all, her appearance, her odour. Instead, she felt a tenderness towards this aged infant, pity, too, certain that in Miriam's lifetime, many people had let her down, never nurtured her as promised.

Speaking in her characteristic short bursts, repetitive phrases, Miriam once again began to tell of her time in Bended Knee. And Stella always listened politely, though she had given up trying to discover any common ground. Miriam only spoke of minor things, such as kittens in a loft, setting out plates on a tablecloth embroidered with fruit, making soup from fish heads with an old woman. Stella thought perhaps Miriam worked in a kitchen, or perhaps she never lived there at all. There was nothing in her descriptions that would lead Stella to believe her one way or another. She had mentioned a man, but he could have been a man from anywhere or anytime. And Miriam had just placed him in Bended Knee because that was a memorable place for her.

"Ellie." Trying to straighten the sharp bend in her back, Miriam looked up at Stella with wide set eyes. "You knows him?"

"Ellie? No, Miss Seary," Stella replied gently, as she did each time Miriam asked this same question. "No, I don't mind that I do." She guessed that Miriam had been born simple, that her childlike manner was not due to senility. "Do you recall his Christian name?"

"He plays the music. Music."

"What sort?" Stella reached up to touch the slight cleft in her own chin, stared at the cleft in Miriam's.

"Lots of keys. Keys opens nothing." She guffawed at her own joke, wide mouth revealing a set of perfectly even greyish-white false teeth.

"Keys?"

"Keys, keys."

"Piano, you means? I never heard you talk about a piano before."

"Oh, yes. Nice music. Good boy."

"Did you play?"

Miriam giggled, slapped her thighs with both hands. "No, no. He gave me nice."

"Music, Miss Seary?"

"Good boy. Nice boy."

"Yes, Miss Seary."

"Dancing. You dance?"

"Not lately, no. But I did. Back in the day."

"Oh, I dance, dance. Missus don't like it."

"Missus?"

"Good girls don't dance. By theyselves." Miriam began to open and close her legs, hoseless thighs slapping slightly.

"To a bit of piano music? I don't see no harm in it. 'Tis harmless."

"Dancing for the devil. Devil dancing."

"That's old nonsense now, Miss Seary." Reaching over, Stella patted Miriam's shoulder. Somehow, Stella had expected her fingers to sink into Miriam's flesh, but instead, she encountered a reassuring firmness. "Whoever filled your head with that don't mean it, I's sure."

As they chatted, Stella's thoughts skipped backwards, flicking through old memories, and at once, she sat upright. With this talk of a piano, a small door cracked open in Stella's mind. Only one person in Bended Knee owned a piano and that was an old widow named Berta May. She had died years ago, but Stella remembered the man who lived with her, helped to take care of the land, few animals, and the house. He was an odd individual, used to wander up and down the laneways in all kinds of weather, would stare at Stella and frighten Elise. But he played beautiful music. The melody often wound its way out through a cracked window, lingered in the air like a foggy charm.

"Was his last name Wood?" She could no longer conjure his first name, though didn't fret over the lapse. That man hadn't crossed her mind in a decade or more, and Stella's memory was about as crisp as a damp rag.

"Got me in trouble. Trouble. It did."

"Oh, come now, Miss Seary."

"Oh my, oh my, oh my. All sorts. Ask missus."

"What sort?" While in the company of Miriam, Stella often had the desire to dig through her purse, find a peppermint knob, offer it up.

"Missus don't like it."

"Probably you misunderstood."

"Shut up. Shut up. Shut up!" Miriam's voice, suddenly shrill, angry.

"Pardon me?" Stella flinched in her seat, put her hands to the knot in her scarf. Miriam had never before spoken in a harsh tone. "Oh, I do apologize, Miss Seary. I didn't mean..." Stella began to stand, slightly nervous now.

"She says shut up. Hurt awful bad. Owww." Miriam slumped forward, praying hands pinched between her knees. "Owww."

On the edge of her seat now, Stella said, "Miss Seary, is you all right?"

"'Twas hot. Hot belly fire."

"Do you want me to get the nurse? A drink of water?"

"Fire down. Down there."

"The washroom? You need the washroom, Miss Seary?"

Miriam opened her eyes, stared at Stella, her gaze reminding Stella of an innocent goat. Open, trusting, a hint of fear.

"I left it. Left it there."

"What did you leave?"

"Left it. Uh-huh. Had to."

"You couldn't go back for it? Whatever it was?"

"No, ma'am. Uh-huh. 'Twas dead. Missus said so."

"I don't understand you, Miss Seary. I don't want you to be upset."

"Dead. Took it away." Miriam sucked in air. "Right quick. Gone."

"Oh my. I'll get the–"

"Before I even seed."

Stella clutched her black vinyl purse, stood up. She placed her hand lightly on Miriam's shoulder, said in a hushed tone, "I'll go and fetch the nurse. I's awful sorry, Miss Seary. I gone and upset you with my questions."

Stella walked out into the fluorescent lights of the hallway, tottering slightly. She leaned her shoulder blades against the wall. At first she hadn't understood, but after a moment, her mind snapped to attention. Miriam Seary had had a baby in Bended Knee. Born still. Or so someone had told her.

With her knuckle, Stella daubed the moistness that had formed in her eyes. She stood as straight as her spine would allow, and took a deep breath. The old woman had surprised her. In her head, Stella had conjured up a magical life for Miriam Seary. A full lifetime as a child, brimming with wonder, absent of misery or sorrow. But now she recognized how foolish that was. Every person experienced loss. Every person, no matter their wits or station, was occasionally enveloped in it, forced to absorb it.

Directly across from where Stella stood hung the portrait of the black bird. Flying straight into a forest of dark green brushstrokes. It angered her suddenly, this image. Of innocence about to be devoured. And she stared at that bird, clenched her fists, willed it to arc upwards, towards the heavens, and avoid the tangle of certain night that lay ahead.

That was the last time Stella saw Miriam Seary. Nettie died within hours of their final visit, and because Stella perceived, at best, a tenuous, and now slightly awkward, connection to Miss Seary, she never went back again.

On a warm day in June, Miss Miriam Seary died while resting peacefully at Pine Ridge Retirement Centre. There was a small farewell with a handful of attendants, nursing staff mostly, a doctor. Though all were fond of Miriam, welcomed the ever-present smile on her sharply tilted head, they recognized that she would not be missed. No husband, no children, no loved ones worth mentioning. They felt a tinge of sadness when they acknowledged that kind Miriam Seary, who everyone joked might live forever, had died completely alone. "It's impossible," one said, "given the constraints we're under, to spend any amount of time seated with one woman."

But they were wrong. Miriam was not alone. Her mind was full, occupied with the good company found inside her recurring dream. Her hands moving over the warm pink udders of the old girls, heavy with milk. Churning sweet butter with all her might. Lying down with a man who was gentle with her. The smell of spring grass, every blade bent and broken beneath her.

On that same day, a woman named Anita Hilliard paid her neighbour, young Henry Tuck, fifteen dollars to repair the squeaky floor of the attic bedroom in the home she had purchased in Bended Knee. With the small inheritance she received when a beloved great uncle died, she had decided to transform the abandoned farmhouse into a lively bed and breakfast. She recognized that those sorts of things were coming into vogue, and she wanted to be seated at the front of the investment bus. Plus, it was a good way for a single mature woman to earn an income while maintaining a respectable home.

The home had once belonged to a married couple named Willard and Berta May. They never had any children, only a few distant, distracted relatives who had no interest in a rundown farmhouse. Anita snapped up the long abandoned home at a steal, and when she toured the rooms, she could practically feel the old-fashioned character oozing out of the walls. Vandals had left behind plenty of smashed beer bottles, some pissy corners, but most of the contents remained intact. Being a thrifty lady, Anita decided to keep much of it. Taking it room by room, she re-papered walls, re-painted doors, re-sugared wilted doilies, vacuumed chairs, bought fresh pillows and sheets. Her handy neighbour, Henry Tuck, assisted with most of the hammer work. While she didn't mind the cosmetic fix-up, she was not one to play with tools.

Though it could have gone under the heading for charm, the squeaking in the attic irritated her. Whenever she would enter the room, she'd shift her weight back and forth over those floorboards, aggravated by the song that rose upwards. As if the floor was trying to tell her something. But Anita, being a poor listener, wanted to shut it up. Stifle the whine. She moved the chatty floorboards to the top of Henry's list, felt a sense of finality as she heard his steady hammering.

If she had gotten down on all fours, which she rarely did, and felt along the floorboards of the attic room, she might have discovered the cause for the irritable squeaking. Several boards were loose, could be lifted easily with a set of eager, prying fingers. But instead, Henry Tuck securely nailed each end of the planks. Nail after nail after nail. Forever locking away a wooden box that was laid on the thick support beams beneath. Inside was a photo, covered lightly in oily loops and arches and whorls. And though no one would ever read them, the box also contained several letters written in scratchy, but legible handwriting. Impeccable spelling. Remarkable, considering the man who penned them. Each one carefully and lovingly addressed to *My darling Mirry.*

My name is Eldred James Wood. I lived in Bended Knee with Mr. and Mrs. Willard May from the age of seventeen years until my death. I wrote those letters, hid them under the floorboards. No one will ever find them and read them, share them. In twenty-three years, a simple swallow of time, the old May farmhouse will burn down because of faulty wiring. My words will be turned to dull ash, then scattered by the very gusts that fed the flames.

Where am I now? Of course, I am long gone. Moved on, as some delicately call it. The narrow pine box, my final resting place, has long since degraded, collapsed under the weight of several feet of damp dirt, a flourishing bed of orange marigolds. There is nothing left of my woollen suit, my watery flesh, the paste that was my bones. With the help of life within the earth, I have travelled outwards, blended in with the soil, disintegrated.

Those in Bended Knee who remember me might think my life was insignificant. Likely they consider me nothing more than the dull-witted farmhand who turned soil on cloudy days. Or the peculiar man who wandered up and down the laneways in thick drizzle. Or perhaps they remember me as the piano player who could never read a note of music. However I exist within their minds, undoubtedly they view me as a lost soul without a purpose. Someone who had simply slipped in and out of existence without leaving as much as a wrinkle.

But they would all be wrong. Though I left a very quiet footprint on this earth, even I have a story to tell. We are all like that. Our lives, when they begin, may fit neatly on the head of a pin, but as we move through the years we are given, our lives expand until we have touched every star in the universe.

So, listen now. Those of you who think I don't belong here. I admit, it is a curious place for me to be, when my story so clearly should have ended near the beginning. But I will tell you what I must, to unravel the sadness, and set it free.

My mother, you see, was an angry woman. And much of that anger was directed towards me. Don't judge her though, as she had every right to be. I let her down, down so deeply, she was never able to recover. In the long light of a warm September afternoon, I destroyed my mother. Only her obligation to me forced her to live like that for years, all the way dead inside. Through and through.

My father passed away when I was seven years old. He slipped off a damp rooftop he'd been helping to shingle, and broke his neck. I spent hours thinking about his last moments. Trying to create them inside my mind. Often I could be found stretched out on the very spot where he fell, staring up towards the now finished rooftop. I'd see his face coming towards me, mouth open, eyes locked with mine. And he would fall on me, into me, over and over again. What had he been thinking when he bungled his footing? Did he try to right himself as he tumbled, or did he accept gravity? Was there an instant, a single drawn out moment, when he knew he had made an irreversible error, and that he was going to die? Did he think of me before he was swathed in light? Knowing that now I would be man of the house.

Before he died, my father put four sons into my mother. I, of course, was one of them. The oldest, in fact. I had three younger brothers. My father always told me how lucky I was to have three shadows. My shadows, he called them. My own personal set of silhouettes. When my father died, my mother would soothe herself by repeating his little jokes. "Where are your shadows?" she'd ask. "Never was a boy so lucky as you, my son. Three shadows." When we'd set out in the morning to turn salt fish on Skipper Murphy's flakes, my mother would say, "Always mind your shadows. Take good care of them."

I promised I would, but I didn't.

There was an old well on our property, hadn't been

used for years. We all knew it was there, but we were forbidden to play near it. According to my mother, an old witch named Agnes lived at the bottom of the wide-mouthed well. She was wretched, frothed at the mouth, had black holes for eyeballs, a hairless scalp of mould, pale worms and water skeeters moved freely in and out of her ears and puckered mouth. "Agnes'll get you, my lovey, if you ever goes near that well. She'll smell you with her tongue, come after you." We never went near the well. Never gave Agnes the chance to catch a whiff of us.

Until one day.

I never figured out who had pried the wooden lid off the well. It doesn't really matter. Someone did. And Ernie, when he saw the edges of the open well, cried out, "Agnes is gone." In a fit of childish bravery, he ran towards the idle well, leaned hard over the side. Two days away from his fourth birthday, and he tumbled over the rim of smooth beach rocks. And I could hear him, my smallest shadow, splashing about inside a pit of darkness.

I was stuck to the spot, as though I was nothing more than a seven-year sapling. Elias, who was five, ran to his younger brother. We could hear his gurgling screams echoing against the dirt walls. Hoisting himself over the side, Elias yelled down with feigned irritation and conviction, "I'll get you out, you little bugger."

Elias slipped slowly, and I watched him disappear. First his forearms, then his hands, then his fingers, for a blinding moment, the very tips of those white fingers, then nothing. I heard the second splash, and Elias was down there, with Ernie and Agnes, screaming out to Eugene and myself.

Eugene looked at me, his pupils wide like a deer who was caught, throat slit, bleeding out. We could both hear our brothers, high-pitched choking pleas, first Ernie, then

Elias, then little Ernie again. We both knew that they were scrambling to stay afloat, each one scraping away at the other, only one head above water at a time. "Maaaaaaaaaaaa, Maaaaaaa." Eugene took quick sips of air, bounced on the spot, looked at me, the well, me, the well, me, the well, then lion-roared as he ran full force towards the well. I don't know what he intended to do, but he toppled into the well, as though diving down, head first. I heard a thud, and not a sound from him after.

My mother was carried across the back of our land on the gust of her continual shriek. She pitched herself against the well, waist hooked by the lip of rock, swiped the rank air with her open hands. "Please," she bawled. "Please, please come out. Eldred. Don't stand there. Please, Eldred. God. God. God. Get them out."

Silence in the well. Hysterical then, she flew towards me. Struck me with her fists. Spit as she spoke. "Get. Them. Out." She fell to the earth, slapping herself in the head, flipping like a netted fish that just couldn't fathom life without water. "They were your shadows," she moaned, her voice like two tall lifeless trees rubbing together in the wind. "Your shadows. Oh. Jesus. My babies. Precious. Drowned."

At that moment, the earth shuddered, made my teeth chatter, blurred my vision. I couldn't take it in. What had happened? Only an hour earlier the four of us were stabbing tree blisters with a stick, coating the stems of dried leaves with turpentine, setting them to sail on a clear puddle. We had been doing that. I was certain. I smelled my fingers for proof, put them in my mouth and sucked the bitter turpentine off. And that's where I wanted to stay, beside the puddle. If only Time had hiccupped then and there. If only I had of grabbed them by their trousers, spoken sternly to all three of them. Now fellers, what good's a shadow that don't stay put?

She clobbered me near unconscious every time the sun cast a dusky reminder behind me. Or in front of me. Beside me, even. Over the years, I learned to fear them, my shadows. They followed me relentlessly. Ghostly evidence of my failure sprouting from my own two feet. Sometimes, when the guilt had rendered my heart into a thin broth, I stepped up to my mother in the soft evening sun, never flinched when I took the best she could give.

She never smiled again. Wore black on her body, black over her head. Proclaimed her hatred of God to anyone who might listen, called him a cruel child-eating son-of-a-bitch. Then, on my sixteenth birthday, when my body had finished growing into a man, she made her way up the hill towards the well, and with a bucket of stale rainwater, a securely tied knot, my mother destroyed herself.

I lived alone for one miserable year. I found it difficult to care for myself, and soon became a burden on my great aunt. After that year had passed, she determined the time was right to sell my mother's house. She meant to include me in the bundle – the purchaser would pay a cut-rate price on the property, home, chattels, and I was to remain on the land. My care would be transferred to the new owner, and in exchange for shelter and a meal, I would work. At first, nobody was interested in the house, the meager furnishings, the wild grassy hill where Agnes continued to reside. Too many spirits. Too much sadness, they said. Until, on the advice of a potential buyer, I moved to Bended Knee. Into the dusty attic of Uncle and Berta May. Then my mother's house sold quickly. Free and clear of shadows.

Uncle and Berta May were kind to me, spoke to me as though I were a man. Uncle Sir never had cause to beat me, all those years, and I did my best for him – working the fields when thick clouds filled the sky, tinkering in the barn or cellar when the sun shone. The Missus fed me, mended my clothes, and on blustery afternoons in the wintertime, she taught me to shape letters and words, to read the Bible. Many years passed, filled with the comfort of predictability.

People thought me simple. And, in some ways that was true. I rarely spoke, found words something of an annoyance. I was often alone. Occasionally, when the evening sky was like a battered tin plate, the air filled with drizzle, I wandered up and down the laneways. Stared into lighted windows, to watch families move around each other, to see husbands and wives embrace. Once, Mr. Johnson caught me outside his bedroom window. I had been watching while Mrs. Johnson unknotted her waist-length brown hair and Mr. Johnson brushed it by the low light of a lantern. I leaned forward when he buried his face in handfuls of her hair, and branches snapped beneath my feet. Mr. Johnson was beside me in a flash, knocked me twice with a fisherman's strong fist, loosening my front teeth, deafening me in my left ear. He never gave me a moment to explain myself. That I wasn't gazing out of depravity, I was trying to learn. To learn how people love.

There was talk about what to do. Uncle Sir and the Missus were too old to be concerned over it, said I was as stun as a flatfish. Nothing more than a curious child. "Anyways, decent folks should draw their curtains," the Missus had offered. She gave me a beginner's piano book, opened the creaky lid that covered the keys, suggested, "Have a go at this. Maybe it'll keep you out of trouble." I could not make sense of the book, but the music still arrived through my fingers.

No woman took an interest in me before Miriam Seary. She arrived at the farm when I was nearly forty years old. At first I was afraid of her, would barely glance over as she lingered near the piano, her back hunched gently, side smile. In hopes of seeing her sway out of the corner of my eye, I played jaunty tunes. Felt incredibly brazen doing so.

I noticed her staring at me frequently, through the streaky windows of the house when I was outside, across the dinner table while we ate. I would swallow my food in lumps, made my stomach feel as though I'd drank a strong cupful of black tea without toast or a biscuit. I didn't understand it, how I felt happy and ill at the same time. For months I wondered on it. Until she came to me in the barn.

Yes, I confess, I had witnessed some tangled antics when I peered into bedroom windows while wandering at night. It all seemed so angry and aggressive, particularly Skipper Whelan, his pinning and his biting and his rocking. The sounds that emerged from his small wife hidden beneath him filled me up with a nervous energy, and I would run for an hour or more, until exhausted. My tightly laced shoes, like Skipper and his missus, slapping, slapping against the damp road.

I couldn't grasp the meaning of it. Not until Miriam placed her warm hand between my shoulder blades in the loft of the barn. I believe it was the first time someone had ever touched me with kindness in their fingers. Her palm released a warmth that traveled through my flannel shirt and flared out through my entire body. I had no idea what I was doing when I balanced my lanky frame on her bulky hips, round abdomen. But Miriam helped me, and while my bones were lost in her folds, I tucked my face into the creases of her neck, her smell like summer butter.

During much of my younger life, I had found Time dragged its hoary heels, now there was never enough of it. Chores on the farm. Errands for the Missus. Tending the animals. There was never enough moments to be with Miriam. She and I lay down together every chance we had. Mostly outdoors during those warmer months. Tall grasses, untouched by scythe or sickle, offered convenient privacy. I never knew a woman could be pleasant and sweet. Never would have guessed that Miriam's body, her quiet ways could become a salve for my childhood guilt. I began to love Miriam Seary, and I was certain that some greater power had brought her towards me as a gift, letting me know that it was time to let go.

As the months went by, her waist became even thicker, and I knew I had put a baby into her. The Missus began to eye me warily, as though she knew what Miriam and I had been doing up over the hill on the fallow land. Uncle Sir became agitated, distant, spent long hours staring at the dull green sea. Miriam fashioned a soft blanket with a fat hook and white wool. Full of tiny holes. "Don't expect that'll keep it much warm," I told her. "Keep it warm, keep it warm," she'd said, whole face smiling before a loud burp escaped from her lips. "Sure, you's no more than a baby yourself, Miriam. Passing gas like that," the Missus had scolded. "I's the baby, I's the baby. I's the babe that sails the ship."

I stayed in the garden when the baby was climbing out, trenched up the same potato plant over and over again. Couldn't stand to hear Miriam screaming. Like she was dying. And I stayed outside, even when the sun threatened to burn through the clouds, because I was all filled up with sick and happy again. My eyes were watering the earth.

Shortly after the child was out of her, Uncle Sir left the

house with a bundle in his arms, what looked like the holey blanket, and he made his way down the laneway. Though I didn't realize at that moment, I soon learned he'd given the child to some capable folks. I forgave him for that, as he knew better than I did. I'd guessed that's what Miriam had wanted. Though I never had the chance to ask her.

When Miriam disappeared, she emptied me out. In some ways, I think it might have been easier to have never felt so full, because it hurt like the devil to have all that goodness drawn out of me. Everything changed when she left, and I decided that this was my punishment. I was with them now, my brothers. Down there inside that abandoned well with the three of them. Darkness and cold, my bargainings with God echoing up the dripping walls, making my poor ears bleed. No one was listening. My Mirry never came back.

For a fleeting moment, I had thought to leave and try to find her. Instead, for weeks I ran circles around Bended Knee in the moonlight, and then again in the mornings before the sun wounded the calm night sky. Silliness, it was, she could've been anywhere. But I didn't stop until I wore holes through my only shoes, through my woolen socks, left tender skin from my soles on the dirt laneways. The Missus told me to give it up, do something I enjoyed. But the songs that emerged when my hands moved over those scratched white keys were mournful. That's all I could manage.

Nothing now for me, but watch the child. Watch her grow. And I did that, as often as I could. I followed Delia Abbott as she strolled along the sea, baby nestled in her slender arms. I watched the girl haul seaweed with her father a few years later. I noticed her eyes, red and swollen, when the young men went off to war. Though the bright day made my legs shake, I stood nearby, as she emerged from the church, a glowing bride. Stella. She was a star. Is a star. Pure light. I wove each image of my child into the fabric of my heart. Though this may sound stale, those glimpses of her sewed me up inside. Kept me breathing for many years.

And now, since my death, I will tell you what is happening. My awareness has been spiraling outwards, in a gradual drift, breaking, re-joining, like an enormous mound of cotton candy, a million tiny fingers pinching off sugary filaments for a million swallowing mouths. At first I felt a deep sense of loss, my memories, my very life was dissolving. But then I came to understand that inside this thinning mass is a stronger core, an energy that clings to itself, holds itself together. My love for Miriam and our daughter resides in that mass. Waiting in that place. So simple.

There are no shadows here.

chapter sixteen

"I've had a vision," Jane Edgecombe announced one morning at the breakfast table. "A simply perfect vision of how to end our little holiday."

"Well?" Elise asked, looking towards her sister-in-law, though never meeting her eyes. Instead, she stared at the contents of the spoon in Jane's hand. It was overflowing with Elise's last bit of good raspberry jam, and Jane was pressing it into a toasted English muffin, going back for more. She was not one to deny herself, even though her body, no more than a spindle, showed little evidence of it. "Well, what sort of vision now?"

"It came to me last night as I was reading the *Telegram* in bed."

"In bed? Who reads a newspaper in bed? You're bound to get black on the sheets."

Jane ignored the comment, dropped the spoon into the near empty jar. "And there it was, a tiny advertisement. Laid out like that, as though it were meant to be."

"My knees are too old for anything crazy now, Jane," Robert said, glancing over his bifocals. "I remember last time–"

"Yes. Knees," she said, face and eyes alight. "But just one. Bended Knee."

"Bended Knee?" Elise leaned her head back, chin lost in a pinkish wattle. "Why on earth would we want to go there?"

"All kinds of reasons, Elise, my dear. I'd love to see where my husband grew up. See your old haunts. You know. Have the boys experience some rustic Newfoundland living. It would be fun."

"Now, Jane, none of us have any interest in flushing out old ghosts."

"Too late. I've already called and booked us all in, Robert. Authentic historic farmhouse from the 1800s, it said. The ad in the paper." Jane nibbled her overloaded toast, sipped her coffee. "Charm galore. Plus, it might nudge you know who out of her funk." She opened her eyes wide, leaned her head sharply to one side.

No one looked directly at the chair, though they all saw the woman in their peripheral vision. A pair of neatly slippered feet, permanently creased pants. Cardigan with easy to handle buttons. Head covered with short, soft, bluish hair. Gnarled fingers moving a crochet hook in and out, in and out, ever so slowly, around the edges of a goliath granny square.

"Bring her around." Another sip of scalding coffee. Wincing. "Let's end this whole thing on a high note, shall we?"

Anita Hilliard, sole proprietor of The May House Bed and Breakfast, was used to young guests, and she knew how to extract a smile out of them. Two boys, she guessed around seven and nine years old, were seated at the kitchen table, staring at her with expectation. "Well now, what do I do for a thrill. Is that the bit of information you're after? Hmmm." Plump hand to her chin. "A few mice, that's what. They's my biggest thrill these days."

Elise Lane cleared her throat. Hard. These boys were her great nephews, but instead of affection, their infantile antics evoked only a general sense of irritation – the emotion she might have while using a dull grater on a carrot. And she guessed, from her sister-in-law's continually flushed cheeks, that Jane's heart housed much the same sentiment. Elise was betting that Jane and her brother Robert were ruing their decision to bring them along when they travelled from Toronto.

"There's nothing more satisfying than checking my traps each morning, seeing a reward for my efforts. Those bright black eyes and grey fur."

"Gross," Jason, the older one, said with a wide grin.

"I uses peanut butter," she confided in a hushed tone. "And more than once you'll get one eating the face right off the other. Talk about ignorant," she said with a snort.

"Ooo, double gross." Andrew, the younger one now.

Elise followed the trail of painted baseboards around the small kitchen, scanning for cracks and holes. Then, she cleared her throat again, ventured with an unintentional squeak, "Many mice here?"

"No, my love. None in here, you needn't worry. The lot of them lives out in the barn. Can't have a barn without a few mice now, could you? Wouldn't be right somehow."

"We can check your traps for you, ma'am. We'll be real careful."

"If you minds your fingers. And your toes."

"That's enough, Jason," Jane cautioned. To Anita, "Did

you ever hear of some place called Devil's Rock?"

Anita Hilliard caught the tone. "Yes. Devil's Rock. 'Tis a peculiar sight. Not far. Down on the beach." She peeled the lid off her bread container, punched her fist deep into the bubbly bread dough.

"Look," Jason squealed, pointing at the two white mounds that billowed up, encased Anita's hand. "There's Granny Stella's backside."

"Christ Almighty," Elise groaned, eyes rolled upwards. "What don't come out of their mouths."

"Never you mind now, about someone's backside. Go on out. Get some fresh air before it starts to rain again."

"Sure, he said the same thing when he saw some rhino pissing on tv," Andrew said, batting his mile-long eyelashes.

"Said what?"

"Said, look, there's Gran's arse."

"Arse?"

"No, he said 'ass.' Ass. That's a swear word."

Elise groaned again.

"Great-Gran was right there too. Heard him say it and all."

"You little rat fink." Jason locked his brother's head in his elbow, squeezed. "Tattle-tail. I'm gonna stick your tongue in one of those traps."

Jane stood up from the table. "Young men!" They disentangled themselves, stared at her as she spoke. "I'm sure Mrs. Hilliard's got a decent bar of soap for your mouths if you keep it up. Believe you me," pushing up her silk sleeves, "I'm up for the task."

The boys tumbled into the porch, jammed feet into sneakers, arms and heads into hooded sweatshirts, slammed the screen door, and pounded down the path in the grass.

"Finally," Jane said, settling in again. "A moment of beloved peace."

"It's apt to be a quiet day. They're having a funeral this afternoon for Alec Parsons."

"Oh, that's too bad. What took him?" Jane asked.

Elise thought Jane's highbrow accent seemed entirely out of place there in the small kitchen. She always spoke with heightened tone, surplus urgency. While Elise's and Anita's chatting tangled together, looping and weaving, Jane's sentences just sunk to the bottom, her words like a bag of mewing kittens tossed in a pond.

"The cancer. Lung, I believe. But he was an old feller. Took beautiful photographs." She sliced through the dough with a long thin blade, quickly shaped a pan of neat supper buns, three loaves. "Going through his stuff, they come across a boxload of photos of his late wife. Had over a thousand of them."

"Must've been true love."

"True love is right. Shouldn't we all be so lucky. She hadn't a stitch on in most of them."

"Oh my Lord." Elise put her hand to her throat.

"And last going off, she was near her age." Anita nodded her head towards Stella, who was seated in a rocker, cup of untouched tea on the pedestal table beside her.

Everyone turned to look at Stella. Smiled at her, and she smiled back. Neat white teeth, gums not quite the right shade of pink.

Ah, yes. Stella. They had quite forgotten she was there at all.

The deterioration was gradual. This point was not lost on Stella. Over the years, she was vaguely aware that the power was shifting, but these shifts were all so understated, there was hardly room to complain. Until the realization of the deep loss struck her in the face. She had forecasted this with some squeamishness decades ago, and now it was reality. She, Stella Edgecombe, had grown old.

In one sense, she knew she was blessed, never having had a serious illness, just a plodding decline of her senses, her body. Bunions, achy knees, temperamental bladder, loss of taste, thinning hair, loose spotted skin. A mildly erratic heart. But whose wasn't? There was a continual off flavour in her mouth that bothered her though. A fetid taste. She might have suspected a tooth, if that had been a feasible guess. But since the only teeth in her mouth were porcelain, she surmised, with some trepidation, that the taste originated from somewhere further within.

Oh, and if she wanted to continue to compile the list of minor ailments, she could not forget the arthritis in her knuckles. She glanced down at her hand as it rested on the pillow near her cheek. Her knuckles reminded her of tubers on thick stubby roots, and she could barely hold a pen to write. But who wanted to write anyway? Didn't she find it difficult to draft a letter to Annette? Robert's granddaughter. Her great granddaughter. Those letters she received from the girl were composed in pink ink, splattered with exclamation marks, dotted with hearts. Brimming with exuberance, this correspondence, while Stella had come to rely mostly on the comma. In fact, in recent years, she required the pause mid-sentence whether one was grammatically correct or not.

Stella closed her eyes, drifted for a moment, opened

them again, glanced about the dimly lit room. She tried to make out the design on the ornate wallpaper, thought it looked like a dull repeated pattern of fat cherubs holding up twisted bouquets of roses. Might well be trucks and cars that surrounded her, she couldn't be certain, though she sensed this tiny room on the first floor of the farmhouse had been a woman's room. Perhaps a mother's room.

She allowed her lids to lower slowly, her mind to wander. If she had to choose a single moment when she realized she was truly an old woman, it would have involved a picnic near Elise's home. Bowring Park, maybe. Or perhaps somewhere entirely different. Stella was uncertain of how long ago it was, or who exactly was present. Elise, she knew. Stella did remember that, her daughter using an ice cream scoop (of all things) to serve potato salad on paper plates, handing out bottles of unnaturally coloured drinks. After the lunch, Elise had cracked open a watermelon with the twist of a long knife. Sounded like a head hitting solid rock. And when the fruit lay open before Stella, its flesh was so brilliant, it had startled her.

Everyone began eating and spitting black seeds and swiping their chins. As Stella watched on, she considered that her attendance there no longer affected the level of etiquette. Once, people seemed to mind themselves, but the effect of her presence had obviously faded. The lot of them consumed the watermelon like animals now, eyes and face pressed into enormous green smiles, rapid breathing, chins and cheeks slathered with wet pinkish tissue.

"Go on, Mother," Elise had urged. "Don't be so stiff."

"I'm just fine, thank you." Stella folded her hands in her lap, wanted to pull her legs underneath the chair, but was fearful that the metal and cloth contraption upon which she was perched might topple over.

Elise swabbed her face with a crumpled napkin. "Too late for you to learn how to have a bit of fun, I suppose."

Stella pursed her thin lips and turned slightly to watch a group of boys in the field, a football drilling the air between them. She watched as one of the boys, some relation to her, or about to become a relation, jumped higher than he needed to in order to catch the ball. Throwing and jogging in the spot, he made exaggerated moves that emulated exercise, but Stella could tell by his shape, his dumpy torso, that he was not well acquainted with physical activity. Then, as she looked on, his hand dove down the back of his tracksuit, slid around the front. And he had groped himself. Handled himself, without the least hint of modesty, as Stella had stared. He had the cheek to shift the whole works around.

In the tiny bedroom, Stella closed her eyes again. Voices from the kitchen drifted in through the thin walls, sounds muted, as though arriving through icy cold water. Likely Jane and Elise were complaining about the costs of caring for Stella. Sharing personal business with that other woman. Asking her opinion on whether or not Stella should be placed in a home? Suggesting it might be better, safer. Stella had heard it all before.

She sighed, ran her fingers over the soft pillowcase. Line-dried freshness. What a simple pleasure, Stella thought. She held the odour high in her nose, in the place particularly sensitive to remembering. No one she knew dried their clothes on a line anymore. Not one single person. She had mentioned this to Miss Parsons, the nurse who came to tend to her, but the nurse took that as a request to use a double dose of fabric softener, causing Stella's bedding to have a smattering of sky blue stains, a strong fake floral scent that nearly gagged her. She inhaled again. Part of her childhood was tucked inside that smell. Salt air and sunshine, winds sharp enough to clip the hide from a bear.

What was she thinking about? Oh, yes. He had returned to the backyard. That boy who was playing football. What was his name? It escaped her completely. She could see his scalp through his thinning hair, his sweaty head glistening in the sun, and he put his hands on her, on the dry, clean shoulders of her ironed blouse. "How you doing, Nanny E?" he had said, leaning down, pressing a hard kiss into her hollow cheek, everyone else smiling on. "Oh, Nanny E," he'd sung, patting her back, "my best old girl."

And there it was. The very instant she had realized how much she had lost. Control over her body. She, an old girl. Stroked on the back as though she were an ancient cow that no longer gave milk. Now, unfamiliar people, dirty people, conceived it well within their rights to touch her. An old girl. To kiss her. An old girl. And this touching and kissing and patting caused others to gaze on with brightened expressions of wonderment. How kind to give the poor elderly soul a flicker of attention.

While this shift of bodily control was taking place, there was movement elsewhere as well. As her only recourse, she had begun to move inwards, spending much more of her time inside her own consciousness. If she considered how often she was fully present, in these papered rooms, beside these chatty people, it would be comfortably limited. The occasion was a rarity. Though she felt slightly snobby to admit it, she no longer enjoyed their company. Preferred the placidness of her memories. They were readily available to her, arrived inside her skull with uncompromised clarity. With minimal effort, she could smell the salt of the snails when she and her brother Amos crushed them for bait. Hear her mother's song as she sat on the daybed, drawing a stretch of thread through a quilt. Taste Nettie's molasses drop cookies, heavier and harder than they should have been. Feel Leander's hand interwoven with hers, that hint of webbing between their fingers touching.

Yet, Stella hadn't shut herself off, bricked herself in. Just this morning, before leaving on the drive to Bended Knee, she and Robert had a lively discussion about the challenges of life on the water. He had been reading the paper at her kitchen table, snorted, and Stella thought it sociable to ask about the latest news.

"There isn't any place they can't reach nowadays."

Robert's voice was strong and clear, words never tangled or dampened in his throat. This was one of the many things Stella adored about her son. He spoke with conviction whether he was describing the weather or a war.

"Mmmhmmm." She nodded. "A lot more trouble back in the day."

"No place is sacred anymore. All the drugs."

"Not like it were."

"Brought an enormous amount of it in, using skiffs," he said. "That's what it says here. If you can believe that." He held up the paper in her direction.

"I can't make it out at all now. I can't make it out, dear."

He folded the paper, dropped it onto the table. "Well, seems a crowd of them was running it. Using boats as a system. Busted by the police. Found an enormous amount of it. Looks like jail time. For a good many years, I'm hoping."

"Ye– right, right," she replied. As opposed to her son's voice, Stella's dentures made her speak with an annoying and embarrassing whistle. So, she spoke slowly, choosing her words as best as she could in order to avoid it. "I can believe it. When I wasss real young, I knowed the big boat would come in ssso far, trap ssskiff bring the flour and what not the ressst of the way."

"Was drugs, Mother. Hash or some such. Selling it to the teenagers."

"Oh. Oh. Didn't have much of that in my day. Hardly even a pill for a headache." She had touched the large pocket on her day dress, felt the hardness of the plastic cylinder containing her heart medication. A light dose. Very light. Hardly even necessary at all. "Had to wait for the good doctor to come round. And that didn't happen but every blue moon."

"Riles me, it does. To no end. I see those boys, Jason and Andrew, rambunctious and all, and it worries me. What's available. What's being pushed. Only another couple of years, and all that garbage will be waiting on their front steps. All they need to do is open the door."

Stella jiggled the medication just enough to confirm the presence of the pills inside. She had wondered if she could stop taking them, her heart felt strong and steady. No more bouts of arrhythmia. But she kept forgetting to mention it to Dr. Simpson. Kept forgetting.

"These young men," he said, peeling off his glasses, jamming them into a leather case, "all they're doing is setting out to destroy. Pad their own pockets off the ruination of others."

Stella nodded again, attempted to portray more sincerity, though she guessed she had missed some crucial aspect of the conversation. "Young men today idn't what they were in my day."

He stopped, smiled at her. "Oh, Mother," he said. Then he crossed the room towards her, touched her face. The kind of touch that Stella appreciated. Honest. Loving. "Yes, those were kinder times, Mom. You've had a lucky life."

She smiled back, looking up at him from her seat. They held each other's gaze longer than usual, and at once, she was girlishly, amusingly aware of her appearance. She desperately hoped her make-up wasn't overly clownish, as it sometimes looked when she caught her reflection. A little too much blush on her gaunt cheeks, too bright lipstick on her mostly hidden lips. Those compounds crept into the wrinkles on her face, created a map of stained lines. Touching the palm of his hand with her dry fingertips, she suddenly wanted to look pretty. To have her only son remember her as a pretty woman. And have that memory, whenever he paused to reflect on her, make him happy.

He broke away first, after another smile. Pacifying, this time, though she didn't like to admit it.

"Miss Parsons?" he called down the hallway of her apartment. "Can you help mother get ready for her overnight outing?"

"Of course, Mr. Edgecombe."

Miss Parsons appeared almost instantly. Stella suspected her nurse was hiding around the corner, listening in on that private conversation with her son. After all, the woman did work for Elise, was paid to know what transpired in Stella's life. Stella glared at Miss Parsons, glared at her starched white cap, white button-up dress, white sweater, white hose, white sneakers without a single scuff. Those sneakers annoyed Stella. She found it rude that someone would walk over her soft carpet wearing sneakers. Clean or not, it was irrelevant. But not wanting to seem focused on petty trivialities, she never mentioned her issue with Miss Parsons to another soul.

"She won't be but a moment now, will you, Mrs. Edgecombe?"

Stella had not wanted to return to Bended Knee. She did not want to see the old buildings torn down, the wild grass shorn with electric mowers, dirt roads paved, and teenagers with painted on clothes loitering underneath electric streetlights. Instead, she preferred the Bended Knee that existed inside her mind. One where Leander still made furniture, where Amos yearned for Nettie, where her father hobbled down the laneway towards a hot Sunday dinner. But her preference was disregarded, and she was packed up like a piece of antique luggage, helped into a van, secured in place with a belt. Flanked by two hot-bodied children, they began to glide down the circular drive in front of Stella's building.

"Stop," Jane had said. And Robert jammed his foot on the break, everyone lunging forward. "Jason. Andrew. Did you empty your bladders?"

"Yes, Grandmother," they chimed, eyes rolling.

"And Mother?"

"What do you want?"

"Did you…you know?"

"You know?"

"Go to the toilet," Elise chimed in. "Tea goes right through you. And I seen you on your second cup."

Stella noticed Robert glancing down at his hands, his fingers curled around the plastic steering wheel. Was it plastic? Or rubber? She had never learned to drive, never gripped a steering wheel, controlled the movement of a car.

"Well, Mother?"

Stella sneezed lightly, a fake sneeze. Something of a habit she had developed when she couldn't say something polite.

"Let's just get going," Robert said. "Not as though we're going to the moon. We're allowed to stop."

Thank you, my son.

After arriving, a cup of tea, two cherry squares later, Elise took Stella by the arm, led her down the long hallway along the back of the house. Elise paused outside the second dark-wooden door on the right, said, "I wonders if this is the one she said. I don't want to go poking around."

As Elise darted back to the kitchen to double-check the room, Stella waited in the hallway, hand on the doorframe. At the end of the hall was a long window that looked on a stretch of closely shorn grass, two burgundy coloured picnic tables. Stella could imagine how it once looked, rows of hearty cabbages and potato plants, a man standing along a row, head bent, hoe in hand, summer sun beating down on his neck. She could picture it clearly.

With the toe of her slipper, she adjusted the hooked rug that was bunched on the floor, heard the sigh escape from her lips. She moved her hand, touched the door, paint somehow sticky even though it was dry. In all her years in Bended Knee, she had never been in this house, but now, something about it felt entirely familiar. She smelled the air, detected the faint scent of onions, even though she was fairly certain there were no onions chopped and waiting on the kitchen counter. How peculiar, Stella thought. She knew the hallway would smell of onions even before she walked through the door.

Elise was beside her again, opened the door with some gusto to reveal a bedroom the size of a large closet. A twin bed jammed into a corner, log cabin quilt hung over the footboard. "Well," Elise said. "A short nap'll do you good, Mother. And you don't need nothing more than you got here."

Stella sneezed lightly.

"You'll feel better afterwards."

As she sat on the edge of the creaky mattress, Stella grunted. The older she got, the more difficult she found it to disguise her annoyance for Elise. Or for anyone else for that matter. Stella's words often emerged before her brain had time to warn her tongue. She couldn't help herself. And she could get away with it too. People attributed her occasional display of crotchetiness to her age.

"Refreshed."

Stella lay her head down, thought about the stupidity in Elise's statement. Feeling refreshed. How was it possible to feel refreshed when her faulty carcass was degrading much faster than it was being born?

"That don't look much like a lamp," Elise said, indicating a pale blue contraption on the nightstand. She reached along the cord, snapped a button, and light emerged from the inside of a hard papery cylinder. The cylinder, decorated with a smattering of cutout stars, began to revolve slowly, coating the walls in moving shapes of light.

"Isn't that nice, Mother?" Elise asked.

"Don't need a nightlight now, Elissse." She hated to whistle her daughter's name. "I idn't a child."

"Not far off," she said with a half smile, and shook the quilt in the air, covered Stella up to her neck.

"God, Elise, I got to breathe."

"I would hope so."

After Elise had receded down the hallway, the house became quiet, except for the gentle knocking of pipes, floorboards creaking as though ghosts were ambling over them. Stella did not mind these noises. They were sounds of ease, well-deserved after more than a century of standing.

She slid her hands under her cheek, began to think about Leander. She often conjured his image before sleeping, pulled him up from her reserves. And there he was, as though by magic, appearing inside her mind's eye, standing on the cliff near their home. His hair was thick and wind-whipped, a tawny brown. He wore black trousers, a crisp white Sunday shirt, and she could see the outline of his undershirt beneath it. Harriet was by his side, yipping and jumping up to kiss Leander's outstretched hand, wiggling her backside to gain height. Behind them, man and dog, the black ocean sparkled with a thousand points of light.

Leander turned, began to meander on the path along those cliffs, Harriet following close on his heels. But there was something different. She noticed Leander's gait was even, balanced. Steady and strong. He wasn't limping as he had done in life.

And when she noticed this, a curious feeling spread throughout Stella's frail bones, a tingling of sorts. She was reminded of being a young child in summertime, sitting on a stretch of rounded beach rocks, dirt-stained feet near the very lip of the ocean. The tide would slowly edge over her toes, her ankles, her legs, slipping in ever so gently. Covering her. Then, as gently, drawing her out. Lying there, she had this sense of being solidly still and in a state of motion at the same time. These images of Leander gave her the same feeling. For a reason she could not grasp, she understood that the Leander in her mind was not a memory, and not quite an imagining. Something ever so slightly different.

He stopped just before the path dipped downwards, the place where earth and frigid water met with sky. As she watched, he looked over his shoulder, waved his hand, beckoning her to follow him. Harriet howled, her furry neck stretched upwards, wide jaw snapping at the clouds.

That feeling again, throughout her entire body now. Leander, like the tide, washing over her, pulling her towards him. She had no desire to rise, shake off her dripping frozen limbs, run towards the house. She desired, more deeply than anything she'd ever experienced, to move with that tide.

"Wait," she managed. "Wait." And with some urgency, she tried to get up from her bed and go. To flow forward. Before he disappeared down over the cut of the cliff. She reached outwards, knocked the lamp with her hand, and it fell, striking the wooden floor, covering her in a blanket of soft-edged stars. The light moved over her eyelids, and ever so gradually, under her eyelids. She barely noticed the shift at all, it was so subtle. Nothing more than a single breath in, a single breath out. "Wait," she said again, as she stood up. "Wait for me, Leander. I'm coming."

The wind had come up out of nowhere, forcing curled leaves to skitter over the pavement, across the sheet of rock, out over the cliffs. As she watched them, Elise thought these tired leaves looked as though they were being propelled towards certain death. Tumbling into nothingness against their will. There was something romantic about it, as though those leaves were unable to resist the wildness of the wind. She liked this weather, would love it, in fact, if only she could excise the raspy whistle from inside her ears. That sound reminded her of her mother's voice. Chiding her.

She held her coat across her chest, ambled up the laneway, then stood for a moment at a curve in the road, stared up at the old farmhouse. It was bright red now, like a fresh wound, when before, the clapboard had been painted blue, perhaps grey. Maybe it had been no colour at all, that last time she had seen it. Close enough to be touching the boards, fingernails scraping the boards. Maybe the farmhouse had been stripped bare of paint, standing there in the salty storms, naked as the day it was built. No, she couldn't remember the colour. Couldn't remember it at all.

In her mind, she decided to continue her walk around Bended Knee, maybe stroll down to the old schoolhouse, rest on the cement stoop, stare at the field where she and Robert had eaten ice cream, bowled with the set of homemade pins her father had fashioned so many years ago. But her body had other ideas. Without thought given to the tall grass, the mucky ditch, her feet stepped off the laneway and onto the property of the bed and breakfast. Secured inside new shoes, her feet cut a line straight across the land until they reached the farmhouse. Elise looked around, wondering how she had arrived on that particular spot, and she hunched down, her back firmly pressed against the wood slats.

Stupid. Forcing herself to sit there and think about that night. Her body wanting her to stay, when her mind longed to meander about, dodging this way and that, blissfully ignorant. Very well. Get on with it. *Not as though one particular day in a life makes a whole lot of difference,* she thought. *It's the culmination of years that shape a person, not a few hours with some boy. Some boy who was worth nothing.* "Lewis Hickey." She whispered his name into the wind, then knotted the tough grass through her fingers, and pulled. Its roots were old, would not let go, and urged her down. No point to focus on that now. Think about something else.

Two empty cola cans, a married pair, rattled down the road side by side, popping over pebbles, rollicking left and right, clanking into each other for a metal kiss. Garbage. Who would throw out garbage like that? Bloody litterbugs. Elise hated trash on the roads, was meticulous about her own garbage. Double-bagged, heavy-duty twist ties. No chance of leakage or emission of foul odours. She took pride in her silver container at the end of her driveway, undented, clean. A much better job than a man would do.

But she hadn't always been like that. One week, she'd missed the truck, and after two weeks of unprecedented summer heat, the mess had begun to liquefy, leak out of newly created holes, trailing down the incline towards her driveway. But that wasn't the worst of it. On the top of each bag she noticed the contents rippling, the black plastic shifting, a faint crackling sound rising up from within. Before her brain could assess the prospects, her hand reached out, tugged away the bag. Her breath caught in her throat when she saw the maggots. Masses of identical fat beige bodies, writhing over and under each other, bathed in filth. *Surely,* Elise thought, *that is the very image of Hell. Right there before her.*

For months, she couldn't get that picture out of her head. Sometimes, when she'd be slipping into a hot bath or just dozing off, it would jump up and startle her. She couldn't help but imagine, in some crevice of her mind, what it might feel like. To be right in the middle of it all. Entities slithering over and under. Lost inside a tangle of identical bodies. In time she came to the conclusion that perhaps it was not so horrible after all. Might even be soothing. No individuals. Just a humming chaos. Common goal.

Elise could see a thin line of the ocean from her perch. Fog, like billowing chalk dust, was tumbling inland. The clouds had dropped lower, and to Elise, they reminded her of injured flesh. Enormously fat arms and legs and backsides, beaten beyond, draped over one another in a haphazard manner. "Lewis Hickey." Spit it out this time. Offered it up to the brutish wind. Just to see if anything might happen.

More than anything else, she always wondered why her mother never tried to help her, never supported her. Looking back on it now, Elise had been nothing more than a young woman, innocent, naïve. But when she tried to tell her mother about Lewis, she was shut down. Told to let it go. Her thighs still bloody, skin scoured from her knees and shins, and already the time had come to let it go. Elise remembered every word they exchanged as her mother stood in the doorway to her bedroom.

"Elise? I'd like to say something to you."

"What's that, Mother. That this mess is my own fault? That you hopes to God I idn't pregnant?"

"No." Silence for a moment. "I want to say. I want... Don't let this get the better of you, is all."

"What do you mean, Mother?"

"Shape your life."

"Stop, Mother."

"This now, what went on 'tween you and Lewis. Idn't nothing every woman don't go through."

"Stop, Mother."

"In some shape or form, Elise. We all goes through it. 'Tis part of who we is."

"I hardly think that's true."

"Put it out of your mind," her mother had said. As though it were that simple. "Decide to be done with it."

Then, Elise scratched her nails in the moist cuts on her knees, and informed her mother that she was leaving Bended Knee. And never coming back. She remembered looking at her mother, leaning against the doorframe, eyes like shadows, body weary. Yes, she remembered looking at her mother, thinking, believing she had never brought that woman an ounce of joy. Not a single ounce of joy.

When she arrived in St. John's, she took her mother's advice, placed that evening with Lewis on a shelf far back in her mind. Allowed it to develop a substantial layer of dust, a cloak of stringy cobwebs. Lived her life, free of the mental kinks such an encounter might create.

Lately though, she wished she hadn't forced it back so

far. Wished she had of taken a week or nine days to feel some sadness over it. Then perhaps, she wouldn't be sitting there on that knoll, a grey-haired about-to-be grandmother, whispering the name of her worst childhood crush. She might be thinking of other more important things, like her bank account. And the fact that Arthur, her second ex-husband, was late once again with the spousal support payment. She would have to contact her lawyer, make an arrangement that was more secure.

Elise put her head into the knees of her jeans, felt the first pecks of rain, tiny shards of icy water on the back of her neck. She shivered, though she did not feel the chill on her skin. Sitting there, on the earth of her childhood, she could practically grasp the quantity of time that had passed. As though all of her adult years were the loop of a wide ribbon, and she was now resting at the knot near the ends.

She looked up, watched a man stride down the laneway ahead of her, salt-and-pepper cap hauled low on his forehead. He stopped, as though he sensed her watching him, made a sharp turn and walked halfway down the driveway towards the bed and breakfast. He hollered towards her. Something about a storm.

Elise leaned forward, wind whistling sharply in her ears. She could see his mouth moving, an arm waving towards the farmhouse, but his words were stolen by the gusts, driven elsewhere. "What's that?" she yelled back.

Another bout of mumbling. "Storm...good...fit... dog..." He pointed his finger towards the sky.

"What?" She scrunched up her face, trying to hear. She stood up, took several steps, resisted taking more. "I can barely catch a word."

He removed his cap, wind immediately seizing the greased fingers of his comb over, making them dance atop his skull. He said something else, "Works...grounds..." stepped towards her, smiled.

He wasn't an unattractive man, this stranger: stocky body, ruddy cheeks, clear eyes. Hands like hammers. Someone who obviously wasn't afraid of a good day's work, and this was a trait Elise valued even more as she grew older.

He smiled again, took another two steps towards her, yelled, "Rising...wicked...tea..."

"I'm sorry, sir." She frowned, shook her head and shrugged. "The wind."

She watched as he held his hair in place, jammed his cap back on, and waved in a somewhat embarrassed gesture, went on about his way. For a moment, she watched him stroll down the drive, lurching this way and that as the wind pressed down upon him. And she wondered who he was. Maybe he had recognized her. Somehow, after all these years. Maybe he was a widower with fully grown, uncomplicated children.

Elise shook her head, frowned at her own stupidity. In the van on the way to Bended Knee, she had the ridiculous fear that she would saunter onto this patch of grass and be gulped down. Devoured by a memory that she now realized had significantly faded. Like an old photo, edges chipped and tattered, image out of focus.

She lifted her face to the rain, let the plump drops strike her eyelids, cheeks. And for several moments, enjoyed the comfort of being alone in growing darkness.

"Read a little something, honey." Jane nestled into Robert's side, head lying on his warm shoulder, soft blue cotton sweater. "You know I love to listen."

Robert reached up, let his hand cover her ear, her coarse hair. She was a decent woman, his wife. He never lacked for affection, never wondered if he were loved, never felt the brunt of a grudge held high. Jane seemed, and likely was, perfectly content to be seated on this musty furniture in the makeshift library of this old house, the firelight mellowing their wrinkles, hiding the dust in the corners.

"Anything in particular, dear?" He stood, began to peruse the shelves. "Mrs. Hilliard has quite the selection of poets."

"Surprise me."

"All right then." He selected a book, settled back beside her, and loosely crossed one leg over the other. Glasses that dangled on a chain lifted to his nose, he flipped through, randomly selected. "Okay. Elizabeth Akers Allen."

Cleared his throat, began to recite:

> "BACKWARD, turn backward, O Time, in your flight,
> Make me a child again just for to-night!"

"Ohhh. Lovely," Jane murmured, slid her arm across Robert's stomach, tucked her hand underneath the bend of his elbow.

> "Mother, come back from the echoless shore,
> Take me again to your heart as of yore;
> Kiss from my forehead the furrows of care,
> Smooth the few silver threads out of my hair;
> Over my slumbers your loving watch keep;—
> Rock me to sleep, mother,—rock me..."

He paused, looked up at his wife, leaned forward, and her arm fell away.

She clasped her hands together, sat up as well. "Why that's beautiful, darling. Um. Who was that again?"

"Shhh."

"Shhh?"

"Shhh!"

He stared towards the door that opened on to the hallway, waited, listening. And after a second or two, he heard a solid thud, something falling from a short height onto the wooden floor. For a reason he could not explain, he had expected to hear that sound. Wanted silence as he listened for it.

"What do you suppose that was?" Jane whispered.

His face fell flat, mouth slightly open, voice cracked ever so slightly. "How long did you say Mom's been asleep?"

chapter seventeen

A young man, not older than eighteen or nineteen years, lingered near the edge of a cliff. He was wearing a long satin cloak, black top hat, and had a cane, carved bird's head handle, hooked over his right wrist. Raising his palms towards the starless heavens, cloak slapping in the wind, he said in a deadly serious tone, "The spirits is agitated. I feels it in the air."

A tiny congregation of four females accompanied the young man. Summer had arrived on the cliffside with her daughter Gemma, and there were two additional teenaged girls. Summer guessed they were locals. It was difficult to determine their age in the hazy darkness that surrounded them. Street lights, wrapped in tendrils of fog, offered little light, and the windows of the many homes appeared farther away than they really were.

Gemma giggled nervously, gripped Summer's mittened hand, leaned against her shoulder. "Will we see anything?" she whispered.

"It's only some stories, Gemma," Summer whispered back. "We can leave if you want."

"I'll be all right."

"Welcome," he continued. "Welcome to what I likes to call 'Weak in the Bended Knee.'" He took a step farther back on the cliff, giving himself some additional height. "This is not for the faint of heart, folks. Tonight, you'll hear stories, true stories, of the tormented souls that wander around our little village of Bended Knee. A history of murder." He paused, stared out through widened eyes, leaned closer. "Stories of unrequited love, affairs of the heart, of the flesh."

One of the two girls snorted, said, "I likes the sound of that, Jamie."

"Shut up, will you?" Snapped back. Then, "I will be calling on these ghosts to have a word to us, to communicate. If you finds you's overwhelmed, folks, let me know and we can take a spell. The portal is open tonight, and they might have a lot to say."

Summer unrolled the cuff of her sweater down over her mittens, silently wished it was a pleasant August evening. She had intended to visit Bended Knee late-summer, but time had gotten away from her. What with Gemma beginning middle school, Tim finishing his doctorate in physics, and her own mythology courses at the university, there just hadn't been a free weekend. First chance came in November, and now it was far too cold to be wandering about in the nighttime, discussing spirits. But her mother Elise had insisted. Jamie Barrett was her step-grandson, and the ghost walk was his latest venture to make a dollar from the tourists who passed through the small community. "He's a right sweet young man," Elise had said. "But business hasn't been that good to him. And the poor feller spent an awful amount of time quizzing the old crowd about way back when."

"I don't know," Summer had replied. "You know how

sensitive Gemma is to that sort of thing. She's always been a little, you know, *in tune*."

Elise, resolute then. "Well, she's almost thirteen. Time to get over that old garbage, if you asks me. Besides, I already paid him and you're going."

They wandered northwards, until rock met road, Jamie leading the way. Winds tugged at his cape, and more than once his top hat lifted from his head, scuttled along the ground. The girls, in their matching cropped sweaters, bleached blue jeans, high-top sneakers, grabbed each other and guffawed each time Jamie chased his hat, popped it back on over his woolen toque, banged the top.

First stop was in front of a one and a half-storey salt-box home, five neat windows on the front, dark painted door neatly in the centre. Lights were on in the upper two outside rooms, blinds half tugged down, giving the home a sedated appearance.

Jamie shifted his feet, poked his hands into pockets of his jacket, pants, finally found a small spiral notepad, flipped it open, flashed a penlight for just a second.

Johnny O'Reilly.

Cards. Devil.

Cleared his throat. "Here, in this house, lives the spirit of a murdered man. One of only two men murdered in Bended Knee. The tale goes that they were playing cards on a winter's night, and the gentlemen's lantern kept going out. Not a window was open, and his wick and his oil was good. He blamed the devil, said he could feel the evil near him, tempting him. 'Leave me, Devil,' he called out, but his fellow card players thought he was up to no good. Cheating, they figured, when the lights was out, he was winning every hand. Scraping all their bits of money towards him. Beat him right bad, they did, and the poor feller died of his injuries. And now, folks say that whenever the current residents of the house is playing a game of cards, the man comes back, trying to blow out their lantern."

"That don't make no sense." One of the girls. "How'd he see to cheat if there weren't no light?"

"Don't people got electric lights now?" the other girl said. "Who uses a lantern?"

He looked nervously at Summer and Gemma, then smirked awkwardly, raised his eyebrows, deep voice. "Well, he probably tries to turn the lights out. Regular lights. Dims them anyways."

Someone hollered at them from the front door of the house, open now like an alarmed mouth. "That you, Jamie?" A stout woman, arms knotted across her chest. "Telling old garbage again?"

"God, Aunt Myrtle," he hollered back. "Can you leave me be? I's just trying to earn a buck."

"Not in front of my house, you don't. Get on with you 'fore I calls your mother. And don't you people listen to him. He don't even get the houses right. Got no idea who lived where. Who done what." Muttering, words carted out courtesy of the wind. "Fool and his money is soon parted."

He ushered the small group several steps forward. "Sensitive types," he said in a hush. "Not wanting to admit they got spirits gliding through their walls."

"I suppose so," Summer offered.

They continued along the shoulder of the road, shoes and sneakers crunching over pebbles, slipping occasionally on patches of rotting leaves. They passed a row of painted houses, angled this way and that. From one of them, the faint sound of tinny country music emerged, weaving through the air. In the ditches, Summer could see the remains of old pumpkins, smashed, empty candy wrappers stuck in the mud. The sweet smell of compost turning into soil hovered just above the ground. She squeezed her daughter's hand. "You okay, Gemma?"

"I'm fine, Mom. Really. It's just made up stuff."

Jamie stopped again. Another flick of the light to illuminate his scribbling. Blue pen.

Effie Hussey.

Babies.

Rattling.

"And here, folks, you've got another kind of haunting. Rumour has it, there's no haunting more persistent or sad than that of a dead baby."

"Oh my," Summer whispered, automatically putting her hand to her stomach. She'd had so many miscarriages before Gemma arrived, and she found it unsettling even to think about it.

"This woman had thirteen children throughout her lifetime."

"Shit," one of the girls said. "Guess they didn't have no rubbers back then."

"They did, then," the second girl announced. "They used sheep guts. In-tes-tins."

"You's joking."

"I idn't, then."

Summer bit her bottom lip, glanced at Gemma.

"Did they tie the end in a knot? How'd they keep?"

"I got no idea, stupid! Sold 'em rolled and dried at the grocery store."

"Hold on, honey. Don't budge an inch. I got to soak my casing. Soften it up."

Jamie scowled. "Come off it." He nodded his head towards Summer and Gemma. "I got some real customers here, and they idn't interested in your take on prehistoric birth control."

He coughed. "So, she had these thirteen babies, and more than half of them died. Sickness. Measles. A couple born still. Her house is boarded up now, but on the nights of their birthdays, you can hear them crying up there. Howling like they was just arrived. Sounds like kittens, they says. Cuts right through your heart, it do." Speaking slowly now. "And sometimes you hears a rattling. Someone shaking a baby rattle. Over and over and over again."

"Ah, you're just making this stuff up now, Jamie."

"Embellishing the bejesus out of it."

"Every time we comes on this walk with you, the stories gets longer."

Ignoring them now, he continued, used his flashlight beneath his cloak to see the list of ghosts.

Leander Edgecombe.

Furniture.

Front Stoop.

"And straight across the street is our next haunting. Notice the shadows moving. This may just look like any regular old home, but there is a dead man who resides here, and he don't like visitors. A long time ago, he spent his time keeping watch over the woman he loved. He's been there for years and years, even though that woman is long gone. Buried."

"What was her name?" Summer interjected.

"Can't tell you that, ma'am," he said with a wink. "Wouldn't be right. Folks round here wouldn't give me their blessing if they knowed I was handing out personal information."

"Oh," she responded. "All right, then."

"What a load of bullshit he gets on with."

"Should cart him off to St. John's to join the politics."

"Can you watch your mouth, please?"

The girl rolled her eyes, opened her mouth to crack her gum. "Yes, ma'am. Thank you, ma'am."

"House of a furniture maker. Pieces he made likely in most old homes around here. By and by, as the village got more populated, he started building coffins for a few extra dollars. They says he cut himself one day, bled awful bad into one of the boxes, and then when it was used to bury a feller, someone from the other side was made aware of him. Took him in jig time. And he left behind his young wife, their whole brood."

"So, he idn't a ghost then. He just took off?"

"No, I weren't finished yet. He was a furniture maker."

"You already said that, Jamie. You gone senile already?"

"And to let everyone know he made furniture, he'd nailed a chair to the roof over his back stoop."

"A chair on the roof?" One pointed. "Dumbest thing I ever heard."

"They used to do that." Summer spoke politely. "As a matter of pride."

She rolled her eyes again. "Yeah, right. Whatever do that got to do with pride?"

"That's right," Jamie said.

"Are you sure a furniture maker lived there?" She could see no stoop, no proper place to nail a chair. Besides, she recalled hearing that her great-grandfather had made furniture, but he had lived several houses up the lane, much farther back from the road. Maybe there were two who did the same work.

"Ah, yes," he said, nodding. "According to my sources." He coughed, voice less authoritative. "Umm, after he died, folks would always see a phantom shadow of him, perched in that chair, elbows on his knees, watching whoever come to the house. And if it were someone he didn't like, their knock made no sound. Couldn't be heard, no matter how hard they struck the door. Weren't let in. And he'd be leaning over, jeering at them."

"Speaking of leaning over, how was your time with Derrick last night?"

"Wicked. Real wicked. Though when we was, you know, he started poking his finger in my ear. Drove me nuts. What the hell was that?"

"The bugger was trying to ear-hump you."

Jamie snapped his cloak together, struck the ground with the cane. "Christ Almighty, Nadine. If you hadn't guessed, I's trying to run a bloody business here. I asked youse to come along to make a bit more of a crowd. That's it. But I don't want you here no more. You hear me? No more."

"Efff you, J.B.," they said as they slunk away, arm in arm, free hands shoved upwards, middle fingers erect. "Looooser."

"I's real sorry," he said, after they swaggered around a corner. "They was just trying to rile me up."

"That's all right," Summer replied. "We're still enjoying ourselves. Right, Gemma?"

"That sure looks haunted," Gemma said, pointing to a drab tall flat-roofed house, windows boarded up. "Who lived there?"

"You got a good sense, miss," Jamie said. "That place got a family of spirits residing together."

Quick glance at his notepad.

Fuller Family.

Father, daughter, grandson.

Talk about the flour.

"Second murder in Bended Knee, though not much more than a shred of evidence on it. That was the old general store, used to sell everything from rubber boots to paint, nails, molasses. A woman lived there with her father, and rumour has it," he lowered his voice considerably, "he used to...to...to interfere with her, shall we say. And this woman went on to have a son, though she never had a husband. No one knows the rights of it, but one day, the father was found stabbed, head jammed into a bag of flour. All kinds of flour sprinkled around him. Folks thought 'twas the devil done it, or else some robber. But the only thing stolen was cards and cards of buttons."

"What happened to the woman and the boy?" Gemma.

"Years and years later, the son choked to death. And the woman died in her sleep."

"And they're ghosts now?"

"They says," he continued, "that when they went to clean up the old woman's room, they found a box filled with those stolen buttons. People say she was half cracked. And now, the ghost of her father wanders about trying to catch her, and the woman is trying to catch her son, and the son is trying to get out through the door. So there's always a fight going on on the top floor of that old general store."

"Fascinating," Summer said, nodding. "God. We're so rich in folklore, aren't we? Greek mythology's got nothing on Bended Knee."

"There's proof too."

"Proof?"

"Yep. People who have gone into the store says they don't see normal dust around. Everything, on both levels, is coated with a thin layer of flour."

"Wow," Gemma said. "Can we go in?"

"You'd want to?" Summer asked. "Are you sure? I'll wait out here, if that's the case."

"Maybe not," Gemma said, blinking. She zipped her

coat all the way up to her neck, tied a knot in her scarf. "Maybe in the daylight."

Next stop was the painted gate in front of the church. Ivy had nearly covered the front of the structure, and with all the leaves fallen, it appeared as though the earth had sent out dozens of criss-crossing fingers, claiming the church as its own.

Jamie consulted his notepad.

Delia Abbott.

Had fit.

"You guys religious?"

"Not particularly."

"Best to ask," he said, "before I tells you about the ghost in the church. Some don't take kindly to the suggestion."

"Go ahead."

"Woman. Fairly young, but poor health. Had all kinds of doctors coming to see her, but she just continued to shrivel away. Some malevolent spirit took hold of her. I'm guessing she had some sort of illness, but you know how people were back in the day.

"Well, she hadn't set foot inside the church for the longest time, and tongues started wagging. Until one day, she strolls in, for no reason whatsoever, and she gets to the middle of the church, falls over backwards. Starts to shake like fish on the wharf. Something's trying to get out of her."

"What was trying to get out of her?"

"Sounds like she just had a seizure, Gemma."

"Likely. But that's not what they believed all those years ago. Wasn't strong enough to handle it, died right there as the devil tried to get free, haul himself out of the church. Folks says she sits in the pew now, right next to where she died. No one'll take her spot. Reckons she needs all the praying she can get."

"What a terrible way to think," Summer said. "The poor woman was just ill."

"Nevertheless, she sits there now. If anyone tries to take her spot, they comes away with a terrible chill. Skin right cold to the touch."

"Well," Summer said, "you might be right. I'm sure there's plenty we know nothing about."

"If we takes a cut through this property," he said as they followed him behind a newer home, "we'll arrive near the last ghost on our walk."

"Do they mind?" Summer asked as they strolled across the frost-filled soil of someone's backyard. Peering in the windows, sheer curtains open, she could see a family of three playing a board game at the kitchen table, the girl drinking from a magenta plastic cup.

"Nah. That's my mom and dad there. And my sister. They don't mind."

They came to a long fence, two stretches of field on either side. On the lower half, belonging to a bed and breakfast, the expanse of lawn was well-kept, but on the higher side, everything had grown wild and snarled. As though the owner had long since given up.

"And now." He lifted the arms of his cape again, peered at his notebook.

Williard May.

"On to our last ghost on tonight's ghost walk. Our oldest and quietest ghost in Bended Knee. He lives right here, in this very spot. You got the May house to the one side and that modest home up there. The fence is new, of course, but he continues to loiter, our old ghost, torn between true love on that side up there and a moral obligation on the other."

"Sounds romantic," Summer said.

"His love for the local midwife festered for fifty years, they says. He pined for her every day, but could do nothing about it because he'd married the wrong woman. Married a woman who wouldn't haul him off the stove."

"Maybe tragic is a better word."

"He lived a life without love, when the true desire of his heart was only a stone's throw away. And when your heart don't get what it wants, it gives out after a spell. And it did for this gentleman, right here on this very spot."

"This very… spot?" Gemma's voice caught.

"Yep. And people says you can see the gate opening and closing, not banging like 'twas wind or something, but gentle like. As he moves from one side to the other. Passing through, and turning back. Passing through and turning back. Lacking the courage to make a change. He's still torn in two, I reckons, even in death. Likely tortured for all eternity."

Summer bent down, one knee on the damp blades of grass, and she lifted some yellowed leaves near the flaking slats of the fence. "Look, Gemma," she said, pointing to a tiny flower clinging to a stem. "A single bleeding heart."

"Yep," Jamie replied. "I idn't surprised."

"Well, thank you, Jamie. That was actually quite fun." Summer pressed a ten-dollar bill into his hand. "Didn't you think so, Gemma?"

Summer glanced at her daughter, saw her jaw agape, staring at the fence. Turning to see what had caught Gemma's attention, she watched the gate slowly creak open, waver. Stopped, poised there, a gap just large enough for a heavyset man to slip through. At once, she was enveloped in a casing of icy air, as though she were reaching into an open deep-freeze. And then, Summer saw Gemma shudder visibly when, in a moment of absolute calm, the gate eased backwards, against the logical pull of gravity, and softly closed.

"Did you do that?" Summer exclaimed. "Is that some sort of trick to end this off? Come on. Tell the truth now, Mr. Barrett."

"No, ma'am. 'Tis the old man. Out for his walk."

"Well, that was something." Summer shook her head, reached forward and shook the gate with her hand. Secure. "Quite a good ending. I'll give you that."

Jamie removed his top hat, tucked it underneath his bent arm, scratched near the edges of his woolen hat. "I didn't do nothing. Honest."

"Must've been a trick of the wind," Summer replied, looking out towards the harbour. "I'll tell Mom we really had a good time."

He opened his hand, a second quick peek at the money. "Thanks. I'm glad." Placing his hand on top of the fence, he began traipsing down the field, letting his hand ride up and down over every point. "Oh," he turned and yelled. "Forgot to say. You can go and get yourselves a warm cup of something at the Captain's Drawers there on Helmet's Hill. Just tell him you was out with me. He knows who you are."

"He knows." Gemma's words were a breath.

Summer wrapped her arms around Gemma, hugged her pre-adolescent body, that lanky construction of bones, stretched skin and muscle. "Should we go for some hot chocolate, honey?"

Gemma dropped her arms, looked up at her mother, burst suddenly into tears. "He knows me."

"Who, honey? Who knows?"

"He really does, Mom. I'm not joking. He knows who I am."

Summer and Gemma nestled into a booth near the front window of the Captain's Drawers. Decorated in a nautical theme, there were worn leather seats, heavy wooden tables, ship wheels and portholes mounted on the walls. Beside the front door, a large glass case held a model replica of a vessel called the HMS *Nipper*, complete with a dozen miniature carved seamen. "'Tis accurate," Mr Atkins, the owner, informed them as they arrived. "Right down to the splinter stuck in the skipper's tooth. Meant to be a toothpick, you sees."

It was good to be inside. Even though there was no one on the streets, Summer sensed the night air was overflowing with energy. Confusion. Like too many people gathered around a dining table, everyone reaching for the serving spoons all at once. Inside the dimly lit pub, it was quiet. Several other patrons were seated nearby, mostly older men perched on bar stools, drinking from tall glasses of amber beer. But with no one dropping coins into the jukebox, there was only a continual soft banter, occasional raucous laugh.

Summer stared out the window. There was little to see. Thick fog had tumbled in, strands of it crawling over the houses, gliding along the open roads, pressing itself into every available crevice. She could actually see the fog moving, lifting and waving, as though it comprised innumerable parts, dozens of milky silhouettes strolling by.

"Do you remember when you were little, Gemma?" Summer asked. "You used to say, 'it's froggy out'?"

"I did?"

Summer smiled, reached across the table, touched her daughter's fingers.

"Here you go, ladies." Mr. Atkins was beside them, a pair of foaming ceramic mugs in his bear-sized hands. "Two of the best hot chocolates in all the province." He slid the mugs across the table, foam jiggling, but staying put. "Will you look at that." He motioned towards the window. "God awful, idn't it? Someone's apt to be killed tonight if they's out around."

"Yes," Summer replied. "It's like we just stepped off the earth."

"Oh, Lard." Full belly laugh, scratch of his balding scalp. "I'm in no rush there."

When Mr. Atkins had left, Summer said, "Are you okay, honey? What happened back there?"

Gemma gripped the handle of her mug. "Nothing, Mom."

"You know you can talk to me about it if you like. But you don't have to."

Gemma blew the foam, stopped when it oozed down the side, clumped on the table. "I thought I felt him, Mom. I really did."

"What did it feel like, my sweetie?"

"Glorious. It felt glorious."

Summer lifted the toes of her shoes up and down, noticed the stickiness of the floor wanting to hold her feet in place. "Well, that's a strong word. A strong feeling."

"There's no other way to explain it." She gazed sideways at Summer, expression serious except for the foam mustache.

"Do you want to come with me tomorrow to see Nanny Stella's grave?"

"I will."

"I don't mind if you don't want to. I just like to go and see. You know. Make sure everything's okay."

"I will, Mom. I don't mind."

Summer wrapped her hands around her mug, noticed

how her chilly palms drew the heat from the ceramic.

"Are we related to that old man?"

"What's that?"

"Are we related to that old man at the gate?"

"Maybe, but I don't think so, honey."

"You're not sure?"

"No. Nan never talked much about her growing up. All I know is that she lived here until she was fairly old and that her parents were not originally from here."

"What about her husband?"

"Don't know much about him at all. Died when Mom was still a child. She doesn't like to talk about him. Neither did your great-grandmother."

"That's too bad."

"Why?"

"I thought we might be. I thought he was trying to let me know."

"Know what, honey?"

Gemma stared out the window, into the thick fog. "That he's okay. That he's happy. He's proud. That he's glad he did what he did."

"What do you think he did?"

"I got no idea. Married that other woman, I guess."

"It was just a story, Gemma. Probably wasn't much truth to it. And you know what the wind is like."

"I guess so. It's just disappointing, is all."

"That you're not related to him?"

"Yeah."

"Well, if it makes you feel any better, I suppose we're all related. If you go back far enough. Search through our histories. Body or spirit, we're all connected somehow. Right?"

"I guess so."

"Remember when your dad was teaching you about Venn diagrams a few days ago?"

"Yeah, math. He's always talking math."

"Well, in my mind, the whole world is kind of like that. Each of us with our own little Venn circle. All of our properties inside that circle. Our lives. Our Venn circle expanding as we age."

"And our circles overlap?"

"I think so. Somehow, our circle overlaps with everyone else's. Sometimes in big, important ways. Sometimes in small ways."

"Yeah, it's complicated though. Dad lost me when he started talking about rotational symmetry and 'n' being prime."

"Yes, it is complicated. Simple, too, though. My smart little darling."

"Mom." Eyes rolling slightly, feigning irritation.

As she watched Gemma, Summer felt a sharp pain in her chest. Where had her daughter come from? This girl with the thin chocolate mustache over her pouty lips. Her hair, a little greasy, pulled into a sloppy ponytail. Mouth moving, talking of Venn diagrams and ghostly admissions and the tissues of life. Just how did she arrive on this very spot?

Of course Summer was not thinking about the business of procreation or birth or their years of growing together or their mother-daughter escape to Bended Knee. No. Something much more ethereal than that. She was once again considering, as she often had before, the innumerable number of events that needed to occur in order to create Gemma. If the mind could skip back through even a handful of generations, just how many happenings were necessary to bring this single body into the light? A rock striking a seagull. A lick of butter. A nibbling goat. A splinter stabbed in a finger. A deadly disease. A slab of overcooked meat. A bonfire. A cookbook in a hidden drawer. A handful of orange beads. A string of ducklings crossing the road. Summer's mind could churn up a million miniscule images, and she was certain each random flicker of thought had somehow nudged Gemma into existence. As though her daughter, as she sat before her now, were the highest grain of sand on one enormous pyramid. Remove one element, the structure would shift, fold, and Gemma would dissolve into oblivion.

Summer stared at her daughter, reached out to touch the cowlick on her forehead, smoothed the strands of baby hair that splayed like a crescent. It was painful almost, to regard something so precious, something that she had created. Painful, and humbling. Her human heart, like a fist inside her chest, struggled to hold the ball of emotion, solid, perfect, like a child's glass marble. A universal sphere of clear pure joy, shot through with bright slivers of cold blue agony and bright red love. Her own peppermint swirlie. Strands of intertwining gain and loss. Visible in the light, no matter the angle. This marble. A prize. It belonged to her now. She would place it in her palm, close her fingers around it.

Trade it for nothing.

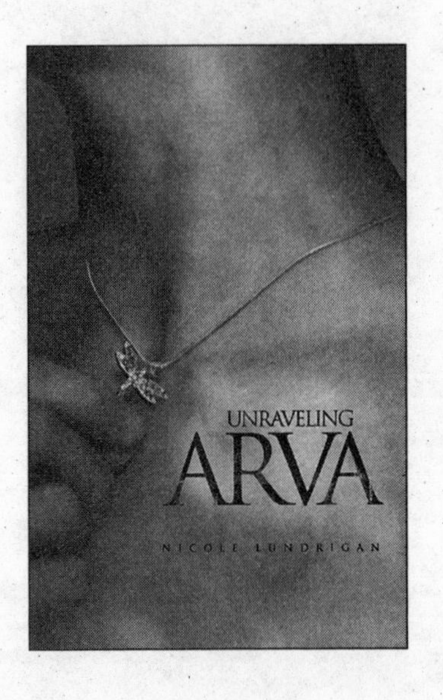

After her eccentric mother's death, young Arva House moves to a close-knit outport with hopes of escaping the past that plagues her. But tangled rumours follow, and she soon becomes the object of speculation. Craving a sense of stability, Arva makes hasty choices, and finds herself enmeshed in a net laden with deceit, infidelity, and latent hostility. Only when the man she thought she loved completely takes her apart, does she realize that all of her unique features somehow fit together to form a whole.

ISBN 978-1-894377-05-8 / $16.95 PB / 5.5 x 8.5 / 240 PP

praise for unraveling arva

"...a superb first novel from an exciting new Canadian talent."

– Margaret Cannon, *The Globe and Mail*
(Selected as a top ten pick for 2004)

"...a blend of magic realism and spot-on vernacular."

– Joan Sullivan, *The Telegram*

"...the author's voice is a slow melt. *Unraveling Arva* teases every experience for sensory detail."

– Paul Butler, *Atlantic Books Today*

On Christmas Eve, 1898, a young widow gives birth while caught outside in a swirling blizzard. Thaw follows the unsettled life of this child, as she grows into a disquieting presence in tranquil Cupboard Cove. Hazel Boone lives life on its border, moving among familiar strangers, her body driven by temptation and an inner fire. Her self-indulgence creates a shame that percolates down through generations, seizing everyone in its path including her son, the painter David Boone, and his young apprentice, Tilley Gover. Seventy years after her birth, during a winter of constriction, a tragedy repeats itself, and the residents of this small outport re-discover that passion can be as destructive as it is redeeming.

ISBN 978-1-894377-11-9 / $19.95 PB / 5.5 x 8.5 / 340 PP

praise for thaw

"...a vivid, rich, galloping story, gothic and true..."

– Lisa Moore, author of *Alligator*

"One of the major pleasures of this excellent novel is reading it aloud."

– Margaret Cannon, *The Globe and Mail*

"Nobody else produces anything like this... she's establishing her own genre, a kind of Newfoundland Gothic... with an arc as relentless and otherworldly as a meteorite."

– Paul Butler, *Atlantic Books Today*